By the same author

RSVP

**SIMON &
SCHUSTER**

London · New York · Sydney · Toronto · New Delhi

A CBS COMPANY

First published in Great Britain by Simon & Schuster UK Ltd, 2012
A CBS COMPANY

Copyright © Helen Warner, 2012

1 3 5 7 9 10 8 6 4 2

Simon & Schuster UK Ltd
1st Floor
222 Gray's Inn Road
London WC1X 8HB

www.simonandschuster.co.uk

Simon & Schuster Australia, Sydney
Simon & Schuster India, New Delhi

A CIP catalogue record for this book
is available from the British Library

Hardback ISBN 978-0-85720-124-9
Trade Paperback ISBN 978-0-85720-125-6

Typeset by M Rules
Printed and bound by CPI Group (UK) Ltd, Croydon, CR0 4YY

Acknowledgements

Firstly, I have to thank my lovely sister, Louise Sears, for her help with the medical research for *IOU*. Louise is a brilliant heart-failure nurse specialist, so any mistakes are my own.

Huge thanks to the truly wonderful Maxine Hitchcock at Simon & Schuster. Your ideas, encouragement and above all, friendship, have made writing this book a dream. I hope I do you proud.

Also at Simon & Schuster, grateful thanks to Nigel Stoneman, Clare Hey, Sara-Jade Virtue and the whole team. It is such a pleasure working with you all and I have really been made to feel like a part of the S&S 'family'.

I am yet again indebted to my agent Sheila Crowley and everyone at Curtis Brown for your continued support.

Endless thanks to Alex Bowley at Channel 4 and to all the amazing producers and presenters I have had the privilege of working with during my time there. Thanks too to the original 'Loose Women', Clare Ely, Jane Beacon and Jacqui Moore, who have been such wonderful friends over the past 12 years and to Jane Moore, who has not only been a great friend, but has also given me the best advice – 'just keep writing!'

Helen Warner

The Warner and Duggan families have, as ever, been incredible in their support. Particular thanks go to my fab sisters-in-law, Claire Warner and Helen Duggan, for buying so many copies of *RSVP* and spreading the word far and wide! Talking of spreading the word – no one can compete with my mum Ann, who has been there for me every step of the way.

And finally, nothing would be possible without my very own little 'team Warner'. Alice, Paddy and Rob make everything worthwhile. Thank you, my darlings – I.O.U!

For Mum
Because I.O.U.

Prologue

The door banged shut behind her and she trudged heavily down the flight of stone steps, clutching the brown envelope in her shaking hand. Taking a deep breath to steady herself, she sat down on the bottom step and stared at the innocuous-looking letter that contained the results. The results that would determine her future. She wanted to know and yet she also had a desperate urge to tear up the envelope into tiny brown pieces and scatter them into the wind, so that she never would.

Minutes passed and still she couldn't bring herself to open it. She watched the traffic on the main road in front of the car park, as cars jostled for position before drawing to a halt at the red traffic lights, the drivers' faces screwed up in concentration as they performed a multitude of different activities. There was an overly made-up woman driving a white Fiat 500, chewing gum with her mouth open and chatting on an iPhone that was clamped to her ear, all the while her eyes darting towards her rear-view mirror. Behind her, a young, white-shirted man in a black BMW was leaning forwards and tapping furiously on the sat nav in the corner of his windscreen, before slamming the dashboard in a fit of temper. As the lights changed to green, they all moved off in a sulky procession, taking this snapshot of their lives with them.

She shivered and pulled her coat around her more tightly as she imagined she heard footsteps behind her. She glanced up to see if there was any sign of him, but the door at the top of the steps remained firmly closed. She wondered briefly if she should wait for him but knew that it was just another delaying tactic.

Nerves danced like butterflies in her stomach as she rewound the movie of her life in her head, smiling to herself as certain memories floated to the surface; but then sank away, to be replaced by long shadows that took her back down a darker path: to somewhere she didn't want to revisit. To somewhere she wished she had never gone in the first place.

She looked up, trying to find solace in the fat, white clouds that were scudding furiously across the cold, blue sky, then shivered again as the wind caught her hair and whipped it around her face. Whatever answer she was hoping to find was not going to be found up there. She bit her lip to stop the tears that tingled and threatened at the back of her eyes and throat. Then, taking a gulp of cold air and screwing up every last drop of courage she could muster, she slid her thumbnail under the flap and sliced the envelope open.

SUMMER

Chapter 1

The fog of steam that had clouded the mirror was beginning to creep silently away as Amy peered closely at her reflection. The pores of her skin looked magnified at such close proximity, but her large, navy-blue eyes were clear and bright and her lips were pink, plump and moist as she pouted back at herself. *Not bad*, she thought, as she smiled at her reflection, amused at her own vanity.

She stepped onto the scales and gazed down at the dial as it lurched drunkenly between the eight and the nine. Finally, it came to rest at exactly eight and a half stone. Amy frowned: how had she put on two pounds in one day? She had worked hard in the gym as usual and had only eaten salad for lunch. *Towels.* Of course! She hopped off the scales as she untwisted the wet turban from her long, damp, honey-coloured hair, then carefully undid the thick, white, fluffy towel she had wrapped around her body sarong-style and let them both drop to the floor. Once again, she stepped onto the scales and this time the dial came to rest where she wanted it to, at eight stone five pounds. She lifted one leg up behind her and balanced on her other foot, grinning as the dial inched a couple of pounds further towards the eight, before leaping off quickly so that it couldn't change its mind. It was a daily battle that had continued over many years. Right now, it was a battle she was winning, but it took an enormous amount of willpower and effort; and it was getting harder with every passing year.

Downstairs, Amy heard a door slam. *That must be the children back from school*, she thought, alarmed at how quickly the day had passed. What had she done with it? She pulled a wide-toothed comb through her hair and slicked on some lip-gloss, before hanging the towels back up on the rail and emerging from her en suite bathroom into the deep-carpeted quiet of her bedroom. She caught sight of her naked body in the full-length mirror and instinctively sucked in her tummy. It was the one bit of her body she had never been happy with, despite her husband Ben's constant reassurance that she looked 'pretty bloody good' to him. Two children meant that no amount of sessions in their basement gym and endless sit-ups made a jot of difference: that strip of fat wasn't budging by natural means. A tummy tuck was likely to be her only option, but she couldn't quite bring herself to do it.

Amy quickly pulled on her favourite jeans and a strappy pale blue top, before bounding barefoot down the stairs. 'Mummy!' yelled Sam, as he stood in the hallway and shrugged off the blazer from his select London day school. In his chubby little hand he clutched a painting, which he proudly presented to her. Amy knelt down and hugged him tightly.

'Hello, handsome,' she said, kissing his slightly sticky cheek. 'What have we got here, then?' She looked at the painting. It was a series of five fat splodges in primary colours and was almost identical to every other painting he had ever done.

'It's our family, silly!' he laughed. 'Me, Flora, Daddy, you and Maria!' Amy laughed but a tiny prickle of discomfort rippled on the back of her neck at the mention of Maria as a member of their family. She looked at her five-year-old son, with his shock of dishevelled white-blond hair. His dark blue eyes, so like her own, danced with mischief in a way that never failed to melt her insides.

His sister Flora, three years his senior and much quieter than her little brother, was busily emptying her satchel. Amy stood up and opened her arms towards her daughter. 'And how's my lovely girl today?' she said. Flora flushed with pleasure and allowed her mother to wrap her in an embrace.

'I'm fine, thanks, Mummy,' replied her daughter. 'Maria says she'll make us her special tortellini for supper.'

Finally, Amy allowed her gaze to settle on Maria, the young Italian nanny who had been with her since Flora was tiny and who had undoubtedly spent more hours with the children than she had. Maria nodded and ruffled Flora's golden hair while Amy beamed. 'How lovely,' she said, thinking her voice sounded shrill in the echoing hallway. Maria's dark eyes met hers and she smiled, one perfectly shaped eyebrow arching like a question mark. Amy nodded her assent and Maria turned towards the kitchen.

It was such a delicate relationship, the one between a mother and a nanny, mused Amy as she sat with the children at the big scrubbed oak table in the sunny day room adjacent to their kitchen. Next to them, Maria moved expertly from one side of the kitchen to the other, lovingly preparing the children's current favourite dish. On the one hand, Amy lived in mortal fear of Maria ever leaving her; but, on the other, she had never quite got used to the idea of another woman playing such a pivotal role in her children's lives, and she often fantasised about letting her go. Sometimes, in her darker moments, she wondered if the children preferred Maria to her, and the thought made her heart constrict with hurt.

'Can I read you the fable I had to write today, Mummy?' asked Flora, in her slightly awkward way that managed to irritate and endear her to Amy in equal measure. She worried about Flora's confidence. She had everything going for her but still she seemed so anxious. Too anxious for such a young child.

'Of course you can, sweetheart,' said Amy, shifting her chair along the hardwood floor so that she was sitting next to her daughter. Flora smiled and began to read fluently in her sweet, clear voice. She was a clever child who had inherited her father's thirst for knowledge, and always seemed happiest when she was lost in a book.

Sam was a different personality altogether. He was loud, funny and affectionate, with extraordinary charisma for such a young child. Everyone, from old age pensioners to babies, seemed to be drawn to him. He had a smile that stretched from ear to ear and a laugh so infectious that Amy and Ben sometimes joked that it should come with a government health warning.

'OK, time for supper!' announced Maria in her brusque voice. 'Clear the table, please.'

Amy helped the children to scoop up their books and her own glossy magazines, wondering for the millionth time why she so often felt like a naughty child in Maria's presence. She was her employer, for God's sake, so why couldn't she do as she pleased in her own house?

'It's because you're setting the kids a good example,' sighed Ben, when she moaned to him later that evening. 'You can hardly sit there with your arms folded defiantly while expecting the children to do as they're told.'

Amy laughed and reached up to kiss him. 'You're so wise,' she said, stroking his face affectionately.

Ben flushed. 'No, I'm not. I'm not wise at all.'

'Yes, you are!' protested Amy, squeezing her arms round his slightly soft middle and burying her face in his chest, drinking in the spicy smell of him that she adored.

'If Maria bothers you so much, maybe we should think about letting her go,' said Ben, his voice muffled as he leaned his face on the top of her head.

Amy looked up to gauge whether he was joking or not. She was shocked to see that his handsome face was taut with strain and his intelligent brown eyes, which normally swam with laughter, were creased with worry.

'But I couldn't *cope* without Maria ... she literally does everything!' Amy half laughed, trying to lighten the mood.

Ben sighed softly. 'It's just that she costs a lot of money and now that the children are at school ...'

'Now that the children are at school, we seem to need her more than ever, with all their clubs and activities to sort out. Seriously, Ben, I think I'll still want Maria here when the kids have left home. She's like a nanny to me, too.'

'Well, then, stop moaning about her treating you like a child!' Ben said with an edge to his voice that Amy had rarely heard him use.

'I'm not really moaning,' she said, back-tracking quickly.

'I'm grateful to have her. And I'm grateful to have *you* ...' she added, kissing him in the way she knew he was never able to resist.

Ben held her tightly for a moment, before she felt the stirring that automatically seemed to follow any kind of physical contact between them. She thought again how lucky she was that after eight years of marriage they still felt such an intense physical pull towards each other. She reached for his hand and started to make her way towards the stairs, leading him behind her.

'Actually, Amy, I'm really tired,' he said, coming to a halt and not meeting her eye as she looked back at him in surprise.

'Don't give me that!' she said with a laugh. 'Since when have you ever been too tired for sex?' Amy had never once known Ben to resist her advances. It didn't seem to matter how stressed he was at work or how little sleep they were getting when the children were babies: he was always, always in the mood for sex.

'Since now,' he replied wearily, and she realised he was serious. She looked at him, his wide shoulders slumped as if he was carrying the weight of the world on them.

'OK,' she said, reaching up and stroking his face. 'I get the message. Let's just get an early night and have a cuddle instead.'

This time, Ben smiled with relief and nodded his agreement. 'That would be good,' he said, sounding exhausted.

Later, unable to sleep, Amy lay her head on Ben's chest, the dark hair there tickling her cheek as she distractedly drew a figure-of-eight on his skin with her nail.

'What?' he said, sleepily. 'What's on your mind?'

'I'm just thinking how lucky I am,' she said, smiling contentedly to herself. 'Handsome husband, gorgeous kids and a beautiful home.'

She felt Ben tense beneath her. 'We're all lucky,' he said quickly. 'Let's just hope it stays that way.'

Looking back, Amy should have heard the alarm bells start to ring there and then. But she didn't. She was enjoying her privileged life far too much to notice.

Chapter 2

'So ... what are you saying, exactly?'

Kate looked into the rheumy eyes of the man sitting in front of her, his forty-seven-year-old face made to look years older by the ravages of illness. His petite wife, not much older than Kate but looking at least twenty years her senior, perched beside him on their faded, once-flowery sofa, clutching his hand so hard her knuckles had turned white; her tiny, ashen face a perfect reflection of her husband's.

'Well,' Kate began carefully, keeping her voice steady, so as not to alarm them any further. 'As you know, you have heart failure.' She paused, allowing her words to sink in before continuing. 'But there are lots of things we can do to help your symptoms, and there's no reason why you can't lead as normal a life as possible.'

She saw both sets of shoulders relax a little as she spoke. There was no point in telling them that although there were plenty of things she could offer to make him more comfortable, he probably wouldn't be around to celebrate his fiftieth birthday. So, instead, she outlined her plans for his treatment over the next year, keeping her tone positive and her voice strong. It was such a huge responsibility to get it right, to not

12

leave these people feeling that there was no hope; but it was so draining. Especially so in the past couple of years, since her own dad's death. Now she knew the true agony of bereavement, and it made her heart ache for those who were about to experience the same thing.

Half an hour later, as she let herself out of the shabby house on a sprawling estate that hummed with tension and the ever-present threat of violence, Kate gave herself a little shake and scurried towards the safety of her ten-year-old red Ford Fiesta, parked on the deserted street in front of her. Looking around her as she put her medical case in the boot, she then climbed into the driver's seat, threw her mobile and stethoscope onto the passenger seat beside her and quickly pressed down the door lock, exhaling with relief as she did so. She started up the engine and the beginning of Steve Wright's afternoon show on Radio 2 filled her ears, the familiarity of the chirruping voices and jangling tunes imme-diately soothing her nerves.

Whenever she and Miles talked about getting a new car – not that they could afford it – Kate always remembered situations like this when she was glad not to own anything worth stealing. *Unlike Amy*, she thought wryly to herself as she drove off the estate on the outskirts of Banntree, the small Suffolk town where she lived, back into the comfort of the main roads and streams of traffic. She imagined how her younger sister would cope in her shoes. Badly, she decided. She wouldn't be able to leave the Range Rover at home and would be mortally offended when she returned from a house call to find it jacked up on bricks and minus every window.

At times, though, Kate felt a jealousy and longing to swap

places with Amy that was almost overwhelming. Not particularly for the material benefits of having Amy's seemingly endless money, big house or flash cars, but more for her lack of pressure and responsibility. The biggest decision she had to make in any one day was whether to have a skinny latte or opt for a smoothie instead.

Kate loved her job as a community-based heart specialist nurse, but the strain was huge. She glanced at herself in the rear-view mirror and inwardly groaned at the prematurely haggard face that greeted her. Her shoulder-length, nut-brown hair badly needed cutting, and she decided that she really should invest in some more Touche Éclat to cover the bags under her eyes. But she hadn't been able to justify forking out for it since the one Amy had bought her had run out. Money was always tight and Miles's job working for the local council paid even less than hers. Paying the mortgage and buying shoes for the children were the priority, not make-up.

She looked up at the clouds that were forming in the summer sky, bringing with them the promise of a rainstorm, then glanced at the dashboard clock. It was just after two. If she hurried, she could squeeze in a visit to the supermarket before the children came out of school but she would need to be quick, especially if it was going to rain. She began to compile a mental shopping list: bread, milk, washing powder ... had they run out of cereal?

As she swung the Fiesta into a parking space in the Tesco car park, Kate was feeling for her mobile phone to call Miles to check their cereal status when she heard the sudden, sickening crunch of metal on metal and her car juddered to an abrupt halt. Kate's neck was jolted violently forwards and her mobile phone and stethoscope went flying into the footwell.

There was a hissing sound, followed by a few moments of silence – broken only by the sound of a Bruce Springsteen song emitting feebly from the damaged car radio – before Kate managed to look up. In front of her, the tailgate of a shiny black SUV sat in a crumpled heap on the bonnet of her Fiesta.

'What the fuck?' yelled a voice and she involuntarily ducked down as a short, red-faced man leapt from the driver's seat of the SUV, looking at the back of his car in disbelief. His mouth opening in shock, he turned his bald head towards Kate, who was still cowering behind the steering wheel of her car.

Taking a deep breath, she gingerly pressed the 'Unlock' button on the dashboard, immediately realising her mistake as he strode over and wrenched her door open. 'What the fuck were you doing?' he yelled, the veins on his pock-marked face bulging dangerously.

Kate looked again at the mess of crumpled metal in front of her. How the hell had she not seen him? 'I, er, I don't know,' she whispered, undoing her seatbelt and gingerly climbing out of the car. Her legs were shaky and pains were shooting through her neck, causing her to wince. She was dimly aware that rain had started to fall in cold, plump drops all around her.

'You stupid, fucking cow!' yelled the man, his eyes blazing. 'You're going to bloody well pay for this!'

Suddenly, there was a rushing sound behind Kate and, just as she was wondering what it was, everything turned black.

'She's coming round!' said a male voice from somewhere above her. Kate opened her eyes and closed them again just as quickly, as a searing pain shot through her head. 'You're OK,' said the voice gently. It was a lovely voice. Deep, resonant, soothing. 'Just lie still. We've called an ambulance and it'll be here any minute.'

Kate did as she was told. She could hear the sound of rain spattering onto concrete and voices speaking in murmurs that were carried up into the air before evaporating. Her head and neck hurt like hell and she couldn't remember where she was or what had happened. She felt someone putting a coat over her and registered a clean, soapy smell from their hands as they smoothed the damp hair back from her forehead.

A few minutes later and, feeling better, Kate opened her eyes again and tried to get her bearings. She was lying on the ground in a car park, a small crowd of people gathered around her. The owner of the voice and hands was kneeling over her, silhouetted against the sullen sky above him. Seeing that she had her eyes open, he knelt down to one side and looked at her with what she could now see were a pair of the darkest brown eyes she had ever seen.

He smiled. 'You're OK,' he said, reaching over to stroke her forehead again. 'The ambulance will be here soon. Can you tell me your name?'

'Kate Robinson,' Kate croaked, enjoying the feeling of being taken care of, despite the pain. Life was such a constant merry-go-round of looking after patients, the kids and Miles that it was nice to be looked after for a change. She hoped the ambulance would be a long while yet, so that she could just lie there, not having to do anything but have her face stroked by a handsome stranger. But, just as that thought faded away, she felt a small rumble in the ground beneath her and saw the reflection of a flashing blue light as an ambulance pulled to a halt beside them.

Suddenly Kate remembered the children, who would by now be waiting in the pouring rain at the school gates and wondering why she wasn't there. It wasn't unusual for her to be late – in fact, she was more often late than not – but she always got there in the end. 'My kids!' she whimpered to the man, who was still kneeling beside her.

'Where's your phone?' he said, immediately understanding and springing into action. 'Tell me who to call and we'll get someone to pick them up.'

Kate pointed towards her car, where her handbag was still sitting on the front seat. 'The front seat – on the floor . . .' she said, her voice hoarse, as she gradually remembered how she had come to be lying on the wet concrete of a supermarket car park.

The man strode to the car, retrieved her phone and grabbed her bag, before coming back to kneel beside her. 'Right,' he said, holding up her phone. 'Who shall I call?'

'Sarah,' she said weakly. 'Sarah Campbell. She's one of the other mums. She'll take the kids home with her until I can get Miles to go and pick them up.'

'Miles?' said the man.

'My husband,' replied Kate, as an ambulance man's cheery young face suddenly loomed over her. As he began to check her over, her new saviour became obscured from view, but she could still hear his voice as he made the call to Sarah.

'Hi, my name's Jack Levine,' she heard him say. 'Your friend, Kate, has had a bit of an accident . . . No, no, she's OK, just whiplash, I think, but she's probably going to have to go to hospital to be checked over and she's worried about picking up the kids . . . You will? That's great, thank you. I'm sure she'll call you herself later. Goodbye.'

By now Kate was being moved onto a stretcher and loaded into the ambulance. 'Can you call my husband, Miles, as well?' she cried out, as the man ended the call. 'Tell him to come to the hospital?'

'Of course,' he said, quickly scanning through her contacts list.

It seemed to take an eternity for the ambulance man to secure the stretcher. Just as he was about to close the doors, a sudden jolt of panic gripped Kate. 'My car!' she said, her eyes darting desperately from side to side as she searched for someone to help her.

Once again, her knight in shining armour appeared as he put her bag into the ambulance beside the stretcher. 'Don't worry,' he said calmly, pulling out his iPhone and tapping on it. 'I'll get all the details for the insurance. Can you quickly give me your phone number?'

'Oh! Er, yes, of course.' Kate rattled off her mobile number, relieved that at least her memory seemed to be intact. He put it into his phone before stepping back to allow the ambulance man to start closing the doors again. 'Thank you so much!' Kate said, tears finally beginning to prick at her eyes as the ambulance doors slammed shut and he disappeared from view.

Chapter 3

Jennifer looked at her watch for the umpteenth time. Ten past ten. She was due to meet him at ten thirty. As she hovered on the doorstep of her pink, chocolate-box cottage, her car keys clutched in her hand, she questioned yet again whether she was doing the right thing. There was still time to back out, and her head swam with indecision. Finally, she nodded to herself and, pulling the cottage door closed behind her, headed out into the morning sunshine towards the old, silver Clio that was parked in its usual higgledy-piggledy fashion on the semicircular gravel driveway.

Driving the short distance into the centre of Banntree, the small Suffolk town where she lived, Jennifer began to wonder how he would look now: whether she would even recognise him after all these years. His Facebook photo hadn't given much away: it featured just his long, slim legs clad in jeans, and a pair of moss-green Hunter wellies, standing next to his black Labrador tagged simply as 'Jess'. Back when she had known him, he had had very dark – almost black – hair and deep, chocolate-coloured eyes that had oozed sensuality. The memory of those eyes still caused her insides to flutter more than thirty years later.

And how would he think *she* looked now, as a pensioner? She knew she had aged well: her long, formerly dark hair was now cut into a severe silver bob that draped over razor-sharp cheekbones, and her figure was still a trim size 10. In her twenties, even though she felt conceited thinking it, she had been known as a 'head-turner'. When she hadn't been working – and therefore wearing her regulation doctor's white coat – her long, slim legs had usually been on display under a tiny suede or leather mini-skirt, topped with a figure-hugging roll-neck, which had clung to her surprisingly ample bust. A pair of knee-length, zip-up leather boots had ensured she got maximum attention; especially when she was astride Michael's motorbike, her arms wrapped around his waist that was clad in his black, James Dean-style leather jacket. The wind rushing through her long, dark hair, they had sped through the streets of London fancying themselves as film stars.

Michael. Jennifer stamped on the brakes as the pain of his loss hit her with its usual crippling ferocity, causing her to swerve violently. Luckily, the winding country road was empty and she took a series of deep breaths to regain her composure before straightening the car and continuing on her journey.

Michael had been dead for just over two years but, if anything, her grief and anger were even more raw now than when first it had happened. The sickening feeling of seeing the police car draw up outside the cottage: Jennifer knowing instantly by the demeanour of the baby-faced officer that it was bad news. And not just bad news but the worst, most agonising news she would ever hear: hit head-on by a drunk, uninsured boy-racer as Michael had been making his way home after a day of consultancy work in London, he had been killed instantly. His Land Rover, normally so protective and safe, hadn't stood a chance as it flew off the road and burst into flames.

His funeral had been beautiful and unusual, just like Michael. He was buried in a natural burial wood, on a hillside just a few miles from their home. The sun had shone down from a clear, cobalt sky and glittered in the silver river at the bottom of the hill on which the wood grew. The sounds of a perfect summer's day had been punctuated only by Kate and Amy's pitiful sobs as they gripped each other for support, both so devastated by the death of the father they had adored. Jennifer, still too shocked to cry then, had stood in silence, consumed with horror that her beloved soul mate had gone. There had been plenty of time for tears later, alone at home, when the enormity of it all had finally crashed upon her with the force of a speeding train. She had contemplated ending it all then – in the hope of being reunited with him – but she knew that Michael would have been disappointed in her. And she couldn't bear to leave her two lovely daughters and her beautiful, precious grandchildren.

It took exactly eight minutes to reach the centre of Banntree. It was one of the oldest towns in England, and consisted of one long street, sprinkled with quaint, medieval buildings housing an old-fashioned variety of shops, a few pubs and one Michelin-starred bistro, which was where Jennifer had arranged to meet him.

Her stomach began to flutter with nerves. She spotted a parking space in front of the village bakery and swung her little car into it. She undid her seatbelt and took a couple of deep breaths before opening the door and stepping out. It was a bright, warm day, with only a few wispy clouds to break up the watercolour blue of the sky – much like the day of

Michael's funeral. Jennifer wondered briefly if she would ever again appreciate what used to be her favourite season: now, every summer's day seemed to taunt her with reminders of what she had lost.

Shaking her head a little to try to dispel her thoughts, she locked the car, swung her large brown Mulberry bag over her shoulder and headed towards the bistro, which she could see was already buzzing with customers calling in for a mid-morning latte or cappuccino.

He didn't mind coming to her, he had said in his message. His son lived in the area, so he knew it well and he would enjoy getting out into the countryside for the day. She hadn't wanted him to come to the cottage: that would have been too intimate for a first meeting. She needed somewhere neutral where they would have the protection of other voices, should their own run out of things to say. Not that they had ever worried about running out of things to say back then: they had never particularly talked much. He was an enigma, whose smooth intelligence acted as a perfect complement to his brooding good looks. He had a compelling magnetism to both women and men. But especially women.

Jennifer glanced in through the lemon-painted sash windows as she passed the front of the bistro. She thought she caught sight of him, leaning against the bar, sipping from an espresso cup. Her heart jolted and she hesitated at the door, her hand hovering over the brushed steel handle, unsure if she could go through with it. Why didn't she just leave things as they were? But even as she stared at her own reflection in the dark glass of the door before her, she knew why. She gripped the handle, pushed it down and walked in impatiently to confront her past.

Chapter 4

'So, that's six hundred and fifty pounds, please,' said the sales assistant, carefully wrapping the pair of Louboutin shoes in white tissue paper before gently encasing them in their signature red shoe bag, and placing them into their buff-coloured box.

Amy took her large leather wallet out of her soft black Prada handbag and opened it, searching for Ben's credit card. Nothing quite compared to the high of buying the most beautiful shoes on the planet. These ones were particularly gorgeous. Peep-toe, with a platform and a skyscraper heel. Amy could just imagine Ben's face when she modelled them for him later. He adored her in high heels and had never once balked at her spending to supplement her already large collection. At least, he never had before. Lately, he had started to comment on her spending but she knew that he wouldn't be able to resist these shoes: especially if she offered to wear them with nothing else.

'Are these for anything in particular?' asked the sales girl, taking the credit card Amy proffered and swiping it through the machine in front of her.

'Like she needs an excuse!' laughed Amy's friend, Jo, from

behind her. She picked up a red patent shoe and gazed at it with her lips pursed, as if studying a painting.

'You can talk!' said Amy, feeling a spark of guilt mixed with irritation, as she gestured pointedly towards Jo's own collection of designer carrier bags. The sales girl laughed but it was a laugh that didn't sound genuine: it was the laugh of someone with an eye on their commission.

'True,' admitted Jo grudgingly, replacing the red shoe and moving languorously towards another shelf. 'But it's all essential . . . I mean, I have to do my bit at all these dinners and events that Tim expects me to go to with him. The least he can do is buy me something to wear.'

'Yes, that's true . . . It's not as if you already have anything in your wardrobe, is it?' Amy smiled as she turned back towards the sales girl, who had swiped the card three times and was now peering at the machine in puzzlement. 'Is there a problem?' she asked, her smile freezing slightly.

A pink rash was starting to spread up the sales girl's neck. 'Er, it's probably the machine but your card has been declined. Have you got another one?'

Amy frowned. 'That's odd,' she murmured, opening her purse again and taking out her emergency credit card, which she rarely used. 'Here, try this one . . .'

The sales girl beamed with relief as she saw her commission come back into view. She swiped the card and nodded emphatically. 'There!' she cried. 'That's fine. Sorry about that,' she added, as she handed over the bag.

'No problem,' said Amy, taking it and throwing a quick glance towards Jo, who, she was relieved to note, was still browsing the shelves further down the shop.

As the two of them stepped out of the shop onto the

Mayfair street where they had already spent most of the morning shopping, Jo said, 'So, what now? A little light lunch?'

They both looked right towards Scott's, just a few metres up the street, where the paparazzi were already gathering in feverish anticipation of the latest celebrity diner to tip them off that they would be arriving for lunch.

'We'll never get a table at such short notice,' said Amy, quietly relieved, but allowing the corners of her mouth to turn down in a display of disappointment.

'Then it's a good job I booked, isn't it?' said Jo triumph-antly, linking her arm through Amy's and steering her towards the large artificial flames and giant awning that formed the front of the restaurant.

Amy allowed herself to be propelled along. She could always put lunch on her own credit card again, but she wished she could shake the gnawing sensation in the pit of her stomach. Something wasn't right; she just didn't know what it was.

'Wow, I need this!' said Jo minutes later, having settled into her seat and taken a large sip of her Kir Royal.

'Me, too,' agreed Amy, gazing at her own Bellini. The rose-coloured bubbles tickled her throat slightly as she sipped it.

'It's hard work, all this shopping and lunching!' said Jo with a glib smile, her eyes darting around the large room in search of celebrities. 'Ooh, that's Victoria Beckham over there! She looks stunning.'

Amy followed Jo's gaze and nodded indifferently, won-dering why she didn't feel as excited as she normally would. Instead, she felt the feeling of guilt that had been pressing down on her shoulders all morning get a little bit heavier, and gave herself a quick shake. She looked across the table at Jo, with her expensive caramel highlights, perfectly manicured nails and gym-toned body, and wondered if *she* ever questioned her role in life. At least Amy had produced two beautiful children, whereas Jo had remained childless by choice, saying she couldn't bear the thought of something ruining her figure and her libido 'only to grow up hating me'.

Jo looked up from the menu she had been studying intently. 'What?' she asked, the corners of her artificially plumped lips turning up in amusement.

Amy blinked back at her, wondering whether to confide in her. They had been friends for years, ever since Tim and Ben had gone into business together. But there was a hardness to Jo that meant Amy had never quite felt that she could fully trust her. Jo had never wanted children and yet she had never wanted a career, either. She seemed happy to be Tim's trophy wife and spend her life spending his money: the guilt that had always dogged Amy about not working didn't appear to trouble Jo. But then Tim and Jo's relationship was very different to Amy and Ben's, and reminded Amy of a business partnership, rather than a marriage. She also knew that both Tim and Jo had been unfaithful in the past, but they seemed happy with the arrangement they had come to.

'Have you . . .' Amy paused and tore off a small piece of bread from the metal bowl full of bread in the centre of the table. She put it in her mouth and chewed slowly; more for something to do rather than because she wanted to eat it. 'Have you noticed anything different about Tim lately?'

Jo frowned as much as her Botox would allow and shook her head slowly. Her shoulder-length hair swung from side to side as she did so and Amy got a waft of her Hermes scent, which always reminded Amy of summer, whatever time of year it was. 'No. Why?'

Amy swallowed the piece of bread and took a deep breath. 'Oh, it's probably nothing. It's just that Ben seems a bit crabby lately, especially whenever I mention work. I just wondered if Tim had said anything.'

Jo shook her head again, but she hesitated for just a fraction of a second and Amy knew she was holding something back. 'Not that I can think of,' she said at last, looking around for a waiter and picking up her menu again. 'Come on, let's order,' she said, brusquely changing the subject. 'This is my treat today – you paid last time. Now I fancy the crab linguine . . .'

'Jesus, Amy!' sighed Ben, nine hours later, lying in their large bed. He looked up at Amy, who had just emerged from her dressing room wearing nothing but her brand new Louboutins.

'Aren't they gorgeous?' she purred, sashaying towards her husband. 'I knew you'd approve.'

But instead of grabbing her and throwing her onto the bed, as she had hoped he would, Ben's face seemed to sag with misery. 'I approve,' he said half-heartedly, 'but I dread to think how much they must have cost . . . I take it they aren't a cheaper, high-street rip-off?'

Amy stopped in her tracks, now feeling ridiculous in her nakedness. She dashed the final few feet towards the bed and dived under the duvet. 'Since when have you cared how much they cost, as long as they were high and sexy?' she said indignantly, pulling the crisp white duvet right up to her chin.

Ben tried to smile but it didn't reach his dark eyes.

Amy looked at him for a moment, before reaching out and starting to stroke his forehead rhythmically with her thumb, the way she did with Sam when she was putting him to bed. Ben closed his eyes and seemed to relax slightly.

'Are you OK, honey?' she asked softly, noticing how clammy his forehead was and wondering if maybe he was coming down with something. It would explain his tetchiness, which was unusual for him.

Ben groaned slightly, before opening his eyes again. He rolled onto his side so that he was facing her, and propped his head up with his hand. The shadows under his eyes had darkened in the half-light from the bedside lamp. 'I'm—' He hesitated and looked away, as if deciding whether or not to continue. 'I'm . . . a bit stressed, that's all.'

'Why?' Amy mirrored his position, her belly filling with coldness as she steeled herself for the answer. 'It's not . . . us, is it?' she added, her heart pounding in her chest. Ben and the children were everything to her: her one reason for being. To think of anything coming between them filled her with a fear that was all consuming.

Ben's face softened and he reached out to stroke her anxious face. 'No! No, of course it's not . . . I love you as much as ever.'

The chill in her belly faded slightly and Amy exhaled with relief. 'Well, what is it, then?'

Ben's hand moved from stroking her face to stroking her breasts. Amy's nipples hardened immediately at his touch. 'It's nothing,' he said, his pupils dilating as he pulled back the duvet and gazed with longing at his wife's body. 'Forget it. Let's try these new shoes out, instead.'

Chapter 5

'Hi, Kate, how are you feeling?' asked Sarah as she slid into the chair beside Kate's hospital bed. 'You poor thing, you must have had such a shock.'

Kate smiled, despite the pain in her neck and shoulder, pleased to see her friend. 'I'm fine really – I feel a bit of a fraud being here. They're keeping me in for observation overnight but they reckon it's probably just whiplash.'

Sarah nodded and bent down to retrieve a bunch of grapes from her oversized shopping bag. She placed them on Kate's lap. 'You look very pale,' she said, her eyes scanning Kate's face. 'Are you sure you're feeling OK?'

'I'm fine. A bit sore, but hopefully after a good night's sleep, I'll be right as rain.' Kate tried to make her voice as upbeat as possible. 'Thanks so much for picking the kids up for me,' she added.

'Don't be daft. It was no problem. Miles has taken them home and my mum is looking after mine.' Sarah's eyes drifted for a moment before she seemed to remember something. 'Oh, and who was that man who called me? He sounded *very* nice on the phone!'

Kate felt her face flush as she recalled Jack's deep voice

and his handsome face, looking down at her with concern as she came round. 'Oh, er, him. Yes, he was very helpful,' she stuttered.

A mischievous glint appeared in Sarah's pale blue eyes. 'Was he good-looking by any chance?' she asked slyly, leaning her blonde head towards Kate. 'Only you appear to be blushing.'

Kate sighed. Sarah had a finely tuned antennae for any kind of gossip or scandal, and she looked like she knew she was on to something. 'I didn't really notice,' Kate replied primly. 'I was too worried about what would happen to the children.'

'Liar!' Sarah said with a laugh, refusing to be deterred. 'What did he look like?'

Kate laughed back, knowing that denial was impossible thanks to her rapidly reddening cheeks. She recalled those delicious brown eyes, framed with the longest lashes she had ever seen on a man. 'He *was* quite handsome,' she began coyly, aware that her pulse had quickened just at the memory of him. 'His name is Jack something. I can't remember—'

'Levine. It's Jack Levine. I remember now,' interrupted Sarah, picking a grape from the bunch and popping it into her mouth. 'Go on,' she said, a trickle of juice spilling from the side of her mouth as she spoke. She dabbed it away carelessly with the back of her hand.

'Well, anyway,' continued Kate, trying to remember the details of what happened. 'I crashed the car ...' she said slowly, then, 'Oh God, I crashed the car!' she groaned, putting her hand over her face. 'Shit! What the hell has happened to the car?'

'It's fine,' said a deep voice to Kate's left, making her jump, then wince, as pain shot through her neck and shoulder again. Tentatively, she glanced in the direction of the voice and felt her heart skip a beat. Standing there, looking just as handsome as she remembered and clutching a bunch of creamy, velvety roses, was her hero from the afternoon.

'Oh, er, hi!' she stammered, knowing that her cheeks were getting pinker by the second. She was about to introduce Sarah, when Sarah leapt out of her chair and almost clambered over Kate's bed to get to him.

'Hi!' she gushed, reaching out to shake his hand. 'You must be Jack! I'm Sarah, Kate's friend. You called me earlier.'

Jack grinned a slightly lopsided smile and shook Sarah's hand, shoving the roses under his other arm as he did so. 'I did, indeed,' he said. 'Did you get to the children on time?'

Sarah stole a look at Kate, who was beaming with pleasure that he had asked about her children before anything else. 'Yes,' Sarah replied. 'They're fine. Miles, Kate's *husband* picked them up from mine about an hour ago.'

'That's good,' said Jack easily, ignoring Sarah's emphasis on the word 'husband'. 'I brought you some flowers,' he added, unnecessarily, his gaze returning to Kate.

'Thank you!' she smiled up at him, wondering if she would ever get to meet him face to face or whether she was destined to only ever see him from the angle of lying down. 'Sarah, can you see if you can find a vase?'

Sarah raised her eyebrows slightly and looked at Kate pointedly. 'Please?' added Kate, looking back at Sarah equally pointedly. After another pause, Sarah reluctantly turned and made her way down the ward towards the nurses' station.

Jack shifted his weight from one foot to the other. 'Sit

down!' urged Kate, motioning towards the empty chair beside her that Sarah had just vacated. Jack smiled again as he walked around the end of her bed and sat down, laying the roses carefully on Kate's bedside table. There was an awkward pause before they both spoke again: 'So!' they both chorused, before stopping and laughing. 'You go first,' said Jack.

'Well, I just want to say "thank you",' began Kate, feeling hot tears starting to prick at her eyes. 'That is, for helping me out so much. For calling Sarah and Miles . . . he's very grateful too, by the way.'

Jack waved his hand dismissively. 'No need,' he said. 'I'm sure he'd have done the same thing. And I'm sure he's just relieved that you're OK.'

It was true. Miles had come racing into the ward earlier, looking panic-stricken, his open face flushed and his bright blue eyes looking perilously damp. 'Oh, thank God!' he had exclaimed when he had found that, apart from her sore neck, she was fine.

Kate had watched him slump down in the chair beside the bed, his tall, wide frame only just fitting into it. He had still been dressed in his smart work clothes of grey trousers and a white shirt and he was panting slightly from exertion, which explained the damp patches spreading from under his arms. Kate was touched by how worried he was about her. 'I'm so sorry about the car,' she had said in a small voice, knowing that as they could only afford third-party insurance – and that the accident had been her fault – they would have to buy a new one, which was the last thing they needed.

Miles had shaken his head and clasped her hand in his.

'Believe me, baby, the car is the last thing I care about right now', he had said, his eyes brimming.

'So,' Kate said again, pushing the thoughts to the back of her mind for the moment and looking back at Jack. 'What were you going to say?'

'Well,' Jack began, 'I came because I wanted to let you know that it wasn't your fault. The crash, I mean.'

Kate frowned in confusion. 'But ... I smashed into the back of him. How could it not be my fault?'

Jack shook his head. 'No, you didn't. I was there, opposite you, when you pulled into the space. It was empty. But he reversed into it out of nowhere, going far too fast, from the other side. *He* reversed into *you*. There was no way you could have avoided him.'

Kate's mouth opened in shock. She had been so sure it was her fault. 'But that man ... he was so aggressive,' she said, as the memory of the other driver's round, red face, veins pulsating with anger, flashed through her mind.

'Of course he was aggressive. He wanted to make out it was your fault. But he hadn't reckoned on witnesses.' Jack smiled, almost proudly. 'I gave the police a witness statement, so hopefully he'll be liable for any costs.'

Kate gazed at him, her heart swelling with gratitude and something else not quite so innocent. 'Thank you,' she whispered. 'Thank you so much. I owe you.'

At that moment Sarah reappeared, clutching an ugly yellow vase. 'This was the only one I could find,' she said, holding it up apologetically, before plonking the flowers into it, still wrapped in their raffia-tied brown paper. 'Sorry, Jack, your lovely flowers deserve better.'

Jack grinned good naturedly, and stood up to let Sarah sit

down. 'It's not the container,' he said. 'It's what's in it that matters.'

Sarah and Kate looked at each other and swooned simultaneously.

'Anyway, I'd better be getting off,' he added, seemingly oblivious to the effect he was having on them. 'I'm glad you're OK, Kate. And, fingers crossed, Mr Angry will have to stump up a fair bit of cash to compensate you for your distress ...'

'Thank you,' Kate said again, happily. 'Thank you so much. Goodbye.'

Sarah, who had sat down, suddenly leapt up again. 'I'll walk out with you, Jack,' she cried, gathering her bags. She bent down and kissed Kate on the cheek. 'Glad you're OK,' she said, beginning to walk off with Jack. 'I'll see you tomorrow.'

Kate grinned at her ruefully. 'Yes, thanks for coming, Sarah. Your concern is truly touching.'

Sarah smiled and stuck her tongue out at Kate over her shoulder. Kate watched them walking out together and felt a prickle of jealousy, before reprimanding herself. She was happily married and in love with Miles, whereas Sarah was single, her husband having walked out on her and the children several years ago, when his PA took her personal assistant duties just that little bit too far. She was happy if Sarah could meet someone, especially someone as lovely as Jack. It was just ... she couldn't help it. She could feel herself being drawn to him by some irresistible force that could only mean one thing: trouble.

Chapter 6

'Hello, Jennifer,' he said, his dark eyes flickering with danger in exactly the same way as they always had. Time seemed to slip into slow motion and Jennifer suddenly felt as though she was wading through water as she approached the bar.

'Hello, Hugh.' Her words seemed to travel slowly over the short distance between them, as if muffled by cotton wool. They both hesitated as she finally reached him, unsure how to greet each other after so long. Eventually, Hugh leaned down and kissed her gently on one cheek, then the other. The shock of his physicality and the smell of him brought so many memories racing to the surface that Jennifer felt her legs go weak, and she stumbled slightly. She shouldn't have come here today. She couldn't cope with seeing him again. Not now. Not ever.

As if sensing her thoughts, Hugh gripped her elbow firmly, partly to steady her; partly, she thought, to keep her from turning and running out of the restaurant. 'Let's get a table, shall we?' He searched her face with his eyes and she nodded hesitantly.

'Sorry,' she stammered, as they sat down at a round

wooden table in the corner, having ordered Jennifer a coffee. 'It's just—'

'I know,' he said, interrupting her. 'I know.'

Jennifer nodded. Even after all this time, there was still a shorthand between them. He hadn't really changed at all. His hair was heavily flecked with grey now, but it suited him: it emphasised the darkness of his eyes and the swarthiness of his skin. Watching him, she was instantly transported back almost four decades, to the day she had first looked into his eyes.

'Is anyone sitting here?' said a voice.

Jennifer looked up in surprise. She had been engrossed in revising for her medical exams. She was tired and stressed, had rowed with Michael and had fled to the little coffee shop on the Kings Road to get some caffeine into her to help her keep going, when all she wanted to do was lie down on the floor and sleep for hours.

'I suppose not,' she replied grumpily to the tall, dark, sharply dressed young man who had asked the question.

As she returned to her books, he sat down opposite her and ordered a black coffee from the pretty young waitress who had instantly and miraculously appeared at his side, before shaking a cigarette out of a pack and lighting it. Seeing her glance up, he motioned the pack of cigarettes towards her and raised his eyebrows. Without either of them speaking, Jennifer took a cigarette and leaned towards him as he lit it for her.

For several moments, they sat in silence, smoking, looking at each other through the columns of smoke rising steadily and seductively from each of their mouths. Jennifer was transfixed by his deep, almost black eyes that seemed to glitter with amusement and – something else, something that she couldn't quite place. Michael's laughing eyes were navy-blue and his hair and skin were fair, giving him a Scandinavian appearance. Jennifer loved Michael's face, yet she couldn't draw her eyes away from this exotic-looking stranger. Still neither of them spoke until, eventually, Jennifer forced herself to look away from him and back down at her books. But she found that the words swam on the page and she couldn't focus properly. She was too aware of him watching her intently.

'What?' she said at last, with a note of exasperation in her voice.

'Nothing,' he replied, in a velvety voice. 'I just like watching you.'

Jennifer tutted to herself and continued to stare in vain at the pages of her book.

'Tell me what's wrong,' he said after a long while, during which he had lit another cigarette and ordered another black coffee from the ever-helpful waitress.

Jennifer bit her lip and felt the tingling in her nose that always preceded tears. 'What makes you think there's anything wrong?' she replied defensively, still not looking up, her voice thick in her throat.

'I just know,' he said simply, taking a long drag on his cigarette and exhaling smoke in rings, expertly puffing them out one after the other like a miniature steam train.

Suddenly, Billy Ocean's 'Love Really Hurts Without You' came onto the jukebox, causing Jennifer's heart to skip and her eyes to swim as the words of the song resonated. It really did hurt without Michael around, especially after they argued. She waited until the tears in her eyes had started to recede before looking up at the young man again, as she stubbed out her cigarette. There was something vaguely hypnotic about him in the way he stared at her without blinking: as if he could see right into her soul.

'Do I know you?' she asked, after yet another long pause.

'No, but I feel like I know you. I've watched you often enough.'

Jennifer's eyes widened in surprise. He gestured his pack of cigarettes towards her and she took another, which she let him light again. 'When?' she said, inhaling deeply, enjoying the kick of nicotine as it combined with the caffeine to give her the buzz she so badly needed.

'I work near here. I see you a lot. Usually with some blond guy.' His eyes narrowed. 'Is that what's wrong? I do hope so,' he drawled.

Jennifer's eyes overflowed before she could stop them. He leaned forwards and handed her a thin paper napkin, which she took and used to wipe her eyes as delicately as she could.

'Good,' he said, the corners of his full mouth turning up.

'It's not funny!' gulped Jennifer, between sobs.

'Not funny, no,' he agreed, looking up to one side, as if he was considering it. 'But good.'

'It's just a tiff,' she protested. 'We haven't broken up. And, for God's sake, I don't even know you!'

'Not yet,' he replied. 'But you will.'

'You've hardly changed,' he said now, slowly and deliberately, breaking through her thoughts. 'You're still very beautiful.'

'Liar,' she said. She took a sip of her cappuccino with a smile, though – secretly pleased with the compliment. Hugh didn't reply. There was no need. They both knew that he wouldn't have said it if he didn't think it was true. One thing she had always loved about him was that there was never any need for small talk. He chose his words carefully and used them sparingly. He wasn't afraid of silence as, just like now, they sat engrossed in their own thoughts and memories.

'So, did you make the right choice, Jennifer?' he said after a long pause, as if emphasising her thoughts.

Jennifer looked into those mesmeric, inky eyes and watched the movie of another life that might have been play out before her. Snapping back into the present, she finally spoke: 'Of course. Did you, Hugh?'

'*I* didn't have a choice,' he replied.

Chapter 7

As Amy drove up the driveway to her mother's pretty cottage, she felt her chest muscles tightening with tension – the way they always did when she visited her. *Surely it should be the other way round,* she thought, parking her Range Rover at an angle to her mum's battered old Clio. *Surely getting out of London should help me to relax?* But it was the disapproval that she knew her mother wouldn't be able to hide that always put her on edge.

As she opened the boot to retrieve her bags, the front door of the cottage opened and her mother appeared. *She's still a strikingly attractive woman,* Amy thought, whose high cheekbones and large, almond-shaped eyes gave her a slightly exotic, other-worldly beauty.

'Hello!' Jennifer called out gaily, opening her arms to the children who propelled themselves towards her at alarming speed.

As the children hugged their grandmother warmly, she looked up and met Amy's eye. 'Hello, darling!' she smiled. '*Another* new car?' Her eyes flitted towards the Range Rover.

'Yes,' replied Amy curtly, kissing her mum on the cheek, then following her into the cottage. She could have sworn that she heard her mother tut but decided to ignore it, choosing not to start a row before she had even closed the front door.

The children raced up the higgledy-piggledy stairs to their bedrooms, hauling their brightly coloured rucksacks behind them. Amy and Jennifer automatically made for the beamed kitchen, where Amy perched at the breakfast bar.

'Cup of tea?' asked Jennifer.

Amy nodded gratefully and stretched. Even though the drive from London was relatively short, it always left her feeling drained and stiff. 'It's so lovely to see you,' said her mum, as she put teabags into mismatched mugs and plonked a carton of milk on the breakfast bar. Amy said nothing, wincing slightly as Jennifer stirred the tea then dropped the teaspoon onto the granite worktop, where it left a miniature brown puddle. As she stared at the spoon, Amy realised with a start that having Maria to clear up after her had made her fastidious in a way that she would never have been if she had had to clear up her own mess. Before she married Ben, she had been more than happy to live in filth, just so long as she didn't have to do any housework. Her university digs had been bordering on a health hazard, mainly because she and her flatmates couldn't be bothered to tidy it up.

'How's Kate?' asked Amy, as Jennifer placed one of the steaming mugs of tea in front of her.

'She's OK, I think,' Jennifer replied, sitting down beside Amy on a high stool. 'She's still a bit sore but I think she'll be fine. More than can be said for their car, apparently. I offered to lend them the money to buy a better one but you know what Miles is like . . .' She tailed off and Amy nodded. Miles was a fiercely proud man who would do everything in his power to avoid taking help from anyone – even if it meant that he and Kate led a frugal existence – when they could have benefited from the fact that her mother was comfortably off and her sister positively wealthy. 'They're coming over tomorrow morning, so you'll be able to see for yourself,' Jennifer added.

'Oh, that's great – the kids will be thrilled.' Amy loved her older sister and adored her sister's two children, Millie and Josh, who at eleven and eight were older than Flora and Sam and were idolised by them.

'So, where's Ben this weekend?' asked Jennifer, a note of pique in her voice.

Amy blew on her tea slightly before taking a sip: an old habit to which she always reverted when in her mother's company. 'Working,' she said carefully, trying to keep the irritation out of her voice.

Jennifer nodded and raised an eyebrow. 'He works too hard,' she murmured, sipping her own tea.

'As opposed to me, you mean?' snapped Amy, unable to stop her hackles from rising.

Jennifer rolled her eyes. 'No, Amy, that's not what I meant as you well know! God, you're a silly girl sometimes!'

A heavy silence descended, as if there was an invisible wall dividing the two women. Finally, Sam came bounding into the kitchen, trailing with him a gust of fresh air that blew the silence away. 'Granny!' he shouted. 'Can I see my greenhouse? Have my cucumbers grown yet?'

Jennifer grinned conspiratorially. 'Well now, you might be in for a bit of a surprise, Sam. Come with me.'

Amy stood at the kitchen window watching her mum bending over a shelf of plants in the greenhouse, explaining and pointing things out to Sam, who was listening with rapt attention. For some reason, he was interested in gardening, which wasn't something he had inherited from her; although Ben often claimed that he loved gardening, he just didn't get the time any more.

She had studied English at university but had found it tough going; everyone else was so much cleverer than she and she only just managed to avoid being kicked off the course. Keeping up with the reading, trying to come up with original thoughts for essays . . . It wasn't what she'd hoped it would be and she barely scraped a third. After university, she had landed a secretarial job, before she had struck lucky and met the love of her life in Ben. He was the young, handsome boss of his own marketing company, and was to go on to make a lot of money as the company rapidly grew in the following years.

When they married, Amy had ignored the advice of her mother to keep working on her own career. She had taken redundancy instead, protesting that she needed to be available full-time to project-manage the restoration of their beautiful new eight-bedroomed house in Notting Hill, complete with swimming pool, games room and large (by the standards of London) garden.

The truth was, Amy had always lived in fear of anyone discovering that she was stupid; thanks to an upbringing with two high-achieving doctors for parents. During her childhood, everyone had always described Amy as 'the pretty one' while her sister Kate had been known as 'the brains'. When she was fourteen, she had overheard her mother joking with a friend that it was a good job Amy had beauty, because 'she certainly didn't appear to have brains'.

Maybe if she had been older Amy would have realised that her mother had been joking but, as a vulnerable fourteen year old, Jennifer's words had burned deep and Amy had never managed to shake off the belief that she wasn't clever. Although she had secretly thought she might like to be a teacher, after that comment – followed by her struggle through university – she had never had the confidence to pursue her dream, and had decided the best course of action was to pre-empt any derogatory comments by pretending that she wasn't interested.

Once the renovation of the house was complete, Ben had suggested to Amy that she might want to get another job, at which point Amy had discovered that she was pregnant with Flora: a happy accident that couldn't have come at a better time, as far as Amy was concerned. She hadn't wanted to return to work, mainly because being away from it had dented her confidence even further: despite the fact that Ben was unfailingly supportive, Amy was terrified that she either wouldn't be able to get a job or, if she did, she wouldn't be able to do it and would end up getting fired.

Ben had been delighted by the arrival of his baby girl and he hadn't raised the slightest objection when Amy had expressed the desire to be a full-time mum. In fact, with his career taking up so much time, it reassured him to know that Amy would be at home, keeping things running smoothly and giving their little girl all the attention she needed.

At home with Flora, for the first time in her life, Amy was finding that she had to work really hard. The relentlessness of the sleepless nights, the incessant feeds and the sheer drudgery of nappy-changing, washing and ironing began to take its toll and, within two months, she was buckling under the strain. She felt isolated, useless, lonely. Flora was a challenging baby and her nerves were shredded. Her mother was as helpful as she could be but Amy always felt that she was thinking that she should just pull herself together and get on with it, like her sister, who had managed quite happily to juggle her two children with a job.

The solution was for Amy to hire help. Along with Maria the nanny (who Amy sometimes referred to as Saint Maria, on the grounds that she had saved her life), she also temporarily hired a cook, a gardener and a cleaner. Before long, her mother was remarking that Amy soon wouldn't need to wipe her own backside as she had so many staff who could do it for her. But Amy had ignored the jibes because she knew that there was no way she could cope by herself and, as long as they could afford it ... well, why shouldn't she get some help?

With so much assistance, Amy was able to indulge her love of reading and painting, meet friends for lunch and get her figure back to its best in the gym she had installed in the basement of their house. She was the perfect corporate wife for Ben, regularly entertaining important contacts for supper and accompanying him to various awards ceremonies and parties, looking suitably glamorous in one of her many designer dresses. Finally, she had found her niche, something she was good at.

She appeared to have the perfect life. But Amy knew that her sister would never swap places with her, despite her privileged existence. Kate often said that she couldn't stand having staff invading her privacy and that it had always been important to her to earn her own money. Sometimes – when

Amy felt bored or lonely – she could understand what her sister meant. But for the most part, she was happy with her life.

As Amy drained the last of her tea and deposited the mug in the dishwasher, her mother and Sam returned from the garden. 'Mummy!' cried Sam, his skin glowing and his eyes shining. 'Guess what? My cucumbers have grown! Granny says next time we come down, we'll be able to pick them and eat them for tea!'

Amy grinned and scooped him up in a bear hug. 'Wow, Sam, that's fantastic!' she enthused, planting a kiss on his dimpled cheek. 'You have such green fingers! Soon, you'll be doing our garden all by yourself and we'll have to get rid of Alf.' Although the housekeeper and cook had long gone, with Maria taking over their chores, Amy had hung onto Alf the gardener.

Jennifer raised an eyebrow. 'One step at a time,' she chided, wagging her finger jokingly.

Amy grinned back. 'OK, well, maybe we'll stick with Granny's greenhouse for now,' she agreed, planting Sam back down on the floor. 'God, you're getting so big and heavy!' she grimaced, rubbing her back. Her mother gave her a look she couldn't read. 'What?' she asked irritably.

'Nothing,' Jennifer murmured, before turning her attention to Sam, who was standing between them like a miniature referee. 'Right then, little love, what are we going to get you for your tea?' she asked, bending down so that she was at eye level with the boy.

'Oh, don't bother cooking – let's go out to Lucca,' said Amy, referring to the local Italian, which the children loved with a passion.

Jennifer shook her head briskly. 'No, Amy. Going out for dinner should be an occasional treat, not a regular occurrence. I never cook for the children any more—'

'Well, you can thank me later for saving you the bother,' interrupted Amy, exasperated and already looking forward to her evening's first glass of red wine.

'Cooking for my grandchildren is not a bother!' remarked Jennifer tartly, already reaching for her apron, which hung nearby on a hook on the wall. 'Now, Sam, how about I make your favourite tuna pasta bake?'

Sam hesitated and Amy's heart melted for him, caught in the crossfire between two warring women, each convinced they knew what was best for him. 'Tuna pasta bake's not my favourite, Granny,' he said eventually, in a small voice.

Jennifer frowned. 'But it always used to be,' she said, sounding puzzled. 'If that's not your favourite any more, then what is?'

Sam raised his big eyes towards Amy, seeking reassurance that he could speak. She nodded wearily, knowing what was coming next. 'Maria's tortellini,' he said.

Jennifer closed her eyes for a second and sighed deeply. 'Well, Maria's not here, is she?' she said finally. 'So you'll just have to make do with my tuna pasta bake.'

'Sam, honey, why don't you go and find Flora?' Amy said quickly, giving him a reassuring pat on the head. Sam's eyes flickered with uncertainty as he sensed that whatever was wrong might be his fault. 'Go on,' urged Amy. 'You can tell her all about your cucumbers,'

Sam's eyes lit up again. 'Ooh, yeah!' he cried, dashing off in search of his sister.

Amy spun round to face Jennifer. 'For God's sake, Mum!' she snapped. 'He's a child! It's not his fault he doesn't want your tuna pasta bake.'

'No,' fumed Jennifer, 'you're right. It's yours!'

Amy's face creased in confusion. 'What the hell are you on about?'

Jennifer undid her apron and bunched it into a ball before sitting down heavily at the breakfast bar, clearly shaken up by the clash with her daughter. 'It's just that you don't seem to play any part in your children's lives at all, Amy, and I think you're going to live to regret it.'

Amy folded her arms, almost shaking with fury. 'How dare you,' she raged. 'I love my children and my husband more than anything in the world.'

Jennifer reached out and took her hand. 'I know that. I really do. But you're not giving yourself the chance to be a proper mother, Amy. You seemed genuinely surprised by how heavy Sam's getting, as if you're some distant relative who only sees him two or three times a year, rather than his mother. And his favourite dish is one that his nanny makes! How can you stand it? I just can't help comparing it to . . .' She tailed off awkwardly.

'To Kate?' interrupted Amy bitterly. 'But how could I ever match up to Miss Goody-two-shoes? She's always been your favourite!'

Jennifer sighed. 'Of course she's not my favourite, Amy. It's just that I see more of her because she lives so close. She has so little time but she does everything for her kids. And I don't mean just buying them things. I'm worried that before you know it, your children will have grown up and you will have missed out on so much of their lives.'

'I don't miss anything!' cried Amy hotly. 'I'm there all the time, Mum! I see them when they come home from school and every morning before they leave.'

Her mum nodded. 'I know, I know. But how often is it just you and them? When are you ever really on your own with them, giving them your undivided attention? No amount of money can ever compensate children for time spent with their parents.'

'Arrrggh!' cried Amy in frustration. 'Flora and Sam spend far more time with me than Kate's two spend with her! It just narks you that I have help because that's not the way you did it. But I'm afraid the only person whose judgement I care about is Ben's, and he's very happy with how we live our lives. He loves me and the children, and we love him! Isn't that all that matters?'

Jennifer's face softened and she leaned over and stroked Amy's face affectionately. 'Yes, darling, it *is* the only thing that matters. But you have so much talent, both as a mother *and* as a person. I just don't want to see it all going to waste.' She sighed. 'But I'm sorry for getting at you. It's none of my business. Come on, let's go to Lucca like you suggested – the children will enjoy it.'

Still feeling shaken, Amy reluctantly picked up her bag. Was Jennifer right? Would she live to regret her choices? She followed her mother out of the kitchen, her appetite gone.

Chapter 8

'Mummy, would you like me to make you a cup of tea?'

Kate looked up at Millie from where she was lying on the sofa with a duvet wrapped around her. At eleven years old, she was already nearly as tall as Kate, with long, thick nut-brown hair just like her own and the same large, dark brown eyes. She was growing into a real beauty, and she had a temperament to match.

'Oh, sweetie, that would be lovely. Thank you.' Kate watched Millie as she walked back out of the room, her long legs clad in her regulation jeans and Converse sneakers. She envied her daughter's carefree spirit; so sweet and pure not yet having been worn down by life. Kate was just thirty-four but somehow she felt like a human gas meter: the years notching up on her face with every passing hour. It had been three days since her accident and she was still feeling tender, as well as slightly tearful and a bit low.

Her life had not turned out quite the way everyone, including she, had hoped. She had been a straight-A student all through school and had been thrilled when she had secured a place at medical school, following a gap year when she had worked as a volunteer for an AIDS charity in Africa.

She fully expected to follow her parents into a career as a doctor, but falling pregnant with Millie had put paid to that particular dream.

Kate had met Miles at the beginning of her first year at university and, to begin with, they were just friends. But, over that first year, they had grown closer and drifted into a relationship. Miles was studying physiotherapy, with the aim of working for a top football club. He was sports-mad, popular and funny. He was Kate's best friend and could always make her laugh, no matter how fed-up or stressed she was feeling. Kate knew she could be a bit uptight, whereas Miles was easy going and preferred to live for the moment: they complemented each other perfectly.

But when the pregnancy test had showed a clear blue line, both Miles and Kate had panicked and dropped out of university immediately, and Kate had known that it was the end of her dream of becoming a doctor. Although she could have taken a year out, before returning to her studies, she couldn't imagine fitting seventy-hour weeks as a junior doctor in with a family. Besides, she had always wanted to be a mum who was there for her children, rather than one who hired a nanny.

They had moved from London to be near her parents in Suffolk, and Miles had quickly accepted the first job he was offered: working for the local council. It was a million miles away from his ambition to be a physio and wasn't well paid, but he was determined to support his new family and seemed desperate to prove to her parents that he was a worthy husband for their daughter. By the time they had married – Kate's bump disguised by a giant bouquet – he was the proudest man in the world.

But in the years since, all his ambition seemed to have drained away. A bad back meant he had had to stop playing sport, which had caused him to put on weight, and he now appeared content to simply plod along in the same job, without really trying to better himself. Whenever they discussed it, he would say he didn't want a high-flying career like Amy's husband, Ben, because it would mean never seeing the children.

Kate would never dispute that Miles was a fantastic father. He gave up endless hours of his free time to coach Josh's football team; he worked hard with Millie when she was struggling with her music; and he never, ever got bored of spending time with them, even if he was just making them giggle over the dinner table with his terrible impressions and tomfoolery. In return, the children and their friends adored him.

But, although he and Kate were very happy together and he undoubtedly loved and supported her, he could sometimes be old-fashioned in the way he treated her.

Once the children had started school, Kate had managed to qualify as a nurse and had worked part-time ever since, yet Miles still expected her to do most things around the house, while he often spent weekends either going to football matches, watching football on TV or coaching Josh's team. An only child whose father had died when he was fifteen, Miles had been molly-coddled by his mother, who had seen it as her role in life to fulfil Miles's every whim. And when his mother died – shortly after he and Kate married – he seemed to expect Kate to pick up where she had left off.

Until her father's death, Kate had been happy to do so.

She felt grateful to have two beautiful children and a husband who made her laugh more than anyone else; who loved her and had given up his dream to support her. But since Michael had died, she had started to feel more unsettled. Her dad had been such an amazing man; and her parents' relationship was so different to her own. Michael and Jennifer had been an equal partnership in every way. They had the same fierce intellect; they had enjoyed the same hobbies, like walking and gardening; and they had clearly still fancied each other rotten. Theirs was a rare and grand passion, the like of which Kate had never experienced and knew that she probably never would. She wondered how different her life would have been if she hadn't got pregnant. Would she have stayed with Miles? She liked to think so, but ever since the chance meeting with Jack, she had been thinking a lot about what she would have done if she had met someone more like him back then.

She sighed and rearranged herself on the sofa. Jack had been on her mind a lot since his visit to the hospital. She couldn't stop thinking about him and hoped, rather than believed, that it was just a stupid crush: after all, he had come dashing to her rescue like some sort of superhero. No one would blame her for being dazzled. But something in the pit of her stomach told her that this was different.

But, she told herself crossly, *forget him*. Sarah was going out to dinner with him that Saturday night and Kate was well aware that Sarah's need was far greater than hers. Sarah had had a rough time in recent years and she was desperate to meet a decent man, while Kate had Miles and knew she should count her blessings. Nevertheless, she was dreading the call from Sarah telling her all about their date, knowing she would be eaten up with jealousy.

At that moment – making her jump guiltily at her illicit musings – she heard a key in the front door. Miles's tall, bulky frame momentarily blocked the light from the warm summer evening behind him as he came through the door, which opened straight into the lounge of their Victorian terrace. Spotting Kate sprawled on the sofa, a brief wave of concern crossed his face, before he turned to close the door behind him, kicking it gently as it stuck slightly; just as it always did after a lot of rain.

'I really must fix that!' he said with a grin, just as he always did; making Kate smile, just as she always did.

'Hi, gorgeous,' he said, coming over to her and bending down to kiss her. 'How are you feeling?' His eyes were hopeful and she knew that his football team, Ipswich Town, were playing at home the next day. He wanted her to tell him that she was fine and he could go to the match with her blessing.

'Well, I'm still very sore . . .' she began, before spotting the twitch of disappointment in his bright blue eyes. It was like kicking a puppy. She couldn't do it. 'I'm fine, though,' she added, as brightly as she could, and Miles's eyes lit up immediately.

'Oh, that's great,' he beamed, slumping down on his favourite old leather chair – perfectly placed for a prime view of the TV – and reaching for the remote control.

'Here's your tea, Mum,' said Millie, emerging from the kitchen and cutting through Kate's thoughts. Miles and Kate both watched her as she placed the hot mug on the old-fashioned wooden chest that served as a coffee table, in front of

Kate. 'Would you like a cup, Dad?' she asked, kissing him on the cheek.

'I'd love one, thank you, darling,' he said, wrapping an arm around his daughter and giving her a squeeze. As Millie once again departed into the kitchen, Miles glanced at Kate and she grinned back at him, knowing exactly what he was feeling for their first-born, precious girl.

They stared at the screen as the evening news blared out for a few moments until Millie reappeared. 'Here you go,' she said proudly, placing the cup down beside Kate's. It was still something of a novelty for her to make tea for her parents, and she seemed to revel in the achievement. She was a very different character to her younger brother, Josh, who was, as usual, ensconced in his bedroom playing on his DS.

'Thanks, little lady,' said Miles with a smile, picking up the cup and taking a long, satisfied slurp. 'Don't suppose you feel like cooking dinner as well, do you?' he added.

'Don't be so bloody lazy, Miles!' Kate snapped, before she could stop herself. '*You* do it! Don't turn Millie into your servant just because your regular one is out of action for a few days!'

Both Millie and Miles turned to look at Kate in shock, and she felt her insides swirl with guilt. 'I'm sorry,' she said quickly. 'I'm just in a bad mood, that's all. Fed up with sitting around.'

'I could do beans on toast?' said Millie tentatively, looking from Kate to Miles. Her face was a mask of uncertainty, not understanding why there was suddenly so much tension between her parents.

Kate sighed. 'Oh, go on then,' she said, forcing a smile to

show Millie that everything was going to be OK. She was glad to be able to gloss over any resentment for another day with something as simple as beans on toast.

Later that night, as she and Miles lay in bed – Miles snoring loudly while Kate stared up at the ceiling – she remembered that they were due to go over to her mother's the next day, to catch up with her sister Amy who was up from London for the weekend. 'Are you awake?' she whispered, nudging Miles hard. He coughed and woke with an almighty snore.

'I am now,' he whispered back. 'Why? What's on your mind?' he added, rolling over onto his side, his head propped up on his elbow.

'I forgot to tell you that we're supposed to be going over to Mum's tomorrow. Amy's down from London with the children.'

Even in the gloom, she could see Miles's face sag with disappointment. 'Oh God!' he sighed. 'Do we have to?'

'Miles!' Kate admonished him, knowing that he was only worried about missing his precious football. 'Don't be such a grump. She's my sister!'

'Well, why don't you go on your own?' he suggested, rubbing his eyes sleepily. 'I'm not in the mood for Princess Amy, showing off her latest designer handbag and her flash new car.'

'That's unfair!' cried Kate, her forehead creasing into a scowl. 'Amy doesn't show off. And she's been bloody generous to us!'

'As if I could ever forget it!' said Miles, rolling onto his back. 'Chucking us a few crumbs from their top-of-the-range table and expecting us to bow and scrape with gratitude.'

Kate sighed deeply. Miles had always had a chip on his

shoulder about Amy and Ben's lavish lifestyle, and had often commented that he thought Kate's parents would have been happier if she'd married someone more like Ben, instead of himself. But she knew that all her parents had ever wanted for her was to settle down with someone who made her happy. And Miles *had* made her happy.

So why wasn't she happy now?

Chapter 9

Just five miles away, Jennifer was also lying awake, unable to sleep. Amy and the two children had gone off to bed after their trip to Lucca but Jennifer had stayed up for a while, drinking another glass of wine, gazing into the dwindling log fire that she had prepared earlier. Amy had laughed when Jennifer had started arranging the logs in the grate and pointed out that it was the middle of summer, but Jennifer had just smiled and ignored the jibes. The cottage, with its long, low ceilings and tiny mullioned windows, was dark inside and stayed cool all year round, and she and Michael had made a habit of lighting a real fire any night that they were alone together, once the girls had left home. It was a habit she couldn't bear to break.

She leaned over to switch on her bedside light and, immediately, the black-and-white photo of her and Michael that she kept there was illuminated, causing her stomach to clench with pain: almost as if she was seeing it for the very first time. She picked it up and gazed at it for a moment, imagining that she was able to feel his presence through the glass. In it, he was standing behind her, his fair head bent to kiss her tanned, bare shoulder as she threw her head back towards him and laughed. Her throat thickened with tears and she clutched the photograph to her stomach, aching with renewed loneliness and loss.

Her meeting with Hugh had made her feel wobbly and unstable again, as if she was walking on shifting sand: her earlier row with Amy was entirely down to her feeling terrified of what she had started. Amy's constant suggestions that Kate was Jennifer's favourite were so far from the truth it was almost laughable. If anything, it was Amy she favoured: she looked so much like Michael. Jennifer had sometimes felt jealous of the close bond Amy had shared with her father, worried that it might somehow dilute the intensity of her own relationship with him. And worried why Kate, although close to her dad, didn't seem to have the same connection with him that Amy did. She worried about what that meant.

She replaced the photo on the bedside table, took a sip of her water and switched the light off again. Lying there, every time she closed her eyes, she could see Hugh's face and was shaken by the effect he was still having on her days later: she felt as if she was betraying Michael by just thinking about him.

They had stayed for hours in the little coffee shop, sometimes talking but mostly not; just reconnecting through a shared secret memory that had been buried for so long now. In fact, it was exactly like the day they had first met . . .

'What was the "tiff" about then?' Hugh asked.

Jennifer looked up at him slowly. She had been pretending to read for what seemed like hours now, without any of the words making sense.

'Shouldn't you be going somewhere?' she said, with narrowed eyes. 'Like, back to work, for instance?'

The corners of Hugh's mouth turned up slightly and she suspected that was the closest he ever came to smiling. 'They'll manage without me,' he drawled, lighting yet another cigarette.

'Do you always smoke so much?' she asked, watching as he inhaled deeply and tilted his head slightly upwards to let the smoke float away from her face. *He suits smoking*, she thought. He looked like some kind of film star, with his sharp black suit, white shirt and loosely knotted black, skinny tie. He looked very at ease with himself, which only succeeded in making her feel deeply uneasy in his company. Somehow he exuded a feeling of danger.

'Yes,' he replied, offering the cigarettes to her again. 'Do *you* always smoke so much?' he added, as she took one and leaned towards him for him to light it.

'I don't smoke,' she replied, drawing heavily on the cigarette. It was true. She hadn't smoked since she had met Michael in her second year at medical school, when he was in the year above her. He thought it was a disgusting habit. Already this total stranger had got her behaving badly.

'Are you going to marry him?'

Jennifer frowned. 'None of your business.'

'If you're not going to marry him, will you marry me?'

Jennifer laughed and shook her head.

'I'm perfectly serious,' he said, a slight note of indignation in his voice.

'Don't be ridiculous. I don't even know your name!'

'If I tell you my name, will you marry me?'

Jennifer sighed and looked at the tip of her cigarette, before stubbing it out in the heavy glass ashtray on the table-top. 'No,' she said at last. Then: 'It's time I was going, I've already been here far too long.' She started to gather up her books and put them into her old, battered leather satchel, which she had found, to her delight, in a jumble sale at her parents' village hall.

'Hugh,' he said. 'My name's Hugh.'

Jennifer finished putting her books away and stood up. 'Well, it's been . . . strange meeting you, Hugh, but I really do have to go now.'

'Tell me your name before you go.' Hugh showed no signs of getting up.

'Jennifer,' she said with a smile, before turning on her heel and walking out, certain that their surreal encounter would be their last.

As she made her way back to her digs, she began to feel rather grubby. A tiny kernel of guilt was taking root deep inside her, as if she had done something she shouldn't have. But then, she reasoned, she hadn't encouraged him. It wasn't her fault that he had come and sat with her. But those eyes . . . she couldn't stop thinking about his eyes.

As she walked down the street towards her building, still preoccupied with the unexpected encounter, she began to make out the figure of someone sitting on the grey stone steps leading up to the front door. Even from this distance she knew it was Michael. The sun was glinting on his shiny, floppy blond hair and she could see his motorbike parked in front of him. She sighed with delight to herself and began to quicken her pace, suddenly desperate to get to him.

As if he sensed her approaching, Michael looked up and leapt to his feet immediately. Jennifer began to run towards him and he did the same. As they met, he scooped her off her feet into a hug so tight she could barely breathe, then he was kissing her with such an intensity and passion that he almost smothered her. 'I'm sorry!' he whispered between kisses. 'I'm so sorry.'

'I'm sorry, too!' she cried, loving him so much at that moment that it was overwhelming. 'I was just—'

'I know,' he interrupted, silencing her with another kiss. 'I'll turn it down. Of course I'll turn it down.' He had been offered a job at St James' Hospital in Leeds, but they both knew that it was one that he couldn't refuse. It would be the first rung on a ladder that Michael would go on to climb right to the very top.

'No!' She put a finger up to his mouth. 'No! I was being unreasonable. It's a great opportunity and you have to take it.'

'But what about …?' He loosened his grip on her and looked at her intently. 'What about us?'

Jennifer took a deep breath. 'Well, I'll have to stay in London and finish my exams, then maybe … well, who knows?' She looked up into his navy-blue eyes, which had filled with tears.

'But what will I do without you?' he said plaintively.

'And what will I do without *you*?' she replied, reaching up and stroking his face. 'But we'll get through it. If our love is strong enough, it will survive our separation. And it's only a few months.'

'That sounds like an eternity right now.'

'I know. But we'll both be so busy with our work – you'll be working crazy hours at the hospital and I'll be slogging away here. You can't turn down this opportunity, Michael; we both know that. I'll visit you whenever I can, and you can come here …'

'With *your* landlady?' Instinctively, they both looked up at the stuccoed white building in which Jennifer had rented a room for the past three years. She was in the tiniest room possible but it was clean and functional and served its purpose. It was in a female-only boarding house, and the landlady was vigilant in what she considered to be her duty to protect 'her girls' from the clutches of any would-be sexual predators: basically, anyone of the opposite sex.

'I'll visit you whenever I can,' repeated Jennifer, smiling up at him. There was a pause as Michael seemed to weigh up what to do next. Then, after glancing around to make sure he wasn't being watched, he dropped to one knee and took her hand in his.

'Michael!' squealed Jennifer. 'What are you doing?'

'Jennifer, will you marry me?' he said, looking up at her with such love in his eyes that her heart instantly melted.

She would never have admitted it – thanks to the feminist principles she publicly espoused – but Jennifer had dreamed of this moment for so long. 'Oh my God!' she said with a gulp. 'Yes! Yes, I'll marry you, Michael!'

Michael scrambled to his feet and once again scooped her up in his arms. 'Thank you!' he shouted, spinning her around. 'Thank you! This is the best day of my life!'

Lying in bed, eyes wide open, staring at the ceiling, Jennifer allowed her tears to run down her cheeks unchecked as the agony of that perfect memory caused her heart to ache savagely. She waited for the pain to subside before allowing herself to close her eyes and try to sleep, hoping she would dream of Michael instead of being tormented by nightmares. Nightmares that opened the darker recesses of her mind and let the horror of past mistakes return to haunt her.

Chapter 10

Kate arrived at Jennifer's cottage the next morning, minus Miles but with Millie and Josh in tow. Amy hugged Kate tightly, shocked by her sister's careworn appearance. She seemed to have diminished in height as well as weight in just the few short days since the crash.

'You look terrible,' she blurted out, before wishing she had kept her big mouth shut.

Kate grimaced. 'Thanks!'

'Sorry. Not terrible, but, well, you look like you've been through the mill. How are you feeling?' Amy peered at Kate with concern as they made their way out into the garden and sat down on one of the pretty blue-painted wrought-iron benches on Jennifer's terrace. The children had greeted each other with squeals of delight and were already chasing each other through the trees of the garden, which was dappled with the late-morning sunshine.

'I just need some more Touche Éclat,' Kate said with a laugh, trying to deflect attention away from her appearance. She wished Amy didn't look so bloody healthy and glamorous: it made her feel even worse. She always thought Amy looked a bit like a mini version of Elle Macpherson.

'You can have mine,' Amy said instantly, reaching for her large Prada handbag and retrieving a leather make-up purse. Kate looked at it as Amy unzipped it. She thought about her own yellow cloth make-up bag, now at least twelve years old, covered in splodges of mascara and foundation and containing a motley selection of ancient cosmetics, most of which were too dried-up to serve any purpose. Amy picked out a Touche Éclat and handed it to Kate.

'No, Amy, I can't,' Kate protested, feeling touched and embarrassed in equal measure.

Amy waved her hand. 'Of course you can. I've got another one at home.'

Of course she had. Kate would never think of spending twenty-five quid on one item of make-up but Amy didn't hesitate to buy two or three at a time. If she wasn't so generous, it would be enough to make Kate green with jealousy; but she knew that Amy had probably bought them with the thought of giving one to Kate and one to Jennifer, anyway. 'Thanks, Amy,' she murmured, reaching for her own handbag. It was the same colour as Amy's but that was where the similarity ended. Hers wasn't even real leather, let alone Prada.

'Where's Mum?' Kate asked now, keen to move on from the moment.

Amy glanced around. 'She's not been up long, actually. I think she must be in the shower.'

Kate frowned. 'Really? That's not like her.'

'She had quite a few glasses of wine last night. Maybe she needed to sleep it off.' Amy's eyes flickered up towards Jennifer's bedroom window, as if worried that she may have been overheard.

'That's not great, is it? Do you think it's ... because of Dad's anniversary?' Kate hesitated, just as she always did, before mentioning her father. Even now, two years on, talking about him still caused another tiny tear in her heart.

Amy's eyes filled instantly and she blinked hard. 'Maybe.'

They sat in silent contemplation for a few minutes, each of them thinking about Michael, before Jennifer's voice brought them back into the moment. 'Kate!' she cried, coming out into the garden in her bare feet, dressed in a long, flowing flowery skirt and a pretty camisole vest.

Kate stood up and hugged her mum gingerly. 'Still sore?' Jennifer said, standing back and holding her daughter at arm's length so that she could look at her properly.

'A bit,' Kate admitted. 'Anyway, lazybones, what are you doing only just getting up?'

Jennifer's eyes darted towards Amy, who was still sitting on the bench. She was watching her mum and Kate, feeling excluded and envious of their easy relationship. She knew it was because they saw each other all the time in the course of their everyday lives, whereas Amy's visits had to be planned and were few and far between. Jennifer occasionally visited her but always said she didn't like coming to London, as it held 'too many bad memories'. What those bad memories were, Amy had never discovered.

'I just slept late, that's all,' Jennifer muttered, raising her hand as if to shield her eyes from the sun. But Kate and Amy both thought she was also trying to hide her face, which had flushed red.

'Hangover, that's what it is.' Kate smiled to show she was ribbing her mother, rather than having a dig at her.

Jennifer's eyelids fluttered for a second before she smiled

back. 'Yes, probably.' She laughed. 'Where are the children?' she added quickly.

Both Kate and Amy gestured towards the bottom of the garden, where the children were playing a game of hide and seek amidst the mature trees and hedges. 'Oh, how lovely!' Jennifer beamed and her shoulders dropped, the tension draining out of her as she watched her grandchildren playing together. 'Hey, you lot!' she called out. 'See if you can find me . . .' With that, she was off, running round the side of the cottage and giggling like a child of the same age as their children, instead of their mother.

Amy and Kate looked at each other and grinned fondly. 'Where's Ben this weekend?' Kate asked, stretching out her legs and raising her face to the sun, which was heating up nicely.

'Working,' Amy sighed. 'Miles?'

'Football!' they chorused in unison. Amy laughed. Kate didn't.

'Everything OK?' Amy prompted.

'Hmmm,' Kate replied, noncommittally.

Amy nodded and waited to see if she would add anything more. Finally, Kate spoke: 'Amy . . . do you ever feel, I don't know . . . *dissatisfied* with Ben?'

Amy thought carefully before she replied. Kate didn't often open up, so it was important not to shut down this opportunity. 'Sometimes,' she said, even though it wasn't strictly true. She had never felt dissatisfied with Ben, just impatient at times. 'Why? Do you?'

'Not with Ben, no,' Kate said, smiling ruefully at her lame joke. 'But, lately . . . Well, I suppose since Dad—' she descended into silence for a second to recover herself, '—

since Dad, I've been feeling more and more pissed off with Miles. I don't really know why.'

Amy nodded and swallowed the lump in her throat. She wanted to say something but didn't think she would be able to: she still found it impossible to talk about Michael without breaking down.

'It's not Miles's fault. He hasn't changed or done anything wrong; but I can't help comparing him to ...' Kate tailed off.

'Grief can often make you reassess your life,' Amy said carefully, after another silence. 'And your accident probably didn't help ... You're still feeling shaken and sore. It's only natural that Miles would bear the brunt of that.'

Kate looked at her for a moment. 'Yes, you're probably right. Anyway, it's a lovely day,' she said briskly, getting to her feet and dusting down her jeans. 'Let's make the most of it and not sit wallowing in misery. Shall we go and rescue Mum?'

As the sun blazed down from a cloudless blue sky, Jennifer fussed like the proverbial mother hen over both her daughters, insisting that they sit in the garden while she prepared a sumptuous lunch for them all.

Amy couldn't put her finger on what it was, but she sensed that something was bothering Jennifer, and she felt that it was more than the fact that the second anniversary of Michael's death had just passed. All of them were still struggling to come to terms with his loss but then, Amy reasoned, she and Kate had their own families to keep them preoccupied, while Jennifer was alone. Maybe that was it. Maybe she needed someone to talk to who wouldn't crumple at the first mention of his name.

IOU

As the day wore on, they ate and chatted in the sunshine of the garden and were cheered by watching the children playing with the garden hose, chasing through the trees and laughing as they sprayed a rainbow of water over each other. For one long, lazy, sunny afternoon, they could all put their troubles to one side and revel in innocent pleasures.

Chapter 11

By the time she drove back on Sunday afternoon, Amy felt optimistic, happy even. But, as she pressed the button to release the electric gate that let them into their driveway, she noticed with a start that Ben's car wasn't there. 'That's odd,' she said aloud.

'What is?' asked Flora, immediately sitting up and looking worried.

Amy reached behind her and patted her daughter's leg reassuringly. 'Oh, it's nothing, sweetie,' she said quickly. 'I was just wondering where Daddy's car was. I thought he would have been at home by now.'

As she ushered the children into the house, Amy reached for her mobile and called Ben. It rang six times before going to voicemail. She frowned as she thought about where he might be. 'Hi, darling,' she said, once prompted to leave a message. 'We're home. I'm just wondering where you are. Give me a call. Love you.'

Amy dumped the children's bags in their rooms and began to unpack her own overnight case, all the while wondering why she felt such unease. With a little chill, she realised it was because she hadn't heard from Ben since Friday evening, when she had called to tell him they had arrived safely at her mum's. Now, as she thought back to their brief conversation, she remembered that he had sounded odd, slightly vague, but she hadn't really thought much of it at the time, putting it down to tiredness. It was the longest period she had gone without speaking to him or texting him in a long while: they were a couple who were in constant contact, always leaving little messages for one another. Why hadn't he been in touch?

With a mounting sense of anxiety – and having settled Flora and Sam in front of the TV and computer respectively – Amy spent the rest of the afternoon calling everyone she could think of who might know where Ben was. She felt strange at first, not wanting to sound neurotic, but equally needing to get the point across that it wasn't like him to be out of contact.

She started with his work colleagues, some of whom she couldn't get hold of, either. Those she did speak to each told the same story: Ben had still been in the office when they had left on Friday night, and they hadn't heard from him since.

'How did he seem?' asked Amy when she spoke to his PA, Carla, who'd worked with Ben since the company had been set up and whom she liked and trusted.

Carla hesitated, as if unsure whether to say what she wanted to say.

'Please, Carla,' urged Amy, trying to fight the rising panic that was bubbling up inside her. 'I'm starting to get really worried, so if there's anything you think wasn't quite right, I need you to tell me.'

Carla sighed. 'Well, he hasn't been himself for a little while, actually,' she said, after a pause.

'In what way?' said Amy, feeling a trail of hot guilt blaze through her as she realised that she, too, had noticed that Ben wasn't himself, but hadn't done anything about it. She'd been too busy enjoying her charmed life, and had chosen to ignore the warning signs.

'Well,' continued Carla. 'You know the company's problems have put such a huge pressure on him these past few months, but I did think on Friday that he seemed to be acting oddly.'

'Company's problems?' repeated Amy. 'What problems?'

There was a long silence before Carla cleared her throat. 'Oh God,' she said, 'I assumed you would know all about it.'

Amy closed her eyes and leaned her head on the wall in front of her. 'No,' she said in a voice that didn't sound like her own. 'This is the first I've heard of it. Please, Carla, tell me everything you know.'

Nearly half an hour later, Amy hung up the phone and slumped down onto the floor. Why hadn't she seen that Ben was struggling? Now that she thought about it, he had been working longer and longer hours for months now, but she had never questioned it. She had never even asked him how things were going, so immersed was she in her own life. He had told her a long time ago that he enjoyed switching off from work when he came home, so she had grown used to never asking him how things were going, beyond a perfunctory enquiry that he'd had a good day.

Once again, she dialled Ben's mobile number and listened as, yet again, it went to voicemail. 'Hi, darling,' she began, her voice trembling. 'Listen, I know that things aren't good for you at work right now, but it's nothing that we can't sort out. Come home, Ben. Let's talk about it and decide where we go from here – together. Don't try and deal with this on your own. I love you so much, darling. Call me, or just come home.' Her voice faltered as she spoke the last few words and, as she ended the call, she spluttered and coughed, tears finally starting to fall.

'Mummy?' asked Flora, her little heart-shaped face creased into a worried frown as she came into the hall to find Amy crouched on the floor, tears streaming down her face. 'What's wrong? Why are you crying?'

Amy stood up quickly and roughly brushed away her tears. 'Nothing, sweetie,' she said, giving her daughter a hug. 'I just got something caught in my throat and it made me choke.'

Flora's eyes flickered with uncertainty, wanting to believe her mother but knowing instinctively that she wasn't telling the truth. 'Really?'

Amy nodded vigorously and pushed back her hair. 'Honestly, I'm fine now. See?' She beamed at her daughter and took her hand. 'Now, how about we get some warm milk and biscuits and watch a film?' Flora's face relaxed into a smile as she followed Amy into the kitchen to help her prepare their TV snack.

As Amy curled up on the sofa with a child snuggled under each arm, she stared unseeingly at the TV screen, all the while silently praying that her husband would come home soon.

A couple of hours later, Amy was tucking Flora into bed when she heard a noise downstairs. Her heart banged with a combination of apprehension and hope and she ran to the top of the stairs. In the hallway below Maria was returning from a day out. 'Hi, Amy!' she waved, before making her way to the room she occupied in the basement of the house.

Amy felt her legs wobble. Where the hell *was* Ben? Should she call the police and report him missing? 'Night night, darling,' she whispered, kissing Flora softly on the forehead as she returned to her room. 'Sleep tight. I love you.'

'I love you, too,' Flora whispered back drowsily, before adding, almost as an afterthought, 'Where's Daddy?'

Amy stroked her daughter's hair and murmured reassuringly, 'Oh, he's got a lot on at work at the moment but he'll be back soon.'

Flora nodded, seemingly satisfied with Amy's explanation. Then she cuddled her beloved bunny, Miffy, to her chest and turned onto her side, already drifting off to sleep. Amy stood and watched her for a moment, loving the way her rosebud mouth opened slightly as she started to breathe rhythmically. She leaned over and switched off her princess light, before padding quietly out of the room.

Out on the landing, the house was still. Amy felt very alone and very scared. Everything in her life revolved around Ben and she didn't know how to function in this strange new situation.

She went down to the kitchen and made herself a cup of tea. As she sat at the big oak table, she noticed for the first time how loud the ticking of the clock was. From where she was sitting, she could see the front door, at the far end of the long, wide hallway. She stared at it, willing it to open and for Ben to come bounding through with a huge smile on his face. But it stayed resolutely shut.

Amy thought back to the first time she had been apart

from Ben: when she was in hospital, having given birth to Flora. It had been agonising being forced to say goodbye to him when he went home for the night. After he had left, she had sat up in her bed, staring through eyes blurred with exhaustion at her perfect new baby girl, and had suddenly been gripped by the worst terror she had ever felt in her life. Somehow, the world suddenly seemed like such a scary and dangerous place, filled with all kinds of shadowy threats to this new life she had helped to create. Only when she had returned to the safety and security of Ben and her home did she begin to finally relax and believe that everything was going to be OK. That she could do it.

Sitting there now, alone at the kitchen table, not knowing if Ben was alive or dead, Amy could feel that terror returning, coursing through her veins and making her blood run cold. If anything had happened to him . . .

After a while, she got up stiffly and put her cup in the dishwasher. She looked around helplessly, not knowing what to do. She leaned forward and gripped the shiny black granite worktop to steady herself. Her heart was pounding and she thought she might be sick. She needed to do *something*: she couldn't just sit there quivering with fright. Should she call the police? She wanted to and yet she was too scared by the sequence of events that might follow.

Finally, her nausea started to subside and Amy felt able to stand up straight. Not knowing what she was looking for, she made her way blindly towards Ben's study, turning the chunky doorknob and swinging open the heavy door.

Amy looked in at the ordered room with a feeling of deep foreboding. She felt sure that the key to Ben's disappearance lay in there. She swallowed before stepping over the threshold, as if she was stepping into a field full of land-mines. On tiptoe, she approached the large desk he had had specially designed so that it could accommodate all his CDs and games, as well as his many books. She smiled slightly as she noticed that all his CDs were filed carefully in alpha-betical order and that the desk surface was clear, except for his large, shiny MacBook. He was so different to her: she was messy and impatient, whereas he was ordered and methodical. Another bolt of fear shot through her: he simply wasn't the type to go missing on a whim. Things must have been building for a long time for it to get to this stage.

To her shame, Amy realised that she rarely came into the room. She had never enquired into Ben's business affairs or ever made the effort to understand how he made the money she was happy to spend so freely. She stared at the MacBook and wondered if she dared open it.

Coming to a decision, she quickly pulled out his ergonom-ically designed chair and lowered herself gratefully into its contours, glad to take the weight off her shaking legs. She lifted the MacBook's titanium lid and watched as the screen immediately fired into life, taking her by surprise. Ben had left it on sleep mode, rather than shutting it down alto-gether, but it had automatically locked and was now prompting her to enter a password. She racked her brains to think what his password would be. The kids' names would be a good bet, she decided. She typed in 'Florasam' but the pass-word box shook defiantly – the sign that it was wrong. Next she tried 'Florriesammy', Ben's nicknames for the children, instead. Wrong again. She sat chewing her thumbnail reflec-tively as she thought, before suddenly remembering that the password needed to be a mixture of letters and numbers. Finally, she tried 'AmyFloraSam.no.1'. This time the password box slid away and the desktop screen came into view.

Amy smiled to herself, touched by Ben's password. She gazed at the screen for a minute, wondering where to begin. Email. That might provide some answers. The screen was much bigger than on her own MacBook Air but the shortcuts were the same, so she was able to navigate quickly to his inbox.

As soon as she clicked on the icon, the screen rolled quickly downwards as dozens of new emails began to appear, stacking one on top of the other.

As the title of each email flashed before her eyes, for a second Amy thought she might be sick. She thrust her head between her knees and took a succession of deep breaths. Although she didn't want to look up, once the feeling had passed she lifted her head and focused on the screen once more.

The most recent email was from Ben's business partner, Tim. It was entitled *That's it then. We're fucked.*

With a shaking hand she scrolled down. There were emails from his bank, from his accountant, from his credit card company. All of them seemed to be increasingly urgent and none of them gave her any comfort. Her mouth dried up. How the hell had she not noticed that he was drowning? Guilt gnawed at her insides. God, only last week she had bought those bloody Louboutin shoes. How must that have made him feel? Six hundred and fifty pounds on a bloody pair of shoes she didn't even need. Amy had never been religious, but now she found herself clenching her hands together so tightly that her knuckles went white as she prayed that Ben was OK. That he hadn't become so desperate that he had harmed himself in some way.

Wiping away the tears that had begun to run down her face, Amy returned to the dayroom and picked up her mobile phone from the table, pressing 'Redial'. Again, it went straight to voicemail. As she tried to speak to leave a message, her composure finally melted away and all she could do was sob into the handset: 'Please!' she wailed. 'Come home!'

She slumped down at the table and rested her head on her hands as her tears continued to fall in an unstoppable torrent. Suddenly, her phone beeped. She looked at it in shock: it was a text message from Ben and her heart suddenly soared with relief and hope. My darling Amy, he wrote. I love you so much but I can't come home yet. I just need time to get my head together. Be strong for me. B x

Amy stared at the message. Why couldn't he come home? Surely it would be better if she could support him through this crisis? Then it hit her: she had never supported Ben. She had never needed to as it had always been the other way round. He was so strong, so dependable, that he had always shouldered the burden for both of them. Now that he needed her support, he clearly didn't think she was strong enough to cope: he would think she would be an additional drain on him. It made her feel ashamed for being so weak in the past.

She thought carefully before replying. She needed to show him that she was there for him; that it was her turn to be strong. Take what time you need, my darling. I promise to be here for you when you are ready and we WILL get through this together. We have each other and we have our perfect children. Nothing else matters. I love you. A x

IOU

Amy pressed 'Send' and, once again, her eyes blurred with tears. She wiped them away irritably. Crying wasn't going to help now. Ben had asked her to be strong and it was the least she could do for him. It was her turn to step up to the mark.

Amy climbed the stairs to bed wearily, her mind racing. She wondered where Ben was spending the night. Was he sleeping rough? As she went to draw the curtains, she looked out of her bedroom window, out over the garden, beyond the rooftops to the bright lights of London. It would be so easy to disappear in amongst the hum and throng of the city, and she could suddenly see the appeal of dropping out of life, even just for a few days. She could understand why Ben had done it: she felt like doing it herself. Her hand hovered by the curtain for a second, before dropping back to her side. She would sleep with them open tonight.

Chapter 12

'That was delicious!' Miles beamed, leaning back in his chair with a satisfied sigh and rubbing his belly.

Josh giggled as he watched his dad lifting his ample stomach up and down so that it began to create its own motion, carrying on quivering after Miles had stopped jiggling.

Kate watched Miles with disdain. 'You're such a show-off!' she snapped. 'A belly that size isn't exactly something to be proud of!'

Miles pulled a face at Josh, which only made him laugh harder. Millie, who was still eating her Sunday roast dinner, looked up and met Kate's eye questioningly, as if she didn't understand why she was being so mean to her dad. Then she, too, looked at Miles and started to giggle a little.

Kate looked away, feeling guilty. She knew she was being a misery guts but she couldn't help it. The feelings of dissatisfaction that had taken root when her dad had died seemed to have intensified dramatically since her accident. Life was so short. So precious. Yet here was Miles just coasting along, happy to stay in his mundane job, happy to keep living in such modest circumstances. Where was his ambition to better himself?

But there was another reason she was being so grumpy with Miles, which Kate could hardly bear to admit, even to herself. Jack. Ever since the day of her accident she had thought about him almost constantly. Whenever she closed her eyes, she could see his dark eyes reflected back at her. And, worse, the two times she and Miles had made love since her accident, she had pictured herself with Jack instead. Last night would have been Sarah's date with him and Kate had tied herself up in knots of jealousy thinking about it, knowing that Sarah would soon be calling to regale her with all the gory details.

Just then, as if on cue, her phone beeped from the kitchen.

She stood up wearily, leaving Miles and the children still giggling to themselves, and made her way into the kitchen.

But, to her surprise, the message was from a number she didn't recognise. It read: Hello you. How are you feeling now? Jack.

Kate's stomach did a little flip. Hello you. Was that him being flirtatious? She glanced furtively towards the living room where Miles and Josh were now loudly discussing their favourite computer game: 'Nothing, I tell you, *nothing* will ever match Lego Star Wars!' Miles cried indignantly, as Josh shook his head violently.

'Wii Sports Resort every time, Dad!' he said, with a finality that suggested the argument was won.

Kate hugged the phone to herself for a second. The realisation that Jack was thinking about her gave her a thrill of excitement. She smiled to herself and thought about how to reply. Tempted though she was to write: All the better for hearing from you, instead she tapped out: Lovely to hear from you. Neck still a bit sore but getting better. K

She looked at the message and deliberated. Should she put a kiss after her initial? Just then Millie appeared in the kitchen carrying the plates from the table, causing Kate to jump and press 'Send'. Decision made.

'Everything OK, Mum?' Millie said, scraping the plates into the bin before dumping them in the sink. 'You seem a bit . . . I don't know . . . moody.'

Kate swallowed down her guilt and smiled at Millie in what she hoped was a reassuring way. 'Sorry, sweetheart. I'm just a bit tired, that's all.'

Millie nodded. 'Well then, why don't you go and put your feet up, and I'll make you a cup of tea?'

'Oh, thanks darling but I think I'll go and have a lie down, actually,' Kate said, as her phone beeped again. She wanted to be alone with Jack's messages. 'Would you three mind doing the dishes?' she said, as she tucked her phone into the back pocket of her jeans.

She made her way into the sitting room and gestured at Miles towards the kitchen. 'I've got a bit of a headache. Can you and Josh give Millie a hand?'

A little frown of concern briefly crossed Miles's brow. ''Course,' he said, playfully swiping Josh's head. 'Come on, buster, let's get moving.'

'Aw, do we have to?' Josh sighed, but he was already standing up.

'Are you OK, babe?' Miles called after Kate, as she made her way up the stairs.

'Fine. Just need some peace and quiet,' she said pointedly, closing the bedroom door behind her.

She retrieved the phone from her jeans pocket and lay on the bed, ready to devour his next words. Her stomach somersaulted as she read: *You should get that lucky husband of yours to give you a neck rub!*

Lucky husband? He was definitely flirting with her. But what was he playing at, when he had only been on a date with Sarah last night?

She thought for a moment before replying: Might just do that! How was last night? Sarah is amazing, isn't she?

There was no reply for a while and Kate wondered if he thought she was being nosey. She closed her eyes, feeling miserable, frumpy and old. Just as she started to drift off to sleep, her phone beeped: Yes, she is. She's going to call you to ask you something. Hope you say yes. Have you got an email address? Want to send you a link about natural cures for whiplash x

Kate frowned, intrigued by the message. What was Sarah going to ask her? The thought of a threesome flashed through her mind and she laughed to herself. Unlikely, she hoped. And she loved that he had been spending time trying to find cures for her whiplash. *It's more than Miles has done,* she thought mutinously.

Nursekate@heatmail.com, she typed. *Thanks for thinking of me x* She knew, deep down, that she shouldn't have given him her email address: now she would be frantically checking both her phone and laptop for messages from him. And that was wrong. She should put a stop to it right now. But she really didn't want to.

'Phone for you,' said Miles, coming into the bedroom a while later as Kate was dozing. He held the handset out towards her. She rolled over and sat up, wincing slightly as her neck twinged.

'Thanks.' She smiled sleepily at him as she took it from him.

'Tea?' he mouthed, as he turned to leave the room.

Kate nodded and waited until he had left the room before she spoke. 'Hello?'

'It's me!' squealed Sarah excitedly, on the other end of the line.

Kate's heart plummeted and she steeled herself for the onslaught. 'Oh, hi, Sarah,' she replied, trying to inject some energy into her voice.

'Oh my God, Kate, he is SO amazing! I think I'm in love!'

'You've had one date!' said Kate drily. She wanted to be pleased for her friend but she couldn't help it: she was jealous as hell.

'I know, but it was the best date I've ever been on!' gushed Sarah, oblivious to Kate's tone. 'He picked me up at eight – did you know he drives a Mercedes by the way? – and we went to that amazing new restaurant, you know, the one that you can't get a table at for *months*? Anyway, he was *such* a gentleman! He opened the car door for me and stood up every time I went to the loo! And then, when it came to ordering, I didn't have a clue what to order, so he said, "Would you like me to order for you?" and then he ordered lobster! And champagne!' Sarah was into her stride now and barely drew breath as she regaled Kate with every minute detail. After a few moments, Kate zoned out. She found herself fantasising about the feel of Jack's hands while he had stroked her forehead as she had lain on the ground, waiting for the ambulance to arrive. Sarah continued her second-by-second analysis for several minutes, until Kate became aware that she was reaching a crescendo.

'Anyway,' Sarah continued, 'so I said, "Would you like to come in for a coffee?" '

'What about the kids?' interrupted Kate, suddenly gripped with fear that she was about to hear all about Jack's prowess in the bedroom in the same intricate detail as Sarah had described the rest of the evening.

'Staying with their bastard of a father!' announced Sarah triumphantly. 'First helpful thing he's done for me in years! Anyway, so I said to Jack, "Would you like to come in for a coffee?" and I gave him one of my best looks – you know, the one I do when I'm on the pull?'

'I know,' replied Kate grimly, having witnessed Sarah in action many times before.

'And guess what he said?' Kate could almost picture Sarah's wide blue eyes brimming with excitement as she spoke.

'"Yes", by any chance?' Kate replied sourly, knowing that she sounded churlish but unable to stop herself. She realised that she was holding her breath as she waited for Sarah's reply.

'No!' Sarah almost yelled and Kate unconsciously exhaled with relief. 'No,' continued Sarah, still burbling with excitement. 'He said he wouldn't dream of it on a first date! *How* gentlemanly is that?'

Kate smiled to herself. In her limited experience of him, that did sound exactly like something Jack would say. 'Did he kiss you?' she blurted out suddenly, surprising herself and Sarah at the same time.

'Yes, but only on the cheek,' replied Sarah. For the first time, Kate could detect a trace of disappointment in her voice. 'I was well up for a full-on snog but I don't think that's his style somehow. Actually, I was well up for a full-on shag to tell the truth, but I don't want him to think I'm a tart.'

'No,' agreed Kate, smiling to herself. *As if he would.* 'So, did he ask to see you again?'

'Yes, he did!' cried Sarah, obviously thrilled at the prospect of seeing him again. 'He's offered to cook for me next weekend! Oh, Kate, I know this sounds awful, but I'm so glad you had that crash. Otherwise I'd never have met him!'

And neither would I, thought Kate, wondering if that would have been best all round.

When Kate didn't reply, Sarah spoke again. 'Oh, honey, I'm sorry, that was insensitive of me. Of course I'm not glad you had a horrible crash, but ... well, you know what I mean!'

'Yes, I know what you mean,' Kate reassured her, looking around her cramped, messy bedroom and thinking how unglamorous her life was. She wanted some excitement, too.

'Oh, and I almost forgot. He asked if you and Miles would like to come, too.' Her tone of voice suggested she was clearly disappointed that Jack hadn't suggested a romantic meal for two.

Sarah's words seemed to come from a long way away and it took Kate several seconds to register what she had just said. 'Sorry?' she replied, her stomach lurching violently as she finally understood. 'Me and Miles? Why would he want us to come?'

'Well, like a sort of double date, I suppose,' Sarah replied. 'He seemed very keen,' she added dubiously.

Kate pictured Miles and Jack together. She couldn't imagine for one moment that they would get on: they were polar opposites in every way. And something at the back of her mind told her that she didn't want Jack to meet Miles – she realised with a stab of shame that it was because she was embarrassed by him. 'I'm not sure about that,' she said quietly. 'I don't think Miles would want to come.'

'Why?' demanded Sarah.

'Oh, you know what he's like . . .' Kate said dismissively.

'What do you mean?' Sarah snapped. She loved Miles and often told Kate that she'd gladly have him if Kate ever got fed up. 'Jack's offering to cook him a free meal,' she pointed out. 'And Miles might be grateful for the opportunity to thank him in person for coming to your rescue like he did.'

'Yeah, maybe,' Kate agreed. 'But he doesn't like feeling indebted to anyone. And he'd probably think Jack was a bit . . .'

'A bit what?' prompted Sarah, when Kate paused just slightly too long.

'A bit . . . up himself,' Kate finished, unable to be more articulate.

'Tell Miles I said he's the one who's a bit up himself if he can't see that he owes Jack big time,' said Sarah grumpily. She was now clearly desperate for Kate and Miles to join them, in case Jack changed his mind about inviting her over. 'Oh, please try and persuade him, will you?'

'I'll try,' agreed Kate reluctantly. Part of her was excited by the idea of seeing Jack again: another part of her was plain terrified. She had a feeling that she was starting something that she shouldn't. But, she reasoned, if Sarah was going to get into a relationship with him, she would be seeing him regularly anyway. Maybe she should get used to it.

Chapter 13

The sun was setting low over the garden but still Jennifer didn't move from her seat on the stone terrace. A goblet-sized glass of white wine sat on the rosewood table in front of her and, after blowing her nose, she picked it up and took a long sip, enjoying the cold kick of the alcohol as it touched her parched throat, still dry from crying.

It was her fourth glass since Amy and the children had left that evening to go back to London. She was drinking too much: she knew it, but didn't want to admit it, even to herself. And it was so easy. Living alone, there was no one to gently suggest that you might have had enough.

As she drained the glass and placed it – unsteadily – back on the table, her head swam. She was grateful that there was no one there expecting her to speak, because she knew her words would be slurred. Drinking had become a crutch: an escape mechanism to help her cope with the agonising, daily pain of missing Michael. If she didn't drink, she would have to resort to more permanent means of forgetting, and she knew that in thinking that way lay madness. Her children and grandchildren still needed her, even if Amy and Kate were grown ups and living their own lives. They still needed her guidance and intervention: she was worried about both of them.

Something was bothering Kate: Jennifer suspected it was more than just the after effects from her car crash. She had seemed down in the dumps and uncharacteristically quiet when she had visited on Saturday and Jennifer wondered if all was well between her and Miles. Jennifer was under no illusions about Miles's faults but, on the whole, she had always liked him – whereas Michael had never seemed to be able to warm to him. He had felt that he wasn't good enough for Kate and that he would 'squash her ambition' as he'd put it.

Certainly, Miles had seemed to grow old before his time over the past ten years. He had looked like he had such a bright future at one point, but now he seemed content to drift along in a dead-end job and didn't seem concerned that Kate might want more out of life. But Kate had never once complained about Miles and had always reacted angrily and defensively if Michael had made even slightly derogatory comments about him. She seemed to think she owed him a debt of gratitude for standing by her when she fell pregnant with Millie.

Jennifer thought that there had been a shift in Kate's attitude towards Miles since Michael's death. Maybe losing her father had made her consider whether he had been right about his son-in-law all along. Jennifer hoped not. Whether or not Miles was lacking in some areas, he was a wonderful father to the two children and however commonplace divorce was, she still thought that it was a terrible curse for any family to be torn apart.

Then there was Amy. Amy was such a complex character.

Jennifer loved her deeply, despite the times in the past when she had sometimes felt jealous of her closeness to Michael. She blamed herself for Amy's low self-esteem, which seemed to stem from a throwaway comment she knew Amy had overheard her make to a friend that Amy wasn't academic. Jennifer could have bitten her own tongue off at the time, and had spent years trying to convince Amy that she hadn't meant it; trying to instil in her the self-confidence she ought to have for someone so beautiful and talented.

She also knew that she should learn to keep her mouth shut and stop criticising Amy's choice to have a nanny, but she just couldn't bear to see the children becoming closer to Maria than to their mother. Jennifer was certain that Amy would thrive as a mum if she was to dispense with all the help and go it alone but, again, Amy didn't have the confidence to try it. Jennifer was worried that one day Amy would wake up and realise that she hadn't made the most of the one thing that she would have excelled at more than any other.

Yes, thought Jennifer, woozily standing up and swaying. *It doesn't matter how old your children are, you never stop worrying about them.* As the last, melon-coloured rays of sun sliced through the encroaching dusk, she picked up the empty glass and made her way back in through the ornate French doors at the back of the cottage, securing the latch behind her. Inside, it was pitch dark and cold. She switched on the lamp on the sideboard and stared at the sitting room, now bathed in an orange glow. All around her, Michael's face stared back at her from the many photos that covered almost every available surface, his eyes twinkling and smiling at her from under his thatch of glossy blond hair. She would never, ever tire of looking at that perfect face. Theirs had been a passion that had lasted almost four decades. Throughout their lives together, they had never lost their desire for each other and sex had been a huge part of their relationship, undiminished through two pregnancies and long periods of separation.

She had tidied up after the children had gone and now everything sat just as it should, in its rightful place. But the room felt empty, the house felt empty; just as it had done since that fateful night when Michael hadn't come home. A wave of sorrow suddenly surged up from deep down inside her, escaping in a strange wail that surprised her. Jennifer slumped down onto the sofa and began to cry tears of grief that were as sharp and raw as the day they had started.

She was woken by the sound of her mobile ringing. Disoriented and confused, she shifted herself into a sitting position and listened carefully to see if she could tell where her phone was. The ringing seemed to be coming from the kitchen, so she hauled herself off the sofa and shuffled through to the next room. Sure enough, her mobile was on the breakfast bar in the kitchen. She looked at the number curiously. It wasn't Amy and it wasn't Kate, and she couldn't think of anyone else who would be calling her at this time on a Sunday night. Eventually, she pressed the 'Answer' button. 'Hello?' she said, coughing slightly to clear her hoarse throat.

'Jennifer?' said an unmistakable, velvety voice.

Jennifer froze, partly with terror, partly with excitement. She had given him her mobile number and he had promised to call, but she hadn't expected him to.

'Jennifer?' he said again, sounding less sure this time.

'Er, yes,' she replied, her voice still gravelly with sleep and alcohol. 'Hello, Hugh.'

'You don't sound like you,' he said, in a slightly accusatory tone.

'No,' she said carefully, trying her voice out to see if she was still slurring. 'Sorry, I was sleeping.' Her confidence grew as she established that she sounded reasonably clear. She glanced towards the clock on the wall and noticed with a start that it was past ten.

'Really? You've changed. You hardly slept at all from what I remember.'

Jennifer closed her eyes as the years reeled back. 'That was a very long time ago, Hugh. More than thirty years.' Her voice was barely a whisper now.

'Is it really that long?' He sounded amused, and there was a long silence. Just as in person, on the phone Hugh never seemed to consider that silence might be unsettling for the person on the other end of the line.

'Did you call for anything in particular?' Jennifer asked, when she decided that the silence had gone on for long enough.

Hugh chuckled. 'I said I would, didn't I?'

Now it was Jennifer's turn to say nothing.

'Can we meet again?'

'I don't know,' she shot back. 'Can we?'

'I think so,' he said slowly.

Jennifer considered for a moment. Sober, she might have told him that she should never have contacted him in the first place. That she had made a terrible mistake, it wasn't one she would be repeating, and that he should have a nice life and say goodbye for good. But she wasn't sober. So she said, 'OK.'

'Shall I come to you again?'

She tried to think clearly through the fog of alcohol. 'Maybe I should come to London? It's quite out of the way for you to come here.'

'I can stay with my son. He lives close by.'

'Stay?' The word echoed through her head as she spoke it, and they both knew what she was thinking.

'Yes, Jennifer, stay. I thought that this time maybe we could meet for dinner, instead of just coffee. I wasn't proposing that you spend the night with me.' The note of amusement had returned to his voice and even though he couldn't see her, Jennifer's face burned with embarrassment. She felt angry that he could still have this effect on her after all these years.

'Although,' he added, 'I will if you insist . . .'

'No, thank you,' she replied curtly.

'You sound desperate to see me, I must say,' Hugh drawled sarcastically. 'I would be offended if I didn't know you so well.'

'You don't know me any more than I know you, Hugh. As I keep saying, it's been well over thirty years. People change.'

'Do they, though?' Once again, Hugh lapsed into a thoughtful silence as he considered the answer to his own question.

As Jennifer finally hung up, having arranged to meet Hugh the following Friday, she flicked the switch on the kettle and hunted through the cupboards for coffee. She knew she would be wide awake at four in the morning as a result of it, but she needed something to help her sober up, to help her focus on how she was feeling. Part of her deeply regretted making contact with Hugh again but at the same time, it felt like something she had to do. She owed it to herself and to Michael to discover, once and for all, what had really happened back then.

'Don't, Jennifer,' pleaded Michael, stroking her long, nut-brown hair back from her face, which was wet with tears.

'I'm sorry,' she sobbed, desperately trying to regain control of her emotions. She had been so determined to be strong and not make him feel bad about leaving. 'I'm just going to miss you so much.'

'And I'm going to miss you, too,' he said, embracing her tightly so that her face was buried in the soft wool of his sweater. She inhaled deeply, trying to hold his smell for as long as possible. He had given her one of his shirts, and she knew she would cuddle up to it in bed every night and would never wash it as long as he was away. 'Promise me you'll write every day. I don't care if you've got nothing to say – just promise to do it.'

Jennifer nodded vigorously. 'I will, of course I will.'

'And it's only eight weeks until you come up to visit,' Michael said, as he lifted her chin to look into her eyes. Although he was trying to comfort her, his words only made her cry harder: eight weeks sounded like an eternity. 'I love you so much, Jennifer,' he said, kissing her tears away one by one.

Behind them a whistle blew shrilly, making them both jump and look at each other in panic. 'Well, I guess I'd better go,' he said, his face contorting with sorrow as he gently unhooked her arms from around his waist and picked up his suitcase.

Jennifer felt faint with grief as she watched him walk away from her to board the train. She tried to memorise his face and his tall, slim frame, topped with the shining blond hair that glinted like gold in the sun. Once he had boarded, Michael leaned out of the window and waved. As the train pulled out, his eyes never left hers for a second.

Jennifer waited until he was out of sight, waving at an empty track, before she turned and slowly made her way back to her digs. Everywhere she looked, other couples seemed to be laughing and affectionate, casually holding hands as they strolled slowly up the Kings Road on a Sunday afternoon, seemingly unaware that, to her, the world had just ended.

For the next week, Jennifer felt as though she was wading through a thick fog that prevented her from both seeing anything clearly or being able to think. Although Michael was the one who had gone away, she felt homesick for him. Her whole body physically ached for his presence, his intelligence, his laughter and his wit. She tried to study but nothing would sink in. She wrote to him every day, just as she had promised, pouring out her heart in long, rambling prose. Each morning, she would race to the small table in her communal hallway to search for his letters back to her, which were equally heartbroken and full of declarations of his love and devotion.

Before he left, Michael had bought her a second-hand, tiny diamond engagement ring, which he insisted would one day be replaced by a diamond ten times bigger. Jennifer thought it was the most exquisite ring she had ever seen and also knew for certain that she would never want to swap it, no matter how rich they became.

The night he gave her the engagement ring, Michael had booked them into a hotel and they were able to spend their first full night together. Whenever they had had sex before, it was always furtively, with Jennifer either smuggling Michael into her room for an hour, or else finding somewhere in the open air, having taken Michael's motorbike out into the countryside. Michael's place was impossible as he shared a room.

That night, with all the time and privacy they needed, it was as if they were making love for the very first time. Jennifer knew with every fibre of her being that it would be perfect and it had been. Michael had undressed her slowly, savouring every part of her as if he was an experienced lover who had seduced dozens of women before, even though she knew he had only slept with two or three women before her. Every time he had touched her or kissed her, he had seemed to set her every nerve ending on fire, until by the time he had finally entered her, her whole body was screaming out for him. Their bodies had worked together so perfectly, right from the very beginning. In the long nights after Michael left, Jennifer sometimes wished that the sex hadn't been so good, so that she wouldn't miss it as much as she did.

Gradually, she developed a new routine without Michael. She threw herself into her studies, which helped to distract her from the ache of missing him, although she still had a calendar on the wall beside her bed on which she carefully counted down the days until she could visit him. Although they limited their phone calls to once a week, Jennifer felt as though hearing his voice was like a drug that sustained her for the following seven days, and she began to grow dependent on them.

Michael, however, was working killer hours and a couple of times when she called at the pre-arranged time, it was only to discover that he was still on the wards, sending Jennifer into a spiral of despair. Gradually, too, his letters became less frequent and she tried not to mind that he seemed to be coping without her and developing a whole new circle of friends that didn't include her. Adding to her paranoia, once or twice on the phone he mentioned another woman called Mary, a junior doctor like him. 'You'd really like her,' he told Jennifer. 'I can't wait for you to meet her when you come up.'

Jennifer didn't reply. She didn't want to meet his new friends, especially not the female ones. She was surprised by the vehemence of her reaction, having always been so confident and sure of Michael's devotion. But the distance between them was feeding her neurosis, and the stress she was under was causing her imagination to travel into dark, jealous spaces.

Her end-of-year exams were looming and she worked harder than she ever had before, so that by the time she sat them she felt confident and prepared. Leaving the hall after her last exam, she was fairly certain that she had passed with flying colours and decided to ring Michael to tell him, even though they hadn't arranged to speak until the next day.

She had butterflies in her stomach as she perched on the stairs in the hallway of her digs and carefully dialled his number, suddenly desperate to hear his voice.

'Hello?' said a male voice. Michael was sharing a flat with three other junior doctors but she wasn't due to meet them until the following week, when she went up to stay for her long-awaited visit.

'Oh, hi,' Jennifer began, 'It's Jennifer, Michael's fiancée. Is Michael there?'

There was a long pause, as if the person on the other end of the line was thinking how best to reply. 'Er, no,' he said at last.

'Oh.' Jennifer was puzzled by the man's reticence. 'Who is this?'

'It's John,' he replied stiffly, as if he didn't want to speak to her.

'Oh, well, hi, John,' she continued, as brightly as she could, despite the feeling of unease that was growing inside her. 'Do you know where he is?'

Another pause. 'No.' Even though it was just one short word, Jennifer knew he was lying.

'Maybe you could take a wild guess?' she said, trying to inject some humour into the stilted conversation.

'Er, with one of the others, maybe?' he said at last and, again, she got the sense that he was hiding something.

'Do you know when he'll be back?' she persevered.

'No,' John replied briskly, clearly having had enough of the conversation. 'Sorry, goodbye.'

The phone line went dead and Jennifer stared at the handset in shock. What the hell was going on? Why had he acted so strangely? Suddenly a horrible thought struck her. Was Michael seeing someone else behind her back? Was it this Mary that he'd mentioned more and more recently? The more she considered it as she sat on the stairs with her head in her hands, the more she decided that it was the only plausible explanation for his flatmate's shiftiness. The realisation struck her like a physical blow and she burst into noisy tears.

Behind her she heard footsteps on the creaky stairs and felt an arm around her shoulders. 'Hey! Jennifer, what's wrong?' said Susie, another of the girls who rented a room in the house. 'Is it the exams? Did they go badly?'

Jennifer shook her head, unable to speak for crying.

'Is it your mum or dad? Has someone died?' Susie prompted, her voice full of concern.

Again, Jennifer shook her head. 'No,' she said at last, when she had managed to compose herself slightly. 'It's Michael . . . I think he might be cheating on me!' As she said the words, she burst into tears again and leaned against Susie, who hugged her tightly.

'Oh, no, surely you must be mistaken. Michael *adores* you.' Susie shook her head emphatically, causing her long, blonde hair to swish around her face. She had spent many evenings out with Michael and Jennifer, and she had become very fond of him.

'He DID adore me!' Jennifer sobbed. 'But I'm sure there's something going on. He keeps mentioning this girl, *Mary*.' She practically spat out her name.

'She's probably just a friend. Michael wouldn't do that to you, I know he wouldn't,' Susie insisted, prompting a fresh bout of tears from Jennifer. 'Hey, shhhhh, it's OK. I'm sure you must be mistaken,' she soothed. 'What makes you so sure?'

In a shuddery voice, Jennifer explained the phone call and the caginess of Michael's flatmate. 'Why would he be so odd, if Michael wasn't up to something?' she wailed, her wide eyes looking to Susie for reassurance. But the new look on Susie's face told her everything she needed to know, despite her protestations that there must be a plausible explanation.

'Come and have some tea in my room,' Susie said firmly, when Jennifer had cried herself out. Jennifer felt too weak to protest and followed her friend up the stairs to her room. For the next couple of hours, over several cups of tea, Jennifer sat cross-legged on Susie's bed and poured her heart out about her fears that she had just lost her soul mate, the love of her life. Susie listened with lots of sympathetic nods and handed out the tea and tissues. Finally, as the sun began to set and the room grew dark, she got up and looked at Jennifer. 'Let's go out,' she said.

'Out?' Jennifer looked back at her, baffled. 'Out where?'

'To a bar,' Susie said, her eyes glinting slightly. 'We've finished our exams, and we deserve a celebration.'

Jennifer shook her head sadly. 'I'm not in the mood,' she said, never having felt less like celebrating in her life.

'I know you're not,' Susie said. 'But that's *exactly* why you're coming. Otherwise you'll just go and sit in your room and cry.'

'That's exactly what I want to do,' Jennifer protested, but she knew that Susie was a determined girl and there was little point in arguing. 'OK,' she finally conceded.

Back in her room, she splashed her face with cold water, brushed her hair and reapplied her make-up at the small basin in her room, peering into the cracked mirror above it. As she changed into her favourite suede mini-skirt and roll-neck sweater, Jennifer's mood hardened. How dare Michael treat her like that? Well, she would bloody well show him that she wasn't going to sit at home moping and waiting for him, while he was out gallivanting with some other woman.

IOU

As she and Susie walked into the noisy bar on the Kings Road, several heads turned to look at them. Jennifer had to admit they were a striking pair. Susie, with her tall, model-thin figure and waist-length blonde hair; beside Jennifer, with her short skirt, long legs and thick, dark hair.

'Hello, ladies,' said a suave-looking man as they approached the bar. 'Can I get you a drink?'

Susie looked at Jennifer and she nodded. 'Thank you!' they chorused, following him through the throng to a table.

As the evening wore on, Jennifer began to enjoy herself. Constantly surrounded by a stream of different men, with an endless supply of drinks, she pushed Michael firmly to the back of her mind. She decided to do what Susie had suggested: celebrate the end of her exams and what she hoped would be the beginning of a glittering medical career.

After several Martinis, her head had begun to swim. She was just thinking that maybe it was time to leave when she heard a voice that made her spine tingle.

'Hello, Jennifer,' the man said, and she looked up into the dark, dangerous eyes that she had almost forgotten. They bore into her with such intensity that she could not tear her own eyes away; her mouth went dry and she swallowed hard as they stared at each other in silence. Without speaking, he reached out his hand: in a daze she took it, and stood up. The noisy bar around them seemed to melt away and there was just the two of them, standing face-to-face, saying nothing.

'Come with me,' he said. It wasn't a question; it was a statement of fact, as if he already knew that she wouldn't be able to refuse.

'Where?' She knew she should look away from him, should leave the bar and never look back, but she couldn't. He had a hypnotising effect on her that rendered her immobile, unable to think coherently.

'Just come with me,' he repeated.

Jennifer woke with a startled cry and immediately looked at the clock on the bedside table. The glowing red digits told her it was four fifteen. She knew she shouldn't have had that coffee, that she would be awake in the small hours, alone with her guilt – and her fear – as a result. But, as the cold sweat poured down her forehead and she waited for the pounding of her heart to slow, she also knew without a doubt that being awake, even if it meant that she would be deathly tired later on, was infinitely better than being engulfed in the nightmares that continued to haunt her sleeping hours.

Chapter 14

The next morning, Amy woke with a start. In those first few claggy moments between sleeping and waking, she knew something was wrong but was unable to remember exactly what it was. She tentatively opened her eyes and, seeing that Ben's side of the bed was empty and the curtains were open, the memories of yesterday came flooding back to her.

She lay in the half-light for a few minutes, trying to gather her courage to face the Monday ahead, before getting up and heading for Flora's bedroom. Flora was sleeping, her tiny pale face framed by a perfect cloud of golden hair. Miffy was still clutched in her fist and each breath from her slightly open mouth ruffled a few strands of her hair, which rhythmically lifted and settled gently again on her cheek. She had kicked off her duvet in the night and only had her white cotton pyjamas for warmth.

Amy walked to the bed and knelt down beside it, her face just inches from Flora's. She could feel each breath from her daughter's body. She watched her quietly for a few seconds before reaching out and stroking Flora's hair. It was silky to the touch and Amy found it comforting to smooth her palm from Flora's forehead to the back of her head. Flora's eyes flickered open and she looked at her mother in confusion. 'What's wrong?' she asked immediately, her little voice croaky.

'Nothing!' hushed Amy. 'Nothing's wrong, darling, but it's time you were getting up. Relax for a few minutes, then get into the shower, OK?'

Flora nodded blearily and instinctively put her bunny to her lips, her eyelids already drooping shut once more.

Amy watched her for a few more seconds before standing up and heading for Sam's room. Unlike Flora's ordered, carefully laid out bedroom, Sam's room was a tsunami of toys, books and games. Amy picked her way through the debris, wincing as she stood on a stray piece of Lego.

Sam was lying on his back, his arms and legs spread out in a star shape, taking up as much space as he could. His dark blue pyjamas had ridden up slightly, exposing a small section of his little belly. He was snoring gently, making Amy smile as she sat down on the edge of the bed and waited until he stirred. Sure enough, a few seconds later he opened his eyes and his sleepy face melted immediately into a wide, mischievous grin at the sight of her. He was such a sunny child, Amy found it impossible not to be captivated by him. She reached out for a hug and he almost leapt into her lap, wrapping himself around her. 'Hello, Mummy,' he said into her neck. The scent of sleep still clung to him and Amy breathed it in deeply, allowing it to soothe her.

'Hello, Sam,' she said, wondering why the shoulder of his pyjama top was damp and realising with a start that it was caused by the tears streaming silently down her face. She didn't want to worry him, so she held him tightly until she had composed herself. 'Right, little man,' she said briskly at last. 'You'd better get up and have a shower.'

'Is it a school day?' asked Sam, leaning back and looking at her, his brow creasing.

' 'Fraid so,' replied Amy, lifting him off her lap and placing him on the floor.

Sam's shoulders slumped. 'Ohhhhhh . . .' he groaned.

Amy clapped her hands together twice. 'Come on now, chop, chop!'

Admitting defeat, Sam slouched off towards his shower room. Amy watched him as he sleepily peed, then stripped off his pyjamas and stepped into the shower where he soon became engrossed in blowing giant bubbles through his cupped hands, using a mixture of soap and shampoo. 'Look, Mummy!' he cried delightedly, as a giant bubble covered his entire tummy.

Amy grinned back at him, pleased and slightly envious that he could be so easily distracted. She was still consumed with unease.

Somehow she knew that Sam's happy little life would never be the same again.

After Maria had taken the children to school, Amy walked despondently from room to room, looking around her as if seeing her house for the very first time. They had employed the very best interior designers and decorators, who had created an exquisite home. Amy had always loved it but, as she gazed now at the paintings and furnishings, she realised that she had never truly appreciated it: she had taken it all so much for granted. But now . . . now that she was slowly starting to realise that there was a real danger of losing it, she suddenly wanted to fight harder than she had ever fought to hang onto it.

In the sitting room, she sat down on the oversized taupe-coloured sofa where she and Ben had spent so many nights snuggled up together watching TV, chatting and sometimes making love. She could picture him smiling his wide smile as she sat astride him while he slowly and deliberately removed her clothes, bit by bit.

The memory hit her like a punch in the stomach and she almost doubled over with pain, aching with his loss. She needed him so badly. After a while, the feeling began to subside and she straightened up, racking her brains to think what she could do that would be of some practical help. As an idea formed in her brain, she headed up the stairs towards her bedroom.

She flung open the door to her dressing room and looked in. As the light automatically came on, it illuminated racks of clothes, shoes, handbags and belts. Her face immediately felt hot with shame at the sheer greed and indulgence contained within those walls. Why hadn't Ben said something when she was spending money that they didn't have? Every time she had come home with another designer bag, it must have been like a kick in the teeth to him, when he was struggling so hard to keep his head above water.

She swallowed hard and made her way over to the 'shoe wall' that she had insisted on having built when they refurbished the house. It consisted of a wall of wooden cubes, in each of which sat a pair of beautiful shoes or boots. Her eyes ran over the designer labels: Jimmy Choo, Prada, Gucci and her favourite, Louboutin. She picked up the pair of Louboutins she had bought just over a week ago and looked at them with a lump in her throat, thinking how much her life had disintegrated in that short time. Ben's credit card had been refused when she had tried to pay for them: why hadn't she listened to the distant alarm bells that had been ringing in her mind that day?

She reached up to the shelf that ran along the top of her clothing rails and retrieved the buff-coloured box and red shoe bag the shoes had come in. She repacked the shoes carefully into their box and retrieved the carrier bag from the pile she had meant to send off for recycling, mentally thanking her lucky stars that she hadn't got round to it yet.

She grabbed her bag and jacket and headed out into the hushed calm of the genteel street where she had lived in such cushioned luxury for the past ten years. Just as inside the house, she now looked around her as she walked along the pavement, noticing her privileged surroundings in a way that she had never done before. She also noticed that the leaves on the trees were starting to crisp at the ends as September encroached – where had the summer gone?

She could hear the bustle of Notting Hill Gate in the distance, but realised that the houses in the square acted as a sound barrier, cutting out most of the noise until she turned the corner and it suddenly hit her, as if someone had just turned up the volume on some headphones.

As she arrived at the busier roads, she automatically glanced around, looking for a cab to hail. Then she stopped. She had hardly any cash left. She reached into her bag and pulled out her wallet. In the change compartment, she counted £1.33. As panic gripped her, she located a £5 note and almost fainted with relief.

She had to get some more cash. Looking up, she realised that she was standing right beside a cashpoint and she took out her debit card, wondering if she dared to use it. With a shaking hand and sense of foreboding, she inserted the card into the cashpoint and tapped in her number. Almost immediately, the machine made an unfamiliar noise and a message appeared on the screen, telling her that the card had been retained and she needed to contact her bank. "Oh God," Amy groaned, her mouth suddenly dry.

Giving herself a stern shake, she spun on her heel and headed for the underground. At least, she reasoned, she still had enough for a travel card. Just.

'Spare any change, love?' said an unkempt young man sitting with a mangy-looking dog on a blanket, as she attempted to pass him to get into the station.

'Sorry,' Amy said with a gulp. Normally she would give beggars a couple of quid: she knew it would go on drink or drugs but she always felt sorry for them. But now, she really *didn't* have any spare change.

Riding the underground, Amy scoured the worn faces of her travelling companions, stupidly praying for a sighting of Ben. But all she saw were the blank faces of people trying not to make eye contact as they dealt with their own cares and worries. Where the hell was he? The face of the beggar flashed back into her mind and she dismissed it quickly. Ben had only been gone a few days, not a few years, and he had texted her.

Amy left the tube train at Bond Street and walked out into the never-ending throng of Oxford Street, where shoppers from all over the world were trying to spend as much money as they possibly could. *What recession?* she thought bitterly as she turned down South Molton Street and headed in the direction of the Louboutin shop. As she walked, she noticed how the crowds gradually thinned out until it was only the chosen few – who could afford to pay obscene prices for top designer clothes – that were left. It was like some kind of grotesque game of musical chairs.

As Amy rounded the corner into Mount Street, she almost collided with Jo coming in the opposite direction. 'Oh!' she cried in surprise, as she reached out to hug her friend. 'Fancy seeing you here!'

'Yes!' said Jo, in an unnaturally high voice, extricating herself from Amy's grip as quickly as she could.

Amy peered at her curiously. Jo was looking furtively from side to side, as if checking to see if anyone had spotted her. 'So ... how are you?' Amy asked, feeling puzzled by Jo's coldness. She must have heard about Ben going missing and would know that Amy was going through hell.

'Good! Good!' Jo chirruped, running her fingers through her mane of caramel-hued hair. Still she refused to meet Amy's eye. Then her gaze settled on the Louboutin bag in Amy's hand and, for a second, as she glanced up, Amy knew that she had just been doing exactly the same thing that she had come for – returning shoes. But, unlike Amy, there was no way Jo would ever admit it.

'So ...' Amy said, almost wanting to laugh at the ridiculousness of the situation, 'I presume you haven't heard from Ben?'

'No ...' Jo said, her Botoxed forehead attempting a wrinkle of concern. 'Erm, look, Amy, I'm really sorry but I'm meeting someone and I'm already running late ...'

'Sure,' said Amy in a flat voice, turning away.

'Let's meet for lunch soon,' Jo called after her. 'I'll give you a bell!'

But Amy knew there would be no call. It was as if she had some kind of contagious disease and Jo couldn't risk being contaminated. Jo would hang on to the death to her lifestyle. She had to. She had nothing else.

Choking back tears, Amy continued down Mount Street until she came to the familiar entrance to Louboutin. Her heart sank as she recognised the same assistant at the till as the one who had served her before.

'Hi again!' the assistant beamed brightly, clearly remembering Amy as someone who usually spent a lot of money. Then the smile on her face died a little as she noticed the bag in Amy's hand.

'I'd like to return these shoes, please,' Amy blurted out, feeling nervous. She had never tried to return anything before: if she decided she didn't like something, she either kept it anyway or gave it to Kate.

'Okaaay,' said the sales assistant, taking the bag. 'Is there a problem with them?'

'No, I just don't think they look right,' Amy gabbled.

'Would you like to exchange them for something else?'

Again, Amy shook her head fiercely, her heart still pounding. 'No. I'd like a refund, please.'

'Do you have the card you paid with?'

The sales assistant was perfectly pleasant but Amy felt paranoid as she scrabbled for her wallet. 'I don't suppose you could refund it in cash?' she asked, her cheeks flaming and her voice trembling.

The sales assistant shook her head and eyed Amy with a

suspicious look. 'Er, no, I'm afraid not. It has to go back onto the card you paid with.'

'But why? Why can't you refund it in cash?' Amy was already thinking how useful the £650 would be, especially if Ben stayed away much longer. What the hell was she supposed to do for cash in the meantime?

For the first time, the sales assistant looked embarrassed. 'I guess it's in case someone found the shoes . . . or had stolen them . . .' She tailed off and bit her lip.

'But you remember me buying them!' Amy tried to laugh, but it came out as a hiccough, instead.

'I know,' the assistant conceded. 'It seems unfair but it's company policy. I think it's true for pretty much all companies.'

'Just thought it would save me a trip to the cash point,' Amy mumbled, handing over her card.

The assistant nodded, in a way that said she knew Amy was lying.

As she stumbled out of the shop, feeling weak with humiliation, Amy glanced back, knowing she would never be there again. Not in this shop, nor in this street. Her days of shopping and lunching were over for good.

Part of her felt strangely relieved.

Arriving home, Amy climbed the front steps despondently. There was still no sign of Ben's car. She opened the front door and disabled the alarm. The silence that greeted her once she had shut the front door seemed to be thick with reproach: for what, she didn't yet know. She felt her throat tightening as tears threatened but, again, she furiously swallowed them down. She would not cry any more. She was going to show Ben that she could be strong. 'Please . . .' she whispered at the walls. 'Please, Ben. Come home soon.'

The front door behind her opened and Amy yelped in shock, her heart swelling with hope. 'Mummy!' cried Sam. 'We're hoooome!'

Flora followed Sam, with Maria bringing up the rear. Amy collected herself, desperately trying not to show any hint of disappointment as she spun round and opened her arms to greet her children, who both snuggled into her. Above their heads Amy met Maria's eye.

'Is everything OK?' the young girl mouthed, her dark, intelligent eyes showing that she understood that something was very wrong.

Amy shook her head but motioned at the children with her eyes, conveying that she didn't want to alarm them. Maria nodded briskly and took each of the children's hands in hers. 'Come on, you two; let's go and make that milkshake I promised you!'

'Yaay!' yelled Sam, immediately extricating himself from Amy's embrace and allowing himself to be led through to the kitchen.

Flora hesitated and looked up at Amy briefly before moving away. Her sensitive nature meant she was quick to pick up on any vibes that things weren't quite right.

As she watched the three of them disappear into the kitchen, Amy suddenly had an idea. Checking that she wasn't being watched, she climbed the stairs to Flora's bedroom. On her white dressing table sat the money box that Jennifer had given Flora last Christmas. Designed so that it could only be accessed by breaking the whole thing, Amy suspected it would be full as Flora wouldn't have been able to get at the £2 coins she was collecting.

She picked it up and, sure enough, it was extremely heavy. She estimated that there could be a couple of hundred pounds in there, enough to tide her over for a few days, or at least until Ben came home.

She almost punched the air with relief, thanking her lucky stars that Flora was such a conscientious saver. She stole out of the bedroom and onto the landing. Once again checking that the coast was clear, Amy slipped into her own room. She sat on the floor looking at the money box, wondering what the best way to break it would be. In the end, she decided to try the simplest approach first. She lifted it up and brought it crashing down onto the floor with all her might.

To her dismay, it simply bounced as the deep carpet absorbed the full force of the impact. 'Shit!' she exclaimed, frowning as she thought of what else she could do.

She moved into her ensuite bathroom, with its hard, sandstone tiles. Crouching down, once again she lifted the money box high above her head. It smashed onto the floor with a satisfying crash and a shiny mountain of coins oozed out amidst the pieces of broken pot. 'Thank God!' Amy smiled to herself.

'Mummy!' cried a voice behind her, and Amy looked around guiltily. Flora was standing in the doorway to the bathroom, looking at the pile of coins and the broken pot in horror. 'What have you done?' she whispered, her little chin trembling.

'Oh, sweetheart!' Amy said, standing up and scooping Flora into her chest. 'I'm so sorry but I needed to borrow some money. I'll pay you back – I promise.'

Flora raised her dark eyes that were so like Ben's and looked at Amy with an expression that pierced Amy's heart. 'But it took me so long to collect all those coins,' she murmured. 'I was going to give the money to the homeless shelter at Christmas.'

If Amy had felt guilty before, now she felt like the worst, most evil mother in the world. Yet another part of her wanted to snap, '*WE* might be living in the homeless shelter by Christmas at this rate!'

'I'll make sure they get every penny,' she said instead, crossing her fingers behind Flora's back. She knew that it might be a promise she couldn't possibly keep.

Chapter 15

As Miles lounged on the sofa watching football, Kate decided to broach the subject of Jack's dinner invitation. She moved over to the sofa, tipped his feet onto the floor and perched beside him, leaning into him the way she had always done when they watched TV together. Miles looked down at her with mild surprise and put his arm around her, kissing the top of her head as he did so.

Kate couldn't remember the last time they had snuggled up together like this. It felt nice and she relaxed into him for a while. She wasn't one of those women who loathed sports; she even liked football. Josh was only nine but he was already showing promise as a footballer himself, and she enjoyed going with Miles to watch him play. But Miles didn't just like football: he was obsessed by it. In his younger days he had hoped to play professionally but, although he had had trials for a couple of clubs, he never made it. Now, he had to content himself with training Josh's team and watching matches whenever the opportunity presented itself.

'Miles . . .' she began, as the half-time whistle blew and his attention on the screen abated for a moment.

'Hmmm?' he replied, affectionately kissing the top of her head again and looking down at her.

'You know I told you that Sarah had been on a date with that guy?'

'What guy?' Miles's face was blank and Kate knew he had absolutely no recollection of her mentioning Jack to him.

'You know, the one who helped me when I had my crash?'

'Oh, him!' Recognition registered at last and Miles nodded. 'Yeah, what about him?'

'Well, Sarah went out on a date with him and he's asked to see her again this Saturday night.'

'That's nice.' Miles's voice was detached in a way that told Kate that he had absolutely zero interest in the intricacies of Sarah's love life, despite the fact that he had always been very fond of her.

'Well, anyway,' Kate soldiered on. 'Jack – that's his name – has invited us to join them for dinner.'

'But we can't afford it,' Miles said automatically. They very rarely went out to dinner and, when they did, it was usually for a birthday or anniversary celebration.

'We don't have to afford it—' Kate began, before Miles interrupted her.

'No, I'm not letting him pay, if that's what you were going to suggest.'

'It wasn't,' said Kate irritably. 'Let me finish. Jack's invited us to dinner at his house. He's cooking.'

Miles looked at her suspiciously. '*Cooking?*' he repeated, looking appalled.

Kate laughed. 'God, you're such a Neanderthal some-times, Miles! Yes, cooking. It's what happens before you actually eat the food that's put on the table in front of you.

I realise it's not something you're very familiar with but, honestly, lots of people do it these days.'

'No need to be so sarky!' He grinned at her. 'I make a mean spaghetti bolognaise – you've said so yourself on many an occasion.'

'That's true, but once a year doesn't really count. *And* you use every pan in the kitchen and expect me to clear up after you. So,' she said, returning to the subject of dinner at Jack's house, slightly surprised by Miles's good-natured reaction to the suggestion, 'what do you think?'

'Oh God, I don't know.' Mile sighed heavily. 'What will I talk to him about? I don't even know the bloke.'

'Well, here's a good opportunity to get to know him,' Kate pointed out. 'You can thank him personally for coming to my rescue like he did. Honestly, Miles, I don't know what I'd have done if he wasn't there. He took care of everything.'

Miles looked at her for a moment before replying. 'He's a regular superhero,' he said drily.

Kate ignored the jibe and continued on a different tack. 'And isn't it nice that Sarah's met someone? She's been really lonely, and deserves a bit of happiness after that bastard Robert walked out on her.'

'True,' Miles agreed. Then he tilted her head up towards him and kissed her on the lips. 'I would never, ever do that to you; you know that, don't you?' he said, looking deep into her eyes.

'Yes,' Kate stuttered, her thoughts jumbled and confused. Why would Miles say that at this moment? Was it because he suspected her of being dissatisfied and bored with their life together? Or, worse, was it because he had an inkling of her guilty thoughts about Jack? She dismissed the thought quickly.

How could he possibly know? She hadn't said anything or done anything that would make him suspicious. Nevertheless, she could feel her cheeks burning as she looked back at him.

'OK, we'll go on Saturday night,' Miles said, turning away from her to face the TV once more, 'but let's not make it a regular thing, eh?'

Kate bit her lip and nodded. It was a simple invitation to dinner at someone's house: someone who appeared to have started seeing her best friend. So why was her heart racing with excitement? Why was she already planning what to wear and wondering if she could possibly afford to have her hair done in the next few days?

Extricating herself from Miles's embrace, Kate picked up her phone and laptop and headed for the football-free calm of their bedroom. She lay on the bed and dialled Sarah's number.

'Miles has agreed to come on Saturday night,' she said, as soon as Sarah picked up.

'Oh, that's fantastic!' Sarah cried, sounding thrilled. 'I'm so glad ... thanks, Kate. We'll have a great night.'

The thought gave Kate a little frisson of excitement. Was Jack as keen to see her again as she was him?

After some more chat with Sarah about the new outfit she'd bought especially for the occasion, Kate hung up and opened her laptop. She clicked onto her inbox and gasped out loud as she saw she had two new emails from Jack Levine.

Her fingers shaking, she opened the first one.

Hey Kate,
Hope your neck is getting better. I promised you I'd send some links to natural whiplash therapies and here are a

couple of articles that might be useful. I do hope you
are coming on Saturday night . . . it would be nice to see
how you look upright!!!
Love Jack
xx

Kate bit her lip and smiled to herself. Then she clicked on
the next email.

Me again. I've been thinking . . . I know a great
masseuse who might be able to help you. She's quite
expensive but I see her regularly, so I'm sure you could
piggyback one of my sessions if you fancy it?
Jack
xx

Kate reread the email. He was definitely sounding as if
he fancied her. She began to tingle in a way that definitely
wasn't platonic, and she knew she should put a stop to this
now: she was entering very dangerous territory. And what
about Sarah? She had been through such a difficult time over
the past few years. This could be her one chance of
happiness and Kate didn't want to be the one to blow it for
her.

She clicked on 'New message'. With shaking fingers and
a pounding heart, she began to type:

Hi Jack
Thanks for these. I think I'll try the links first and see if
they do any good before taking you up on the masseuse
offer! I've spoken to Miles and we'd love to come for

dinner with you and Sarah on Saturday night. Let me
know if there's anything you'd like us to bring.
Kate
xx

Kate pressed 'Send', feeling satisfied that she had reminded
him that he was supposed to be with Sarah and that she was
with Miles, while remaining friendly. Just then, the bedroom
door opened and Miles ducked as he stepped through, carrying a cup of tea.

'Hi, babe,' he beamed, putting the brimming mug down
beside her on the bedside table. 'What're you up to?'

'Oh, just catching up on some emails,' Kate replied airily,
surreptitiously closing the lid of the laptop.

'How are you feeling?' Miles looked at her solicitously.

'A bit better, actually,' Kate said automatically. She wasn't
really concentrating on Miles, instead wishing that her emotions would stop tumbling over each other and that her heart
would stop racing. Maybe she would take one look at Jack
and realise that she had been building him up into something he wasn't? That would be the best solution all round,
she decided.

Yet something deep inside told her that wasn't going to
happen.

Chapter 16

Once the children were in bed, Amy walked disconsolately down the stairs and headed for the kitchen. She made herself a cup of tea; more to give her something to do than because she wanted one. She sat down and tried to ignore the silence that seemed to envelop her like a suffocating blanket. Even though Ben had spent time away from home in the past on business trips, the house had never felt as empty as it did now.

From where she was sitting, she could see the front door. As she stared at it, it suddenly opened and Ben walked through it. He closed the door behind him and stood swaying slightly under the shadow of an elaborate light fitting. Wincing slightly at the light, his eyes finally focused and he locked eyes with Amy.

Amy's nose tingled: she knew she was on the verge of crying but knew that it was important that she stayed calm. She breathed deeply and blinked quickly until the tingling sensation stopped and her eyes cleared. 'You're home!' she said, trying to smile.

Ben continued swaying, looking straight at Amy, his eyes brimming with misery. Suddenly his shoulders drooped and he seemed to melt down onto the wooden floor of the hall-way. He landed on all fours and suddenly let out a keening sound that had Amy leaping out of her seat and running to him, almost skidding the last few yards on her knees as she dropped to hold him in her arms.

'Please, Ben!' she cried. 'Don't!' She managed to manoeu-vre him up into a kneeling position and wrap her arms around him so that his head was supported on her shoulder like a baby's. She cradled him for several minutes, trying to ignore the wafts of alcohol every time another sob left his body.

'Let's get you upstairs,' she said eventually, when she felt that she couldn't support him there any more. Somehow she dragged him into a standing position and, with his arm slung over her shoulder, managed to haul him down the hallway and up the stairs. Panting with exhaustion as she finally deposited him onto their bed, she watched helplessly as he curled up into the foetal position, still sobbing pitifully.

'Ben, sweetheart?' she said, louder than she had intended. Ben seemed to jump at the sound of her voice but didn't reply. 'You need to go to sleep now,' she continued. 'But whatever's wrong, we can fix it. Together. Nothing is so bad that it can't be fixed,' she murmured, undoing the laces of his shoes and gently removing them. Without his shoes, Ben seemed to curl up even tighter but he stopped crying, and seemed to nod slightly, his body juddering with leftover sobs. Amy wondered whether to try to get him under the covers so that she could get in beside him, but decided that she simply didn't have enough energy left to move him again. She would have to sleep in the spare room.

She went into her bathroom and collected some toiletries

and her robe, which was hanging from a hook on the door. With one final look back at Ben, who already appeared to have fallen into a deep sleep, she closed the door behind her and leaned heavily against it, as a shiver of fear shot through her. *What the hell do I do now?* she thought bleakly, as she headed for the spare room.

The next morning, she awoke early with a start. She immediately got up and made her way into her and Ben's room, expecting to find him still curled up on top of the covers where she had left him the previous night. Instead the bed was empty, and Amy's stomach swirled with fear. *Oh God, not again!* she begged silently, whirling around and running down the stairs in her robe. Unthinkingly, instinctively, she headed for the front door and, opening it, was just about to run out into the dawn light when a voice stopped her in her tracks. 'It's OK,' said Ben. 'I'm here.'

Amy felt as though she might faint with relief as she turned around and closed the door again. 'Oh, thank God for that!' she whispered. She walked quickly towards Ben, who was standing in the kitchen clutching a mug of coffee. His hands, she noticed, were shaking so much that dark splashes of black coffee had slopped out onto the polished wood floor.

She took the mug from him and placed it carefully on the table before reaching up and cupping his face in her hands. He was still wearing the same clothes he had worn since he had last left the house, and his eyes were black and sunken. His stubble pricked her smooth palms but she held him fast, gazing into the eyes that she loved so much. 'Whatever is wrong,' she said quietly but firmly, 'we can sort it out. We've got each other and we've got our children. Nothing else matters.'

As soon as the words left her mouth, Ben crumpled. 'But it's really bad, Amy! You have no idea how bad it is!' he wailed, before slumping down onto a chair and burying his face in his hands.

The question, 'How bad?' hung in the air between them but Amy was too terrified to ask it. Instead, she bent down and kissed the top of his head, before quickly turning away so that he wouldn't see the panic in her own eyes. 'Tea,' she said. 'I'll make some tea.'

'Amy?' said Ben, as she busied herself putting the kettle on and throwing some teabags into a teapot. His voice was tremulous, desperate.

With an almighty effort, Amy forced herself to look at him. 'Let me just go and get the children up,' she said quietly, smiling at him with a smile that didn't reach her eyes. 'Then how about we talk later?'

Ben's eyes burned into her retreating back as she picked up her tea and headed upstairs. At the top of the stairs she paused suddenly and bent over slightly, gripping her stomach with her free hand, trying to stop the pain that was spreading from her chest into her abdomen. She felt truly scared: it must be worse than she had even contemplated. Had he done something illegal?

After a moment, the pain started to subside and she straightened up, distracting herself by looking around at the walls, which were tastefully painted with muted colours and hung with dozens of expensively framed paintings and prints. Again, it was almost as if she was seeing them for the first time and, now that she thought about it, maybe she was.

*

Once Maria had taken the children to school, Amy made some more tea and went in search of Ben, who was in his office. She knocked on the door gently, before turning the knob and walking in. Ben was sitting at his desk with his back to her; his computer was switched off and he was resting his head in his hands. She hesitated, sensing that there was some kind of invisible barrier around him that she shouldn't try to cross. 'Ben?' she said softly.

He didn't move so she walked over and put the tea down in front of him. Her eyes scanned the desk, which was now littered with scraps of paper and dozens of Post-it notes, all of which were covered in random scribbles and numbers. The room felt thick with silence, broken only by Ben's laboured breathing. The smell of stale alcohol, unwashed hair and body odour emanated from his skin, making her feel slightly nauseous.

Amy stood about a metre away from Ben, her arms folded defensively, wondering how to get through to him. 'Ben?' she said again, at last.

When he didn't answer again, she stepped forward and, without fully realising what she was doing, she half pushed, half slapped him on the shoulder. To her surprise, he fell to one side and slid onto the floor. Amy's mouth dropped open in shock as she watched him start to repeatedly bang his head on the hardwood floor.

'Ben! For fuck's sake!' she shouted. 'Stop it! You're scaring me.'

Ben paused for a second, as if he was registering her words, before resuming his head banging, this time accompanied by indecipherable muttering. Panic washed over Amy as she watched her tall, handsome husband reduced to a weak, gibbering wreck. She looked around her as if searching for someone to take over and help, but she quickly remembered that she was the only other person in the house. She walked out into the hallway, beads of sweat forming on her forehead as she tried to think clearly and decide what to do. Her eyes rested on her mobile phone, lying on the hall table.

She snatched up the handset and pressed 999. She was about to press 'Dial', when something made her hesitate. By now Ben was keening the way he had last night, the noise growing louder and louder as it echoed through the house. If she called an ambulance, she realised that Ben might be sectioned for his own safety. How could she allow that to happen? The humiliation and ignominy would be too much for him to ever recover from. And he would always blame her.

She pressed 'Cancel' and returned to Ben's office, where he had stopped banging his head but was now screaming, as if in agony. Decisively, Amy knelt down beside him and lifted his head into her lap. She stroked his forehead with both her thumbs rhythmically until he stopped and started to sob uncontrollably instead. She continued to apply gentle pressure, taking deep, exaggerated breaths in the hope that he would copy her, which he quickly did. As quiet descended once more, broken only by the two of them breathing in unison, Ben seemed to grow calmer. His eyes, which had been wide-open in terror, now gently drooped shut. His skin was damp and clammy to Amy's touch and she could see that his cheeks, even under the stubble, were a deathly pale. She continued to massage his forehead and started to sing gently to him the lullaby that she sometimes sang to the children if they couldn't sleep. Her voice was tremulous but pure and he calmed further as she sang. Gradually, the stiffness in his body seemed to leave him and he became more relaxed.

They remained in that position for another half-hour, until the pins and needles in Amy's legs became unbearable and she needed to shift position. 'Ben?' she said softly, lifting his head gently from her lap.

Ben's eyes shot open and he gripped her wrist desperately. 'Don't leave me!' he pleaded.

'Shhhhh, I'm not leaving you, sweetheart,' Amy said, keeping her voice as level as possible, despite her heart beginning to pound once more. 'I'm just changing position. My legs have gone to sleep,' she said, with a half-laugh. Ben's grip loosened on her wrist and she gave it a surreptitious rub as she shifted from kneeling; to crossing her legs into one of her yoga poses. It felt good to sit up straight, and her vertebrae clicked back into place one by one.

Ben's eyes were closed as he lay face up on the floor. 'What happened?' he said, after a few minutes. 'Amy, I'm scared!' A tear escaped from the side of his closed eyelid and Amy instinctively reached out to wipe it away, only for it to be followed by another. This one she left to trickle its way through his stubble, before settling at the edge of his jawline. She watched in fascination as it hung there for several seconds before finally dropping off and splashing onto the shoulder of his shirt.

'Shhhhh,' she said again, not because she was trying to calm him but because she had no idea what else to say or do. Amy's life thus far had been one of love, laughter and indulgence but, as she rolled her aching shoulders, seated on the floor with her husband crying silently in front of her, she knew that for both of them there was no way back from this.

Chapter 17

Kate spent almost the whole week thinking about what she was going to wear for dinner at Jack's. She didn't have an enormous wardrobe; there was never much money spare for her to buy clothes, but she had some great things that Amy had given her.

As she rummaged along the clothes rail in her cupboard, she mulled over what sort of look she was going for. So far, Jack had seen her in her deeply unsexy work uniform of trousers and a plain blue smock top, worn with clumpy black Hush Puppies, then later, he had seen her when she was in another deeply unflattering outfit: a hospital gown. She wanted to show him that she was actually a not bad-looking thirty-four year old with a pretty good figure, considering she had had two children.

Her fingers came to rest on a soft, black All Saints dress. It was clingy, with gathers in all the right places so that it showed off her toned arms and ample cleavage, while hiding the lumps and bumps left over from the caesarean scars on her tummy. She picked it up and held it up against her, looking across the small room into the full-length mirror hanging on the wall. *Hmm, definitely a possibility*, she thought, before her eyes rose and rested on the reflection of her face. God, she looked a mess: her hair was in desperate need of a cut and colour, and her eyes had dark circles underneath them.

A little surge of resentment spread through her as she tried to remember when she had last treated herself to some new make-up or a haircut: it was so many months ago that she couldn't actually recall, as she always told herself that they couldn't afford it. But now, as she stood gazing as the prematurely aging specimen staring back at her mournfully from the mirror, she could feel herself rebelling. *Fuck it*, she thought angrily. If Miles could afford to follow his bloody football team all over the country, she could sure as hell afford to buy herself some foundation and get her hair cut.

Before she could change her mind, she dropped the dress on the bed, stormed out of the room and down the stairs, scanning the tiny sitting room for her phone. Snatching it up, she scrolled through her contacts list, looking for the number of her hairdresser and pressing 'Call' with a defiantly heavy prod of the button.

Having established that they could fit her in later that afternoon, Kate grabbed her bag and headed out to the car. Both children were having tea with friends so she was free to prowl around the shops without either of them traipsing behind her, moaning that they were hungry, thirsty or tired.

As she drove into the car park on the high street, she felt a flutter of excitement – the kind that she hadn't felt in years – at the prospect of treating *herself* for a change. She found a space near to the exit leading to the town's exclusive department store, parked and entered the shop. Still filled with the same defiance that had materialised out of nowhere earlier, she marched purposefully towards the Benefit make-up counter.

She had passed the counter many times in the past and watched enviously as other women had had expertly applied makeovers before buying the products the assistant had recommended. Well, today it was her turn to be one of those women.

'Hi, can I help you?' said a pretty, dark-eyed girl, with shiny chestnut hair swept back into a ponytail.

'I don't know.' Kate laughed, suddenly nervous. 'But I hope so.'

'OK, well, take a seat,' the girl said sweetly, guiding Kate into a high black make-up chair and looking closely at her face. 'What sort of look were you after?'

'Yours?' Kate said with a smile, before adding, 'Or anyone else's, apart from mine.'

'Nonsense,' the assistant smiled. 'You're gorgeous. I'm Alex, by the way. Shall I just do what I think?'

'Yes, please!' Kate nodded vigorously before relaxing back into the soft leather of the chair and submitting herself to Alex's expert touch.

For the next forty-five minutes, she was stroked, prodded, patted and painted. Finally, Alex narrowed her eyes, giving her one last, appraising look. 'There,' she said proudly, 'you're done. Your husband is one lucky man – you look amazing!'

'Really?' asked Kate shyly: she sometimes thought Miles wouldn't notice if she came into the room with her head tucked under one arm. But Jack, on the other hand – she had a feeling he would notice. 'Can I see?' she urged excitedly.

'Sure.' Alex swung the chair around so that Kate was facing herself in the mirror. 'Oh my God!' she gasped. 'Is that really me?' Even with her hair scraped back in an unflattering elastic hair band, her face looked transformed. Her skin was flawless; her high, sharp cheekbones subtly defined with a flattering dark rose blusher. Her full mouth had been shaped into a perfect, pouting bow and slicked with a pale pink gloss, while her deep brown eyes were now smoky and smouldering.

'You look like a model,' said Alex proudly.

Kate stared at herself in wonder. She felt arrogant even thinking it, but Alex was right. She looked sophisticated and sexy in a way that she had never, ever done before.

'Do you think you could do it yourself?' Alex asked, still grinning at Kate in the mirror.

Kate nodded slowly. 'I think so. Can you get me all the products you've used?'

'*All* of them?' Alex said, her eyebrows raised in surprise. 'Don't you have any make-up at home already?'

'Not really,' Kate said airily, determined to throw away every single crappy piece of make-up and the threadbare make-up bag they lived in just as soon as she got home.

By the time she had paid for her hair too, Kate had spent almost £300. She drove home feeling sick with guilt. The make-up sat accusingly on the seat beside her, expensively wrapped in cheeky little stiff card bags, tied with bright pink ribbon: she loved the packaging almost as much as the products themselves, never having owned anything so luxurious in her life. But the thought of what Miles would say when he saw the credit card bill filled her with dread. They paid it off every month, as Miles steadfastly refused to get into debt. Aside from the mortgage, they owned everything else outright. His mantra was, 'If you can't afford it, don't buy it' which, most of the time, Kate agreed with. But it was just so bloody boring living like that, especially when she saw Amy splashing out on make-up, clothes and shoes every single week without giving it a second thought. And Ben never seemed to begrudge her a penny, even though it was entirely his money, whereas Miles definitely felt that Kate shouldn't 'fritter money away' as he put it, on trivialities. He didn't seem to understand the concept of a woman's need to treat herself occasionally.

Locking the car door and looking up at the house, she tried to ascertain if Miles was home from work yet. *It doesn't look like it*, she thought with relief, opening the front door and creeping into the sitting room nervously. 'Hello?' she called out. No answer. Kate almost danced with delight, taking the stairs to their bedroom two at a time. She sat on the bed and took each item of make-up out of its bag, as carefully as if she was lifting a new-born baby out of its cot. She stroked each one lovingly, before placing it in her new make-up bag. When she was done, she tucked each little bag inside the other and put them reluctantly at the bottom of her underwear drawer, knowing that she would take them out from time to time and remember how good it felt to own something so new and beautiful.

Next, she dashed into the bathroom, and retrieved her ugly, dirty old cosmetics purse from the bathroom cabinet. She looked at it for a second, trying to remember how long she had owned it and its contents. *Nearly thirteen years*, she decided, before hurling it into the bin scornfully and covering it up with lavatory paper so that Miles wouldn't notice it. Not that he ever emptied the bins, but she didn't want to take the risk.

Just as she had finished hiding the evidence, she heard the front door opening downstairs. 'Oooh eee!' called Miles jokingly, and her heart softened immediately.

'Oooh eee yourself!' she called back, trotting happily down the stairs to greet him. 'How was your day?' she asked, taking him by surprise with a kiss and a hug.

'Good.' He smiled, looking down at her. 'You look . . .'

'What?' she asked with a grin, amazed that he might have noticed her makeover.

'Different,' he said.

'Good different or bad different?' She stepped away from him so that he could get a proper look at her.

Miles considered for a minute. 'A bit of both,' he said at last, causing Kate's heart to sink.

'What do you mean?' How bloody typical of him to put her on a downer, when she had been feeling so good about herself.

'You look . . . very well,' he said slowly. 'But I don't like all that make-up. You don't need it.'

Normally, Kate would have felt flattered by such a comment but not today. Today she wanted to kill him for giving her such a backhanded compliment. 'Well, *I* like it,' she said stiffly. 'So get used to it.'

Miles looked at her in surprise and she could see that he genuinely didn't know what he'd done wrong.

'Is this anything to do with tomorrow night?' he asked, his eyes narrowing.

Kate inwardly flinched. 'Don't be ridiculous!' she snapped.

'It's because I am only thirty-four but I look and feel about a hundred and I decided that it's time I did something about it.'

'It's just a bit strange that you would suddenly decide that, the day before we're supposed to be going to see this bloke for dinner,' he said quietly.

Kate tutted and turned on her heel towards the kitchen, but she was struck by how unusually perceptive Miles was being. Far from not noticing that she had had a makeover, he seemed to have noticed both that and the reasons behind it. And he seemed to feel threatened by Jack in a way that she had never known him feel before. He wasn't a jealous man and had always been relaxed about her having male friends, so why was he different about Jack? Was it because *she* felt differently about Jack than she had about any other man? Maybe Miles knew her better than she knew herself.

Then she had a thought. Had Miles seen the emails she and Jack had been exchanging? After the first few initially polite exchanges, their emails had begun to get increasingly personal. Somehow Jack seemed able to get Kate to tell him things about herself that she had never told Miles, or anyone else for that matter. They had discovered that they had a shared love of books and film and had talked at length about the merits of different authors, novels and movie adaptations, before moving on to talk about their childhoods, their first loves and their hopes and dreams for the future. Jack wrote as if he knew her deepest thoughts intimately and she found herself responding. The thought of Miles reading them suddenly made her insides curdle.

'What's made you get jealous all of a sudden?' she called back to him, tentatively.

Miles made his way towards the kitchen and stood in the doorway, watching her. 'Oh, nothing. It's just that it seems a bit coincidental that you would suddenly decide that you're not happy with how you look. I think you look gorgeous just the way you are.'

Kate felt prickles of guilt shoot through her. 'But I just feel so old and dowdy, Miles. It's probably to do with the accident – I've just felt a bit down since then.'

Miles's eyes clouded over as he absorbed her words. He came into the kitchen and wrapped his arms around her from behind. 'I'm sorry,' he said. 'You look lovely. Really lovely,' he added, kissing the side of her neck. Kate allowed herself to fall back into him and relaxed against his body. As he continued to plant tiny kisses over her neck and face, she felt an unfamiliar swirl of desire start to ignite within her. 'What time are the kids back?' he whispered, as she turned to face him and kissed him back passionately.

'Not for at least another hour,' she said with a smile, as he took her hand and led her up the stairs to their bedroom.

Chapter 18

Across town, Jennifer was also preparing for a night out. Hugh was coming to collect her from the cottage, which scared her: she hadn't wanted him to be anywhere near what was once Michael's space. Somehow it seemed wrong and only served to increase her feelings of guilt, but there was no other option. She couldn't drive, having loaned the Clio to Kate and Miles until they got the insurance money for a new car, and she didn't want to rely on the only local taxi firm, who might send a car but only if they had one available: it was more likely that they wouldn't, and she would be left stranded.

She dressed carefully, in a green, patterned wrap-dress, which was elegant but not too dressy, and her favourite pair of tan, knee-length, leather boots with a low heel. She applied enough make-up to make her feel confident, but not so much that she looked like she was making too much effort for him. Hugh's arrogance would lead him naturally to assume it was all for his benefit but Jennifer knew differently. Meeting up with him again, making contact, getting to know him again, was all for *her* confidence.

She checked herself one last time in the mirror, before

deciding that she was happy with what she saw and going downstairs to await his arrival. Instinctively, she headed for the fridge, took out a bottle of rosé and poured herself a large glass. Taking a long sip and feeling herself relax as the cold alcohol entered her system, she was instantly transported back to that fateful night, when she had made the biggest mistake of her life.

'Where is he?' Hugh asked, lighting up a cigarette as they walked down the Kings Road side by side.

Jennifer wasn't cold but she shivered and pulled her jacket more tightly around her. 'Who?' she asked, reaching out to take the cigarette he offered and drawing heavily on it.

'The boyfriend.'

'Fiancé,' she corrected, giving him the cigarette back and waving her diamond ring at him as she did so.

Hugh looked at her but said nothing. They continued walking for several minutes – with Jennifer having no idea where they were going – before she answered him. 'I think he might be cheating on me.' She was pleased her voice sounded strong and even, rather than tearful and small, as it had earlier. She had definitely toughened up during the evening.

'Oh,' Hugh said, before he suddenly stopped walking, causing Jennifer to draw to an abrupt halt beside him. In one movement, he finished his cigarette and dropped it to the pavement, before he turned towards her and grabbed her tightly around the waist, then kissed her hard on the lips.

Taken by surprise, Jennifer resisted at first but his grip was so firm that she was unable to move away; and she suddenly found herself responding with a passion she didn't know she possessed. His taste and smell were so different to Michael's, coupled with the mesmerising sense of danger he exuded, that her whole body filled with lust. At that moment, all she wanted to do was have sex with him: it was as if her mind had been taken over by her body.

As they broke apart, Jennifer gasping slightly and feeling weak with desire, Hugh took her hand and looked deep into her eyes. 'Will you sleep with me tonight?' he asked.

She nodded slowly and he smiled a long, slow smile that turned her insides to liquid, before turning and leading her up the stone steps of a large white townhouse that they had stopped in front of. 'Where are we?' she asked, suddenly anxious.

'Relax,' he said, sliding his arm around her waist. He guided her through a shiny black front door into a wide, palatial hallway with an ornate sweeping staircase leading up from a black-and-white tiled floor. 'This is my home.'

'What?' Jennifer looked around in amazement. It was one of the most luxurious houses she had ever set foot in. 'Your parents' home, surely?' she said, watching aghast as he headed up the stairs and motioned for her to follow him.

Hugh turned on the stairs and looked back at her with an amused grin. 'No, Jennifer, *my* house.'

Something inside her seemed to click and she looked up at him in horror. What the hell was she doing here, with this stranger she knew absolutely nothing about? But as if he could sense what she was thinking, he walked back down the stairs and grabbed her wrist. 'Don't,' he said in an urgent, quiet voice. 'Don't go.'

'I think I must,' she said, refusing to look into the eyes she already knew could persuade her to do anything. 'I don't know you. I don't know anything about you.' She was about to turn and walk away when he tilted her chin up and kissed her on the lips. Not passionately this time but gently, seductively; she could feel herself responding to him as his tongue began to explore her mouth, every nerve ending in her body seeming to respond. He lifted her sweater over her head and unhooked her bra, gazing at her breasts with a hungry expression, before bending to kiss and lick her already hardened nipples.

With shaking hands – knowing all the time that she should leave – Jennifer unzipped his jeans and pushed them down over his slim hips. It didn't surprise her that he wore no underwear, and his erection sprang out towards her as she dropped to her knees and took him in her mouth. Hugh groaned loudly as she sucked and teased him, hardly knowing where she had learnt such techniques. With Michael, she had enjoyed plenty of sex but it had never been like this, where it was all about lust and nothing to do with love.

Moaning as he pulled her to her feet, Hugh put his thumb into her mouth and watched her with liquid eyes as she sucked hard on it. He pushed his hand under the waistband of her skirt and his fingers began to explore her, making Jennifer's knees buckle beneath her.

Still watching her intently, Hugh kicked his jeans off over his feet and reached down to slide off her skirt and knickers, which he threw onto the hall floor behind him. Jennifer was shaking as he found her mouth again with his, and entered her. He thrust hard and deep inside her with rhythmic, almost aggressive movements until she came. He looked at her triumphantly and resumed thrusting until she shuddered to another climax almost within seconds.

Abruptly, Hugh pulled out of her and stood up, motioning for her to do the same; but her legs were too shaky, and she almost crumpled as she tried to get to her feet. As if she weighed nothing, he scooped her up in his arms and carried her the rest of the way up the stairs. He took her into an ornately decorated, surprisingly feminine room, where he laid her gently on top of a wide bed with chocolate-brown silk covers.

For the rest of the night, they alternated between having energetic, animalistic bouts of sex and sleeping exhausted in each other's arms. By the time the sun came up the next morning, Jennifer felt she had learnt more about sex in one night than she had her whole life. It was so different to what she experienced with Michael. With Michael she made love. With Hugh, she had wild, uninhibited *sex*.

Beside her, Hugh stirred and Jennifer felt a jolt of alarm. Yes, Michael might have been cheating on her but now she was no better than he. As Hugh slipped back into sleep, she edged tentatively to the side of the bed. Keeping her eyes on him to make sure he didn't wake, she placed her feet on the deep-piled carpet and stood up. Still he didn't move, so she tiptoed noiselessly towards the open door. With one last glance back at his sleeping form, she shuddered slightly and left the room.

One look down the stairs brought the memories of the hedonistic night flooding back. Hugh's jeans lay discarded across the steps, while her clothes were strewn across the hallway. Still tiptoeing, she scooped them up and dressed with a sudden, desperate need to get out of his house. To get away from the scene of her crime and try to forget that it had ever happened.

She snatched up her bag and opened the heavy door, breathing a sigh of shocked relief as she closed it behind her. Concerned now that the noise of the door closing would have woken Hugh, she ran down the stone steps like a soul possessed and sprinted towards the Kings Road, where she knew she would be able to melt into the early bustle of the Saturday morning crowds. Sure enough, although it wasn't yet eight o'clock, when she got there, the traffic noise and sounds of the street waking up were enough to make her feel camouflaged and safe.

As she slowed to a walk and caught her breath, she began to feel like she was coming back into herself: she realised that for the whole night, she had been feeling a strange sense of detachment. It was as if she had been watching someone else's feet on the pavement beneath her as she walked along with Hugh; as if someone else's body had succumbed to his like a starving person, desperate for food; as if the whole thing had been an out-of-body experience that had happened to someone else entirely.

As she turned off the Kings Road into the road where she lived, she smiled to herself and began to feel a sense of release. Maybe it hadn't happened to her? Maybe it had all been a strange dream that she would gradually forget through the mists of time. She let herself in through the front door and crept up the stairs to her room. She would pretend to have spent the night in her own bed and no one would be any the wiser.

She was just about to open her door when Susie appeared on the stairs in her robe, looking pale and worried. 'Jennifer!' she hissed. 'Where the hell have you been? Michael's been here looking for you.'

Jennifer's stomach seemed to freeze and she heard a rushing sound that made her think she was going to faint. 'What?' she whispered, her voice trembling with shock. She sank down onto the stair where Susie was standing and looked up her. 'When?'

'Last night, when I got back.' Susie was still talking in a whisper: they both knew better than to alert their landlady to the fact that one of them had spent the night elsewhere. 'He was waiting outside. That's why his flatmate was acting so strangely – Michael wanted to surprise you for the end of your exams by coming to visit! Oh, shit, Jennifer, where the hell have you been?'

Time seemed to grind to a halt and suddenly Jennifer couldn't think: it was as if she had been turned to stone. Finally, she shook her head helplessly. 'I don't know what to do, Susie,' she whispered, her lips pale with horror.

Susie reached down and put her arm around her. 'Let's go into your room. We can't talk out here.'

Jennifer nodded and stood up shakily. They slipped into her room and Susie sank down on her bed, her knees curled up under her and her back to the wall. Jennifer looked around. Everything was exactly as it had been when she had left last night, and yet nothing would ever be the same again. Her world had fallen off on its axis.

'What did you tell him?' she said at last, sitting on the bed beside Susie. She couldn't meet her friend's eye, too overwhelmed as she was with shame and regret.

'I told him that a load of us went out and that you probably stayed over at one of the other girls' houses.'

Jennifer closed her eyes. 'Did he believe you?'

'I think so,' Susie said. 'Well, you know what Michael's

like,' she added, and Jennifer opened her eyes and nodded, unable to speak. She *knew* what Michael was like, so why the hell had she suspected him of cheating on her when it was the last thing in the world that he would ever do to her? Shame was enveloping her like a blanket and she began to shake violently.

'Was it ... did you ... spend the night with that guy?' Susie whispered, her eyes wide with worry.

Still Jennifer couldn't speak as the horror of what she'd done crawled over her like a cockroach, but she nodded miserably.

There was a sharp intake of breath from Susie before she reached out and took Jennifer's hand, stroking it in an effort to calm her. 'It'll be OK,' she said quietly. 'No one knows and no one needs to know.'

Again, Jennifer closed her eyes and leaned against the wall, covering her face with her hand in an effort to hide the disgust she was feeling for herself.

'Come on, Jennifer,' Susie urged her. 'You've got to forget about it now. If you behave like this he'll know in an instant. Have a bath, wash your face and brush your hair. Go to find him and laugh at the mix-up. Push it to the corner of your mind, never to be thought of again.'

After a long pause, Jennifer opened her eyes, looked at her friend and smiled. 'Thank you,' she whispered. 'Thank you so much. And you'll never, ever tell anyone?'

Susie shook her head slowly. 'There's nothing to tell,' she said emphatically.

Outside, Jennifer heard a car pulling onto the gravel driveway to the cottage and she jumped involuntarily. Her glass was empty and her cheeks burned with fresh shame yet again, as she tumbled forwards through time to the present day.

Getting up and trying to ignore the faintness she felt, she placed her glass in the sink and picked up her jacket. The interior light was on in Hugh's black Range Rover and she could see his face, illuminated as he looked at her, his eyes holding hers – as if he could tell exactly where she had been in her mind for the past hour. She hesitated slightly on the doorstep but there was no backing out now; she had opened Pandora's box, and there was no way to close it again.

Chapter 19

Ben took to his bed where he slept sporadically, while Amy prowled around the house wondering what on earth to do. The children, who were used to their father working long hours, didn't question why he wasn't around.

Only Maria seemed to grasp what had happened. She gently put her hand on Amy's shoulder at lunchtime one day, as Amy sat at the kitchen table with her head in her hands, and told her that she had made some chicken soup. 'Maybe Ben would like some, too?' she added, her meaning clear.

Amy wiped her face to remove any trace of tears and fixed a smile on her face, before looking up. 'Thanks. That's a good idea,' she said, so grateful for Maria's presence. And for her presence of mind. It hadn't even occurred to Amy that Ben must be starving. Maria was only a few years younger than Amy but, at that moment, she seemed so much older and wiser. 'I'll take some up,' she said, getting up.

'I could do it?' offered Maria.

Amy shook her head and patted Maria's arm. 'No, thank you – I'll do it. You go and have a break.'

She switched on the hob under the giant vat of chicken

soup, before taking two bowls out of the cupboard and placing them on a tray, along with some spoons. She stared out of the window while the soup heated, hating the muted colours and dampness that were creeping into the garden, heralding the imminent arrival of autumn. To Amy, at that moment, autumn only signified more depression.

Behind her, the soup started to bubble and a delicious smell filled the room. Amy stirred it gently before carefully ladling it out into the bowls.

She climbed the stairs slowly, biting her lip with concentration as she struggled to balance the tray. Kicking the door to their bedroom open with her bare foot, she carried it to the bedside table nearest to Ben, who was sleeping, and placed it down gingerly. He didn't stir but as she sat on the mattress beside him, his eyes flickered open. Amy was shocked yet again by the deterioration in his appearance in such a short space of time. His dark eyes were rheumy and bloodshot; his skin was clammy and had a slight greenish tinge; while his stubble had now grown into a full beard. 'I brought you some chicken soup,' she said.

'I'm not hungry,' whimpered Ben, and Amy felt the first spark of irritation ignite within her.

'Well, hungry or not, you need to eat,' she replied firmly. 'Come on, sit up.' Her tone was clipped as she pulled the pillows out from beneath his head and propped them up against the headboard, giving him no choice but to sit up. She handed him a bowl of steaming soup, which he took with shaking hands. 'Careful,' she said, as the soup swirled threateningly towards the edges of the bowl. Quickly, she took her own bowl off the tray and put it on the bedside table, before sliding the tray onto his lap to catch any splashes.

Ben stared uneasily at the soup for a while but, eventually, he picked up his spoon and began to eat, slowly at first but with increasing speed. Amy watched him slurping greedily, obviously ravenous after several days of not eating. He finished the whole bowl in seconds, tilting it to his lips to get the last few dregs. 'Well, you obviously needed that!' she said with a smile.

Ben nodded and eyed Amy's bowl on the bedside table. She laughed and replaced his empty one with her full one. Again, he quickly dispatched the contents, and sighed with satisfaction.

'I think you should take a long, hot bath,' she said. 'Why don't I run you one?'

Ben smiled weakly and nodded. 'OK,' he said meekly.

Amy walked to their bathroom and turned on the taps, taking repeated deep breaths and swallowing hard to stop herself from crying. She couldn't allow herself to crumble. She had to stay strong.

Once Ben was in the bath, Amy slipped into his office and picked up his mobile, scanning through his contacts list to find a number for Tim. With shaking hands, she pressed 'Dial', closing the office door behind her to ensure that she couldn't be heard.

Tim answered almost immediately. 'Where the fuck have you been?' he said angrily, without preamble.

Amy was momentarily speechless, then it dawned on her that Ben's number would have come up on Tim's phone. 'Er, Tim, it's not Ben,' she said, clearing her throat as she spoke. 'It's Amy.'

'Oh, Christ. Sorry, Amy, I thought it was Ben ...' he mumbled contritely.

Amy nodded. 'Yes, I can see why you might have thought that.' She half laughed. 'And why you might be so angry with him for disappearing for a bit. But Tim, Ben's not well.'

There was silence on the other end of the line while Tim digested what Amy had said. 'In what way, "not well"?' he asked eventually, his tone suspicious.

'Well, I'm not entirely sure myself,' she began, suddenly feeling an urge to cry again. She gulped before continuing. 'I think he's had some kind of breakdown.'

There was silence on the other end of the line. After a while, Amy wondered if he had hung up. 'Tim?' she prompted.

Tim coughed softly. 'I'm still here,' he said. 'I'm just a bit shocked. I don't know what to say.'

'Did you see it coming? Was he behaving differently?'

Tim sighed heavily. 'No ... well, yes, I guess so. God, it's so difficult to say. Things have been very tense because of the business going down the pan, so we've all been behaving differently. I suppose I was too busy thinking about myself to worry about Ben. How serious is it?'

Amy felt tears flush into her eyes again and blinked them away furiously. 'I don't know,' she whispered. 'It's never happened before so I've got nothing to compare it with. Is the business really going down the pan?' she added.

'Looks that way,' said Tim quietly.

'How come? Everything was going so well!' Amy exclaimed, desperate for it not to be true.

'Worldwide recession. Other companies who owe us a lot of money have gone down, and it looks like they'll take us with them. It's like a giant game of dominoes.' Tim's tone was matter-of-fact, but there was a crack in his voice as he spoke.

Amy stared at the phone, scared to ask the next question. 'Is there any chance that the company will survive?'

There was a long pause, as if Tim was trying to weigh up what to say next. 'I don't think so.' He paused, then continued, 'Amy, are you aware of what's tied up in the business?'

Amy's insides turned to ice. 'Well, I've never been that involved.' She shook her head as she spoke, ashamed of her ignorance. 'But while Ben was away I had a look through his computer. Tim, it looks like we might lose the house ... is that true?'

'I don't want to be the one to tell you,' Tim said, sounding agonised.

'Please!' Amy begged. 'Please, Tim. I need to know what I'm dealing with here. Be honest.'

Tim hesitated and exhaled loudly. 'Then I think losing the house is just the start.'

Later that evening, after the children were in bed, Ben finally got up and came downstairs to join Amy in the sitting room. She was sprawled on the sofa, staring unseeingly at the TV; she started slightly as he shuffled barefoot into the room, wearing a pair of dark grey pyjama bottoms and a white T-shirt. He still hadn't shaved but he had washed his hair and his skin now smelt clean and soapy. Amy sat up and tucked her feet underneath her, before patting the space beside her.

Ben nodded slightly, almost to himself, and sat down exactly where she had patted. He sat stiffly, with his back straight and his arms hanging beside him. Amy looked at his hands and noticed that both were clenched into a tight fist, as if he might launch a vicious assault at any minute. Neither of them spoke as Amy waited for him to give some kind of explanation for the bomb that had just dropped into the middle of their lives, but Ben remained defiantly silent, his eyes fixed on the TV screen, seemingly transfixed by the property programme that was blaring out.

Eventually, she couldn't stand it any longer and picked up the remote control, pressing the 'Off' button. As the picture disappeared into blackness, Ben sighed deeply and frowned, as if he was struggling to understand where it had gone. Amy's unease grew by the second as she watched him twitch and frown. 'Ben,' she said, her voice alarmingly loud in the quiet room.

'Yes?' he replied politely, his voice robotic and detached.

'Look at me,' she said, more quietly this time.

Ben hesitated and scratched his chin. Finally, he turned his head in her direction but couldn't meet her eye.

'Ben, look at me,' she repeated.

This time, he raised his eyes and Amy recoiled at the sorrow she saw there. Ben's eyes filled with fat tears that rolled over his lashes and splashed onto his cheeks, before plopping onto his lap.

Amy reached out and took one of his hands, still tightly curled into a fist. One by one, she uncurled his fingers and smoothed her fingers over his palm. 'What's happened, Ben?' she whispered.

Ben shook his head. 'I don't know,' he whispered back. 'But I can't ever go back into that office. I can't, Amy! Please don't make me go back!' he pleaded.

'Ssshhhhh,' she said, hugging him and rubbing his back gently, shocked at his response to her question. 'OK, let's not talk about that now. Just get some sleep and let's see how you feel in the morning.' Her voice sounded much brighter and more optimistic than she felt: she knew instinctively that whatever kind of breakdown Ben had had, and regardless of whether he felt better after a good night's sleep, he would never be returning to his old job.

Ben nodded and wiped his eyes. 'Will you come up to bed with me, Amy?' he asked pleadingly, as he stood up. 'I'm scared to go up there on my own.'

Amy felt her shoulders sag under the weight of this new responsibility; it was as if she now had three children to care for instead of two. But she nodded wearily and followed her husband out of the door and up the stairs.

Chapter 20

'Beautiful cottage,' said Hugh, holding open the door to the Range Rover and standing back as Jennifer climbed into the passenger seat.

'Thank you,' she said.

'How long have you lived here?'

Jennifer glanced at him and noticed a muscle pulsating in his cheek. It wasn't like him to make small talk, and she wondered if perhaps he was nervous. Somehow the thought that he was feeling as discomfited by this situation as she was made her feel better. Stronger. She thought for a moment and tried to calculate how long they had owned the house. 'About thirty years,' she said at last. 'Do you still live in ...' She tailed off as the memory of his beautiful house flashed through her mind and, with it, the memory of what they had done there.

'Lost it in my divorce,' he said quickly, as if reading her thoughts. He seemed to do that a lot.

Jennifer nodded and they lapsed into silence for a while. 'Who was she?' she said, surprising herself with a prickle of jealousy.

'She wasn't you.' His reply made her heart contract, and

she realised she was angry with both him and herself that he could still have this effect on her, even after so many years.

'Children?' She wanted to move the conversation on to new territory for them both – into their lives outside the bubble that was theirs.

'Just the one.'

Jennifer assumed he must be referring to the son that he had mentioned previously.

'You?'

'Two daughters,' she said, feeling herself swell with pride, just as she always did when she talked about the girls.

'How old?'

'Thirty-f—' Jennifer stopped suddenly. 'Both in their thirties now,' she corrected herself.

Hugh nodded, and they continued their journey in a comfortable silence. He drove to a well-known restaurant in Banntree, making her wonder how he knew about it when apparently he hadn't visited the town before meeting her in the coffee shop last week. He slowed down as they passed the restaurant and parked in a space a short distance up the road.

He jumped out and came round to open her door, reaching to take her hand as she climbed out. As their skin touched, she felt a jolt in her stomach and looked up at him in shock. He seemed unperturbed and smiled at her in a slow, lazy way, before crooking his arm and offering it to her. Jennifer hesitated. She didn't want anyone she might know to see them and assume they were a couple. 'It's OK,' he said, again reading her mind and dropping his arm good-naturedly. 'I get it.'

He locked the car and they were walking towards the

restaurant when he suddenly spoke. 'Did he ever know?' he asked.

Jennifer almost stumbled at his words. 'I'm ... I'm not sure,' she stuttered, her head swimming with the miserable, sluggish guilt that had dogged her every move for so long now.

Had Michael known?

'Go to see him,' said Susie, as Jennifer dithered, unsure whether she could carry off the deception. Surely he would take one look at her face and know the truth? 'It'll be fine!' Susie added, prodding Jennifer to get up from the bed where she had been sitting.

Reluctantly, Jennifer got to her feet, unsure what to do first. 'How do I find him?' she asked in a dazed voice. 'I don't even know where he is.'

'He left me the address. Go on, go and have that bath, get dressed and get over there before you change your mind.' Susie was already lifting Jennifer's towel off the rail and gathering up her wash bag. 'Go on!' she urged.

Jennifer took her things and headed for the communal bathroom, praying that she would be able to wipe the guilt and regret from her mind as easily as she would be able to wash the smell of Hugh from her skin.

Once she had bathed, she suddenly couldn't wait to see her Michael again. After a good luck hug from Susie, she hurried down the stairs and raced to the underground, clutching the piece of paper with the address he was staying at in her hand.

It was still before ten o'clock when she arrived at the house belonging to a friend of his. She walked up the front steps and rang the doorbell with shaking hands. There was no answer but she looked through the letterbox hopefully. 'Hello?' she called into an empty, echoing hallway. Still there was no response and she turned disconsolately to walk back down the steps when she heard a noise from above.

Looking up, she saw a sash window sliding up and Michael's blond head and bright blue eyes appeared. 'Jennifer!' he yelled in delight. 'Don't go! I'm coming! Wait right there!'

Her heart danced with joy as she waited for him. After several moments, during which she imagined him pulling on some trousers and racing down the stairs, the front door was flung open and he scooped her up in his arms. 'Oh, darling!' he laughed. 'I thought you'd had second thoughts and run out on me!'

Jennifer laughed back, returning his kisses. 'I will never, *ever* run out on you,' she told him vehemently, meaning it. She knew then that she had no choice but to do what Susie had advised and push the whole Hugh experience into a recess of her brain, never to be spoken of again.

After Michael returned to Leeds – with Jennifer planning to go and visit him the following week – she set about packing up in London and saying goodbye to that part of her life for ever. She was going to try to get a job in Leeds to be near Michael so that they could start their married life living in the same city. They had booked the wedding for October in a church in the Suffolk village where Jennifer's parents still lived and where she had grown up. Her parents adored Michael and were delighted that she had found such a suitable young man to marry.

Jennifer was determined to forget about Hugh and pretend that it all had never happened. But, as she dashed back from the post office one morning, her mind full of the numerous things she still had to sort out before leaving London, she spotted him sitting on the front steps of her house, smoking. 'Oh God, no,' she whispered to herself, panicking as she tried to think what to do. Hoping that he hadn't seen her, she spun on her heel and began to walk blindly back the way she had come, picking up speed with every stride until she was almost running. *But what if he's still there when I get back?* she suddenly thought, her heart racing. She couldn't stay away indefinitely; she had to face him and tell him in no uncertain terms that she never wanted to see him again.

Gradually, she came to a halt and slowly turned back round, expecting to see him still sitting there, in the distance. But he had vanished. Relief washed over her and, hesitatingly, she began to take tentative steps towards her house again.

'Hello, Jennifer.' He stepped out from behind a hedge and stood facing her, blocking her path.

'Oh my God!' she screamed, coming to an abrupt halt. 'Hugh! You frightened me!'

Hugh looked at her with an amused expression. 'Did I?' he said, in a voice that suggested he was extremely pleased with himself.

Jennifer took a deep breath and ran her hand through her hair. 'Please, Hugh,' she said, in a gentler voice. 'I can't see you again. I think we both know that.' She looked up at him with a beseeching expression, begging him to understand.

'He's not right for you. He's too boring,' Hugh said, as if she hadn't spoken.

Jennifer folded her arms defensively around herself. 'He's as far from boring as it's possible to be, and he is *completely* right for me,' she said, piqued.

Hugh took out his cigarettes and shook one out of the packet, lighting it with an expert flick of his lighter. He took a heavy drag before passing it to her.

Jennifer waved the cigarette away with her hand, before folding her arms again. 'No,' she said irritably, registering the look of surprise that crossed his face. She realised then that Hugh wasn't a man who had ever been turned down.

'I bet the sex isn't the same with him as it is with me.'

Jennifer sighed. It was all very well her pushing the memory to a far corner of her brain but the truth was, she realised, that once you had done it, you couldn't undo it. She flushed at the recollection of Hugh's hard body against hers.

'*Was*,' she whispered. 'Past tense. It's never happening again.' She paused before continuing, 'But you're right, sex with Michael isn't the same as it was with you ...' She watched a light come on in the dark pools of Hugh's eyes before she delivered the killer blow. 'It's so much *better*.'

'Come and have a coffee with me,' he said quietly, and she was shocked and slightly scared by the desperation on his face.

Jennifer shook her head. 'Don't you think it's best for both of us if we say goodbye now?'

'I'll marry you,' he said, causing another little charge of fear to shoot through her.

'Hugh,' she said, trying to keep her voice firm but gentle at the same time. 'You don't know me. I know nothing about you. I don't want to get married to you. I want to marry Michael.'

'I will make you happy,' he said, reaching out to take her hand.

Jennifer looked down at their clasped hands, his skin dark, hers paler, and for a fleeting instant she wondered what would happen if she took that moment to jump off the cliff. As their fingers entwined, the story of a different life that she could possibly live was beginning to write itself in her head. She would live in luxury, never wanting for anything; her children would have their father's sultry, dark, irresistible eyes, and their passion for each other would only grow with each passing year.

But, even as those delicious thoughts reeled through her brain, she could also write the story of a relationship built on the weak foundations of lust and sex, with marriage to a man who she would never truly know, who was dangerous. She could see that the end of the story would most likely be a bitter divorce years down the line, on the grounds of his adultery. Having given up her beautiful Michael for the sake of her lust for Hugh, she would be left wrung out and regretful.

'No,' she said, looking up at Hugh for the last time. 'You couldn't make me happy. Goodbye, Hugh.' She reached up and kissed his full lips, trying to commit the feel and taste of him to memory.

'I don't think Michael knew,' she said now, as she and Hugh took their seats in the restaurant. 'If he had, I don't think he would have been able to keep it a secret for all of those years.'

'Why not?' Hugh said, picking up a menu and studying it, deliberately not looking at her. 'You did.'

Chapter 21

'I wish we hadn't agreed to go to this bloody meal,' moaned Miles as he emerged from the bathroom, a towel wrapped around his waist and another wrapped turban-style around his head.

Kate looked up at him in the reflection of her dressing-table mirror. She was trying to recreate the look Alex had given her yesterday in the shop, using all her new products. The problem was that she wasn't used to applying make-up and she was struggling to perfect her technique. 'Don't be such a misery guts,' she said, resisting the urge to laugh at Miles's comic appearance. His belly was hanging over the top of the towel around his waist and the turban made him look like an extra from a *Carry On* film. 'It's very nice of him to invite us and, really, it ought to be us cooking for him. We owe him big time, Miles.'

Miles sniffed and removed the turban from his head, dropping the wet towel onto the carpet – where she knew it would stay – and running his hands through his damp hair. That would be the extent of his efforts at styling it, but Kate envied how easily it fell into place. *He's still a handsome man*, she thought, *although he could definitely do with losing some weight.*

She knew why Miles didn't want to go that night: it was because he felt he owed Jack, and if there was one thing Miles hated, it was being in debt to anyone.

'Why are you putting all that muck on your face?' he asked, narrowing his eyes suspiciously at Kate. 'And where did you get it all? Is it new?'

'So what if it is?' she snapped back, defiantly. 'I thought it was about time I treated myself to some new make-up, seeing as the eighties have been on the phone asking for the last lot back.'

Miles grinned. 'Can we afford it, though?' He picked up his jeans off the chair, where he had slung them earlier, and perched on the edge of the bed as he pushed his feet into them.

Kate watched him in the mirror, feeling a rising sense of anger. 'Miles! Can you wear something other than your dirty old jeans that you've been wearing all day?' she hissed. 'And as for whether we can afford some new make-up for me, I'd say that if we can afford for you to go to your precious football every week, then we can afford to buy me some new make-up. Stop being such a tight-arse.'

Miles's mouth dropped open indignantly. 'I'm not tight!' he protested.

'OK, you're not tight,' she conceded, still fumbling with an eye shadow applicator brush loaded with 'Evening Smoke' eye shadow. 'But when was the last time you told me to treat myself to something nice?'

'But we can't—' he began.

'—afford it. Yes, so you keep saying,' Kate interrupted him. 'But I noticed that our budget always seems to stretch to a season ticket and you don't seem to struggle with paying for the travel to away games. Why is that, Miles, do you think?'

Miles harrumphed as he reluctantly kicked off his jeans again. 'Well, it is *my* money . . .' he began.

'Don't you DARE claim that it's YOUR money!' Kate shouted now, turning to look at him with blazing eyes. 'In case you hadn't noticed, I earn just as much as you and every fucking penny goes on food, the kids, the house! I don't ever spend anything on myself because I'm too busy putting everyone else first, whereas *you*, you selfish git, make sure you always have enough cash to do whatever you want!'

Kate was losing control, she knew, because she was feeling defensive and guilty about spending so much money on herself for the first time in her married life but, as she ranted, she realised just how much she had begun to resent Miles for his lack of generosity towards her.

As she finally stopped, feeling exhausted by her uncharacteristic outburst, Miles slumped onto the bed in just his boxer shorts and looked at her in shock. 'I didn't know you felt like that,' he said in a small voice, which made Kate's face redden with shame.

'Oh, just forget it,' she sighed, turning around to look at herself again in the mirror. 'Mum will be here soon to babysit. Get dressed and let's get this evening over with.'

'Wow, you look lovely, sweetheart,' said Jennifer, as Kate opened the door and greeted her with a hug. Miles and Kate rarely went out so didn't often require a babysitter but, when they did, Jennifer was always ridiculously excited at the prospect of spending an evening with her grandchildren. 'So, who is this mysterious chap you're having dinner with?' she added, putting her purse away from paying the taxi and taking off her jacket. She hung it on one of the already overflowing hooks by the front door.

Kate glanced round to check if Miles was within earshot but she could hear him upstairs, talking to Josh in his bedroom. 'He was my knight in shining armour when I had the crash,' she said in a loud whisper. 'He met Sarah when he visited me in hospital and they've had a couple of dates. So I think this is just a sort of "getting-to-know-you" dinner with the two of them.'

Jennifer looked at Kate. 'Any particular reason why you've made so much effort with your appearance? And you *do* look gorgeous, by the way.'

Kate flushed under her mother's gaze; Jennifer knew her so well. 'I just decided that it was about time I put myself first for once and made a bit more effort with my appearance, that's all. I've been feeling so old and frumpy lately.'

'Good for you,' said Jennifer, looking at her appraisingly. 'And you look anything but old and frumpy – that dress is very flattering.'

Kate glowed at the compliment. 'Cast-off of Amy's,' she explained. 'But I am really pleased with it.' She ushered her mum into the sitting room before turning to shout up the stairs. 'Millie!' she yelled, before obedient footsteps could be heard trotting down the stairs. 'Granny's here,' she added, unnecessarily, as Millie ran into the sitting room and straight into Jennifer's embrace. Kate watched her mum and her daughter as they curled up on the sofa together and immediately started chatting about Millie's school, delighted to be in each other's company. Like her mother before her, Millie was a grade-A student who was passionate about science and was determined to become a doctor like her grandparents. She was very close to Jennifer, having grown up living so near to her, and they were more like best friends than grand-parent and granddaughter. It warmed Kate's heart to see them together: the children had been such a comfort to them all since Michael had died.

'Well, see you later then,' said Kate as Miles joined her in the sitting room, having changed into a white shirt and black trousers.

'Have fun,' chorused Jennifer and Millie as they closed the door behind them.

'Wonder if Josh will actually come out of his room at all?' Kate said with a laugh, as they got into Jennifer's car.

'I doubt it,' Miles said, seemingly glad she had apparently got over her earlier tantrum. 'Have you got the directions?' he asked, starting the engine.

Kate nodded. Sarah had called her yesterday to give her Jack's address, although Jack had already emailed it, along with a map and sat nav coordinates. *As if we have sat nav,* Kate thought wryly. She didn't recognise the address as it was in a village she didn't know, about five or six miles away. As they pulled away, she could tell Miles was itching to put the radio on to listen to the sports updates. 'Go on, then!' she said jokingly, keen to dispel any lingering tension between them. 'I know you're desperate to!'

Miles glanced at her with a smile. 'Have I told you lately that I love yoooouuu!' he warbled, switching the radio on. Kate was glad of the distraction, as she could now assess how she was feeling about seeing Jack again. Her heart was pound-ing at the thought. Mentally, she chided herself for even thinking about him in that way: Sarah was her best friend and she was clearly smitten with him. And Kate was married. Whatever connection she thought she perceived between her and Jack, Kate knew she needed to push it to the back of her mind and forget about it. He was taken and so was she. But, she told herself, no one could censor her mind and so when she was alone, she could allow herself to fantasise about him all she liked and no one need ever know. And, hopefully, like all the other crushes she had had in the past, such as the infatuation she had had with Robbie Williams when she was fourteen, this one would quickly fade too.

'Christ, do you think that's it?' said Miles, as they rounded a corner and drove up a hill, upon which perched a beautiful, sprawling sandstone house that glowed warmly in the rays of the evening sun.

Kate's eyes widened. 'I reckon it is,' she said quietly. 'Sarah said he's very rich.' She was suddenly reminded of the line from *Pride and Prejudice* when Elizabeth Bennet is asked when she first realised she might be in love with Mr Darcy and she replied that it was from the moment she first saw his family home, Pemberley. Certainly, Jack's rather impressive pile could only have added to his attraction for Sarah.

Drawing up at the large, wrought-iron gates, Kate got out of the car and pressed the intercom buzzer there. 'Hello!' said an unmistakable voice. 'Come on up.' Kate found herself staring at the buzzer as if expecting Jack to materialise out of it, but was woken from her reverie when from in front of her there came a low, swishing sound as the huge gates swung open.

As she got back into the car, Kate looked at Miles, who was staring up at the house in awe. He looked more uncomfortable than ever in Jennifer's battered old Clio, already able to see several top-of-the-range cars parked on the sweeping gravel circle directly in front of the house.

'Oh, look, there's Sarah's car.' Kate pointed to a little yellow Mini Cooper that had been hidden by the other cars as they trundled up the drive. She felt relieved and comforted to see it, and was suddenly keen to see Sarah again. It felt like ages since they had last seen each other.

The grand front door opened and both Sarah and Jack emerged from the house, smiling broadly. Kate wasn't sure, but she thought Sarah's smile tightened slightly when she spotted Kate. 'Ooh, you look nice!' she said, greeting her with a kiss and a hug. 'I don't think I've ever seen you in a dress before! Or with so much make-up!'

Kate looked back at her friend. 'Is it too much?' she whispered as quietly as she could, but Jack stepped forward before Sarah could answer.

'Hello you,' he said, and Kate's stomach flipped. Oh God, he looked so effortlessly gorgeous in a blue chambray shirt, tucked casually into a pair of jeans that clung to his long legs and showed off his toned physique. He kissed her on each cheek and Kate instantly remembered that soapy, clean smell from his hands as they had stroked her face on the day of the crash. 'How lovely to see you upright!' he laughed, his eyes dancing with mischief as he scanned her face, which was flushed with embarrassment.

'Er, Jack, this is Miles, my husband.' She was all too aware of Miles standing behind her, looking awkward in such unfamiliar surroundings.

'Good to meet you, Miles!' said Jack, his face open and friendly as he shook hands with him.

Miles seemed to relax at Jack's friendly approach. 'Good to meet you too,' he smiled back. 'Thanks so much for your help – with the crash and everything,' he added. Kate looked at him proudly. It would have taken Miles a lot of effort to express his gratitude so warmly: it didn't come naturally to him.

'Oh, don't mention it!' said Jack, shaking his head and batting away Miles's thanks. 'I'm glad I was able to help. I have to say, that other guy was a nasty piece of work.'

'Well, if it hadn't been for you, he would have got away with making me think it was all my fault,' Kate joined in, and Miles nodded his agreement.

'Yes, well, he was banged to rights luckily.' Jack smiled again and looked around at everyone. 'Now, let's not stand around out here getting cold – come on in.'

'Wow,' breathed Kate, looking around her as they entered the imposing hallway. She caught Sarah's eye and Sarah pulled an, 'I know I can't believe it either' face, making Kate smile.

Jack showed them into a beautiful sitting room, with glass doors at the back that opened out onto stunningly landscaped gardens that swept down to a wide, blue river. Bright, white sails from boats were just visible, bobbing about. 'You've got a lovely home, Jack,' Kate breathed, feeling completely overwhelmed by the grandeur of it all.

'Thank you,' he smiled. 'Now, what can I get you to drink? Sarah, would you like another glass of champagne?'

Sarah glanced at Kate as she spoke. 'Er, yes, please, although I won't be able to drive home if I have another . . .' Her words hung in the air unanswered, as Kate and Miles looked awkwardly at the ceiling, the floor, or anywhere that didn't involve looking at Jack.

'Well, maybe Kate and Miles would give you a lift home if you needed one ...?' Jack said eventually, looking expectantly and, Kate thought, slightly desperately at Miles.

Miles nodded quickly. 'Of course,' he said, causing Sarah's face to drop slightly. 'So, what do you do then, Jack?' asked Miles, voicing what Kate had been dying to ask.

'I own an ad agency,' Jack replied with a smile. 'Well, it was my father's, and I've taken it over.'

Miles and Kate nodded; Kate feeling inferior and, she suspected, Miles feeling the same.

'How about you?' Jack asked Miles.

'I work for the local council,' Miles replied in a clipped tone, clearly not wanting to elaborate. 'But it pays the bills.'

Kate's hackles rose. 'Well, it pays *some* of the bills,' she corrected him, before wishing she hadn't opened her mouth. Miles was probably feeling insecure enough without her adding to it. 'And allows you to indulge your passion for football ...' she added quickly.

'Oh, you're into football?' Jack quickly and expertly picked up Kate's conversational ball. 'Come with me to get the drinks and we can talk about it without these two giving us the evil eye ...'

Miles followed Jack out of the room, leaving Sarah and Kate alone. 'So, how's it going then?' Kate whispered, as soon as they were out of earshot. 'He seems lovely.'

Sarah's face took on a dreamy expression. 'Oh, he is!' she gushed. 'He's such easy company and he's funny, generous, sweet ...' She hesitated for a moment.

'But?' Kate prompted her.

Sarah sighed. 'It's just that I don't think he's as into me as I'm into him.'

'What makes you think that?' Kate said with a tut. 'You've only had two dates! Surely he wouldn't have asked to see you again if he wasn't bothered about you?'

Sarah's eyes clouded slightly. 'Hmmm. It's just . . .'

'What?'

'Well, I think I'm keener on him than he is on me. And he seemed very eager for me to invite you to dinner with us. I've been beginning to wonder if maybe it's *you* he's really interested in.'

Kate's stomach flipped again, and it was a couple of moments before she was able to speak. 'He invited me and my *husband*,' she said at last.

'True.' There was a pause as Sarah considered the thought. 'I don't know . . . But, seeing you tonight, I wouldn't blame him! You look gorgeous.' There was a trace of bitterness in her voice, as if Kate had somehow betrayed her by looking so uncharacteristically glamorous.

'So do *you*!' Kate shot back, trying to cover up the guilt she was feeling. She *had* made more effort than usual and it was undoubtedly for Jack's benefit, no matter what she had said about feeling frumpy. What the hell was she playing at? If she could, she would have run upstairs and wiped off all her new make-up and changed into a pair of jeans.

As the two men returned to the sitting room, carrying their drinks, Kate took hold of Miles's hand and stood on tiptoe to kiss his cheek. 'Thank you, darling,' she said, as he handed her a glass of champagne. 'Would you like me to drive? I don't mind.'

Miles looked at her in surprise, unused to her offering to drive home so that he could drink. 'That would be great!'

He grinned back at her. Out of the corner of her eye, Kate could feel Jack watching them and she felt her face flush. She was going to show him that she wasn't available, however attractive she might find him. And she wanted to give Sarah a clear run at him. It was the least she could do for her friend, who deserved a bit of happiness after such a tough few years.

For the rest of the evening, Kate stuck to water, while the others demolished bottle after bottle of wine and laughed raucously at each other's jokes. She was pleased to see Miles relaxing and enjoying himself, apparently having hit it off with Jack through a shared love of football. Sarah kept shooting seductive glances at Jack – which seemed to go unnoticed – as he played the perfect host by making sure his guests had full glasses and keeping them supplied with a succession of delicious dishes.

'Did you cook all this yourself, Jack?' Kate asked, as she finished off a sublime chocolate mousse.

Jack fixed his eyes on her in a way that made her feel like he was stripping her naked. 'Well, I've always thought that the way to a woman's heart is through her stomach. Don't you agree, Kate?' he said quietly, and she realised that he wasn't drunk at all, unlike the others.

Kate looked around in alarm but Sarah and Miles were playing a game of 'Hold the teaspoon on the end of your nose' and hadn't even noticed. They had always got on well but they appeared to have completely bonded that evening. She looked back at Jack, who was still staring at her intently, making her feel flustered. 'Maybe,' she replied at last.

'Why don't you come into the kitchen and you can help me make the coffee?' he said, still staring at her.

Kate hesitated. She didn't want to appear rude but equally she didn't want to put herself in a compromising position.

'Don't worry,' he said, again in a voice that only she could hear. 'You'll be perfectly safe.'

As if in a daze, Kate stood up and collected the mousse glasses before following Jack out into the vast kitchen, leaving Miles and Sarah still giggling like two naughty schoolchildren as they hunted for a dropped spoon under the table. As Jack headed for the dishwasher – cleverly built into an island, topped with shiny black granite – Kate stood immobile, clutching two glasses and wondering where to put them. 'Over here,' Jack prompted, motioning for her to join him. She walked over and bent down to put the glasses into the rack. 'Here,' he said, leaning in to take them from her. 'I'll do it.' Their faces were millimetres apart and she could feel his breath on her cheek. Knowing that she shouldn't, she looked up and locked eyes with him. He leaned closer and their lips touched, sending what felt like a million electric shocks racing through her body. She pulled away but, as if drawn to him like a magnet, she somehow found herself kissing him again as they straightened up. He pulled her towards him, crushing her, his tongue exploring her mouth with darting movements that made her insides swim with lust.

'No!' she hissed suddenly, her face crumpling in confusion and guilt as she leapt away from him.

'I knew it wasn't just me,' he said, facing her with a look of longing. 'I knew you felt it too.'

'I can't,' she whispered, her features twisting with anguish. 'I just can't.'

'I know,' he said, sadness flickering across his face. 'But I just needed to find out.'

Kate paused. 'We should go.'

'If you must . . .' Jack said, still gazing at her.

As they emerged from the kitchen, Kate felt that she must have guilt written all over her face, but Miles and Sarah seemed none the wiser and were happily slurring jokes at one another.

'It's time we should be going,' Kate said, more loudly than she intended, and both Miles and Sarah looked up in surprise.

'Awww,' said Miles. 'We're only just getting started. Do we have to?'

Kate walked over to him and took his arm as she helped him stand up. 'Yes,' she said firmly. 'I think we have to.'

Sarah looked longingly at Jack. 'I could always stay here tonight, Jack?' she said in a sultry voice, ruining the effect somewhat with a hiccough at the end.

Kate's heart ached for her friend as Jack shook his head. 'No, sweetie, I think it's best if you get a lift home with Kate and Miles.' Like Kate, he walked over to Sarah and helped her up. 'I'll call you tomorrow, OK?'

'Well, that was a lot better than I thought it was going to be!' Miles said happily as he sat heavily on the edge of their bed and took off his trousers. 'I really like Jack. He's a nice bloke.'

When Kate didn't answer, he looked round at her curiously. 'You've been very quiet since we got home,' he said. 'Didn't you like him?'

Kate climbed into bed and pulled the duvet up to her neck. 'Yes,' she said quickly. 'He was nice.'

'Good,' Miles replied amiably, blissfully oblivious to the turmoil his wife was feeling as she lay down to face another sleepless night.

AUTUMN

Chapter 22

Amy and Ben circled each other like two predatory animals, confined in the same cage but never communicating beyond eyeing each other warily. Amy didn't know what to do for the best and veered wildly between wanting to get Ben help and not wanting him to have mental illness on his medical records. In the end, she called Kate in desperation. Kate was the practical one. She always knew what to do in any situation.

'What's up?' Kate said, picking up Amy's call, even though she was in the middle of a home visit with an elderly lady, who was now confined to one room of her house. Amy never rang her during work hours, so she knew it was something important. She excused herself from the woman and went out into the chilly hallway, where she perched on the bottom step of the scratchy, hideously carpeted stairs.

Amy felt tears threatening and had to take a deep breath before she could speak.

'Amy?' Kate prompted, a feeling of alarm growing. 'What's happened?'

'I think Ben has had a breakdown,' Amy managed to blurt out, before she had to stop to compose herself.

There was a shocked silence at the other end of the phone as Kate digested what her sister had just said. In her mind's eye, she pictured Ben, with his wide, perfect smile and his sparkling eyes, always the life and soul of any party; charisma oozing out of every pore. He was absolutely the last person she could imagine having a breakdown. Finally, she spoke. 'Are you sure? What makes you think that?'

In a shuddering voice, Amy explained everything that had happened over the past weeks. 'So, it looks like the business has collapsed,' she finished. 'And we're broke. But worse, Ben is broken. Really broken. I just don't know what to do with him. I'm scared, Kate!'

'Oh God, Amy, I'm so sorry,' Kate said, her mind reeling.

Amy was grateful that there wasn't a trace of gloating or pleasure at her misfortune in Kate's voice: her sister was genuinely devastated for them. 'Poor you,' Kate continued. 'And poor Ben. What does the doctor suggest?'

Amy flushed and shook her head. 'I haven't taken him yet.'

'Oh, Amy, you must! You've got to get him some help as soon as possible.'

'But I'm worried about him having that on his notes,' Amy said, again feeling as if she was about to cry. 'What if it affects his future prospects?'

'He won't *have* any future prospects if you don't get him help.' Kate knew she sounded brutal but she had experience of patients who had had breakdowns, and suicide was a very real danger, especially in the first few weeks.

Kate's words hit Amy with a thunderous force, causing her to snap to her senses. 'You're right,' she said quietly, vowing to call the doctor as soon as she got off the phone.

'And what about everything else?' Kate prompted, feeling as scared as Amy sounded. 'Will you lose the house?'

'Yes,' Amy replied emphatically. 'I found letters from the mortgage company that Ben had just ignored—'

'But if you contact them and explain what's happened, I'm sure there's a way through it—' Kate interrupted.

'No.' Amy stopped her with a flat voice. 'It's too late for that. He also ignored a summons and they've now sent us a letter with a date that we have to move out by. It's just before Christmas, which is nice.'

'Oh God, Amy, I'm so sorry,' Kate gasped, feeling helpless.

'According to his business partner, Tim, that's just the start of it, so Christ knows what else we owe,' Amy continued.

'Oh God,' Kate said again, thinking of Amy and Ben's lavish lifestyle. It didn't seem possible that it could all disappear so suddenly. Then another thought hit her. 'Oh Amy ... will the kids have to leave their school?' she asked in a voice that was barely above a whisper.

Amy slumped onto the hard wooden floor as the mention of Flora and Sam caused her legs to buckle under her. 'Yes!' she wailed. 'Oh, Kate, what the hell am I going to do? We don't have the money to pay the school fees. Come to that, we don't actually have any money!'

Kate didn't reply for a few moments, not knowing what to say. For the first time, she was grateful that she and Miles had never really had any money: it would be so much worse to have it and lose it, than never to have had it at all. On the other end of the line, as Amy waited for Kate to speak, she took the opportunity to blow her nose and regain her composure.

'Could you take the children out now?' Kate said. 'It's just coming up to half-term. Maybe you could get a refund of their fees for the rest of the term?'

Amy closed her eyes as she considered the thought, her stomach churning. The money would help to pay for essentials and Maria's wages for at least another couple of months. 'Maybe,' she said. 'But where the hell would they go to school? I couldn't put them into one of the state schools around here – they'd be ripped to pieces in seconds.'

On the other end of the line, Kate nodded. Suddenly, she had an idea. 'Maybe you could get the kids into St Marks?' St Marks was the school that both Amy and Kate had attended when they were young, and where Millie and Josh now went.

'Move out of London?' Amy echoed, her heart racing at the prospect. 'But what about all our friends? What about the children's friends?'

Kate didn't answer; she didn't need to. They both knew that she was thinking exactly the same as Amy: that their friends would all disappear just as fast as their money had.

'Amy,' Kate said kindly, interrupting her thoughts. 'The most important thing is you, Ben and the children. Everything else can be dealt with. Please remember that. I know that it feels like the end of the world right now but I promise you everything will be OK, as long as you get Ben the help he needs and you keep the people who love you closest.' She stopped as a thought occurred to her. 'You could move in with Mum for a while – she would love to have you living with her, and it'll help her, too.'

'How?' Amy couldn't imagine how being landed with a

whole family to feed and look after could possibly benefit her mum.

'Haven't you noticed how she's been?' Kate asked, and Amy realised to her shame that she hadn't really given her mother much thought, except for getting annoyed when she questioned how much money Amy was spending.

'Not really,' she said, sniffing. 'Why?'

'I think she's drinking too much,' Kate said. Her voice was tight as she spoke, and Amy could tell that she was genuinely concerned. Now that she thought about it, Amy *had* noticed that Jennifer had seemed to drink rather a lot when they had stayed with her last. 'I think she's desperately lonely,' Kate added. 'She misses Dad so much and having you there with the children would be the perfect distraction for her. Give her a ring, Amy. I'm sure it's the right thing to do.' Kate could hear the old lady calling her from the next room. 'Look, I've got to go but call me anytime. And get Ben to a doctor, now. Love you,' she added, before hanging up and returning to the warmth of the sparsely furnished sitting room, where yet another life was ebbing slowly away. If her job taught her anything, it was that life was a house of cards that could come tumbling down at any moment.

Amy put the phone down, feeling a swirl of gratitude for her sensible older sister. Kate had never let her down before and, yet again, she was there with a solution. Amy still wasn't sure if it was the right solution, and she didn't know how Ben would feel about the idea of living with her mum, but with no other ideas on how to get through their current crisis presenting themselves, it might be all they had.

After calling the doctor and making an appointment, Amy mentally braced herself and rang her mum. She couldn't help but wonder if a part of Jennifer might be pleased by what had happened, thinking it served Amy right.

Jennifer was in the garden when the phone rang and she dashed into the cottage, picking it up just in time to stop it going to the answerphone and cursing herself for not taking the handset into the garden with her. 'Hello, sweetheart,' she panted, as she recognised Amy's number.

'Oh, Mum!' Amy cried, her resolve not to cry finally melting away in a torrent of tears and sobs.

Jennifer's heart almost stopped. She suddenly had the same feeling she had had when she had seen that young policeman walking towards the front door to tell her about Michael. She almost wanted to hang up on Amy so that whatever devastating words she was about to utter could be left unsaid. 'What is it?' she managed to gasp, unable to swallow, her throat suddenly feeling as stiff as cardboard.

'It's Ben,' Amy sobbed, and Jennifer's heart began to beat again. God forgive her but at least it wasn't one of the children. 'He's had a breakdown.'

Jennifer sat down heavily on the sofa, not caring that she might have mud from the garden on her clothes. She was trying to digest what Amy was saying, her mind already reenacting so many horrific scenarios in a few split seconds that she couldn't compute what Amy meant by 'breakdown'. Did she mean the car? Gradually, as realisation dawned, her voice returned. 'Oh, darling, I'm so sorry,' she said, feeling an overwhelming urge to hold Amy in her arms and rock her, just as she had when she was a little girl. 'What can I do to help?'

Amy hesitated and sniffed loudly as she tried and failed to regain her composure. 'Well, the immediate problem is that we're going to lose the house,' she began, dissolving into anguished tears again.

Jennifer's brain was still struggling to keep up with her daughter's words. 'Why?' she asked, almost to herself.

'Because the business has collapsed and we've lost everything. We're completely broke.'

'What if I was to give you some money?' Jennifer suddenly felt a spark of hope that she might be able to help Amy out of the mess she was in. 'I'd be glad to give it to you.'

'Thanks, Mum,' Amy replied sadly. 'But the fact is, we're in deeper than that. Ten thousand pounds wouldn't even cover a month's outgoings.'

Jennifer gasped with shock, unable to speak for several seconds.

'But, Mum,' Amy continued. 'We will need somewhere to live. So I know it's a huge thing to ask but—'

'Of course you must come here,' Jennifer interrupted her briskly, overwhelmed with relief that she was able to help. Being needed again after so long feeling surplus to requirements was almost a boost to her self-esteem, which had been at rock bottom since losing Michael. At once, her mind started to whirl with what she would need to do to prepare for their arrival. There were beds to be made, groceries to be bought ... 'When will you need to leave?' she asked, as gently as she could.

'Just before Christmas,' Amy replied and her voice sounded so young and vulnerable that Jennifer's heart ached for her. 'We just got the court order to leave by December the sixteenth.'

Jennifer wanted to ask about the children and their school but she didn't want to risk upsetting Amy any more than she was already. And the nanny would have to go, which, although Jennifer had always resented her playing such a huge role in the children's lives, she knew would devastate Flora and Sam. They loved Maria.

She felt as if she could cry along with Amy for the earthquake that was about to rip through her grandchildren's little lives.

After Amy hung up the phone, she went into the kitchen and poured herself a glass of cold water from the huge American fridge. She stared at it for a moment. She looked around the vast room, at the bespoke units, the top-of-the-range granite worktops and the chrome designer appliances, and wondered what would happen to the house when they were gone. Who would live there, in the home where they had had their babies and which had been filled with so much love and laughter over the years? She hoped that whoever owned it next would love it as much as she did.

In a strange way, losing the house was a relief. Although she knew that it was too late, she had tried hard to stop it happening by taking back any shoes or clothes that were still within the return window and selling most of her designer gear on eBay. But even as the dribs and drabs of cash came in, she began to realise that it was the equivalent of putting her finger in the dam wall. It provided them with enough cash to scrape by day to day – just – but their monthly outgoings were huge, and no amount of clothes sold on eBay was going to cover even one month's payments.

She gulped down the last of the water, suddenly thirsty after so much crying, and went in search of Ben. She found him in their bedroom, sitting on the floor beside the bed, switching the lamp on and off in a robotic, rhythmic way that scared and irritated her in equal measure. She watched him for a moment to see if he would notice her; he stared past her with unblinking eyes and seemed totally unaware of her presence.

'Ben?' she said at last. 'Ben, sweetheart, we need to talk.'

When he didn't respond, Amy walked over to where he was sitting and perched cross-legged on the floor beside him. Still he didn't seem to notice her, and continued to click the light on, then off again. They sat for several minutes, neither of them speaking, listening to the click of the light switch every second, which Amy soon found comforting too. Finally, she reached out and took the switch out of Ben's hand. 'Stop, now,' she said quietly, tucking the cord back around the bedside table.

Ben frowned and looked down at his hand, as if he couldn't understand where the switch had gone.

'I've made an appointment with Doctor Green,' Amy said. 'For tomorrow. Isn't it lucky that we were able to see him so quickly?' She realised that she was talking to Ben in the same voice she used for Sam, trying to coax and cajole him.

Ben didn't say anything and Amy picked up his trembling, clammy hand in hers. 'We're going to get you some help,' she said, putting his hand to her lips and kissing it.

As her lips touched his skin, he seemed to jump, as if she had given him an electric shock. 'No!' he said, looking at her with wide, terrified eyes. 'I don't need a doctor. I don't want to see a doctor.'

Amy looked back at him with eyes that she knew must be reflecting his terror, because she felt as if she was falling into some kind of black hole and she didn't know how to climb back out. There was nothing to hold on to, to help her get a grip. 'You do, Ben. You're not well. It's not your fault but you do need something to help you get better. Do you understand what I'm saying?'

A tiny chink of light appeared in Ben's eyes and he nodded. Then he took his hand back out of Amy's grasp and reached out to find the light switch, before resuming his rhythmic clicking. Amy sighed and looked at him helplessly. She decided that it probably wasn't the time to tell him that they would soon have to leave their beautiful house and move in with her mum.

Chapter 23

As Kate arrived to pick up the children from school, she spotted Sarah's yellow Mini parked just down the road from her. 'Hi!' she called to her friend as she went up to her window and knocked on it.

Sarah jumped as if she had been caught doing something she shouldn't and pressed the button to drop the window. 'Oh, hi, Kate, I was miles away,' she said, looking up at her with a heavy expression. Kate could tell instantly that there was something wrong.

'What's up?' she said, stuffing her hands into the pockets of her jacket against the autumn chill that was permeating the air.

Sarah shook her head and sighed. 'Jack said he thinks it's best if we don't see each other again.'

She didn't meet Kate's eye as she spoke, and Kate immediately sensed that Sarah somehow blamed her. 'I'm sorry,' she said helplessly. More than that, she felt guilty.

Sarah shrugged her shoulders. 'I told you I didn't think he liked me as much as I liked him.'

Kate didn't reply; she didn't know what to say.

'Have you heard from him?' Sarah said, catching Kate off guard.

'Me? No! Of course not,' she stuttered. She sounded like she was lying, because she was. She and Jack had been emailing for weeks now. Kate wanted to stop but she couldn't: she was becoming addicted to hearing from him. He wrote beautifully, with an intenseness that seemed to leap off the computer screen and straight into her heart. It was wrong, she knew. But she felt helpless to stop it.

Still Sarah wouldn't look at Kate. 'He asked me for your number quite early on. Said he needed to speak to you about something to do with the crash, but I think he just wanted to speak to you.' Finally, she looked up at Kate. 'I know it's you he's interested in.'

Kate's mouth dropped open in shock. 'No!' she said quickly, her heart racing with fear that she might be about to be caught. 'Don't be daft.'

'I'm not being daft,' Sarah said, putting the window up and getting out of the car. 'I know the signs, remember? I bloody well knew Robert was having an affair with that slut of a secretary of his.'

'Sarah!' Kate exclaimed hotly. 'I'm not having an affair with Jack! I haven't even seen him since that dinner at his house.'

Sarah looked intently as Kate for a few moments before linking her arm through hers and walking with her through the school gates towards the playground. 'OK,' she sighed. 'And I know you're not having an affair with him,' she continued in a conciliatory tone. 'I'm just feeling a bit gutted, you know? I really, really liked him.'

Kate gave Sarah's arm a squeeze. 'Of course,' she said,

grateful that she was apparently off the hook. She hated herself anew for what she was doing and suddenly wished she could force Jack to fall in love with Sarah. However painful that might be for her, it would be the right thing to do. As the thought entered her head, almost immediately she started to plan how she might make that happen. Maybe she should meet him, try to persuade him? If she could convince him that nothing was ever going to happen between them, he might reconsider and give Sarah another chance. But could she convince him that nothing was ever going to happen when they both seemed to be tumbling inexorably towards . . . something? *And hadn't something happened already,* she thought, remembering with shame some of the emails she had written. Did that constitute an affair?

At that moment, Josh came sauntering out of his classroom, side by side with Sarah's son Daniel. Josh frowned as he saw Kate but she knew it was for show. At nine years old, he was at the stage where he still wanted his mum to pick him up from school and read to him before bed, but he didn't want any of his friends to know it. 'Hi, gorgeous,' she said, ruffling his hair in the way she knew he loved but would never admit.

'Hi, Mum,' he replied, flattening his hair again with a furtive glance at Daniel, who was going through exactly the same procedure with Sarah. 'Can Daniel come round?'

Kate looked at Sarah, who raised her eyes to heaven goodnaturedly and nodded. 'Oh, go on, then,' said Kate, pleased that Sarah seemed to have relaxed towards her. It made her determined to try to do something to persuade Jack that he should give Sarah another chance. 'Don't forget Flora and Sam are coming to tea, too,' she added to Josh.

187

'Flora? What sort of a name is that?' snorted Daniel, look-ing at Josh aghast.

'It's a lovely name!' Kate cried indignantly, knowing that this was just a taste of the sort of ribbing Flora was likely to get if she started at this school: her studious nature and posh voice would make her stand out. 'They're coming to meet Mr Carter, to see about joining the school, remember?' she added to Josh, ignoring the still-snorting Daniel.

Josh nodded. 'Cool,' he said quietly. Josh loved his two cousins and Kate felt a swell of pride knowing that he would protect them from any nastiness when they first arrived. He might be her baby but he was one of the big boys at the pri-mary school now, both in age and stature.

Arriving home, Kate settled the two boys and Millie with a drink and a biscuit before dashing up to get to her com-puter. Feeling breathless, she opened it and, sure enough, a fresh email from Jack sprang up on the screen, entitled *My very own Florence Nightingale*.

Closing her eyes for a second, trying to breathe deeply to stop her heart racing, she created a new message and tried to think what to write. Eventually, she typed:

I think we should meet . . .

WINTER

Chapter 24

Amy felt momentarily dizzy as she approached the school building, Flora and Sam trailing miserably beside her. They were staying overnight with her mum to be able to come in and have a look around St Marks and meet the headmaster. In the weeks since Ben's business had collapsed, they had become practically penniless and worse, saddled with debts that they couldn't pay.

At first, Amy had been optimistic about their prospects, certain that they must have millions tied up in investments that would pay off any outstanding bills and leave them a couple of million to live on. But with every day's post, she seemed to uncover some new debt that she hadn't known about.

To her horror, she discovered that Ben had put almost everything up as collateral for loans for the business, and they now had nothing. She had yelled at him in terror that she had never known what he was up to, but her signature had been there in black and white on the papers that he had showed her in his shaking hands. She couldn't remember signing them and wondered briefly if he had forged them, but then she realised that as long as Ben had kept bringing in the money and paying the bills, she hadn't shown the slightest bit of interest in what he was doing – or what she was signing.

The cars were gone, except for the little run-around they had bought for Maria, along with the state-of-the-art TVs and sound system. But Amy didn't really care about any of that any more. The thing that most broke her heart was the effect all this would have on the children. She was having to move them out of the family home, and take them out of their much-loved school. Their miniature lives seemed shattered as they said their heartbreaking goodbyes to their better-off friends, who would all be returning the next term and continuing their education as if nothing had happened. They made heartfelt promises to be friends for ever and to keep in touch, but Amy knew the way these things worked. Now that she and Ben were broke, their rich friends would quietly melt away, and it would be the same for the children's friends. It wasn't cruelty on their part; it was embarrassment. They didn't mix with anyone other than those in the same income bracket as they didn't know how to react to poverty, so they simply stayed away.

Maria had said she would continue working for nothing until they had to leave the house, which touched Amy deeply and made her feel even worse about any spiteful thoughts she had previously had about her. It also reassured her that Maria truly loved the children and had not treated caring for them as just a job. She had vowed fervently to Maria that she would do whatever she could to somehow find a role for her in their future lives, but they both knew that it was wishful thinking. In the end, however, Maria was soon offered another job and her new employers wanted her to start immediately, so yet another building block of the children's lives was knocked down when their beloved nanny departed. Sam, who always wore his heart on his sleeve, had reacted with his typical open-heartedness and wailed loudly as he hung onto Maria's arm and begged her not to go. Flora had tried to be stoic but she, too, had descended into sobs as Maria finally left for the last time.

'It'll do you and the children good,' her mother had insisted when Amy had broken the news of Maria's departure on the phone.

'Gee, thanks for your support, Mum,' Amy had replied bitterly. The truth was, Jennifer had been incredibly supportive since Ben's breakdown, regularly sending her cash and doing all she could to help. But although Amy was grateful, she also felt unbelievably humiliated every time she had to ask for money.

'Oh, darling, I don't mean to sound harsh,' had said Jennifer in a softer tone. 'But you'll have the chance to be a full-time mother to those children, and you'll rise to the challenge magnificently. I know it's hard now, but I truly believe that one day you'll look back and thank your lucky stars that fate gave you this opportunity.'

Amy had shrugged. She wished she shared her mother's optimism.

Amy stared up at the grey building in front of them now. It was a seventies monstrosity that managed to be both modern and decaying at the same time. Flora and Sam clutched each of her hands tightly as the three of them stood rooted to the spot, paralysed with fear.

Amy looked down at Flora, whose worried expression was

the one she had been wearing for weeks now. Her little cheeks were pale and tight, while her eyes seemed to have grown even larger in her small face. Sam was sobbing loudly, his white-blond head bobbing up and down as he moved agitatedly from foot to foot.

'Well, come on, then,' she said as brightly as she could. 'Mr Carter said he would be waiting for us in his office.'

'I don't want to go in!' wailed Sam loudly. 'I hate it!'

'Shhhh.' Amy bent down on one knee and wrapped her arm around Sam, while keeping hold of Flora's hand. 'C'mon, Sam, it'll be OK. Let's at least go inside and take a look.'

'But I don't want to!' yelled Sam. 'I want to go back to my old school!'

'Mrs Osborne?' said a tall man of around forty, coming out of his office and into the reception area where Amy was sitting with the children. 'I'm Ian Carter, the headmaster.'

Amy stood up and shook his outstretched hand, noticing as she did how cool and dry it felt compared to Ben's hands, which were permanently clammy these days. 'But . . . you're so young!' she blurted out, before reddening slightly.

Mr Carter laughed good-naturedly. 'Not *that* young, I assure you! So, who have we here?'

Amy looked down at the children, who were a picture of misery as they both tried to shrink further back into their seats. Sam's eyes were still red from crying and he was sniffing loudly. Flora's misery was more self-contained but no less apparent, as her eyes darted in terror from side to side and her small body stiffened under the adults' gaze.

'This is quite difficult for them,' Amy said, aware that she was apologising for the children's lack of enthusiasm for their surroundings.

Mr Carter nodded briskly. 'I understand. Why don't you come into my office and we can have a chat.'

Amy motioned to the children to follow her and they reluctantly climbed off their chairs and shuffled behind her. Inside the office – a rather cramped room, dominated by a desk overflowing with books and papers – Amy pulled Sam onto her lap and clutched Flora's hand as she perched awkwardly on the chair beside her. There was something eternally terrifying about being in a headmaster's office, even as a grown woman.

Mr Carter took a seat behind his desk and smiled again. 'So, Sam, isn't it? You're wanting to join us after Christmas, are you?'

'No!' cried Sam, as fresh tears trickled down his chubby cheeks. 'I want to go back to my old school!'

'Sam!' cried Amy, turning crimson with embarrassment. 'I'm terribly sorry,' she stammered to Mr Carter, who waved his hand dismissively.

'Don't be,' he said. 'It must be very hard for them both. But, Sam, Flora … listen to me,' he said, looking from one to the other as he addressed them kindly. 'You aren't the first children to have to change schools and I promise you won't be the last. There are other children here in the same situation. It isn't easy and I understand how you're feeling, but you will make lots of new friends here, I promise.'

Amy looked at Flora, who seemed to relax slightly as Mr Carter spoke. 'Really?' she said, her soft voice almost inaudible.

'Really,' he assured her. 'And we're not monsters here, either. Some of the teachers are actually quite nice. Ugly. But nice.'

Amy felt a little gurgle of laughter move up through Sam's body and escape from his mouth. Immediately, he clapped his hands over his face, as if to try to stop any further outbursts. She looked down at Flora, whose lips were twitching slightly and whose eyes were starting to glimmer. Suddenly, she let go of Amy's hand and folded her arms, as if to show Amy that she was going to be able to stand on her own two feet. That she was going to be OK.

Amy looked up at Mr Carter and smiled a full beam of relief at him. She felt an overwhelming sense of gratitude at having someone else in control for this matter, instead of her having to shoulder all the responsibility.

Arriving back at the house in London the next day, she found Ben lounging on the sofa reading a free newspaper. 'How are you feeling?' she asked, trying to sound sympathetic, rather than irritable. It felt like she hadn't sat down for weeks: there was so much to do to keep the house running without anyone to help her, and she was starting to feel overwhelmed with exhaustion.

'I feel great.' He grinned up at her and folded the newspaper. 'I went for a walk to clear my head; then I picked up this paper and sat in the park reading it. It was very ... liberating.'

'Ben!' snapped Amy. 'It's bloody freezing out there! What were you doing sitting in the park with a load of drunks? People might think you're one of them.'

'So?' Ben shot back, like a cheeky child. 'Who cares what

people think? I don't. I'm beginning to realise how much pressure I've been under all these years. I've never had time for *me* to really find myself.'

Amy felt her eyes narrow as she looked down at him.

'What?' he demanded. 'Why are you looking at me like that?'

'Nothing,' she sighed dispiritedly. 'I'm going to get the children's tea.'

'What are they having?' Ben asked eagerly, swinging his legs onto the floor and sitting up.

Amy unwound her scarf and gritted her teeth. 'Beans on toast – just like every other bloody night lately,' she muttered mutinously, shrugging her coat off her shoulders as she left the room.

'Great!' cried Ben, as if she'd announced she was making a slap-up, three-course meal. 'I'll have the same!' he added, as he followed her into the kitchen, where the children were sitting on the floor making Christmas decorations from pine cones they had collected before leaving Suffolk that afternoon.

'We got on fine at our appointment with the new school, thanks for asking,' said Amy sarcastically, as she put bread in the toaster and hunted in the cupboard for a tin of beans.

'Oh ... good,' said Ben distractedly, stretching and beaming at the children. 'I was thinking ... maybe I might have a go at painting tomorrow. I was quite good once. It'll be good for me.'

Something in Amy gave way. 'What *might* be good for you—' she hissed, unable to stop the words tumbling out, even though the doctor had advised her that she wasn't supposed to challenge him or give him any cause for stress, particularly in front of the children, '—is if you stopped thinking so much about yourself and started paying attention to your family, because we're not having quite such a nice time as you are . . . Not that you've bloody well noticed, you selfish shit!'

Ben's jaw dropped and he stared at her in shock. 'What are you on about?' he asked, frowning in bemusement. 'I don't know what you're talking about.'

Amy sighed. 'Maybe I should record your conversation and play it back to you, because then you'd realise just how much you use the words "me", "I" and "myself"!'

Ben continued staring at her and didn't reply. Behind him, Amy could see Flora looking up at her in concern.

'Oh, forget it!' she said wearily, spooning the beans into a saucepan and stirring them as they heated. Ben trudged out of the kitchen with the same puzzled expression on his face, and Amy had to close her eyes and count to ten to stop herself from storming after him and throwing the pan at his head. She was struggling to cope with her own feelings, let alone dealing with Ben's depression. His medication was very slowly starting to have an effect and he was no longer a danger to himself, but an unfortunate side effect was that he had become unbelievably self-absorbed and Amy was running out of patience. He seemed to have retreated into himself just when she needed him most. Her husband had gone and in his place was a shell of a man who seemed incapable of making even the most basic decisions. Every night as she went to sleep, Amy prayed that the man she loved would be back by the next morning.

Chapter 25

'So you're going to have a full house again?' Hugh said.

'Looks like it,' Jennifer said, nodding. They were sitting in a quaint pub a few miles away in a village called Brickley. Jennifer had never been there before, which was why she had suggested it. Hugh was becoming a regular visitor and although she had begun to look forward to his visits, she didn't want to risk anyone she knew meeting him. She had found some new, out-of-the-way haunts where they could be together, unobserved.

For his part, Hugh was beginning to talk more. Instead of sitting smoking and staring at her – like he had back then – he had begun to engage in proper conversations.

'Will you still be able to come out to play?' he asked, with a mischievous glint in his eyes.

Jennifer looked at him. She shouldn't have allowed this to go on for so long. She should have done what needed to be done and said goodbye to him once and for all. What she was doing was a betrayal of Michael.

'Please don't say that we'll have to stop our little rendezvous,' he continued.

Jennifer took a sip of her wine and looked up at Hugh. 'I think we must,' she said quietly.

'You're going to run out on us all over again, aren't you?'

Jennifer shook her head. 'No, Hugh, I'm not running out on "us", just as I didn't run out on "us" back then. There was no "us".'

'You and I both know that's not true.'

Jennifer opened her mouth to protest but she closed it again as she realised that he was right. He wasn't just a one-night stand, to be regretted, then forgotten; no matter how much she would wish that to be the case. He had got under her skin. Into her soul.

After spending a blissful week with Michael in Leeds – where she finally met Michael's friend Mary and was reassured to find that she was a rather plain-looking, gregarious girl who was desperately in love with one of his flatmates – Jennifer moved back to her parents' house in Suffolk and threw herself into planning their wedding. Michael was still working the long hours of a junior doctor, so she needed to find a distraction and this was perfect. An only child, her parents were thrilled that she was marrying and they were prepared to pay whatever she wanted for a lavish do. But Jennifer wasn't the showy type and she was happy to plan a small affair in the local village church where she had been christened, followed by a reception in the church hall.

Her dress was being made by a dressmaker she had had recommended to her in London, and she travelled down to the city for her final fitting, feeling sick with excitement. Susie was her bridesmaid, and was also having her dress made by the same woman. They met outside the address in Battersea and Jennifer hugged her friend with delight.

'Not long now!' Susie grinned, squeezing Jennifer in an embrace. 'How are you feeling?'

Jennifer beamed back. 'Permanently sick, actually. I suspect it's nerves. I'm just so excited!'

Susie nodded. 'I bet you are! And how have you been coping without Michael? That must be hard.'

Jennifer nodded. 'Oh, it is! It's awful but we speak on the phone whenever we can and write all the time. It's only been a few months but it feels like an eternity. Still, he's coming down next weekend and it'll make me appreciate him all the more.'

'It most certainly will,' Susie agreed. 'Come on, then; let's go in and face Greta!'

Greta was a Dutch woman in her fifties and she was the scariest woman either Jennifer or Susie had ever known. She was tall and broad-shouldered, with a clipped accent that made her seem more stern than her appearance suggested. She never complimented the wearers of her garments or even smiled at them, but she was renowned for being the best dressmaker in London.

'Hello, Greta!' Jennifer and Susie chimed in unison as she answered the shiny green door to her terraced house.

Greta nodded by way of greeting and stood aside for the two girls to walk past her, down a long hallway, into her workroom at the back of the house.

Jennifer had taken off her jacket and was placing it over the back of a chair when she noticed that Greta was casting her eyes over her in a critical, beady way. 'You hev gained weight,' she said, in an accusatory tone.

Jennifer almost laughed with shock. 'Oh! Have I?' she cried, looking at Susie for confirmation.

Susie pulled a dismissive face. 'No, not at all!' she insisted, looking Jennifer up and down.

Greta shook her head and tutted. 'I em telling you,' she said with a huff, 'that you hev put on weight. Eef you do not believe this, your dress will be the proof!'

Susie and Jennifer both gaped in silence as Greta lifted out Jennifer's dress from a large built-in wardrobe and showed it to her. It was made of white silk, with long sleeves and a full skirt that had been embroidered and decorated with hundreds of tiny pearls. Neither of them spoke for a few seconds as they gazed in awe at Greta's gorgeous creation. 'It . . . it's perfect,' Jennifer said at last.

'Eet *vas* perfect but I think it will not be now. Please try on.' Greta was unmoved by their appreciation of her work.

Jennifer went behind the screen Greta used as a dressing room and removed her clothes. 'Ready!' she called, when she was standing in just her bra and knickers. Greta's bulk appeared around the back of the screen and she held the dress out, the buttons undone so that Jennifer could step straight into it. Greta pulled up the bodice and gripped Jennifer around the waist to spin her around so that she could do up the buttons. The first two did up easily but from the third button up, Greta had to pull the fabric harder and harder to get it to reach around Jennifer's body.

Jennifer started to sweat as it became obvious that the dress wasn't going to do up. Greta tried one last time, before dropping the sides of the dress and throwing her arms up in the air in exasperation. 'Ees no good!' she snapped. 'You hev

202

put on weight and it will not do up. I hev to make the top part all over again!'

Jennifer stared up at her in horror, Greta's beady blue eyes were looking even icier than usual as she tried and failed to conceal her anger. Before she could stop herself, Jennifer burst into a torrent of noisy tears, bringing Susie running to the other side of the screen.

'What's wrong?' she cried, putting her arms around Jennifer, her face a mask of concern.

Greta tutted and, ignoring Jennifer's tears, dropped the dress to the floor again, before motioning to her to step out of it. Shaking, Jennifer obeyed and Greta stomped back around the screen into her workroom, with the dress un-ceremoniously bunched up into a ball under her arm.

'It won't do up!' whispered Jennifer tearfully.

'Oh, don't worry,' Susie comforted her, hugging her tightly. 'You look fine to me. Maybe it's just with Michael away you've been eating a bit more than usual?'

Jennifer nodded slowly, although she was thinking that if anything, she had been eating less than normal because she was feeling so sick with nerves as the wedding got closer.

Suddenly, a cold realisation began to take shape in the pit of her stomach, while at the same time as the thought entered her head, Susie seemed to reach the same con-clusion. The two girls looked at each other in shock. Instinctively, Susie's eyes travelled to Jennifer's belly and widened as they did so. Jennifer followed her friend's gaze and saw to her horror that her normally flat, brown stom-ach had grown distinctly rounder. There wasn't yet a bump but it was obvious that something was different. And her breasts, which were already large in proportion to her slender frame, were now straining to be contained in the cups of her bra.

'Oh my God!' whispered Susie, looking as terrified as Jennifer felt. 'You're pregnant.'

Hearing the words triggered a fresh bout of tears from Jennifer as she began to get dressed. Her head was swimming with confusion as a million questions presented themselves. But the worst, biggest question of all was the one she couldn't bear to ask herself. It couldn't possibly be . . .

As she and Susie left Greta's house, with Greta promising grudgingly to have the dress remade by the following week, Susie put an arm around Jennifer's shoulders and gave her a squeeze. 'It'll be OK, you know,' she said and Jennifer nodded. Of course it would be OK. Michael would stand by her and no one would be any the wiser. Except the one person she had to look at in the mirror every day.

As if sensing what Jennifer was thinking, Susie suddenly said: 'He's been round, you know, several times. I haven't had a chance to tell you before now.'

'Who?' Jennifer knew exactly who she meant but was stalling for time.

'That guy. The one you met in the bar that night.'

Susie's words hung in the air as they walked along the tree-lined street, Susie drawing admiring glances. Jennifer wondered if she would ever draw those sorts of glances again: already she felt old, fat and frumpy.

'It wasn't the first time I'd met him that night,' she said quietly. 'I already knew him.'

Susie nodded but didn't say anything.

'What did he want?'

'He wanted to know where you'd gone. He wanted your address.'

'Did you give it to him?' Jennifer asked in alarm. She had thought that she was safe, hidden away in the wilds of Suffolk. It unnerved her to think of him knowing where she lived.

'No, of course not,' Susie said quickly. 'But I can't vouch for anyone else. You never know what sort of tricks he might have pulled to get it.'

Jennifer took a deep breath and tried to think calmly and clearly. She was on the pill. She couldn't possibly be pregnant from her one night with Hugh. It was far more likely that it was from the many times she and Michael had been together. The more she thought rationally, the calmer she began to feel. She was going to bury the pernicious thought somewhere in her brain where it could never come out again. She would forget all about Hugh and concentrate on making a life with Michael that was as perfect as it could be.

After she returned to Suffolk, Jennifer knew she had to break the news to Michael. She didn't want to tell him over the telephone, as he would be surrounded by his flatmates and unable to talk properly. He was coming to visit for the weekend so, although it almost killed her to keep the secret to herself, she waited until he arrived.

Back from the station where she had picked Michael up, Jennifer knew she couldn't wait any longer. Having waved goodbye to her parents – who had greeted Michael like the long-lost son they had always wanted – they set off on a walk. 'You look so beautiful,' Michael said, stroking the hair off her face and kissing her passionately once they had found a spot deep in the wood behind her house where they could be alone together, unobserved. 'It's been hell without you,' he whispered, reaching under her sweater and unclasping her bra, his warm hands exploring her breasts before moving downwards. Jennifer sighed with pleasure as she relaxed into his touch, her senses heightened after so long without him. She unzipped his trousers and pulled them down, before sliding him inside her.

Afterwards, as they lay together on a patch of mossy ground, Jennifer's head resting on his chest, she decided the time was right. 'Michael,' she began in a faltering voice, looking up at him. 'I've got something to tell you.'

'Hmmm?' he smiled, kissing the top of her head as he looked down at her quizzically.

Jennifer took a deep breath. 'I'm pregnant,' she said with a gulp. It was the first time she had said the words out loud and she sensed a wave of emotion threatening to overwhelm her as she spoke. She felt Michael stiffen beside her as he digested her words, then he shuffled to sit up, forcing her to sit up too. His mouth had dropped open in shock but, gradually, a smile formed on his lips. 'Are you sure?' he said, his brimming eyes showing that his reaction was a positive one.

Jennifer nodded. 'I'm sure.'

Michael reached down to touch her belly, a look of wonder on his face. 'That's amazing!' he cried, kissing her tenderly. 'We're going to have a baby!'

A single tear escaped from Jennifer's eye and she swept it away quickly, but not before Michael had seen it. 'Oh, darling,' he said, looking at her in concern. 'You must have been so worried, keeping this to yourself. But it's going to be fine – we're getting married anyway, so it'll just be a case of the baby arriving a little bit sooner than we planned.'

Jennifer nodded, unable to speak she loved Michael so much. She just wished she could turn back the hands of time and undo that awful night. She knew that the rest of her life would be spent not knowing, consumed with guilt, and trying to make it up to Michael for the biggest mistake she could ever have made.

'Do your parents know?'

Jennifer shook her head, still unable to make any sound.

'Shall we tell them together?'

Jennifer smiled and nodded as relief flooded through her. She never had to do anything on her own again. From now on, Michael would be with her every step of the way.

The conversation with her parents was excruciating. Her mother burst into tears and her father looked as if he wanted to murder Michael but, gently and persistently, he assured them that although it wasn't how they had planned it, he would look after Jennifer and that everything would be OK.

'But what about your medical career?' her mother had wailed plaintively at Jennifer.

'I can still practise, Mum. I'll just have to fit it in around the baby. At least I've finished my training,' Jennifer replied, in a voice that sounded more confident than she felt.

'I promise you,' Michael interjected, looking from her mother to her father with his open, honest stare, 'that not only will Jennifer be the best mother in the world, she will also – one day – be the best doctor too.' At his words, both her parents seemed to relax and Jennifer knew that it was going to be fine. They loved Michael almost as much as they loved her, and they would believe anything he said.

As she waved Michael off back to Leeds the following day, Jennifer turned to leave when she saw something out of the corner of her eye: a figure dressed in dark clothes, smoking quietly, leaning against the station's railings and watching her. She didn't look at him properly but she knew it was Hugh: she realised that she had felt the same sensation of being watched several times recently, but this was the first time she had actually seen him.

She stumbled down the path, away from the station, hoping that she was mistaken and that he was just a stranger waiting to meet someone off a train; but, as she was formulating all sorts of explanations, she heard the fall of his footsteps behind her. Summoning up every ounce of courage she possessed, she turned suddenly and found herself face-to-face with him.

He looked dishevelled and had lost weight from his already slender frame, but Jennifer's heart lurched with longing at the sight of his beautiful face. His large, dark eyes looked like black pools in their hollow sockets; his strong, square jaw was covered with stubble; and his cheekbones were sharply defined, giving him the appearance of a Romantic poet.

'Why are you here?' she asked in a shaking voice.

Hugh took a long drag on his cigarette with a trembling hand, his eyes never leaving hers. 'You know why.'

'Please, Hugh—' she began.

'Please, Jennifer,' he interrupted, in the resonant drawl that seemed to go right through her. 'Don't marry him. You're making the wrong choice.'

Jennifer bristled. 'How can you say that? You don't *know* me. You don't know anything about me.'

His eyes narrowed as he exhaled and dropped his cigarette

to the ground, where he ground it out with his boot. 'Oh, but I do. I know everything about you. I have been watching you for so long now.'

'Spying on me is not the same as knowing me, Hugh.'

'I've done a lot more than spy on you, don't forget,' he said, making her feel suddenly faint.

'You need to leave now, Hugh. I am not going to change my mind.' She tried to keep her voice firm. 'I am going to marry Michael and I can never see you again. You need to accept that and move on with your life.'

'But I want you,' he said, in a steely tone.

'Well, you can't have me,' she said with equal resolve. 'I know you're used to getting your own way, Hugh, but you're not getting it this time. I mean it – leave me alone and don't come here again.'

Hugh nodded slowly. As he leaned forward to kiss her she felt the scratch of his stubble on her skin, then the soft pressure of his warm lips as they made contact with her cheek, and lingered there.

'I'll always be here – you'll never be able to forget me,' he whispered, sending another chill through Jennifer as she wondered what he meant. Did he mean physically, emotionally or – Jennifer prayed it wasn't so – did he somehow know about the baby?

She turned around and continued to walk down the path towards her parents' home, when something made her turn around and look back. Hugh hadn't moved from where he had been standing and was watching her with a desperate intensity. She hesitated slightly, before resuming her journey down the footpath. This time she didn't look back.

*

For many years after, Jennifer had often had the sense that she was being watched but, whenever she had looked around, she had never seen him again and, over time, she convinced herself that she was imagining it. But now, sitting there with Hugh, she knew that it hadn't been a figment of her imagination: she could sense his presence a mile off.

'You watched me, didn't you?' she said suddenly, making Hugh look up at her in surprise.

But instead of demanding further explanation, or furiously denying it, Hugh simply corroborated what she had known all along. 'Of course,' he said quietly.

'Why?'

'We both know why.'

Jennifer picked up her glass with trembling hands and took a sip of wine. She was playing for time: she didn't want to say too much in case she gave the game away about something he knew nothing about.

'I don't,' she said, equally quietly.

Hugh raised an eyebrow and looked at her in a way that made her feel emotionally and physically naked. 'Liar,' he mouthed.

Chapter 26

It wasn't just lunch, they both knew that.

Kate knew that she had arranged to meet a man that she had spent a great deal of the past couple of months conducting an on-line affair with. But although she was going to see if she could persuade Jack to give Sarah another chance, Kate also knew that, deep down, she just wanted to see him. She couldn't help it. Her head told her to send him an email cancelling their lunch date, yet her heart told her to go. She felt as if she was standing on the edge of a precipice and she could choose to stay where she was, or jump. In the end she chose to jump. And the vertiginous feeling was incredible.

They arranged to meet on Saturday afternoon in the centre of town. Kate knew that Miles would be at football and she could ask her mother to have the children; she could say she was going Christmas shopping without attracting suspicion. She prickled with guilt as she realised that already she was behaving in a deceitful way, exactly like someone who was having an affair.

'What are you doing this weekend?' Sarah asked her as they walked the children out of school on Friday afternoon.

Kate reddened immediately and shrugged her shoulders. 'I might do a bit of Christmas shopping,' she said casually.

'Ooh, maybe we could go together!' Sarah cried delightedly. 'I've got loads still to do. I could give you a lift.'

'Erm, well, I don't want to sound ungrateful,' Kate stammered, her mind searching for a plausible excuse, 'but I think I'd be better off on my own ... only because I'll be too easily distracted if you're there too,' she added, seeing Sarah's crestfallen face. 'The temptation to stop for skinny lattes every five minutes would be too great!'

'Yeah, you're probably right,' Sarah agreed, to Kate's relief. 'I'm going to do most of mine online anyway. Why don't you do the same?'

'Oh, you know what I'm like – I'm such a technophobe.' Kate realised she was almost babbling. 'I'd end up ordering all the wrong things. No, I prefer to see what I'm buying for myself.'

Sarah nodded, apparently satisfied with Kate's explanation. Kate breathed a sigh of relief, wondering yet again why she didn't just put a stop to all this immediately.

Millie and Josh were delighted to be spending the afternoon with Jennifer. She opened the door to the cottage with a beaming smile, her arms held out in welcome to the three of them. 'Hello, my darlings!' she cried, as they hugged each other. 'Josh, I see you've brought your DS – very wise. I've made some chocolate-chip cookies you can scoff while you play.'

'Cool,' said Josh, heading for Jennifer's squashy cream sofa and diving onto it, after obediently kicking off his trainers first.

'And Millie – how about you, my darling? Do you want to help me do some Christmas wrapping?'

Millie nodded. 'Sure, Granny,' she agreed, smiling easily. 'And I've got some homework you could help me with, if you didn't mind?'

Jennifer glowed with pleasure, loving the feeling of being needed by her family. 'Of course I don't! Kate ... go on ahead, darling. Don't worry about these two – they'll be absolutely fine.'

'Thanks, Mum. Oh, and I've finally got the money through to buy a new car, so you'll be able to have yours back soon.'

Jennifer smiled. 'Well, keep it as long as you need it. I haven't missed it at all.'

Kate looked at her mother curiously. 'How have you been getting about? You said you went out the other night – how did you get there?'

'Oh!' stumbled Jennifer, trying to hide the flush spreading up her face by busying herself with some letters on the hall table. 'I just get various friends to pick me up,' she finished lamely.

'That's good.' It didn't occur to Kate to wonder which friends Jennifer was talking about. She had never been a very social animal, mainly because she and Michael had never needed anyone else and had relied on each other for company. Now that he was gone, there were few people her mum saw outside her immediate family. 'I'll see you later, anyway,' Kate added, closing the front door behind her.

As Kate entered the car park, she was shocked to find that she was shaking. She tried to picture what Jack looked like, but his face had faded from her memory.

They had arranged to meet in a coffee shop that was

tucked away down a small alleyway. Kate knew about it because she had walked past it occasionally but she had never been inside, and she thought it unlikely that anyone she knew would go there, either.

It was dimly lit inside, with old-fashioned red lamps on each table making it look like evening all day long, even on the brightest days. With a cold wind and heavy, threatening-looking rainclouds outside, Kate was glad of the wall of warmth and cosiness that hit her as she stood squinting into the gloom.

She didn't see Jack at first: he had his back to her and was sitting at a table in the far right-hand corner. Once she spotted him, she hung up her coat at the front of the room and headed towards him, her heart lurching as he turned to look at her. He had on a chunky, expensive-looking navy jumper, with a plain white T-shirt underneath and a pair of well-cut jeans. He looked devastating, and she knew immediately that it had been a mistake arranging to see him again.

'Hello, Kate.' He smiled shyly and she wondered if he sensed that she was contemplating turning around and running back out of the place. She stood rooted to the spot a few yards away from him, unable to move in any direction. Jack stood up and took her hand, guiding her into the chair opposite him. 'You look well,' he said, smiling warmly.

'Thank you, you too,' Kate replied, wondering if he felt as nervous as she did. 'I got the insurance money for the car, by the way, so thank you – again!' she laughed shrilly.

'I'm glad,' he said, looking at her closely. 'Thank you for meeting me.'

There was an awkward pause as they both looked away, unsure of what to say next. A waitress – who reminded Kate of Millie – broke the silence when she came over to their table. 'What can I get you guys?' she asked brightly, her long hair falling in strands across her face where it had escaped from her ponytail. Thinking of Millie made Kate's stomach churn again.

Jack looked at Kate expectantly. 'Oh!' she said, feeling flustered and groping for the menu. 'I'll just have a cappuccino,' she replied, once she had glanced at the handwritten menu and found that she couldn't focus on anything.

'Another espresso.' Jack smiled at the girl, who was gazing at him through fluttering eyelashes, making Kate start with surprise. She couldn't have been more than seventeen – Jack was almost twice her age. But he did seem to have that effect on people.

'So,' said Jack, turning back to Kate, apparently impervious to the girl's charms.

Kate cleared her throat, as the girl huffed off to get their order. 'I hear that you called it a day with Sarah,' she said awkwardly.

Jack looked away quickly. 'Er, yes, I thought it was probably for the best.'

'But why? The two of you got on well enough, didn't you?'

'We did. But I think she wanted more out of it than I did.'

'Why, what did you want out of it?'

Jack took a deep breath and looked back at Kate. 'Honestly?' he asked, holding her gaze in a way that made her feel exposed.

'Honestly.'

'I wanted you.'

Now it was Kate's turn to look down. 'That's not going to happen, Jack,' she said gently, her heart pounding.

'Then why are you here?'

The warmth in her face turned to red-hot heat and she opened her mouth to speak, but no words would come out. 'I, er, I . . .' she stammered. Why *was* she there? The truth was that she felt an attraction to him that she had never felt for any man before, even Miles; while the excuse for why she was there was that she wanted to persuade him to give Sarah another chance.

She decided that dishonesty was the best policy.

'I thought I might be able to convince you that Sarah is worth another go. She's bright, she's pretty and she's the best fun. Far more fun than me,' she added, as she got into her stride. 'Seriously, Jack, I think you would be great together. Why don't you give her another chance? She really liked you.'

'And I really liked her,' he said, his face showing that he was genuine. 'But, the truth is, Kate, I just didn't feel the same connection.'

'The same connection as what?'

Jack raised an eyebrow. 'You know,' he said in a low voice. 'The same connection that I feel with you.'

'Jack, don't,' Kate whispered, relieved when the waitress returned with their drinks: it gave her time to collect her thoughts. 'It doesn't matter what either of us feels; it can't ever happen. I have a husband and two children who I love very much. I would never do anything to hurt them.'

Jack's eyes clouded with disappointment. 'I know,' he said quietly. 'I respect that. I just think that you can't deny that there is something between us. All those emails . . . I feel like we've seen inside each other's souls. It's so much more than just physical attraction.'

'Oh!' The sound escaped Kate's lips before she could stop it. She could almost see the waves of attraction shimmering between them, pulling them into one another.

Unable to bear the intensity of Jack's stare, Kate looked down into her cappuccino and watched the bubbles of froth melting away one by one into the creamy coffee below. She didn't speak because she didn't need to. Jack was right: it was as if there was a magnetic force field around both of them that neither of them was strong enough to resist. Fate had thrown them into each other's path, but it was a less innocent connection that was bringing them together now.

Kate looked up and saw Jack watching her intently, as if hoping that he could persuade her with his eyes. She knew she needed to break the connection for a few minutes – it was becoming too overwhelming. 'What about you?' she said at last. 'Why are you single?'

It did the trick: Jack's eyes widened in shock. 'Where did that come from?'

Kate smiled. 'Sorry, I didn't mean it to sound quite so harsh. But tell me about yourself. How did you get here?'

'In my car?' he grinned, clearly stalling for time.

Kate tutted, jokingly. 'No, come on, Jack. You know plenty about me. I want to know about *you* now. Fill in the blanks for me.'

Jack sighed deeply. 'Don't know where to begin really . . .' He paused and looked into the distance, as if deciding what to tell her. 'There was someone . . .' he began again. 'We were together for six years.' Kate felt a prickle of discomfort. She could sense that this story didn't end happily. 'Anyway,' Jack continued hesitatingly. 'She was . . . complicated, I suppose you'd say.'

'In what way?' Kate took a sip of cappuccino, hoping she hadn't left a moustache of froth on her upper lip.

Jack looked as though he had drifted off into another world. Neither of them spoke for a while, as she waited for him to continue. 'She was a model.'

Kate nodded. *That figures*, she thought, slightly bitterly.

'She was like a man magnet,' he added. 'She was always being propositioned and because she didn't have much self-confidence, she always made sure I found out about it. She seemed to want to goad me. Finally, it turned me a bit crazy and I got jealous. Ironically, even though that seemed to be what she wanted, it drove her away. It didn't end well, and it put me off relationships for a long time. Until you.'

Kate's mouth dropped open in shock. 'Don't, Jack,' she said, her emotions swirling. She looked at the pain in Jack's eyes and wanted to be able to stop it.

'How long ago did you break up?'

'Several years ago, now. Well, three years, four months, two weeks and one day, to be precise,' he said, smiling slightly. Kate felt the threat of tears behind her eyes and blinked quickly. 'You're the first person I've met since her that I've felt anything for.'

Kate didn't reply: her thoughts were going haywire. She imagined for a moment the impact it would have on Millie and Josh if she were to have an affair with Jack.

She didn't consider for a moment that she wouldn't get caught; she already knew she would. Kate was an open book and wouldn't be able to handle the deceit and the lies that it would take to get away with it. The children would be damaged for ever, with Josh probably never able to trust another woman and Millie's little world blown to pieces as she was torn between the two people she loved most in the world. And what about Miles? Yes, she had been feeling unsettled recently but she loved him. He made her laugh, he was her best friend and she felt like she owed him so much: especially the children, who were everything to her.

As she thought, Jack drank his espresso and watched her, a spark of hope in his eyes but, as she made her decision, the spark died, as if he could read her thoughts.

'It's OK,' he said. 'I get it.'

Kate felt as if she was on a raft, drifting out to sea, further and further away from what might have been. 'In another lifetime—' she said apologetically. 'Who knows?'

'But not in this one?' He seemed to want to hear her say it, to confirm what he already knew.

'No,' she said sadly. 'Not in this lifetime.'

She picked up her bag and stood up. 'I should go,' she said, suddenly desperate to get back to the life she had chosen over Jack, as if to confirm to herself that she had done the right thing.

'Will I see you again?' Jack said, his voice wavering slightly.

Kate bent down and kissed the top of his head, drinking in the scent of him as she did so. 'I don't think so. Goodbye, Jack. I hope you find what you're looking for.' As she walked away from the table she heard him say, 'I've already found it.'

Kate stumbled back to the car park, blindly pushing her way through the throng of Christmas shoppers, hating the proximity of other people and desperate for the privacy of her car. Once there, she unlocked the door and climbed into the driver's seat, where she laid her head on the steering wheel and cried her heart out for what she had lost.

After a while, she had the sense that she was being watched and looked up, blowing her nose with a tissue as she did so. She scanned the car park but couldn't see anyone, except for anonymous shoppers hurrying to their cars, their heads down against the wind and the rain, which had started to fall.

Suddenly, there was a knock on the passenger car window, making her jump violently. She looked sharply to her left and saw Jack's unmistakable eyes looking at her with a pleading expression. She hesitated slightly, her emotions suspended with shock, before she nodded softly. He opened the door and climbed into the passenger seat.

'Don't leave like this, Kate,' he said, as he clambered in and tucked his long legs in front of him into the cramped footwell. 'You're breaking your heart. I'm breaking mine. Surely that must tell you something?'

Kate could feel herself being drawn towards him in that same, strange magnetic way she had when they had first kissed. Before she could reply, he was kissing her again and, this time, she was responding with a fierce passion that seemed to have taken her over completely. She wanted to drink in the taste and feel of him so that she would never forget it.

Eventually, with a massive force of effort, she managed to pull away from him. 'I can't,' she said, her throat thick with tears once more. 'I just can't, Jack.'

'But you want to?' He was staring at her as if he could see right into her soul. 'I know you want to.' He answered his own question.

Kate shook her head. 'It makes no difference whether I want to. I can't. It's not me.'

'Can I email you? Or ring you?'

'I don't think so,' Kate sighed.

'But I want to be *with* you,' Jack said, taking her shaking hand in his.

Kate half laughed. 'Oh, Jack, you don't even really know me. I'm boring, really.'

'I'd like you to bore me,' he said, smiling at her.

'I'm married.'

'I'd like to be married to you,' he replied emphatically.

Kate looked at him. 'As I said, you don't even know me.'

'I know you.'

Jack's words hung in the space between them, like a taut wire that was about to snap.

'Goodbye, Jack,' Kate said, snapping the invisible wire.

Jack's shoulders slumped and his dark eyes turned black. Kate leaned over and cupped his face in her hands, gazing at him, trying to memorise every part of his face. Then she kissed him gently before pulling away. 'I need to go.'

Jack held her gaze before nodding. 'I know,' he said. 'Goodbye, Kate.'

The rain started to fall harder in fat splatters across the windscreen as Kate watched Jack climb out of the car. He walked across the car park, his head bent against the downpour, leaving Kate with rivulets of tears running down her face.

Once she had calmed, she fished in her bag for a tissue and wiped her eyes. Taking a deep breath, she started the car and began to make her way shakily towards the exit.

'You're back early,' said Jennifer, opening the door to her as she arrived back at the cottage. 'I thought you'd be hours.'

'No,' Kate replied in a small voice.

Jennifer held her at arm's length so that she could look at her. 'What's wrong?' she said.

As soon as her mum spoke, Kate burst into tears and fell against Jennifer.

Jennifer looked around to make sure that Millie and Josh weren't within earshot, relieved to hear the TV blaring out from the sitting room. She held Kate tightly for a few moments, trying to calm her, before ushering her up the stairs to her bedroom.

She sat Kate on the side of her bed and sat down next to her, taking her hand in hers and stroking it softly. 'Tell me what's wrong,' she said, feeling anguished for her daughter, who was always so strong and resilient. She had never seen her like this before.

Kate shook her head and said nothing, watching as the tears splashed onto her jeans leaving tiny, dark patches.

'Is it . . .?' Jennifer hesitated, wondering if Kate would trust her enough to confide in her about her marriage. She never had before; but, she decided, maybe she had never needed to before. 'Is it to do with you and Miles?'

As she spoke the words, Kate cried out loudly, making Jennifer think that she was right. But Kate quickly corrected her. 'No!' she sobbed. 'Well, not about us specifically.' She looked up at her mum with sorrowful dark eyes, as if weighing up what to say next.

'You can tell me, sweetheart,' Jennifer said, squeezing Kate's hand reassuringly. 'Whatever is wrong, you need to talk about it; and I promise you I will never discuss it with anyone or judge you in any way.'

Kate nodded. 'Well . . . I've met someone,' she said in a shuddering voice. 'A man.'

Jennifer immediately thought of the two children lying on her sofa downstairs, blissfully oblivious. 'OK,' she said.

'It's Jack.' She looked at Jennifer to see if the name meant anything, but her face was blank. 'You know, the one who helped me when I had the crash?'

'Oh,' said Jennifer slowly, as understanding dawned. She knew that Kate had been different since the crash but she had put it down to her being shaken-up and sore. Now, everything became clear. 'The one you went to dinner with?'

Kate bit her lip.

'Isn't he with Sarah?' Jennifer was struggling to get a full picture of what had happened between them.

'Was,' said Kate, glancing again at Jennifer. 'He called it a day.'

'Because of you?'

Kate nodded and felt the tears brimming again.

Jennifer's mind was racing. She didn't want to ask how far the relationship had gone, but she needed to know if it was just a fling or if Kate was thinking of leaving her marriage for this man. 'Do you love him?' she asked tentatively.

Kate blinked in surprise. 'No!' she said quickly, and Jennifer felt relief flooding through her until Kate added, 'I don't know! I hardly know him, really.'

Jennifer frowned. 'I assume you had a relationship with him?'

Kate winced. 'Not a physical relationship,' she sighed. 'Nothing happened between us sexually. But we have been emailing each other for months now and it got ... quite intense. There was definitely a connection between us.' Jennifer waited, holding her breath. 'I just ... well, I just met up with him and told him that it couldn't go any further.

223

And I'm so upset because ...' Kate burst into noisy sobs again, unable to continue speaking.

Jennifer put her arm around her shoulder and hugged her tightly. 'I think I understand,' she said.

Kate looked up at her gratefully. 'Really?'

Jennifer nodded and Kate could see in her eyes that she genuinely did. 'I've been where you are, Kate,' she said quietly.

Kate's tears stopped in their tracks as she stared at her mum in astonishment. 'When?' she asked, her jaw dropping.

Jennifer looked wistful as she thought about Hugh and the choice she had had to make years before. Then she looked at Kate. 'Another lifetime ago,' she said.

Kate smiled. 'Another lifetime. That's what we both talked about. In another lifetime, maybe Jack and I ... but it's not another lifetime. It's this one and that's all we get.' She sighed. 'I really felt a connection with him, though, Mum. That's why it's so hard.' Her bottom lip quivered and she thought she might cry again; she swallowed hard to try to get rid of the lump in her throat. 'Was it between Dad and someone else? That you had to choose between, I mean?'

Jennifer nodded and squeezed Kate's hand, more for her own benefit than for Kate's. Kate had never seen her mum like this: had never thought about her like this. Like a human being with a hinterland that preceded her and Amy.

'And you chose Dad?'

A half-smile played on Jennifer's lips. 'Yes, I chose your dad,' she said, again with a wistful look in her eyes as if she was remembering something from a long time ago.

'Was it the right choice?' Kate's words seemed to hang in

the air in the tiny gap between their two heads.

Jennifer looked right into Kate's eyes. 'Yes, it was the right choice,' she said emphatically. 'And you have made the right choice, too. I know it. Attraction is powerful. So powerful,' she said, almost aggressively. 'But love and friendship are enduring. And you have put a stop to this before it is too late, unlike—' She stopped herself, and suddenly Kate could see that she was almost panting from the effect of what she had just said.

'Unlike what?' Kate looked at Jennifer curiously.

'Unlike some people,' Jennifer whispered, before continuing in a stronger voice: 'I am so proud of you, Kate. I promise you I understand how hard this must have been for you, but you will never, ever regret it. Yet you might have regretted the alternative "lifetime".'

Kate felt something shift inside her as her mum spoke. She was stunned that Jennifer was so intuitive about what she was feeling. 'Thank you, Mum,' she said, leaning into her mum's embrace. Tears began to course down her cheeks again but, this time, they weren't tears of sorrow for what might have been. This time, they were tears of relief that it never was.

Chapter 27

With their leaving date and their move in with Jennifer looming, Amy began to pack up the house. Not that there was much left to pack: she had sold as much as she could to get some cash. Ben's parents lived in France and Amy had wanted to keep their problems from them, so there had been no hope of getting any financial assistance from them. Amy had told them that they would be moving house but hadn't explained any more than that. Ben didn't seem overly concerned with what his parents thought, but Amy knew that it would break their hearts to see their only son in such a broken state.

His sister, Alex, had gone off to India to find herself several years previously, and they hadn't heard much from her since. It occurred to Amy that maybe self-indulgence ran in the family but she dismissed the thought quickly. Ben might have had a breakdown and be suffering from depression but, up until then, he had been a wonderful husband and father. *Once the drugs kick in, he will return to his old self*, she reassured herself over and over again.

Amy had confided in her mum about everything, and had found her to be more supportive than she could ever have imagined. 'I promise you,' Jennifer had told her one evening, when Amy had been in the depths of despair, 'you will come through this a stronger person. And although it's difficult now, if you pull together, it will make your relationship with Ben and the children better.'

'We already have a good relationship!' Amy had snapped back, immediately lapsing into her default defensive mode.

'Shhhh,' her mum had hushed her gently. 'I know that. I meant that it'll be *even* better. You will come through this, Amy. There is more to life than money.'

'I know you're right,' Amy had agreed, reluctantly. 'But I'm dreading Christmas – how the hell am I going to buy the kids' presents?' she had wailed.

Jennifer had immediately offered to give her some money, and Amy had had no choice but to accept her mum's offer. She thought back to the previous year when she had congratulated herself for managing to do all her shopping online. She had never once stopped to add up how much she was spending. She had never needed to.

So, as they packed up what was left of their possessions and prepared to move out, Amy found herself scouring eBay for bargains and trying to think of creative presents that she could make for free.

'What are you doing?' asked Ben one evening, as she pored over the computer in his office.

Amy started with surprise and spun round. Ben was leaning against the doorframe with both hands tucked into his jeans pockets. His hair had grown and he had lost the extra pounds he had been carrying before his breakdown. His eyes looked bigger and darker, and his skin clearer. She realised with a stab of pain just how distant they had become with each other in a short space of time. She hadn't looked at him properly for many weeks, and she almost didn't recognise the man now standing in front of her.

'I'm ... er, I'm just trying to find Christmas presents for the kids,' she said, pushing back some strands of hair that had fallen loose, conscious that while Ben's looks had improved, hers had suffered. Her highlights badly needed doing, her skin was puffy and spotty, and her eyes now sported two dark circles beneath them due to lack of sleep, even though she was desperately tired.

Ben looked at her for a long moment and she tried not to flinch under his gaze. 'What?' she said eventually, slightly irritably.

'You've been amazing,' he half whispered. 'I'm so sorry.'

Amy's eyes brimmed with tears, which she tried to blink away. She pulled out the scrunchy that was holding her hair back so that, as her hair came down, she had some camouflage. Ben came over to where she was sitting and knelt down in front of her. He took one of her hands in his and stroked her face with the other. 'I don't know what happened,' he said, his eyes searching hers. 'I disappeared for a while there.'

Amy smiled ruefully and sniffed loudly as tears began to course down her cheeks unchecked. 'Yes, you did. Oh God, Ben, I've been so scared!' she sobbed. 'I thought you had gone for good.'

She buried her face in his T-shirt and let all the angst of the past weeks and months pour out in a torrent. Ben wrapped his arms around her and held her tightly, rubbing her back until she calmed. 'I'm so sorry,' he said again, when she finally looked back up at him. 'I didn't know what to do. I lost everything.'

'Not everything,' hiccoughed Amy. 'You didn't lose us.'

'Didn't I?' he said, his eyes pleading. 'Please tell me I didn't lose you.'

Amy shook her head. 'No. We're still here,' she smiled, kissing him. He kissed her back, hungrily, and began to run his hands over her body. Amy pushed him away shyly, unused to his physicality after so long without him. 'I look so awful,' she whispered self-consciously.

Ben leaned forward and kissed her again, with even greater intensity. 'You have never looked more beautiful,' he said gruffly.

Relief flooded through Amy and she found herself responding, her senses reawakening with every touch. Ben pulled back and looked at her, a smile playing on his lips.

'What?' she said, desperate for him not to stop.

'I was just thinking,' he said, taking her hand and pulling her to her feet as he stood up himself. 'There's one thing that's still free . . .'

Chapter 28

'Sarah!' Kate called loudly, having spotted her friend dashing out of the windswept, rainy playground ahead of her. Sarah turned quickly at the sound of Kate's voice, her blonde hair flying around her face in the wind, and gave a dismissive wave. Kate began to jog towards her but, to her surprise, Sarah turned back to the direction she was heading, her arm around Daniel, and continued almost running towards her yellow Mini. She scrabbled furiously in her large bag for her keys, before unlocking it and jumping in; Daniel scrambling into the passenger seat beside her. She then started the car and drove off so fast that the tyres screeched slightly as she pulled away.

Kate stood on the slippery pavement with Millie and Josh on either side of her, watching her drive off. 'Well, that's odd,' she said aloud, frowning.

Millie looked up at her. 'Why didn't Sarah want to speak to you?' she said, looking puzzled.

Kate shrugged in an effort to look like she didn't care but the truth was, Sarah had been avoiding her for the past week now, and she couldn't for the life of her understand why. She sensed it had something to do with Jack but she honestly didn't know what she had done wrong, or why Sarah had become so distant so suddenly.

Arriving home, feeling disconcerted and gloomy, she found Miles – a tea towel wrapped around his waist as a makeshift apron – standing at the cooker in their galley kitchen, stirring sauce in a pan. Numerous pans were discarded on the worktops and the detritus of his ingredients were everywhere. His face was a mask of concentration as he looked from the Jamie Oliver cookbook back to the saucepan, as if checking that the concoction on the hob was, in fact, the same as that in the picture.

'What the heck are you doing?' Kate asked, taking off her coat and hanging it up.

Miles looked up at her and grinned sheepishly. 'I'm cooking.' He nodded towards the simmering pan.

'I can see that.' Kate smiled back at him. 'But why? You never cook.'

'Well, maybe it's about time I started,' Miles replied shortly, before squinting back at the picture in the book. 'Not that I'm very good at it.'

Kate wandered further into the kitchen and leant against the worktop, watching him. 'Well, it smells good,' she said, feeling hungry as the garlicky aroma filled the kitchen.

Miles beamed. 'It does, doesn't it? Why don't you go and put your feet up, and I'll call you when it's done?'

Kate's eyes narrowed in suspicion. 'What are you up to, Miles?'

Miles's big blue eyes widened even further. 'Nothing! Can't I make a meal for my family without it becoming an international incident?'

Kate frowned. 'Er, well, no, actually. It's freaking me out.'

Miles turned away from the hob and looked at her with an expression she couldn't read. 'I just want to make you happy,' he said, in a quiet voice.

Kate froze under the spotlight of his gaze. 'You do make me happy,' she replied, suddenly scared that Miles might be able to read her mind. Yet how could he possibly know? She had been careful to delete all emails from Jack and the ones she had sent him. And what was there to know, anyway? It wasn't as if she had slept with him.

Miles nodded to himself, before turning back towards the hob. 'It'll be ready in twenty minutes,' he said. 'Seriously, why don't you go and have a bath or something, until then?'

'Well, OK,' Kate agreed reluctantly, before turning and going up the stairs. She wondered what the hell was going on.

Chapter 29

'Wow!' yelled Sam, ripping the wrapping paper off a parcel. 'Dinosaur Top Trumps! Daddy, will you play with me?'

Amy watched in amazement as Sam, still wearing his fleecy blue pyjamas, bounced up and down with delight at such a tiny gift. She thought back to the previous year when she had ordered the latest computer console and numerous games, costing hundreds of pounds. Sam had been pleased but had simply put the boxes to one side and continued to methodically plough through the mountain of presents still waiting to be opened.

This year, the children had still been greeted by a decent pile of presents, but there wasn't one big, expensive centre-piece. Yet neither of them had even noticed. They unwrapped packets of felt-tip pens and drawing books with as much glee as if they had been given something worth much more. Flora was already engrossed in one of the books she had been given, sitting cross-legged in front of her granny's crackling fire, her blonde hair pulled back to reveal a face that showed no signs of the worry she seemed to have worn permanently for the last several months.

Amy curled her feet underneath her and sighed, taking a

sip from the steaming mug of tea she was clutching. She watched Ben, stretched out on the floor on his tummy, frowning with concentration as he examined his Top Trumps. He was getting better all the time but it sometimes felt as if it was one step forward, two steps back. He would appear to rally completely for a day or two, but then be engulfed by depression again, as if he had had the stuffing knocked out of him. He was still a shadow of his former self.

Leaving their house had hit them all very hard. Amy had taken Flora and Sam by the hand and walked from empty room to empty room, mentally saying goodbye to their old life. Even Sam had seemed to understand the magnitude of what was happening and had pursed his lips with quiet sto-icism instead of crying loudly with his usual noisy emotion. Flora had clutched Miffy to her chest and gazed with worried eyes up at Amy, seemingly more concerned with how her mum was coping than herself, while Ben had waited by the front door with his head down and shoulders slumped, unable to accompany them on their tour.

As she closed the door behind her for the last time, Amy had been almost overwhelmed by the mixture of emotions she was experiencing. She was devastated to be leaving the home where they had started their family and where they had been so proud and happy together. But at the same time, she felt a massive sense of release from all the pressure and worry she had endured over the past few months.

They had driven to Amy's mum's house straight from London, all of them keen to forget their troubles in the crisp beauty of the rolling Suffolk countryside, and the children excited at the prospect of living with their granny for a while. As they had driven through the outskirts of London, Amy had reached over and put her hand on Ben's leg. She was driving as his breakdown had led to him being too anxious to get behind the wheel: just one of many symptoms he had developed which Amy fervently hoped were temporary. Ben had reached down and squeezed Amy's hand, while staring straight ahead.

'You OK?' she had asked, her own stomach roiling with fear.

Ben had nodded but hadn't spoken.

'I'm scared,' Amy had blurted out, glancing in the rearview mirror at the two children. They were sleeping soundly, leaning against each other in a way that made Amy's heart contract.

Ben had still not said anything and Amy had started to feel a familiar twinge of irritation rise through her. It had disappeared completely in the last week they had spent in their house, but now that they were heading off towards her mother's like a family of refugees, the desperation of their situation loomed large once more.

'I'm sorry,' Ben had whispered quietly, and Amy had immediately felt her face burn with shame.

'No!' she had insisted quickly. 'Don't be sorry. We'll get through it.'

'I'm scared, too,' he had said, dragging his eyes away from the road and looking at her.

Amy had reached down and switched on the car radio, wanting to cut through the thick silence. An Adele song was playing and Amy's eyes had blurred hopelessly with tears as the sad, haunting tune of 'Someone Like You' had filled the air.

Ben's fingers had started to stroke Amy's face, catching her tears as they fell. She had stared straight ahead as the windscreen wipers moved robotically from side to side, clearing the rain so that she could see the road clearly. She had tilted her head slightly towards Ben, so that his hand was cupping the side of her face. Neither of them had spoken as they reached the motorway, both too weary and churned up with emotion to voice what they were thinking. Amy had driven on autopilot towards Suffolk, realising with a jolt that it might be the last time she drove the route from London. 'We haven't got a home any more,' she said aloud, almost to herself.

Ben looked at her with an odd expression on his face. 'I'm not sure we ever really did,' he replied.

Amy had felt exhausted by the time she finally pulled onto the gravel driveway in front of Jennifer's cottage. She had turned off the engine and she and Ben had gazed up at the welcoming lights burning in the small leaded windows. As they did so, the front door had been thrown open and Jennifer had come running out. Amy undid her seatbelt and got out, falling gratefully into her mother's arms, feeling like a child again. 'Welcome home,' Jennifer had whispered, immediately making Amy feel like everything was going to be all right.

Even now, it was strange being back in the cottage where she had grown up and still had her own bedroom – now occupied by Flora – but they were all loving being there. Jennifer was briskly comforting and seemed to enjoy looking after them as much as they loved being looked after. Amy realised that they had never stayed there all together before, and romantically imagined them to be like a family sheltering from the Blitz, huddled together and taking comfort from each other's proximity.

Already, by eight in the morning on Christmas Day, delicious smells were wafting from the kitchen. Amy could hear her mum buzzing about, clattering plates and pans, humming along to the Christmas carols that were blaring out from the radio.

She got up and wandered into the kitchen. 'Anything I can do?' she asked, as she perched on a stool at the breakfast bar and watched as Jennifer expertly prepared the turkey. She popped it into the oven as if it weighed nothing, instead of being a fifteen-pound whopper. Jennifer pushed back a strand of her silver hair and looked at Amy, her hands on her hips. 'Um ... well, I guess you could peel the potatoes,' she said dubiously. She knew Amy's ability in the kitchen wasn't exactly up to Delia's standards.

Amy nodded and obediently hopped off her stool. She took a giant bag of potatoes from the vegetable rack and tipped them into the sink, which she filled with warm water. As she began to peel slowly, her mum took another knife out of the drawer and joined Amy at the sink, where she deftly peeled three potatoes to every one that Amy did, her hands moving at the speed of lightning. 'Wow!' Amy laughed. 'You could enter the Olympics if they had a potato-peeling category. I don't know how you do it so fast.'

Jennifer grinned at Amy good-naturedly. 'I've had plenty of practice. Mind you, it's been a while since I've had a houseful like this. It's so lovely to have you back.'

Amy felt her eyes smarting and couldn't risk speaking in case her voice betrayed the emotion she was feeling, so she said nothing.

'So, what are you going to do now, love?' Jennifer said, after a pause.

Amy concentrated hard on the potato she was working on. 'Well, we've got a roof over our heads, thanks to you . . .' Jennifer batted the remark away as Amy continued, 'And getting them into the school is at least one less thing to worry about.'

Jennifer dropped her knife into the sink and wiped her hands on the front of her apron. 'I meant, what are *you* going to do now?' she said, leaning against the worktop as she looked closely at Amy.

'Oh, I see,' said Amy, buying time by scooping up handfuls of peelings, which she deposited in her mum's 'compost' bin. 'Well, I'm not really sure.'

'You'll have to get a job, won't you?' said Jennifer, slightly nervously. The thought of Amy at home all day was a terrifying proposition.

Again, Amy busied herself by putting the kettle on, as if by ignoring the question it could become unasked.

'Amy?' her mum prompted.

'Yes! I bloody well will!' snapped Amy. 'There. Happy now?'

Jennifer frowned. 'Whatever do you mean?'

Amy sighed and slumped down again on the stool, looking around the chaotic, steamy kitchen and feeling a helplessness wash over her. 'I mean, you've always said I should have my own way of earning money and now you've been proved right, haven't you? I'm fucked.'

A flicker of irritation passed over Jennifer's face at Amy's bad language but she walked over to her daughter and wrapped her arms around her. 'I know you, Amy. You don't have to pretend with me. You have zero confidence, which is something I feel partly responsible for. You feel that you won't be able to get a job because no one will want you and there's nothing you can do because you're not trained in anything.'

Amy opened her mouth to protest but closed it again. Jennifer was right. That was *exactly* how she felt.

'But you're wrong,' her mum continued. 'There are lots of jobs you could do. You're still young and you have got – despite what you might think – a lot to offer. I am so proud of the way you have coped these past few months. Lots of others would have crumbled completely, but you stuck your chin in the air and got on with it. You have been amazing, and you wouldn't have coped as well as you did if you weren't a strong person.'

Amy shook her head hopelessly. 'But I don't know where to begin,' she whispered, burying her head in the soft wool of her mum's jumper and inhaling her familiar White Linen perfume. She wished she could stay there for ever, away from any responsibility.

Jennifer pushed Amy back and held her at arm's length, looking at her full in the face. 'Begin at the beginning,' she suggested with a smile.

Amy took a deep breath in. 'You make it sound so easy,' she said, exhaling loudly.

'That's because it *is*,' replied Jennifer.

Chapter 30

Kate and Miles took the children to join the rest of the family for Christmas lunch at Jennifer's. It was the first time since Michael's funeral that they had all been together at the cottage and, although this time there wasn't the same sad purpose for getting together, nevertheless all of them were feeling a sense of loss for different reasons. As they all sat around Jennifer's giant table, on the surface gaily celebrating Christmas, each one of them was nursing a secret dread of what the future might hold.

Ben's recovery was slow but sure and being at Jennifer's seemed to soothe his nerves, but it was still a shock for Jennifer and Kate to see how badly he had fallen apart. They had only ever known Ben as the good-looking, gregarious, über-successful boss of his own company. Now, he looked thin and drawn, and was nervous and shaky. He was distant with everyone except Amy, whom he followed around like a lost puppy, panicking whenever she wasn't around.

Amy was enjoying being at Jennifer's because she felt safe and secure, but she was terrified of what the future held for them all. She loved Ben as much as ever but she couldn't picture how their relationship would work now that they had swapped roles: both mentally and literally. Now, it was Amy who was the strong one holding the family together and the one who would have to go out and find a job, while Ben was the one with no confidence, who would stay at home and possibly take over looking after the children. They hadn't discussed it but it was the obvious solution, although as Ben had always worked such killer hours and earned such good money – something that Amy knew she couldn't realistically match – it was going to take them all a long time to adjust to such a seismic shift in their lives.

Kate had been dreading Christmas, with all the forced jollity that it entailed: all she really wanted to do was sit in a darkened room and cry. She knew she had done the right thing in putting a stop to anything more happening between her and Jack, but she hadn't been prepared for how bereft she would feel afterwards. She thought about him constantly and was irritable with Miles, despite the fact that he seemed to sense that something had happened in their marriage and had suddenly started behaving differently towards her. As well as helping around the house, he had started to cook regularly, he was attentive towards her and he had even missed a football match to take her Christmas shopping. But despite his best efforts, Kate still felt dissatisfied and unsettled. At the moment, it felt as if it was only the children that kept her going.

Meanwhile, Jennifer was in a permanent state of worry and turmoil. Having Amy, Ben and the two children to stay was one thing, but she was nervous about how they would all cope if it turned into a long-term arrangement. Amy was still so prickly and defensive, and Jennifer hadn't dared to ask how long they were intending to stay in case she took it as a sign that they weren't welcome. Jennifer was worried about Amy. She was certain that she would come through this awful episode a stronger person but, at the moment, it was hard to watch her struggling with her fears for the future, without really being able to help. Yes, Jennifer could provide a roof over their heads and food for them to eat but she knew that, ultimately, it was the equivalent of her putting a sticking plaster over a cut knee. In the end it would have to be up to Amy to carry her little family through the storm, and it broke Jennifer's heart to see her uncertain of which way to go.

Kate was such a different person to Amy but Jennifer was equally concerned about her eldest daughter. Kate had always been the good girl, the one who could be relied upon by everyone and who never seemed to struggle with knowing which way to go with her life. Until now, she had accepted her lot with a cheery grace and practical attitude. But since Kate had confided in her about Jack, Jennifer had realised just how many parallels there were between her and her daughter. Both had had to get married because they were pregnant and, although Kate didn't know Jennifer's secret, both of them had had another man in the background of their marriages. But in Jennifer's case, the man she had married *was* the love of her life and her soul mate, whereas she suspected Kate had settled for Miles out of a sense of duty and gratitude. Jack had offered her a glimpse into another life and now she couldn't be satisfied with what she had; she wanted a taste of what might have been.

And then there was Hugh. Jennifer had grown used to meeting him on a weekly basis and she was confused about her feelings for him, now that she had had to put a stop to their liaisons for a while. It annoyed her that he still had a sexual power over her that she seemed unable to resist, and it only compounded her sense of guilt. She had made a terrible mistake when she hadn't resisted him back then: surely the least she owed to Michael's memory was to be able to resist him now?

For his part, Hugh had made it very clear that he wanted Jennifer as much he had wanted her when they first met. He was a man who always got his own way and she felt that he had never recovered from the fact that he didn't get her. She could see that – in some ways mirroring her own experience – he had spent the intervening years that they had been apart with her hovering in the background of every relationship he had had. For him, reuniting with her now was a case of finally completing the circle, dealing with unfinished business. She could see that he had always expected her call. Always known that in the end, he would get what he wanted.

Jennifer had been profoundly shaken by the realisation that Hugh had known all along about the baby. She had assumed that when she finally got round to speaking to him about it he would be stunned, hurt, and maybe even angry; but the one thing she never, ever expected was for him to already know. She had spent days agonising over how to broach the subject with him, only to find that she hadn't needed to.

It had been almost three weeks since she had last seen him and, since then, she had had a sick feeling in her stomach as she had tried to work out how or when she might re-establish contact. And on what basis? There was no need to keep seeing him regularly if he already knew what she had been building up to telling him. So why couldn't she shake her desperate yearning to look into his eyes, and to hear his voice again?

As the children drifted off to play with their various toys and games, Kate and Amy began to clear the table. Jennifer got up to help but they both insisted that she stay seated and have another glass of port with the two men.

Ben and Miles appeared to have reached an uneasy truce, having always been wary of each other in the past. Miles seemed shocked by Ben's collapse but equally seemed to feel more comfortable being with him, as if they were somehow on an equal footing now. Before, the chip on his shoulder was so big he could barely walk: he had told himself that Jennifer and Michael preferred their more successful son-in-law with his charm, wit and, of course, not inconsiderable wealth. Now, with Ben a nervous wreck, it was Miles who seemed like the successful one and it gave him the confidence to hold his own in family situations in a way he never had before. This was the first family dinner he could remember that he had actually enjoyed, instead of simmering with resentment at the slightest real or perceived barb from his in-laws.

'Ben's awful, isn't he?' whispered Amy, as she and Kate loaded the plates into the dishwasher.

Kate hesitated for a moment before looking at her sister. Amy herself had undergone a dramatic change in appearance over the past few months. She had lost weight but she had already been very slim, and the extra pounds she had lost had only made her look tired and drawn. Her blonde highlights badly needed touching up, the dark roots making it look lank and lifeless. But it was her skin that gave away just how much stress she had been under. Amy had been blessed with a peaches-and-cream complexion that gave her a glow all year round and emphasised the navy-blue of her large eyes. Now, her skin had a grey tinge and she had broken out in spots. Kate had never known Amy to suffer from spots, not even during their teenage years when she had often cursed her own misfortune to be blessed with an olive skin, but one with an oily complexion that was prone to acne.

'He's slightly better than I thought,' she said at last, not wanting to add to Amy's misery by telling her that she was shocked to the core by Ben's deterioration. She knew that she herself would have struggled to cope with him as he was now, in his clingy, nervy state. For the first time in many weeks, it made her appreciate Miles's steadiness. Yes, she might sometimes wish he was more dynamic in his job, but seeing Ben had jolted her into the realisation that with tremendous highs, there often came terrible lows. 'What are you going to do now?' she asked, as they finished stacking the plates and put the kettle on to make coffee.

Amy ran her hand through her hair and shrugged help-lessly. 'Who knows? I don't have any training for anything; I've got no proper CV. Serves me right, I suppose, for sitting on my backside all these years enjoying the high life while the rest of you were busy forging a career for yourselves. God, Kate, what I wouldn't give to swap places with you right now!'

Kate perched on one of the stools at the breakfast bar and motioned for Amy to do the same. 'That's ironic,' she grinned, taking Amy's hand in hers and stroking it to show that she was ribbing her, rather than being unsympathetic.

Amy smiled back. 'I know! I know!' She waved both hands in the air in a gesture of surrender. 'There must have been so many times when things were hard financially for you and Miles that you would have happily swapped places with me. But, you know what? I don't think you ever really wanted my life, did you?'

Kate shook her head slowly. 'No. Your money, maybe. But not your life.'

'You used to say you wouldn't have been able to stand having another person living in your house when we took on Maria.'

Kate said, 'That's true. I would have hated the invasion of privacy, but that's not to say I was right and you were wrong. You did what you thought was best for you and your family, Amy. You can't start beating yourself up now for things that were right for you at the time.'

'But I feel such a fool!' Amy cried, and Kate could see that she was on the verge of tears.

'You have absolutely no reason to feel foolish!' Kate reassured her hotly. 'You've been the best wife and mum you could be, and your family adore you!'

'Yes, but you've been the same and yet you've got a back-up plan as well. You've got your career if Miles's job ever hits the buffers. I should have listened to Mum all those times she told me how important it was to earn my own money.'

Kate opened her mouth to speak, but it was as if she had run out of things to say. Amy was right. Jennifer had always drummed into the girls that they should always have their own job, their own career, so that they were never reliant on a man for money. But while the message had been heard loud and clear by Kate, somehow Amy hadn't had the confidence to do the same. She had been lucky meeting Ben, who had happily supported her financially and never really expected her to go out to work, especially once the children had come along.

'I'm going to have to get a job,' Amy said. 'I know that. I just don't know how to start.' She swallowed. 'Will you help me, Kate?'

Kate nodded furiously. 'Of course I'll help you! You are not on your own here, Amy. Mum and I will support you all we can.'

Amy's shoulders seemed to relax slightly as Kate spoke and she took a deep breath. 'And do you think ... do you think we might be entitled to anything?'

It took Kate a moment to understand what she was saying and she frowned slightly as she replied, 'Benefits, you mean?'

Amy nodded miserably. 'It's just that at the moment we have absolutely no money coming in. We could ask Ben's parents for money, but I don't want them to know what's going on. They'd be so devastated to see Ben like this.'

'That's true,' Kate agreed. 'I think you're doing the right thing keeping it from them, but I don't know what you'd be entitled to, if anything, by way of benefits.' Suddenly, she had a thought: 'Mind you, Miles might know, working for the council. Do you want me to ask him?'

Amy blushed, embarrassed at finding herself in this situation. She had always felt that Miles disapproved of her lavish lifestyle and she wondered if he might take the opportunity to gloat at her and Ben's misfortune. She liked Miles, but had sometimes thought he was boring, and too chippy when it came to borrowing money. Now, she couldn't think of anything more appealing than someone who refused to get into debt and who took responsibility for their finances. 'That would be great,' she said in a small voice.

They sat in companionable silence while the kettle hissed its way to boiling point, before turning itself off with a satisfied click. Kate got up to make the coffee, just as she always did. 'No!' said Amy, suddenly getting up. 'I'll do it! You sit back down. It's time I learned to pull my weight. I've got to earn my keep somehow.'

Kate hesitated. She was so used to doing all the work that it felt alien to her to sit watching someone else do it – especially Amy. 'OK,' she agreed, slightly reluctantly, as she sat back down. She sensed that it was important to Amy to try to give something back now that she could no longer pay her way with money and, as she watched her cack-handedly pouring the boiling water into a cafetière, into which she had already spooned far too much coffee, she resisted the urge to either help or correct her.

'So,' said Amy, as she proudly poured the treacly coffee into two mugs. 'How are *you*, Kate?'

Kate looked at her questioningly. 'Fine. Why?'

Amy sat down and looked at her with narrowed eyes. 'Because I think you're not fine at all.' Kate glanced from side to side as if she had been cornered and was looking for an escape route. 'Kate?' Amy prompted. 'What's wrong? You haven't been yourself since the crash.'

At the mention of the crash, Kate's stomach dropped. If only she hadn't had that crash: she would never have met Jack and would have been continuing happily with her life. But as she looked at Amy, who was worn down with her own, much more serious worries, she knew that she couldn't possibly confide in her. Offloading might make Kate feel a little bit better but it would only add to the burden Amy was already carrying. She knew that Amy had always looked up to her and had never known her be anything other than solid and dependable. By blowing that myth apart, Kate knew she would take another of the building blocks that were supporting Amy and destabilise her further. 'I'm fine,' she said, rubbing her neck, as if the memory of the crash was making it ache again. 'It's just that it was a bit of a jolt to my system. I think it's taken me longer than I thought to get over it.'

Amy lifted her head and leaned back to look critically at her sister, as she tried to decide whether or not to accept Kate's explanation. In the end, although she didn't believe her and sensed that she was holding something back, she decided that she simply had too many other things to worry about, without adding to them. 'OK,' she said, signalling that she was willing to let the matter drop – for now. 'Let's take some coffee into the others, shall we?'

Kate nodded, grateful not to have to go through why she was feeling so low. She knew it was unsettling for everyone else; that she was always the calm, dependable one who took everything in her stride. She wanted to shake herself out of it and told herself sternly to get a grip. Sooner or later, surely her subconscious self would listen to her own good advice?

In the dining room, Jennifer, Ben and Miles were still seated around the table, chatting easily. Well, Jennifer and Miles were chatting easily, Amy thought. Ben was physically present but his mind was obviously elsewhere as he watched them silently, his dark eyes large and frightened in their sockets.

Jennifer glanced at her as she laid the tray on the table and sat down beside her, and Amy knew without being told that Ben had been alarming Miles and Jennifer with his strange behaviour. She poured the coffee and, as she did so, she noticed that Ben's fists were clenched tightly into a ball once again. 'Coffee, sweetheart?' she said, as light-heartedly as she could.

Ben shook his head vehemently.

'I'll take that as a no then, shall I?' Amy snapped, as the other three stole glances at each other.

Jennifer watched them all helplessly as they drank their awful, thick, overly strong coffee in a heavy silence. How had it come to this? How had her happy little family managed to fall apart so comprehensively in such a short space of time? For the first time, and completely irrationally, she blamed Michael for leaving her alone to cope with it all.

Chapter 31

As Christmas faded, and the new year dawned in a blanket of mist and drizzle that hung over the countryside for days, Amy steeled herself for the children's start at St Mark's. It had broken her heart to see the way their London friends had already melted away – not that the children seemed to have noticed – and she wondered how her old friend, Jo, was coping with being ostracised from the wealthy 'in-crowd' they had both once been part of.

She hadn't heard from Jo – not that she was surprised. She had always known that their friendship was one based purely on shopping, lunching and pampering themselves. Now that those pastimes were no longer an option for either of them, there was very little left beneath the surface of the friendship. She had never really trusted Jo, or confided in her.

Amy had wondered if she should maybe call her, but something had stopped her. It was the sense that Jo was nothing if not a survivor, and she would be doing all she could to hang on to the vestiges of her old life: by her false fingernails, if necessary. She wouldn't want to be reminded of how dire their situation was or want to be contaminated

251

any further by the odour of failure that must surely be clinging to both Amy and Ben, whether they were aware of it or not.

The children, however, were proving to be more resilient than Amy had dared hope. They had taken their house move, school move and their father's illness entirely in their stride, treating their change in circumstances like some sort of adventure. They adored their granny and were enjoying seeing much more of her than they normally would. If anything, Flora seemed happier and more secure since they had come to Jennifer's. She had never complained about the fact that she hardly ever saw her dad when he was working ridiculous hours in London but it was noticeable that, even though he was still a long way from being back to his old self, Flora felt happier having him and her mum around all the time. She was more confident, and seemed to be blossoming by the day.

Sam bounded into Amy and Ben's room at 6.30 a.m., already dressed in his uniform of grey trousers and royal-blue sweatshirt, which he had put on back to front. His bright, blond hair was sticking up in every conceivable direction and his shoes were on the wrong feet. 'Get up, Mummy! Get up, Daddy! We can't be late on our first day!' he cried, bouncing onto their bed delightedly.

Amy had already been awake for hours, staring up at the ceiling. Beside her, Ben had slept deeply but fitfully, thrashing around as if he was fighting the demons in his head with all his might. His medication helped him to sleep but it had a sedative effect that made him wake late, with a woozy head and slurred speech.

'Morning, darling,' Amy smiled, reaching out to pull Sam into bed beside her. He squirmed and resisted at first, saying 'I've got my shoes on!' but Amy ignored him and, having quickly slid his shoes off, tucked him under the duvet so that he was cocooned spoon-like against her stomach. His hair smelt of shampoo and his little body felt warm. 'Let's just have a quick cuddle before we have to get up, shall we?' she whispered as she kissed the top of his head, wishing they could stay there for ever. Sam's body relaxed against her and she squeezed him to her, wanting to put a protective force field around him so that none of the horrible stuff in life could dent his sunny little personality.

After a few moments, Flora appeared in the doorway, silhouetted against the landing light. She hesitated, watching her mum and Sam for a few moments before Amy motioned for her to come and join them. Flora smiled and scampered towards the bed as Amy and Sam shuffled over to make room. She slipped under the duvet and the three of them lay huddled together. Beside her, Amy suddenly felt Ben stirring and she reached out to take his hand that, even first thing in the morning, was scrunched into a tight fist. One by one, she uncurled his fingers, before stretching his arm gently over towards the children so that he was embracing them all at once. She twisted her head to look up at him and for the first time in months, she saw a light in his eyes. It made her feel that as long as they all had each other, they might just be OK.

By the time they reached the school gates, there were already a number of parents milling around, having dropped their children off already. Gripping Flora and Sam's hands tightly, her insides churning ominously, Amy smiled shyly at a trio of mums who looked at her curiously as she passed them. Her eyes searched hopefully for Kate but she was nowhere to be seen and Amy suddenly realised that Kate would have had to drop Millie and Josh off early so that she could get to work. Amy wondered if she had already missed her as she led the children through an outer porch door and into a lobby that was screened by a security door. She pressed the call button and waited. After a couple of moments, the tall figure of Mr Carter appeared and released the door to let them in. 'Hello!' he greeted them warmly, reaching out to shake Amy's hand. 'How nice to see you again, Mrs Osborne and Flora . . . and Sam, isn't it?'

Both Flora and Sam beamed up at the kind, open face of their new headmaster and Amy could have kissed him in gratitude for making them feel so at ease. 'Right, let's get you inside into the warm, and I can take you to meet your new classmates!' Mr Carter said with a smile. Amy loved how he talked to the children directly and not over their heads at her, the way their old teachers and headmistress used to do. Dutifully, Flora and Sam followed him into the corridor.

She hesitated in the lobby, watching her children as they headed off with Mr Carter, one either side of him, as the door began to swing slowly shut.

'Oh!' he said, spinning suddenly on his heel. 'How silly of me. I completely forgot. You'll want to give Mummy a kiss goodbye, won't you?'

Amy's composure melted as both Flora and Sam hurtled back towards her and flung themselves into her outstretched arms. 'Have a lovely day!' she said with a gulp, trying to hide her tears behind her hair as she kissed and hugged them both. They had been so brave and uncomplaining about all the awful things that had happened lately that it made it all the more heartbreaking to see them having to deal with yet another strange, new situation like this.

As Amy looked up, she caught Mr Carter's eye. He nodded at her, and she could tell immediately what message he was giving her: without speaking, he was telling her that it was OK to feel the way she did and that everything was going to be fine. She blinked hard and gave her face a cursory wipe with the back of her hand, before nodding back at him. 'Thank you,' she mouthed, as the children returned to his side, and they all headed off again.

As Amy trudged down the school driveway, her head bowed against the seemingly never-ending drizzle – which seemed to echo and reflect her own feelings so perfectly – she heard a voice.

'Hey! Hello!' said an attractive blonde woman who looked to be in her mid-thirties, as she fell into step beside Amy.

'Oh, hi!' Amy tried to sound as bright and friendly as she could, despite the fact that she felt anything but, right then.

'You must be Amy.'

Amy looked quizzically at the woman. 'Yes . . . sorry, do I know you?' She didn't want to appear snooty and she was suddenly worried that she might have met this woman before and not remembered.

'I'm Sarah, Kate's friend,' the woman prompted.

'Aha!' Amy smiled and nodded as recognition dawned. She had heard Kate talk about Sarah many times before.

'I saw you coming out of the office and presumed you'd just dropped the kids off . . . How was it? It can't be easy . . .' She tailed off, as if she was wary of saying too much.

'No,' Amy agreed solemnly. 'But, Mr Carter seems so nice ... that helped.'

Sarah nodded. 'He's great. When my husband did a runner, the kids were distraught but he really helped them through it. Helped us all, actually. He seems to know exactly what to say, and when. There aren't many like him around.'

'No,' Amy agreed, as they reached the end of the drive and stopped. 'He's very good with kids. Does he have a family of his own?'

Sarah shook her head. 'He's married to the job.' She smiled then asked: 'What are you doing now, then?'

Amy pulled a face. 'Not much – I've got to start looking for a job. I suppose I may as well get cracking, now that I've got this bit over with. It was what I was dreading most.'

'Well, if you want to go for a coffee, I could help you come up with a plan?'

'Don't you work?' Amy blurted out before she realised how judgemental it must have sounded – especially coming from her, who hadn't worked for years. 'Sorry,' she said, and corrected herself: 'I mean, I would love to have a coffee; I just don't want to disrupt your plans.'

'No, not at all,' Sarah insisted. 'I work from home, doing HR consultancy. I can fit in my hours to suit. I can certainly spare the time for a coffee!'

Amy looked at her. She sounded more than a little over-eager, but then Amy remembered Kate telling her about what a rough time Sarah had had when her husband left her: she could see that she was lonely. *That makes two of us*, Amy thought, realising just how alone she felt herself at the moment. 'A coffee would be lovely,' she said with a grateful smile.

When Amy returned back to the cottage a couple of hours later, she went in search of Ben. She found him sitting cross-legged in front of the open fire in the sitting room, staring into the flames, a look of fascination on his face.

Jennifer came in from the kitchen. 'Oh, you're back!' she said, walking over to give Amy a hug. 'How did it go?'

Amy shrugged, all the while watching Ben with a rising sense of frustration. He seemed to have forgotten that she had just dropped their children off for their first day at a new school. Either that, or he didn't care. Immediately, she shook that thought from her head. Ben adored his children. He was ill, but that didn't mean he didn't care about them. She looked at her mum and tried to raise a smile. 'It went as well as it possibly could,' she said. 'The headmaster's great.'

'Oh, that's Ian Carter. Yes, he's fantastic,' Jennifer agreed enthusiastically, as Amy followed her into the kitchen.

'Anything I can do to help?' Amy said, looking around the kitchen in wonder at all the dishes Jennifer had on the go at once. Jennifer was an incredible cook and she seemed to have treated the arrival of Amy and the family as an excuse to try out all her best recipes: Amy had never eaten so well or so much. For her part, Jennifer had more or less stopped cooking altogether since Michael's death, saying she hated preparing meals for one. Now that she had her family back around her, she was making up for lost time.

'No, not at all!' Jennifer said briskly. 'You can put the kettle on and make us a cup of tea instead.'

Obediently, Amy filled the kettle and flicked the switch,

before perching on one of the kitchen stools and watching while her mum continued to stir the huge vat of bolognaise sauce she had prepared earlier. Even though it was still only midday, the lights were on because it was so dark outside and the kitchen was filled with an incredible aroma of garlic and herbs, giving it a cosy, comforting atmosphere. 'I went for a coffee with Kate's friend, Sarah,' she said, watching as her mum used a teaspoon to taste the sauce, before deftly adding another dash of herbs and red wine to her simmering concoction.

'Oh, that's nice,' Jennifer said, as she lifted a large ball of dough out of a glass bowl where it had been proving. She began kneading it on the scrubbed oak kitchen table. 'She's a sweet girl, Sarah.'

'Isn't she?' Amy agreed, getting up and taking two mugs from the mug tree and popping a teabag into each one. In the past, the fact that the mugs were old and mismatched had annoyed her: now she found it curiously comforting. 'But I thought it was a bit strange that she kept going on about that guy ...'

Jennifer stopped kneading for a second and smoothed a stray hair off her forehead with the back of her hand. She frowned. 'Who? The ex-husband?'

Amy finished making the tea and put her mum's cup down on the table beside her. 'No, that other one. The one who looked after Kate when she had the crash. Jack.'

At the mention of Jack's name, Amy thought she saw Jennifer flush. 'Oh,' she said eventually, still kneading the dough furiously.

'She seems to think that he had a thing about Kate and she kept insinuating that Kate had a thing about him, too.'

Jennifer didn't reply.

'Yes,' Amy continued, 'I think she's really disappointed because she quite liked him. But she seemed to be pumping me for information. Kept asking if Kate had mentioned him much or if I knew whether she'd seen him at all.'

Jennifer finished kneading the dough and began to tear it into smaller, bread-roll size chunks, which she began to roll into equally sized balls. 'And what did you say?' she asked carefully.

Amy blew on her tea and took a sip. 'I said she hadn't mentioned him and so I didn't think she'd seen him at all. But then, as I pointed out, Kate's married and even if he had a thing for her, she's not the type to have an affair.'

'No,' agreed Jennifer: quite forcefully, Amy felt.

'Mum?' she said, wondering why Jennifer wouldn't look at her. '*Did* something go on between them? Kate has been acting really strangely ever since the crash and Sarah seemed very suspicious. I was thinking about it on the way home … I put it down to her suffering from some kind of delayed shock but maybe it's more than that? Maybe she *is* having an affair?'

'She isn't,' Jennifer said emphatically. She took her time putting the tray of rolls into the oven, then she washed her hands and dried them on her apron, before she picked up her tea and perched heavily on the stool beside Amy, finally looking her in the eye. 'She could have. He was very keen on her and I think she was very keen on him but, as you say, that's not our Kate's style. She told him it couldn't possibly happen.'

Amy's mouth dropped open. She wasn't sure if she was more shocked that goody-two-shoes, dependable Kate had contemplated having an affair, or that she had confided in Jennifer about it.

As if Jennifer could sense what she was thinking, she said quickly, 'She didn't tell you because she didn't want to add to your worries at the moment. She thought you already had enough on your plate.'

Amy nodded slowly and sipped her tea as she thought about how this news made her feel. She somehow felt betrayed that Kate hadn't felt she could confide in her and simultaneously touched that she didn't want to upset or worry her. 'So, how come she told you about it?' she said at last.

Jennifer shrugged. 'I think I'd guessed what was up with her. I caught her at a low moment and she confided in me.'

'Did you tell her not to do it?' Amy was suddenly curious – and seeing her mother in a whole different light. She couldn't imagine discussing something as intimate as having an affair with her, let alone taking her advice on the matter.

'No, of course not!' Jennifer insisted indignantly. 'She had already decided that for herself. Maybe I helped to make her see that she made the right decision,' she added, looking into the distance thoughtfully.

'Wow,' mouthed Amy, still stunned by the revelation. 'When did all this happen?'

'A couple of weeks before Christmas,' replied Jennifer, after a short pause.

'But she's still acting strangely,' Amy persisted. 'Surely if nothing happened, she's got no reason to act so oddly?'

'I think it's made her look at her life a bit more closely. Made her question things she always took for granted before.'

'Like Miles, you mean?' Amy prompted, thinking about

her brother-in-law and how much she would appreciate someone that steady and dependable right then.

'Maybe,' agreed Jennifer tactfully. 'I think it's all shaken her up a bit but, hopefully, she'll get over it. Anyway, what about you, my love? How are you coping?' she said, deftly changing the subject.

Amy felt her eyes burning again and cursed herself for being so emotional. 'Oh ... you know,' she shrugged, her gaze automatically moving to the door into the sitting room, where Ben was still sitting staring into the fire. 'Has he been like that all morning?' she asked.

Jennifer nodded. 'But it's fine, Amy. We're going to have to go with him a bit on this; it's not a path any of us has gone down before. I think we just need to take each day as it comes and deal with each new symptom as it arises. He *will* get better. In fact, I think he's already a lot better than he was. He's been doing quite a bit in the garden, and I think that helps him. Soothes him.'

'Do you think he's getting better?' Amy asked her mum hopefully. 'Do you really?'

'Yes,' Jennifer replied firmly. 'He just needs time. And he's got all the time in the world here, so he can heal at his own pace. I've treated many patients with depression and he's fairly typical.' Jennifer wasn't a psychiatrist but her medical career had entailed a long period as a GP, and she recognised Ben's symptoms as the same as numerous patients she had had in the past. 'It's *you* I'm more concerned about,' she added, her eyes searching Amy's face. 'I worry about the impact all this is having on you. Having a partner with depression is incredibly difficult, darling. Don't think I'm not aware of that.'

At Jennifer's words, something hard and solid in Amy's chest cracked, and she burst into uncontrolled sobs.

Jennifer opened her arms and Amy fell against her mum's breast. Jennifer rocked her backwards and forwards as if she was a child, saying, 'It's OK,' over and over again, until Amy began to calm. Finally, Amy got up and pulled a tissue from a box on the windowsill. She blew her nose and wiped her face and looked at Jennifer with a blotchy smile. 'Well, crying isn't going to do any good,' she said in a shuddery breath.

'No, but sometimes it's necessary,' Jennifer said calmly. 'What can I do to help you, Amy?'

'Get me a job?' Amy replied with a half-grin, sitting back down beside Jennifer.

'OK. What sort of job do you want?'

'One that pays,' Amy replied drily. 'Except that I'm not qualified to do anything. I should have listened to you all those times you told me to make sure I always earned my own money, shouldn't I?'

Jennifer frowned. She hated being reminded of how she had contributed to Amy's lack of confidence by nagging her. 'Well, let's not think about that now,' she said quickly. 'Was Sarah able to help at all? She works in HR, doesn't she?'

Amy's face lit up as Jennifer spoke. 'Yes! Actually, I forgot to mention it! She suggested I talk to the school about being a teaching assistant. Apparently, they're looking for one.'

'Oh, yes!' Jennifer cried, thrilled at the idea. 'That would be perfect! You always used to say that you would love to be a teacher and—'

'But,' Amy broke in, her eyes clouding over, 'why would

they employ me? There must be loads of mums better qualified than me who'll be going after that job.'

'Why *wouldn't* they employ you?' Jennifer countered. 'You're clever; you're capable. Just look how well you've coped these past few months, Amy! Other women in your situation used to having lots of money and help would have completely crumbled. But you've been incredible, especially in protecting the children from too much upset over what's happened. Seriously, darling, you should get an application in immediately.'

Amy hesitated. She really wanted to apply for the job but she was genuinely scared of not getting it. She knew it would be a pitiful salary but it would mean so much to her to be able to say she was earning money – any money – for the first time in her married life. And it would take the pressure off Ben, meaning he would be able to take his time to decide what he wanted to do next. 'OK,' she said, after a while, butterflies of excitement beginning to dance in her stomach. 'Will you help me, Mum?'

Jennifer jumped off the stool. 'Of course,' she said, immediately taking off her apron and heading for the door like a woman possessed.

'Mum!' Amy said with a laugh, 'Shouldn't you take the rolls out of the oven first?'

SPRING

Chapter 32

The arrival of spring had done nothing to lift Kate's spirits. In fact, the sight of daffodils bursting into vivid colour along the roadside and the blossom on the trees seemed to mock the darkness of her mood. It seemed to her as though everyone else was getting their lives together, and she was the only one left feeling lonely and disorientated. She was enjoying having Amy, Ben and the children living closer and she now saw them regularly but, catching her off-guard and confusing her, Amy and Sarah had quickly struck up a friendship, at the same time as Sarah had seemingly decided to dump Kate. She was pleased that Amy had found a friend so quickly, but she just wished it wasn't *her* friend that she had found. Sarah had been increasingly off with her ever since the Jack situation and was now ignoring her calls and texts altogether. Kate thought how ironic the whole thing was. Nothing had really happened between her and Jack, yet Sarah blamed Kate for him not being interested in her.

She wondered how long it would take for her to stop thinking about him: he had left an indelible impression on her. Jack had emailed her a couple of times since their meeting and it had taken every ounce of willpower she possessed to delete his messages and not reply. She knew that it would only be starting the whole cycle of emotional infidelity all over again.

At home, Miles was still on his best behaviour. He was paying far more attention to Kate than he ever had before, and Kate sometimes wondered if it was because he had an inkling that he had come so very close to losing her. It had helped calm things between them, while seeing so much more of Ben and Amy – particularly after Ben's breakdown – was making Kate appreciate anew Miles's steadiness, in a way that she hadn't for many years.

Amy had applied for a job as a teaching assistant at St Marks, surprising herself and everyone else in the process. She and Ben seemed to have settled into a whole new routine, with Ben taking over the childcare while Amy scoured the local newspapers and job sites. She would earn nothing like as much money as Ben used to bring in but, after Miles's advice, they had managed to get some income support too, which meant they could just about get by.

They seemed quite happy to be living with Jennifer, which had surprised Kate. She had expected them to hate not having their own space and having to depend on Jennifer for a roof over their heads, but they appeared to be adapting to their new, much more meagre way of life without a backward glance. Jennifer too, was apparently loving having a family to look after again. She had been lost and lonely since Michael's death and it was as if having Amy, Ben and the children there had given her a new lease of life.

She hated to admit it, but Kate was feeling jealous of the fact that Amy now got so much of their mum's attention. She missed her mum's company: it was now rare that they were on their own together. If she wanted to see her, she had to arrange for her to come round to Kate's in the evenings after work, which somehow made it a more formal and less spontaneous relationship.

As if trying to compensate for Jennifer's increasing absence, Kate had found herself visiting Michael's grave more and more. She would wander through the trees of the natural burial wood until she found his plot, sit down on one of the fallen logs that acted as benches, and talk to Michael as if he was still alive and sitting with her, listening. She could feel his presence strongly and each time she visited, she could feel the agony of his loss start to lessen slightly, reviving her and giving her strength.

On the days she visited Michael's grave, she had time to think about her own situation and how much it mirrored Jennifer's all those years ago. She was still reeling from her mum's revelation that there had been another man on the scene when she first got together with Michael and that, like Kate, she had had to make a choice between the two of them. It had made her look at her mum in a whole new light and had helped her to see that her own decision was really the only one she could have made. But she would always wonder what might have happened if she had chosen the other path.

One day, in early spring, as she sat on the fallen log talking to Michael, she heard the sound of footsteps approaching through the trees and turned to see Jennifer walking down the path towards her. If Jennifer was surprised to see Kate, she didn't show it.

'Hello, sweetheart,' she smiled, perching beside her. It was a perfect spring day, with blossom bursting forth in the trees and wild daffodils creating a golden rug on the ground in front of them. The air smelt fresh with hope and new life, and the river at the bottom of the hill glinted a silvery-blue under the pale cornflower sky.

For a while, neither of them spoke as they absorbed their surroundings.

'What was he like?' Kate said finally, realising that it was one of the few times they had been alone together since she had confided in her mum about Jack, just before Christmas.

Jennifer frowned. 'Who? What was who like?'

'Your "other man",' Kate grinned impishly. She made quotation mark signs with her fingers as she spoke.

An expression of guilt crossed Jennifer's face as she glanced towards Michael's grave. 'How do you know about him?' she said, playing for time as her mind whirred.

'You told me, don't you remember? When I told you about . . . you know.'

'Jack?' Jennifer prompted, still trying to stall. She suddenly regretted telling Kate about Hugh and wondered why she couldn't have kept her mouth shut: just as she had done for the past thirty-four years.

Kate's face dropped at the mention of Jack's name. 'Yes, Jack,' she said quietly. 'Anyway,' she continued, 'you said that you had to make a choice between this other guy and Dad. I just wondered what he was like. Tell me about him.'

The flush on Jennifer's face spread down her neck as she reddened at the thought of Hugh. She hadn't seen him since before Christmas and it was now like picking at a scab to think about him. She had deliberately and forcefully banished him from her thoughts, concentrating instead on looking after her family, but now that Kate was inviting her to talk about him, it was as if all of her pent-up emotion – whether regret or lust or guilt – was racing to the surface and manifesting itself on her face.

Kate looked at her curiously. 'Are you OK? Sorry, I shouldn't have asked . . . especially not here . . .' She tailed off.

'No!' Jennifer jumped in quickly, taking Kate's hand in hers. It was cold, despite the sun slicing through the trees. 'It's not that . . . It's just . . .'

'What?'

'It's just difficult to talk about it, that's all.' Jennifer looked up at Kate and she could see that Kate didn't understand why it was so hard to talk about someone that, as far as she knew, Jennifer hadn't seen for years. How *could* she understand, when she didn't know that Hugh had come back into her life so recently and had made every bit as much of an impression on her as he had the first time around? Nor did she know what sort of devastating impact he could potentially have on Kate's own life; if Jennifer were to continue down the path she had started on.

'Nothing, it's OK,' she said carefully, trying to compose herself. 'It's just . . . strange, thinking about him. I feel guilty,' she added, glancing again at Michael's plot, before looking up and meeting Kate's eye, willing her to understand.

To Jennifer's relief, Kate's eyes registered understanding. 'Well, yes, I know how that feels,' she agreed. 'But it's not a sin to talk about him, is it?'

Jennifer hesitated. 'No, I suppose not.'

'So?' Kate prompted, clearly not to be deterred from her questioning.

Jennifer sighed and thought about what to tell her. As

there was the possibility that this man could, in fact, be Kate's biological father, somehow it felt important to get his description right and to make sure that Kate wouldn't have any reason to think ill of him.

'He was about as different to Michael ... I mean, your dad—' she began haltingly, '—as it's possible to be.'

Kate smiled and looked towards Michael's plot fondly, before sitting back slightly. 'In what way?'

Jennifer leaned her head back and looked up, trying to absorb some warmth from the weak sunshine as thoughts of Hugh as a young man floated through her brain, making her head swim. 'He was tall, very slim and very dark,' she began, turning to look at Kate's own dark complexion, wondering for the millionth time if she had inherited it from her. Or from Hugh.

'I can't imagine you with someone dark,' Kate said. 'You always looked so right with Dad, him being so fair. You complemented each other perfectly.'

Jennifer smiled at the memory of Michael. They *had* looked good together. She had never told anyone, but she sometimes fancied them as looking a bit like Ali MacGraw and Ryan O'Neal in *Love Story*.

'He had very dark eyes. Dangerous eyes, I always used to think.'

Kate raised an eyebrow. 'He sounds hot,' she said in what she hoped was a conclusive way. She had a feeling her mother might be about to go into detail about his sex appeal. She wasn't sure she was quite ready for that yet – or ever.

But Jennifer didn't seem to notice. Her eyes were glassy as she was transported back to an earlier time in her life, thinking about someone who had left a deep impression on her.

'He didn't waste words and sometimes it could be quite uncomfortable being around him,' she continued, as Kate watched her intently. 'But he was incredibly charismatic. And he was so persistent . . .' She faltered, and Kate felt for a moment that she was intruding into something she shouldn't.

After a few minutes' silence, Jennifer continued, 'I have to admit it was flattering, having this rich, handsome young man pursuing me.'

'Rich?' Kate said, mock-sharply. 'You never mentioned he was rich . . . Why on earth did you choose Dad over him?'

Jennifer laughed, the spell seemingly broken. 'Because I loved your dad more than Hugh,' she said simply. 'And then Dad made some money too, so we weren't exactly poor.'

'Hugh?' Kate said. 'Was that his name?'

Jennifer nodded, cursing inwardly before they lapsed into silence again for a few seconds.

'Did you ever regret your decision?' Kate felt as if she was holding her breath as she waited for Jennifer to reply. To her surprise and consternation, Jennifer didn't answer immediately. 'Mum?' she prompted, her forehead creasing in concern.

Jennifer took a deep breath. 'No,' she said, yet there was a sadness to her voice that suggested the answer wasn't as simple as that one short word suggested. 'No,' she repeated, as if trying to convince herself. 'I have many regrets,' she added. 'But I have never, ever regretted choosing Michael. He was everything to me.' Her pupils dilated as she spoke and her dark eyes became even darker.

Kate felt her heart squeezing with sorrow as her mother's grief raged as raw as ever in front of her. She immediately felt guilty for giving her cause to dwell on her loss again.

'Sorry,' she said, reaching out and taking Jennifer's hand.

Jennifer shook her head quickly. 'No, it's helpful to talk about it – really,' she said, smiling briefly. 'I love talking about your dad. It's just strange thinking about Hugh, that's all.'

'Do you know what happened to him?'

Jennifer looked away guiltily. She would have liked to talk to Kate about him, to be honest about the fact that she had made contact with him again after all these years, but that might lead to questions she couldn't possibly answer yet. 'No,' she muttered. 'I hear about him from time to time and I think he's fine, but that's about it.'

'Have you thought about getting in touch with him again?'

Jennifer looked up sharply, unsure if Kate was somehow telling her that she knew; she could see from her face that she didn't. 'I haven't thought about it,' she said, choosing her words carefully, not wanting to lie outright.

'Well, maybe you should. It's so easy to track people down these days with Facebook and things like that.'

'What makes you think I should?'

Kate hesitated. 'Well, I suppose there are a couple of reasons really. Firstly, I worry about you being lonely—'

'Not much chance of being lonely with Amy and Ben there!' Jennifer said with a laugh.

'Well, no, maybe not,' Kate agreed. 'But also . . . no, this is going to sound silly.' She stopped talking and looked down at her hands, which she was twisting around one another.

'Go on,' Jennifer prompted. 'What were you going to say?'

Kate cleared her throat and said, 'Well, maybe if you were to make contact with this Hugh again after all these years and then if you were to get together with him again—' Kate realised she was babbling '—it would mean that you didn't have to choose one or the other. You could have both. See, I told you it was silly . . .' She tailed off apologetically.

'A bit like you wish you didn't have to choose between Jack and Miles?' Jennifer probed gently.

Kate reddened. 'Something like that,' she admitted. 'Not that I'm saying for one moment that I wish Miles would die so that I could have Jack,' she added hastily.

'Good,' Jennifer smiled sadly, staring at Michael's plot. 'Because I certainly wouldn't recommend it.'

Kate's eyes brimmed as she thought about the pain her mum had been through over the past two years since Michael's death. She knew – even though she would never have said it out loud to anyone – that her mum and dad's passion had been far greater than anything she and Miles had ever had, so for another man to have even tempted her mother, he must have had something incredible about him. Somehow, it seemed important to her that her mum re-establish contact with him. Maybe it was because it gave her hope.

'I should go,' Jennifer said, after a while. She stood up and, as she did so, seemed to stumble slightly, as if she might faint.

'Mum?' Kate cried in alarm, jumping up and holding Jennifer's arm to steady her. 'Are you OK? I'm sorry, I should never have brought it up.'

Jennifer sat back down on the log and took a series of deep breaths. She felt as though her heart might explode. 'No, I'm OK,' she croaked eventually. 'I just had a funny turn, that's all.'

'What sort of funny turn?' Kate urged, thinking that

maybe it was connected to Jennifer's drinking. She leaned in close but couldn't detect any alcohol fumes.

'Oh, I just go a bit woozy, that's all. It always passes quickly.'

'You should see a doctor,' Kate said, feeling cross with herself that she hadn't noticed anything amiss before.

Jennifer laughed. 'I *am* a doctor, don't forget! I promise you, it's nothing. I haven't been sleeping well and it's probably to do with that.'

Kate frowned but could see that the colour had returned to her mum's cheeks and that she appeared to be fine again. 'Well, *I'm* a nurse – don't forget that either – and I'm ordering you to take it easy, OK?' she said as sternly as she could. 'Don't overdo it running around after Amy and her lot. Amy's not as helpless as she makes out, you know.'

Jennifer grinned again and gave Kate a mini salute. 'Yes, sir!' she smiled, before blowing a kiss towards Michael's plot and heading back up the hill.

After Jennifer left, Kate sat gazing into the distance, thinking. She felt so alone. She missed Michael, she missed Jennifer and, more than anything, she missed Jack.

Chapter 33

Amy smoothed down her navy pencil skirt and looked at herself in the full-length mirror in the small bedroom she and Ben shared in Jennifer's cottage. She thought back to a year ago when she used to spend ages prancing around her huge, luxurious bedroom trying on her endless designer outfits and planning what to wear to the next work function she would be going to with Ben. Now, here she was wearing a pair of sensible heels, a smart skirt and a crisp white shirt, as she prepared for the first interview of her adult life.

'Will I do?' she said into the mirror.

'Yes. You'll do,' said Ben gently from the bed where he was reclining, watching Amy as she got ready.

Amy raised her eyes so that they met his in the mirror. She noticed with a start that she couldn't just see him in the reflection: she could also see all her fears and worries reflected in his face. She felt sick with nerves and tried to breathe steadily, reassuring herself that this was a low-paid job for which she was likely to be as qualified as anyone else applying. But however much she told herself that it didn't matter if she didn't get it, right then she felt as if her whole life depended on it.

She applied some lipstick with shaking hands and quickly wiped it off again after seeing what a mess she had made of it. Instead, she took out her small tin of Vaseline and smeared a slick of it over her dry lips, rubbing them together and peering at her skin, which was finally starting to clear of the spots that had dogged her for months. Stress, she realised.

She picked up her hairbrush and pulled it through her shoulder-length hair, which was blonde again after she had finally had her highlights retouched. Jennifer had paid for her to have it done at the local salon in Banntree.

Amy had had to quash her instinctive squeamishness about the dated décor of the salon and the chewed nails of the young stylist who didn't look old enough to have left school. It was so very different to the salon she had visited every four weeks in London, where she was treated like a member of a exclusive club and pampered with good coffee and expensive chocolates, before handing over £250 without blinking. But to her surprise and delight, the young girl had made her laugh with hilariously indiscreet stories about her drunken exploits and disastrous love life as she deftly and professionally completed the highlights, which looked miles better than her London stylist had ever managed. When she announced that the total bill was just £45, Amy had almost fainted with shock and shame at how much money she had frittered away over the years on her hair alone.

Her heart was banging and she could already feel a trickle of sweat running down her back. Panic was setting in that she would be shown up for the useless fraud she was, and that she would embarrass herself totally in the interview. What the hell was she thinking of, going for this job? In the old days, she could at least have asked Ben to talk her through everything she needed to do and he would have coached her in the right way to answer any tricky questions but, now, the best he could manage was a shy smile and kiss, before telling her gently to 'Knock 'em dead'.

'Mum?' she called out, walking into the kitchen to look for Jennifer. She desperately needed a pep talk but her mum was nowhere to be seen. Just as she was about to turn disconsolately away, Jennifer came bursting in through the back door from the garden, her cheeks red from the fresh air, beaming at Amy.

'Oh, darling, you look perfect!' she cried proudly, slipping off her muddy clogs and padding barefoot over to Amy, where she appraised her with a nod of satisfaction. 'Just perfect,' she repeated. 'How are you feeling?'

'Sick,' Amy admitted. 'I'm wondering whether to call and cancel. What the hell am I thinking? I'm just going to make a complete fool of myself.'

Jennifer shook her head quickly. 'Of course you're not, sweetheart! You'll surprise yourself at how brilliant you are.'

Amy looked at her sceptically. 'I seriously doubt that,' she muttered, biting her lip nervously.

Jennifer picked up Amy's hand in her own and tilted Amy's chin so that she was looking into her eyes. 'Treat it as practice for future interviews. Tell yourself you're not bothered whether you get the job or not—'

'But I *am* bothered!' Amy interrupted. 'I wish I wasn't, Mum, but I'm *really* bothered!'

'I know that,' Jennifer continued quietly. 'So, pretend. Tell yourself that you don't really want it but you're going to use this interview to practise for the future. It's purely to give you experience of interviews, that's all.'

Amy looked at her mum gratefully. 'And do you really think that'll work?'

'It always worked for me,' Jennifer said emphatically. 'And I always got the job. If nothing else, it'll help you to stop stressing and calm you down.'

Amy nodded. 'It has already,' she said, smiling as the tightness in her chest ebbed away. 'Thanks, Mum,' she added, before kissing Jennifer on the cheek and heading out of the door.

Walking up the path to the school office, Amy suddenly felt self-conscious in her smart interview outfit as the heels of her shoes made a clicking sound on the pavement. She had only ever worn jeans and Converse trainers at the school before, when she was picking up or dropping off the children.

Through the glass window to the office, she could make out the silhouette of Ian Carter as he bent over to show something to the school secretary, Mrs Deans, a woman so relentlessly kind and cheerful that she was universally adored by the children and parents alike. As she watched him, he looked up and caught her eye, giving her a brief, slightly stilted wave. He walked into the lobby and pressed the release button to open the door for her.

'Good morning, Mrs Osborne!' he said, smiling easily, reaching out to shake her by the hand. His skin felt cool and smooth to the touch and Amy remembered the first time she had shaken his hand all those weeks ago, when she had brought the children to see the school for the first time. She had been struck then by how much of a contrast his skin was to Ben's clammy palms, and she was struck by it again now.

Mr Carter stood to one side and gestured for Amy to enter

in front of him. As she did so, she could feel him watching her. 'Take a seat in my office,' he said, motioning towards his room, whose door was ajar. 'I'll go and get Miss Swanley, whose class you would be assisting.'

Amy's heart dropped as she made her way into the office – still just as messy as the last time she had seen it – and she took a seat in the same chair she had sat in when she had first been there. Miss Swanley was Sam's classroom teacher and the children loved her, but many of the parents found her abrasive and slightly cold. 'I don't want this job,' Amy told herself over and over again, taking deep breaths to calm herself. 'This is just for the experience.'

After a few minutes, she heard footsteps and Mr Carter and Miss Swanley came into the room. Mr Carter walked around to his own side of the desk, while Miss Swanley hesitated slightly before sitting in the chair next to Amy and fixing her with a grin that seemed more sinister than friendly. Amy regarded her cautiously, thinking that she looked so much older than her years because of the way she was dressed and the extra weight she was carrying. She couldn't have been much more than forty-two or forty-three, but she looked at least ten years older.

'So,' Mr Carter began, picking up a paperclip and rolling it between a perfectly manicured finger and thumb. 'Thank you for coming, Mrs Osborne. Why don't you begin by telling us a bit about yourself?'

Amy licked her lips as her mouth dried. 'Well,' she began, a small nervous laugh escaping from her throat before she could stop it. 'I'm thirty-four years old. I have two children, Flora and Sam, who joined the school at Christmas and I would really, really love to work here.' *Hell, where had that come from?* She was supposed to be pretending she wasn't bothered about the job.

Mr Carter's grey-green eyes crinkled as he smiled at her, as if she had just cracked a joke. Amy glanced at Miss Swanley, who was also smiling slightly, although her smile didn't reach her eyes.

'You don't seem to have much experience of working,' Miss Swanley said sharply and suddenly, peering at Amy's CV, which she had picked up from Mr Carter's desk. Amy noticed that her nails were bitten and that she wasn't wearing a wedding ring.

'Not in an office, no,' she agreed. 'But I was very happy being a full-time mum,' she countered nervously. 'And I think any mum would tell you that that's extremely hard work.' She paused, wondering if Miss Swanley might nod in acknowledgement but, when she didn't, Amy knew she was right in her assumption that she was childless and married to her job. 'So I think I've gained a lot of experience that would help me in this role, if I was lucky enough to get it,' she added quickly.

'Well, if you were so happy being a full-time mother, why do you suddenly want to go out to work now?' Miss Swanley had a triumphant glint in her eye as she spoke.

Amy opened her mouth to reply but Mr Carter spoke first. 'Well, I'd say that's obvious, wouldn't you, Mrs Osborne?' he said, raising his eyebrows encouragingly at Amy, while simultaneously shooting Miss Swanley a reproving look. 'The children have started school. That changes everything, I would imagine.'

Amy nodded gratefully. 'Yes!' she agreed enthusiastically, glad that neither Mr Carter nor Miss Swanley knew that she had had staff in London, that she had kept on even after the children had started school. 'And I want to do my bit to support the family, as my husband is unable to work at the moment.'

Suddenly, the glint in Miss Swanley's eyes vanished. 'Oh, I'm sorry to hear that,' she said sweetly, making Amy frown in confusion before comprehension dawned. Miss Swanley was clearly nursing an enormous crush on Mr Carter and she didn't want any threats from single mothers on the lookout for a father-figure for their children. Now that Amy had effectively ruled herself out of that category by mentioning Ben, maybe she would be in with a chance after all.

Amy's phone started to ring as she and Jennifer were loading groceries into the car at the supermarket two days later. It was a sunny, blustery day and Amy's hair swirled around her face as she put the phone to her ear. Jennifer finished putting the last of the bags into the boot as Amy took the call.

'Is that Mrs Osborne?' said an unmistakable voice.

Amy's heart seemed to stop. 'Yes, hello, Mr Carter,' she said in a hoarse whisper as Jennifer looked up, her dark eyes wide with expectation.

'I'm very pleased to be able to offer you the role of classroom assistant, if you would still like the job?' he said. Amy thought she could detect a slight nervousness on his part, but was too excited to let this register with her.

'Oh my God, yes!' she laughed. 'I mean, yes, thank you! I would be delighted to accept the role. Thank you, Mr Carter!'

In front of her, Jennifer squeezed her palms together and then clapped with excitement, before giving Amy a little thumbs-up. Amy thought Jennifer looked like the proudest mum in the world and for the first time in her adult life, she felt she had really achieved something worthwhile, and on her own merit too.

At the other end of the line, Mr Carter laughed. 'I think you can call me Ian now.'

'And you can call me Amy,' she replied, unable to stop the beam from spreading across her face. 'And Miss Swanley . . . what's her name?'

Ian Carter laughed again. 'Oh, I think you'd better stick with Miss Swanley!'

Chapter 34

Hugh was already waiting in the pub in Brickley by the time Jennifer arrived. She would have liked him to pick her up but she couldn't risk Amy seeing him and starting to ask too many questions, so she had driven herself there. She had felt like a naughty teenager that evening, furtively getting ready and sneaking out of the door without anyone seeing. It hadn't escaped her notice that it had used to be Amy who had been the one creeping out to meet boys, hoping her parents wouldn't catch her out. Now it was her sixty-year-old mother.

Jennifer had found herself shaking like a teenager too as she applied what she hoped was her most understated make-up, and dressed in a long, flowing moss-green skirt and fitted flowery top. Then, feeling too exposed, she had added a long, draped, pale green cashmere cardigan, which immediately made her feel more comfortable, yet still sophisticated. Her stomach fluttered with nervous anticipation as she pulled on her favourite knee-length boots.

Hugh had answered her call immediately: as if they had only spoken yesterday, instead of several months ago. She could tell that he had known without a shadow of doubt that

285

the call would come; that she wouldn't be able to keep away from him now that she had started something she couldn't possibly stop.

He was sitting in a booth, his head bent over a book and a half pint of beer on the table in front of him. She stood for a minute, watching him, before she approached. He had such a natural elegance about him, with his chiselled cheekbones and his aquiline nose; and his salt and pepper hair flopped forward and shone where it caught the light, while his long fingers toyed with the corners of the pages as he read. As she watched him, it was as if he sensed her presence for he looked up and, for the first time she could remember, he smiled at her properly. It was a slow, languorous smile but it transformed his face, and she felt a sudden urge to run into his arms and kiss him and never stop.

Instead, she smiled back at him and walked towards his table. There was a moment's hesitation as he stood up and bent to kiss her. She turned her head to the side but only slightly, so that his lips made contact with part of her lips. The effect on both of them was instant and electrifying and she blinked at him in shock, seeing that her expression was mirrored in his. 'Jennifer,' he said at last.

'Hello, Hugh,' she managed to stutter as she edged past him. She slid her bag onto the padded bench before shuffling in beside it.

'What can I get you?' The smile was gone but he looked happy and excited to see her, his eyes dancing as he spoke.

'I'll have a gin and tonic, please,' she said. 'But I'm driving, so that'll have to be it.'

Hugh nodded and made his way to the bar. Jennifer tried to pretend not to watch him but it was difficult to tear her eyes away: she noticed that all the other women in the pub were furtively shooting glances in his direction, too. The barmaid took his order with a flutter of her eyelashes. She was young enough to be his daughter and could probably have had her pick of men. *She can keep her mitts off Hugh,* thought Jennifer murderously, surprising herself with her venom.

She picked up Hugh's book. It was a battered copy of *Brighton Rock*: even his choice of reading material oozed cool. By the time he returned with their drinks, Jennifer had begun to feel old and dowdy.

Hugh placed her drink on the table and slid onto the seat opposite her, fixing her with his stare. 'You look beautiful,' he said. Instantly, her shoulders, which had sagged somewhat, began to straighten, her spirits lifting with them.

'Thank you,' she muttered, taking a sip of her drink and noticing with a start that several of the other women in the pub were now looking at her with a mixture of curiosity and admiration.

'I've missed you,' he said, speaking as if he was stating a fact, instead of describing how he was feeling.

Jennifer savoured the deliciously tart taste of the gin and tonic on her tongue as she thought about how to respond. 'Have you?' she said at last, knowing that her teasing tone belied how desperate she was to hear him tell her that again.

Hugh's eyes darkened even more as his pupils dilated. 'I've missed you as much as you've missed me,' he said.

Jennifer raised her eyebrows sardonically. 'Really?'

'Really,' he confirmed, still gazing at her with an unblinking stare.

Jennifer looked away, suddenly unable to bear his scrutiny a second longer. Her emotions were tumbling over each other; she hadn't expected to feel so unnerved by him again. She so wanted to be in control and had thought that having some distance from him these past few months would have helped her to do that, but it seemed to have had the opposite effect: it was as if being away from him had heightened her desire for him. Every nerve ending in her body seemed to be screaming out for him and, worst of all, she knew that he could tell.

They sat for several minutes in silence, the only sound the music that was playing in the bar and the muted conversations of the people around them. She watched as the ice in her drink began to melt with tiny cracking sounds, all the time aware of his brooding presence, and the fact that he never once took his eyes off her.

The music changed and she looked up at him sharply as 'Love Really Hurts Without You' began to play. Without blinking, he seemed to register the significance of the song. 'I remember,' he said softly.

'That first day,' she smiled, casting her mind back through the prism of decades. She was twenty-six again, sitting in a coffee bar on the Kings Road, trying to study, while an enigmatic stranger sat opposite her smoking and watching her: just as he was doing now. 'When did you stop smoking?' she said suddenly.

Hugh's eyes crinkled slightly. 'I didn't,' he drawled. 'Bloody smoking ban.'

Jennifer nodded, glad; although she didn't know why. Hugh suited smoking and now she too cursed the smoking ban. She used to love looking at him through the haze of cigarette smoke – it added to his film-star appeal and his sense of mystery, as if nothing with him was ever quite clear. As she thought about it, she realised that that was in fact the perfect metaphor for their relationship: always seen through a haze that distorted the true picture.

'How was your Christmas?' she asked, determined to try to regain some control over whatever was going on between them.

Hugh's eyes finally left hers and he looked away. 'Quite difficult, actually,' he said, in a staccato way, which suggested that it was hard for him to say the words.

'In what way?' Jennifer had never asked him much about his own life. Without ever saying so, he had made her feel that it was off-limits.

'My son ... he's had a rough time over the past few years. We're not particularly close but things had improved since ... well, since I had been coming down here to see you. I spent Christmas with him but as he had just broken up with someone and I wasn't seeing you ... well, we weren't very good for each other. Both too preoccupied with ourselves, I suppose.'

Jennifer nodded, intrigued. She felt a frisson knowing that he had been close by over Christmas without her being aware of it. She wondered if he had done what he used to do, and watched her from afar.

'Yes,' he said, his eyes narrowing slightly.

She mirrored his expression as she looked back at him. Was he able to read her mind or was he just a lucky guesser? He unnerved her so much and yet she felt so comfortable with him. She wondered how such a state could be possible.

'How was yours?' he asked, taking a long sip of his drink before leaning back in his seat as if he was settling down to listen to a good story.

'Don't you know already?' she replied cheekily, her mind reeling as she wondered when and where he might have watched her. She hadn't gone out much, beyond visiting Michael's grave or going to the supermarket. She recoiled slightly at the thought of being watched as she did either of those things.

'I don't think yours was much better than mine,' he said. Again, his tone was unequivocal. It wasn't a question.

Jennifer felt a shiver travel down her spine as she briefly relived the horror of a Christmas with a family who were all broken in some way or other. Only the children had brought any light into the dark, bleak picture. 'You're right. I missed you,' she blurted out, surprising both herself and Hugh, who seemed to flinch without moving a muscle.

Hugh reached out and cupped his hands around hers. It was such a tiny gesture but it was somehow erotic and intimate at the same time. She stared down at his fingers encircling hers and was struck by how similar their colouring was. Michael's hands had been large and fair, with a smattering of fine, pale hair; whereas Hugh's were dark and elegant, with long, slim fingers that seemed to perfectly reflect his exoticism.

'Jennifer, will you sleep with me tonight?' His voice was barely a whisper but she could hear him loud and clear, even over the banging of her heart within her chest. 'I *need* to sleep with you,' he added, and she could hear the agonised tone that emphasised each word.

She raised her eyes to meet his. 'I . . . can't,' she whispered back, already knowing that resistance was futile. She needed him and wanted him in turn. It felt as if she had been lifted up into a typhoon that was carrying her irrevocably towards something; she didn't know if it was her future or her destiny, but she did know that she couldn't stop it.

'Yes, you can,' he urged, the tips of his fingers beginning to caress hers rhythmically, turning her insides to pure, liquid lust.

'Where? How?'

Hugh shook his head slowly. 'Here. Now.'

Jennifer's forehead creased slightly in confusion as she asked the question without speaking.

'We have a room booked.'

A flicker of indignation was over-ridden by a wave of excitement. Thoughts of Amy and Ben and the children floated briefly through her head, before drifting away. They would be fine. She wasn't responsible for them. She was a free agent who could do whatever she wanted. And what she wanted to do was sleep with Hugh.

She picked up her glass and drained the last of her gin and tonic, knowing that Hugh was watching her, literally holding his breath as he waited for her response. She liked having that power over him – for once. She lifted her eyes to meet his and held them for a few moments before she finally spoke. 'Then let's go and check in.'

Chapter 35

Cuts in funding were affecting the NHS, meaning that Kate's workload was growing by the day. Already feeling low, the nature and responsibility of her work meant she was beginning to struggle: it felt like yet another area of her life where she had made the wrong decision. If she hadn't dropped out of medical school she would have qualified as a GP and by now she would have been earning very good money, with a fraction of the stress she was under in her current role. *And maybe I wouldn't have married Miles,* she thought, before pushing it crossly to a corner of her mind.

Every time she went to the supermarket where she had had the crash, she looked out for Jack's car, hoping that she might spot him. She never did. Their meeting had been a once-in-a-lifetime, chance encounter. He wasn't in the habit of going to Tesco, unlike her. His life was one of glamour and luxury. *One that involves getting the housekeeper to do the shopping,* she thought bitterly. One that might have been hers if she had taken another path. She knew that she would never accidentally bump into him again in the course of her humdrum, ordinary little life. If she wanted to see him, she would need to go out of her way to contact him; but that was something she couldn't bring herself to do.

Every day she ached to see him again, and she wondered how he felt about her. Was he as consumed by thoughts of her as she was of him? If she was honest, she was disappointed that he hadn't made any further effort to contact her after the initial emails, even though she had made it clear that he shouldn't. And he wouldn't know whether she might be with Miles or the children if he was to call, or if Miles might have access to her voicemail or texts if he was to try to contact her that way. In the end, she convinced herself that Jack must have decided to forget about her and get on with his life.

In contrast to her, Amy was already revelling in her new role at the school. She was popular with the children and the other staff, particularly Mr Carter the headmaster, who seemed to have taken a shine to her.

'Don't be silly,' Amy laughed, reddening, when Kate mentioned it to her.

'Why have you gone red, then?' Kate teased. They were at a coffee shop in the centre of town; Jennifer having agreed to have all the children for an afternoon while Kate and Amy went shopping.

In stark contrast to Amy's old life, she had very little spare money but she needed to buy some bits for the children, and Jennifer had given her £50 for her birthday, which she had insisted that Amy should spend on herself. Kate had never had any money so she was used to confining herself to window shopping, or tagging along with Amy while she bought whatever she wanted, so it felt a bit like old times to her.

Amy put a hand to her cheek as if checking for heat. 'Have I?' she muttered. 'Well, I don't know why if I have.'

'I bet I can guess why,' Kate said, eyeing her sister sceptically. 'And who could blame you? He's lovely.'

'So's Ben,' said Amy sharply, her smooth forehead wrinkling slightly as she took a sip of her cappuccino.

Kate bit her lip guiltily. As a nurse, she of all people should know that Ben couldn't help his illness but she also knew that she wouldn't have been able to cope with it as well as Amy had. She seemed to have endless patience with him, and Kate wondered how she would deal with Miles in the same situation. Would she have stuck by him the way Amy had stuck by Ben? Maybe. But maybe not. She loved Miles, but she didn't seem to feel the same all-consuming passion that Amy felt for Ben and that Jennifer had always had for her father. It made her wonder if it was her fault, and whether she should have held out for someone who really ignited her passionate streak. Someone like Jack.

'What's wrong?' Amy was looking at her curiously and, for a second, Kate worried that she might have been thinking aloud.

'Oh ... nothing.' Kate shook her head to try to disperse the image of Jack's face from her mind. 'Just remembering something.'

'I wish you'd confide in me!' Amy suddenly blurted out, sounding hurt and frustrated at the same time. 'I know there's something wrong with you, Kate. I've known since Christmas. And I feel like it's something to do with that guy. The crash guy.'

Kate looked back at Amy with an unblinking stare. 'Jack,' she said quietly. 'His name's Jack. And you're right. There has been something wrong and it is to do with Jack. I just didn't want to burden you any further.' She paused and then continued. 'You've had so much on your plate, what with Ben, moving house, the children moving schools and you starting your new job. The last thing you needed was me whining away about something that wasn't really anything, anyway. Nothing happened.' To her horror, she realised that giant tears were spilling from her eyes and running down her cheeks. Brushing them away in embarrassment, she repeated, 'Nothing happened.'

Amy reached out and took Kate's hand in hers. 'It wasn't nothing, Kate. If it's affected you this badly, it's very significant.' She paused for a moment to give Kate time to compose herself. 'Have you seen him again?' she asked gently.

Kate shook her head, her throat too constricted with tears to speak.

Amy's dark blue eyes crinkled in sympathy as she stroked Kate's hand. 'Do you want to see him again?'

Kate looked away and out at the street, thronging with shoppers on a busy Saturday afternoon. It was a lot like the day she had last seen him, the only difference being that instead of gaudy Christmas decorations adorning every shop window, there were now pretty hanging baskets of spring flowers instead. 'I don't know,' she shrugged at last. 'Yes, but no.'

Amy smiled. 'It's a strange one. Maybe if you saw more of each other, you would get over whatever it is you're feeling for him. But because your experience of him is so limited, it could be that you're building him up into something he's not.'

Kate fished in her bag for a tissue and wiped away the last vestiges of her tears as she considered what Amy had said. It was true that she knew very little about Jack, but she strongly suspected that seeing him again would only intensify whatever it was they had between them. 'I think I like that idea but for all the wrong reasons,' she said with a watery smile. 'It would give me an excuse for making contact with him again, and I just don't think I can risk it. I made the decision to put all my effort into my marriage and try to forget about Jack and, even though it's been incredibly hard, I do still think it was the right decision. I just couldn't do anything to jeopardise the children's happiness. And they love us both so much . . .' Her voice shook and she knew that if she carried on speaking, she would dissolve back into tears, so she stopped talking and took a deep breath instead.

Amy nodded as she contemplated her own situation and compared it to Kate's. She wondered whether it would make Kate feel better or worse if Amy confided how she had been feeling. In the end, she decided she had nothing to lose. 'The truth is . . . I *have* noticed that Ian Carter seems to have taken a shine to me,' she began. 'And I've got to be honest – I've been flattered and boosted by all the attention, however much I might deny it. During the day, I've got the headmaster of the school being all dynamic and inspirational and supportive, then I go home to Ben to find him slouching on the sofa aimlessly watching TV, or shuffling around the house in his scruffy old clothes. It's hard not to compare them.' She paused as Kate nodded. 'More and more, I've begun to fantasise about what it would be like to be with someone like Ian, so I can totally understand how you're feeling, Kate. But, whenever those fantasies start to get a little out of control, I always manage to rein them in by reminding myself that Ben might be unwell, but that he's still dynamic and inspirational at heart, too. What I mean is, I remind myself of all the reasons why I loved him so much in the first place. Maybe you should try doing the same with Miles?' She looked up expectantly at Kate as she finished speaking, her cheeks flushed with the weight of her admission.

'I have,' Kate replied wearily. 'But I don't need reminding of why I love him because I've never forgotten ... it's just that it's a steadier kind of love. Jack and I, well, we spent a lot of time emailing each other and I know it sounds pathetic but we had such a *connection*. We love the same books, the same films; we have the same hopes and dreams. It's like we're two halves of a whole. Even in the short time I knew him, I could tell that if I went for it, it would be passionate ... exciting,' she added, feeling embarrassed.

'Listen to me, Kate,' Amy said earnestly. 'You have no idea how many times I have wanted to swap places with you since Ben's breakdown. The thought of someone steady and reliable *is* exciting to me. And, don't forget, great passion can often mean great heartbreak too.'

Kate looked at Amy and thought how far she had come in such a short space of time. A year ago, she had been so absorbed in her own privileged little world she would never have been able to give her older sister such wise advice. 'It's not always the case,' she said quietly. 'Mum and Dad never seemed to have any lows in their relationship, and look at how crazy they were about each other.'

Amy raised an eyebrow and took a sip of her cappuccino.

'What?' prompted Kate. 'Why are you looking like that?'

Amy hesitated and, for a moment, Kate thought she wasn't going to answer. 'Well,' she said finally, 'it's just that, living with Mum; it's made me see her in a new light. I know she loved Dad very much but I definitely get the impression she's hiding something.'

Kate looked down and stirred her cappuccino. Clearly Jennifer hadn't confided in Amy about having to choose between their father and another man. The realisation pleased her and she felt bad for that. She was becoming a terrible person lately.

'And she's definitely up to something at the moment,' Amy continued.

'Like what?'

'She's seeing someone, I'm sure of it.'

'Another man, you mean?' Kate's mouth dropped open in shock. She certainly hadn't expected to hear *that*. Jennifer hadn't mentioned anything more about Hugh since their conversation weeks ago. Immediately, she felt hurt that her mum hadn't confided in her: she had felt certain that she would have done. 'No, that can't be right,' she decided aloud.

Amy shrugged. 'Well, why else would she start going out for dinner regularly without telling me who with and then—' she paused for dramatic effect, '—not come home until the early morning!'

'What?' Kate couldn't take it in. 'You mean she's been staying out all night?'

Amy giggled. 'Listen to us two! Talk about role reversal – it's the kids getting all het up about their mum sneaking out with a boyfriend and staying out all night! Shouldn't it be the other way round?'

Kate grinned back. 'True,' she acknowledged, still reeling from Amy's revelation. 'But, and without wanting to sound too Victorian about it all . . . are you *sure*? Could there be a more innocent explanation?'

Amy thought for a moment. 'No,' she said firmly, 'I don't think there could. I only spotted her coming home by accident because I couldn't sleep. I was standing at the window looking out. It must have been about five in the morning – she pulled up in her car and sneaked into the house all furtively. Then she pretended to get up as normal with me and the children at seven.'

Kate shook her head in amazement. 'And you didn't ask her about it?'

'I was waiting for her to mention it!' Amy said with a laugh. 'I couldn't believe it when she didn't say a word and acted as if she'd been in her own bed all night.'

'The dirty little stop-out!' said Kate mock-primly, then paused. 'How do you feel about it?'

Amy thought for a moment. 'A bit weird, actually,' she said, looking slightly bashful. 'In one way I'm glad because she could do with someone . . . but in another, well, it feels a bit like a betrayal of Dad—'

'It's been more than two years,' Kate interjected.

'I know, I know,' said Amy. 'But don't *you* feel a bit strange about it?'

Kate motioned to the waitress for the bill. 'Not strange, no. But I am fascinated. I wonder when she'll mention it to us?'

'*If* she mentions it to us . . .'

As they arrived back at Jennifer's cottage, both Kate and Amy were looking at their mother from a whole new perspective. Jennifer could tell she had been discussed and she felt herself getting flustered under the scrutiny.

'So, are you going out again tonight, Mum?' Amy asked, winking slyly at Kate as the three women congregated in the kitchen.

Jennifer, at the island worktop where she was rolling out pastry for an apple pie, looked up sharply. 'Er, yes, actually.' She avoided making eye contact with them both and immediately Kate understood.

'Anyone we know?' Kate asked mischievously, trying to convey that if it was Hugh, she was OK with it: Jennifer should trust her enough to tell her.

Jennifer looked at Kate. 'No, no one you know,' she said, giving Kate a stern look that told her not to reveal what she had confessed about Hugh to Amy.

Kate nodded slightly. 'Well, have a nice time,' she smiled, kissing Jennifer on the cheek to show her that all was well between them. 'I'd better get home. Miles and Josh will be back from the football shortly.'

'Everything OK with him?' Jennifer said, deftly dropping the pastry lid onto the pie and beginning to brush it with beaten egg. Kate almost laughed at the way they were all talking in riddles to keep their secrets from one another.

'Everything's . . . fine,' she replied carefully.

Jennifer pricked the top of the pie with a fork and popped it into the oven, before turning back to Kate. 'You seem better,' she said. 'Happier.'

Kate looked at Amy. 'I am,' she lied.

Chapter 36

'Wow, that looks fantastic,' said Ian Carter, as Amy stapled the last of a collage of Easter paintings by the children to the wall in the main hall.

Amy flushed, aware that her legs were level with Ian's eyes as she stood on a small step-ladder. 'Thank you,' she smiled, surveying her handiwork before descending the three steps. 'You're right, it looks great, even if I do say so myself.'

Ian laughed. She noticed as he did so that his teeth were white and even. 'So, how are you then, Amy? The children seem to have settled in really well.'

'They have,' Amy said, nodding as she began to tidy the remaining sheets of coloured card she had been using into the paper cupboard. 'Thank you so much for your help with them,' she continued.

Ian shrugged. 'They're lovely children. You've done a great job with them.'

'Really?' Amy smiled proudly. 'Thank you for saying that – it means a lot.'

'And what about the job?' he continued, sitting down on a nearby wooden bench. 'It seems to be going well – how are you finding it?'

'Oh, I love it!' Amy didn't need to exaggerate how much she was enjoying it to impress her boss. She got to do all the same things as Miss Swanley, but she didn't have the same frightening level of responsibility and, best of all, as she was the teaching assistant for the reception class, Sam was one of her pupils. Despite her being concerned that it might have been a problem, it was perfect: she was able to keep a close eye on him to make sure he was settling in OK and for Sam's part, he still hadn't got over the sheer novelty value of having his mummy as one of his teachers. She had never felt so fulfilled in her life, and was bursting with inspiration and ideas for the children. 'It's yet another thing to thank you for!' she said.

'Not at all.'

Amy closed the paper cupboard and perched beside him. 'No, seriously, it's changed my life, this job. My life in London ... well, it couldn't have been more different.'

'Tell me about it,' Ian said, his eyes glinting slightly.

Amy grinned up at him to buy herself some time. 'Oh God, I don't know where to begin. Well, it was a bit self-indulgent, if I'm honest.'

'Nothing wrong with that!' he interjected, raising one eyebrow.

'Hmm. I didn't think so at the time but now, looking back, I'm not so sure. We had a lot of money ... well, that's not strictly true. My husband had a lot of money.'

Ian nodded but said nothing, gesturing for her to continue.

'Well, we had a fabulous life. Beautiful house in an exclusive part of London, the children went to a great school ... Not that this isn't a great school!' she added quickly.

Ian smiled.

'And a great social life. We ate out most nights and I spent my days shopping and lunching. I didn't have to worry about a thing.'

'You must miss it.'

Amy ran her hand through her hair as she thought about it for a moment. 'I don't miss it at all, actually,' she said, surprising herself. She looked up at Ian. 'You know, I've only just realised at this very moment how empty it all was.'

'What happened to make it stop?'

Amy hesitated. 'My husband's company crashed, and so did he,' she replied at last.

'That must have been very tough.'

'It was,' Amy admitted. 'Still is, if the truth be told.'

Ian threw her a sympathetic look. 'Well, you certainly keep that under wraps. I would have had no idea there was anything wrong from the way you are at work. You're doing so well, and you're very good with the children, Amy.'

Amy felt herself reddening with pride and looked down, afraid she might cry. 'Thank you,' she said, with a small gulp.

'Have you ever thought about training to be a teacher?'

Amy looked up at him quizzically. 'No!' She laughed. 'I'm not clever enough!'

'You've got a degree, haven't you?' Ian shot back. 'And of course you're clever enough!'

Amy opened her mouth to speak but the words wouldn't come. She was reeling with shock, with pride and with something that felt very like excitement as the kernel of an idea began to take root.

'I wouldn't know where to begin . . .' she muttered.

'I could help you.'

Amy frowned. 'But you're so busy. And why would you want to do that, anyway?'

'Because I think you've got real potential. Maybe we should go for a drink or a coffee one day, to discuss it a bit further. If you want to, that is?'

'Er, yes, that would be great,' Amy stuttered, unsure how to respond. He was her boss, so she didn't want to appear rude but, equally, she didn't want to give him any kind of signal that she might be interested in him romantically. 'I'd better get on, Miss Swanley will be looking for me . . .' she added apologetically.

'Of course, but think about it, won't you?' Ian said, looking at her with an amused expression.

'What?' Amy suddenly felt self-conscious. 'Why are you looking at me like that?'

'You've got glitter in your hair,' he replied, using his fingers to flick it away.

Just as he did so, Amy caught a glimpse of Miss Swanley as she appeared in the doorway to the hall. Through the glass panel in the door, Amy could see the expression darkening on her podgy, pale face.

'Sorry to interrupt,' Miss Swanley said pointedly as she opened the door and came bustling into the room, looking to Amy's eyes as if she was positively quivering with pent-up fury.

Ian turned sharply to look at her. 'You're not interrupting anything,' he replied casually, but in a tone of voice that somehow conveyed that he was annoyed with her. 'What was it you wanted?'

Miss Swanley's eyes widened, her double chin wobbling slightly as she nodded furiously. 'I'm not interrupting? Oh, that's good. It was Mrs Osborne I was after, actually.' She emphasised the word 'Mrs' as if to make a point.

Ian stood up from where he was seated. 'Well, in that case I'd better not keep you any longer,' he smiled. Amy was sure he had also winked at her surreptitiously. 'Keep up the good work!' he added as he walked past Miss Swanley, giving her a wide, beaming smile as he went.

'Well!' Miss Swanley said, looking puzzled as she watched Mr Carter leave the hall. 'He seems to be in a funny mood.'

Amy checked that all the paper was safely stored away, and picked up her stapler. 'OK, Miss Swanley, show me what's next on the agenda,' she said cheerily, ignoring the older woman's suspicious gaze.

'Hello!' Amy bellowed from the flagstoned hallway as she and the children came through the front door after school. Immediately, Sam took off in the direction of his beloved garden, while Flora headed upstairs to start on her homework, just as she did conscientiously every day. 'Ben?' Amy called out as she shook off her linen jacket and hung it up on an old wooden hat-stand that had been there for as long as she could remember.

When there was no reply, she followed the sound of the TV into the sitting room and peered through the weak, early evening sunshine that was glinting through the French doors at the back of the room. At first she couldn't see anyone and was about to walk back out when she noticed a pair of stripy-socked feet sticking up from the deep recesses of one of the three squashy, stone-coloured sofas.

'Ben?' she said, more sharply than she intended. The feet didn't move, so she walked into the room and towards the end of the sofa, where she turned to face him. Although the television was blaring out loudly as Noel Edmonds entreated a large woman to open the distinctive red box on the bench in front of her, Ben was fast asleep.

Anger suddenly surged through Amy with the same force as if someone had switched on a power hose. She picked up the remote control and pressed the 'Off' button so forcefully that it actually hurt her thumb. As she did so, and the picture fled into a tiny white dot, Ben's eyes flashed open and he sat up suddenly, looking disoriented and shocked, as if he thought he might be under attack.

Amy's eyes narrowed as she looked at him. His dark hair was long and wavy and he had more stubble than looked either trendy or even deliberate. He was very thin in his dark navy T-shirt, and his jeans hung loosely around his hips. He looked like a faded boy-band member with a drug habit. 'Ben!' she said again, putting her hands on her hips without quite realising what she was doing. 'You've fallen asleep again with the telly on!'

Ben's face took on an insolent expression, which she had been noticing more and more recently. 'So?' he said rudely, in a voice that almost dared her to criticise him. 'And I'd prefer it if you didn't put your hands on your hips like that. I'm not one of your pupils!'

Amy gritted her teeth in fury. She had been in her new job for a month now and she was loving it. She didn't know if she would be able to take the pressure of being a proper teacher as Ian had suggested, but being a teaching assistant was perfect for now.

The only thing that wasn't working out so well was Ben's reaction to their change in roles. He was supposed to look after the children whenever Amy had to stay late to help prepare for the following day's lessons and to assist in after-school activities, but he seemed to have decided that his childcare duties were confined to walking to the school to pick them up and bringing them home. He refused to help with the cooking and seemed unembarrassed to let Jennifer prepare all the meals, saying simply that she was better at it than he. When Amy had suggested that he could help with the cleaning and washing as a way of earning their keep, he had simply laughed at her. As far as she could tell, Ben's days were spent relaxing in front of the TV or sleeping.

'He's depressed, Amy,' Jennifer had reminded her often, when she complained to her mum, more through embarrassment than anything else. 'I know how hard it is, sweetheart, but it will pass.'

'Are you sure?' Amy had pressed her. She had been patient for so long that she was beginning to wonder how much longer she could cope.

Jennifer would hug her tightly. 'I *am* sure,' she would say, looking into Amy's worried eyes. 'He will get back to normal. I can't tell you exactly when it will happen, but I can tell you that I'm sure it will.'

Now, Amy wondered if her regaining some confidence and starting work had had the unexpected effect of knocking back Ben's recovery. He had never seemed to mind that she didn't work but, now that she thought about it, she wondered if it was more than just because he wanted her to be there for him and the children. Maybe he had also enjoyed her lack of confidence because it made her more dependent on him and bolstered his own self-esteem? The worst thing was that she couldn't recognise the Ben she had loved so

307

much in the man in front of her. Every day that passed with him behaving like a selfish, spoilt child just made her feel more and more distant from him.

She knew for sure that even if Ben ever did get back to normal, it would take a very long time for their relationship to do the same.

Amy left Ben lying on the sofa – where he was already reaching for the remote control to turn the TV back on – and walked out of the room to go and find Jennifer. The kitchen was empty but the smell of shepherd's pie was wafting from the oven, making Amy's stomach rumble. She picked up an apple from the fruit bowl on the scrubbed wooden table and took a bite, before looking out into the garden, which was slowly coming back to life after a long, hard winter. *A bit like us*, Amy mused as she watched Jennifer and Sam digging in one of the flowerbeds together.

Sam had blossomed since coming to live in the countryside: it seemed to be his natural habitat. As Amy thought back over the past year to the previous spring, she realised that her mum had been right all along. However upsetting and difficult things had been, it did seem as though they would all come out of it on the other side much stronger, and maybe even much happier. Certainly the children were already more relaxed and content. They had settled quickly and easily into their new school – far more easily than Amy had dared hope. Flora had had a few shy days when Amy feared she might struggle but Josh was in the same class as she was, and he had quickly introduced her into the middle of everything. She was now part of a gang of four little girls who seemed to have become firm friends.

Amy had always felt that Sam would have been fine

wherever they went and so it had proved. It helped that he was so much younger than Flora and that he hadn't been fully established in his old school, but even Amy had been surprised at how quickly he had adapted. Flora was a deeper, more complicated child and Amy could now see what her mum had always said – but which she had always deliberately ignored – that she needed her parents' attention and time far more than she had ever needed a big house, nice cars or an expensive education.

As Amy watched Jennifer and Sam, Jennifer seemed to sense her looking and stood up and waved at her. Amy waved back and felt a lurch of the deepest love possible at the sight of Sam's little pale blond head bobbing around in the muddy flowerbed.

He grinned up at Jennifer as she said something to him, and nodded. Jennifer took off her gardening gloves and made her way back down the garden towards the kitchen where Amy was standing. At the back door, she paused to slip off the old clogs she always wore when she was working on the garden and came into the kitchen.

'Hello, darling,' she said brightly, walking over to the oven and bending to check on the shepherd's pie, before proceeding to the sink and washing her hands. 'How was your day?'

Amy nodded and smiled at the same time. It was so lovely to have someone show an interest in what she was doing and so good to feel that she was contributing to the wellbeing of her family. Days spent shopping and lunching with Jo had never left her feeling the same sense of satisfaction.

'It was great!' she enthused, flicking the switch on the kettle and setting out two mugs. 'I really love this job, Mum!'

Jennifer finished drying her hands and smiled warmly. 'And you're obviously brilliant at it too,' she said proudly. 'Sam's just been telling me that all the children in the class think you're "very pretty and very lovely" and that you're "the best teacher".'

'Did he really say that?' exclaimed Amy, feeling herself swell with pride as she glanced towards Sam, who was still using his tiny shovel to dig holes in the flowerbed, his little face a chubby mask of concentration.

'He did,' Jennifer assured her, coming to perch on a stool beside Amy at the breakfast bar.

'Well, guess what? Today Ian told me I should think about doing a PGCE and training to become a proper teacher.'

Jennifer's eyes widened with delight as she looked at Amy. 'But that's fantastic, darling! And he's right, you definitely should.'

Amy sighed. 'But it's not really an option, is it?'

'Why not?' Jennifer shot back.

'Because one of us needs to go out to work,' Amy replied, a trace of bitterness in her voice. 'If I were to do a PGCE, neither of us would be earning anything.'

Jennifer pushed a few stray hairs back from her forehead. 'I'm sure there's some kind of grant these days for anyone training to be a teacher – and it probably wouldn't be that much less than you're earning.'

Amy felt a little glimmer of hope start to ignite. 'Really?' she said, her mind whirling. 'But—'

'But what?' Jennifer interrupted.

'But we would have to stay with you for a lot longer than any of us planned,' Amy said quickly, looking at Jennifer to gauge her reaction. 'How do you think you would feel having us here on a semi-permanent basis?'

Jennifer was about to answer that it would be no problem at all when something made her hesitate. Although she loved having them there, it would mean she had no privacy to continue her relationship with Hugh.

'You see?' Amy said, clocking her mum's hesitation and smiling sadly. 'It's a pipe dream.'

'No, it's not!' Jennifer insisted, her mind suddenly made up. 'I don't care how long it takes, Amy. If it means you achieve your dream, you can stay forever as far as I'm concerned.'

Amy smiled, suddenly embarrassed. 'Thank you, Mum.' She got up and busied herself making two mugs of tea, one of which she pushed towards Jennifer. 'Something smells good,' she said, nodding towards the oven.

Jennifer took a sip of her tea. 'You need to give it another ten minutes and it'll be done.'

Amy looked at her in surprise. 'Are you not eating with us?'

Jennifer shook her head quickly. *Guiltily*, Amy thought. 'No ... I'm, er, I'm eating out tonight.'

'Again?' Amy frowned. 'And who with?' She hadn't meant the question to sound as nosy or as rude as it did but she thought it was about time Jennifer came clean about who she was seeing and what she was up to.

Jennifer wouldn't meet her eye. 'Oh, just with a friend,' she said, causing Amy to raise an expectant eyebrow, which Jennifer either didn't notice or chose to ignore. Instead, she took another sip of her tea, before taking the mug over to the sink, tipping away the rest and rinsing out the cup, which she left to dry on the draining board.

Amy watched her in puzzled silence. She really wanted Jennifer to confide in her about who she was seeing. 'Anyone I know?' she prompted.

Jennifer hesitated with her back to her daughter, as if she might be about to open up to her. Then her shoulders seemed to drop slightly. 'No,' she said, turning and looking at Amy with eyes that seemed to will her not to ask anything more, 'no one you know,' before leaving the room briskly.

Amy stared around the empty kitchen feeling nonplussed and confused. Jennifer was the one bedrock in her life at the moment: Kate was moody and down, just as she had been since way before Christmas; while Ben was distant and plagued by his own demons. If Jennifer was now going to start behaving oddly too, Amy honestly didn't know if she could cope.

SUMMER

Chapter 37

'You can't keep doing this,' said Hugh sleepily, turning over and opening one eye lazily as Jennifer pulled on her clothes in the pink-tinged dawn light seeping in around the curtains.

Jennifer didn't answer but pulled up the zip on her skirt and scrabbled around for her boots, which she found under the bed. Sitting back onto the bed to pull them on, she felt Hugh sitting up. He leaned towards her and wrapped his arms around her waist from behind, nuzzling her neck. Jennifer breathed in the scent of him: almost spicy, but not the artificial spiciness of aftershave. This was a raw, natural smell that seemed to have an immediate aphrodisiac effect on her. 'Don't,' she said half-heartedly as he planted tiny kisses on the back of her neck, sending a shiver of pleasure down her spine.

'Are you going to tell them?' Hugh whispered, his hands roaming up the front of her top. 'Or are you just going to keep me as your dirty little secret?'

Jennifer smiled. 'Yet another dirty little secret to add to the list,' she sighed, reluctantly pushing his hands away and standing up. She turned to look back at him in the dim light.

He looks ridiculously sexy, she thought. *Not at all like a man in his sixties.* Or was that just her impression? Maybe as you got older, you didn't notice the signs of age – you just continued to see yourself and your lovers as looking just the way they always had.

'When will I see you again?' Hugh asked, pushing back the sheet and standing up, entirely unembarrassed by his nakedness as he reached for his cigarettes and opened the window, before lighting up and leaning out to exhale into the still-chilly early morning air.

'Same time next week?' Jennifer gathered up her bag and hooked it over her shoulder.

'I can't do that. I'm supposed to be having dinner with my son.' He turned to look back at Jennifer and, noticing the look of disappointment on her face, he shrugged slightly. 'Sorry, but you aren't always available, are you?' Then, as an idea struck him, he continued, 'Maybe you could come too?'

'You've told him about me?' Jennifer asked in horror, her emotions tumbling over one another. Hugh had more or less moved in with his son now that he was regularly seeing her, so it made sense that he should have told him about her. But the thought still shocked her.

'Of course I've told him about you!' Hugh drawled, taking another long drag on his cigarette, before extinguishing it on the windowsill and flicking it expertly out of the window. 'How else would I explain where I've been all these nights?'

Jennifer blinked at him in confusion. He was right, but the thought of someone else knowing about their relationship made her feel uneasy. It made it feel more real; and more wrong, somehow.

'How did he take it?' she asked nervously, thinking of the reaction of her own girls and imagining for a moment how good it would feel to be honest with them. To trust them enough to tell them.

'He was fine,' Hugh said with a smile, closing the window and walking around the bed to where Jennifer was still standing fully clothed, her bag over her shoulder. She felt incongruous beside his nakedness. Hugh wrapped his arms around her and kissed her on the lips. 'I might go as far as to say he was happy for me,' he added, taking her hands in his and trying to pull her back down onto the bed.

Jennifer resisted for a few seconds, then allowed herself to fall on top of him, laughing with abandon as she did so. He made her feel so young again, so happy and so alive. 'I love you,' he whispered in her ear as he rolled on top of her and looked into her eyes. 'Marry me.'

Jennifer's mouth dropped open in shock. 'What?' she stammered. 'What did you say?'

Hugh's pupils dilated. 'You heard me,' he said quietly. 'I lost you once, Jennifer; I don't want to lose you again. Marry me.'

'But . . .' she shook her head as a million different reasons why it wasn't possible ricocheted through her mind. 'I can't. I just can't.'

'You can,' he said, in a matter-of-fact voice. 'But you won't. You won't admit to yourself or to your children that you've found happiness again.'

Jennifer opened her mouth to say something but the words wouldn't come. He was right.

'You're scared,' he added, as always reading her with stunning accuracy.

317

'I am scared,' she admitted, tearing her eyes away from his, which were probing her face with an intensity that left her feeling exposed. 'I'm scared of what the children will think. I'm scared of—'

'I know,' he said, kissing her lips gently. 'I know what you're scared of. And I'm scared of that too. But maybe it's time to confront it. Maybe it's time to be honest after all these years of lying.'

Jennifer shook her head fiercely as the tears began to fall. 'I can't do it to her, I just can't,' she sobbed as Hugh kissed away her tears. 'I'm not ready.'

'You'll never be ready. *I'll* never be ready and she'll never be ready. It's not something anyone can prepare for but we only have one life, Jennifer. I want to meet her, before it's too late ...' He tailed off and Jennifer's tears stopped abruptly as she looked up at him.

'Too late for what?'

Hugh cleared his throat. 'I just want to meet her, that's all.'

Jennifer rolled to one side so that Hugh slid off her, and she sat up again.

'Will you at least come next week? To meet my son?'

Jennifer's insides plummeted with fear at the prospect but she screwed up her courage. 'OK,' she said, looking shakily at Hugh. 'OK. Now, I really had better go ...'

Hugh sat up and kissed her on the lips again. 'Thank you,' he murmured. 'That means so much.'

Jennifer nodded as she stood up. 'I'll meet you both here at our usual time?'

Hugh looked at her. 'No, we'll go into town. I don't want anyone else knowing about here. It's our little secret,' he mused. 'Anyway, let's say eight o'clock – at Antonio's?'

'OK,' Jennifer agreed, scooping up her bag again and putting her hand on the doorknob. 'Oh, by the way,' she said. 'I don't even know his name.'

'Jack,' said Hugh easily. 'His name's Jack.'

Chapter 38

All the way home, Jennifer's mind reeled. It couldn't be. It couldn't possibly be the same Jack. It was the most common name for boys; she'd seen that in a survey somewhere. But something inside told her that it *was* the same Jack that Kate had fallen for. It was too much of a coincidence, and hadn't Hugh said that his son had been miserable at Christmas because he had just been dumped by someone he was very keen on? As the road ahead twisted and undulated before her in the glow of the slowly rising pale Suffolk sun, Jennifer thought how apt it seemed as a symbol for her life: just when she thought she was on the right path, it would twist again and take her off in a direction she didn't know she wanted to go.

And then there was Hugh's marriage proposal. It wasn't the first, and she strongly suspected that it wouldn't be the last. But there was something about the way he had said it this time: it was as if his patience was starting to run out. And he had been patient. So patient. He had waited a whole lifetime for her. *Kate's lifetime*.

Kate. Jennifer's insides turned to ice at the thought of how all this would devastate Kate. Not only might she find out that Michael wasn't her real father, but that her real father could be the man her mother was sneaking around seeing behind everyone's backs. And, oh God forbid: Jack, who Kate had felt such a strong attraction for, who had come into her life and devastated it with the impact of a nuclear bomb; Jack could, in fact, be her half-brother.

At the thought, Jennifer pulled the car into the side of the road and leapt out, already retching. Afterwards, she stood at the roadside, gulping in great lungfuls of air, leaning one hand on the side of her car to stop herself from fainting as an invisible metal band seemed to tighten around her chest. She looked around her, across acres of wide, flat, golden fields, trying to breathe slowly and deeply, hoping to find the answer to all her problems in the still dawn.

Then, as if someone had spoken, she heard a voice in her head, clear and crisp, telling her what to do. She nodded to herself, feeling calm again, and the band around her chest loosened momentarily. It was as if she was coming to the end of a journey.

Pulling into the driveway of the cottage, Jennifer saw the curtain in Amy and Ben's room twitch as if it had just been hurriedly closed again. She smiled to herself. Again, she felt that strange calmness that had come over her earlier. She knew that Amy had seen her before, sneaking home in the dawn light after a night of illicit passion with Hugh. It was time to stop pretending to both Amy and Kate. She hoped that they were old enough now to cope with the idea of her as more than just a mother and grandmother. That she was a person in her own right, with needs and desires that were just as strong as either of theirs.

She got out of the car and let herself into the cottage. All was quiet, except for the rhythmic ticking of the grandfather clock in the hallway, which showed six fifteen. As it was a Sunday morning, she didn't expect there to be any signs of life for at least another hour, when Sam would come bounding down the stairs, full of energy and vigour as he bounced into the new day with his usual sparky enthusiasm.

Instead of going up to her bedroom, she went into the kitchen, automatically reaching for the kettle that she filled and put on to boil. She stood looking out of the window onto her lovingly tended garden that had given her so much pleasure, especially since losing Michael. He had adored their garden and being in it made her feel closer to him. She sometimes felt as though she could feel him standing beside her as she dug and clipped and pruned.

'Morning, Mum,' said a voice, startling Jennifer from her reverie.

'Oh! Morning, darling,' she replied, feeling her face redden with guilt as Amy came into the kitchen. Jennifer watched her for a moment, struck by how fresh and beautiful she looked, dressed simply in a pair of white cotton pyjamas, her feet bare and her shiny blonde hair pulled messily into a scrunchy at the back of her head. 'You're up early,' she added at last.

Amy perched on a stool at the breakfast bar and smiled at Jennifer. 'Yes, but not quite as early as you,' she said, a note of mischief in her voice. 'And if I'm not very much mistaken, those are the clothes you went out in last night.'

Jennifer looked down as if noticing for the first time what she was wearing. 'It appears you might be right,' she agreed, taking a deep breath and looking up at her daughter. 'That might be because I stayed out all night,' she blurted out, looking at Amy with an expression that begged understanding.

Amy's eyes widened in surprise but she didn't say anything.

'Aren't you going to ask who I was with?'

Amy shrugged, looking uncomfortable and slightly embarrassed. 'I'm not sure I want to know, now that you're offering to tell me,' she said at last.

Jennifer's spirits plunged. Kate had seemed open-minded and encouraging about her meeting Hugh; she had somehow imagined Amy would be the same. But Amy had always been a daddy's girl, closer to Michael than she was to Jennifer: with Kate it was the other way round.

'Well,' Jennifer said, putting teabags into two mugs and filling them with boiling water. 'When you're ready, I'm happy to tell you.'

'OK.' Amy took one of the steaming mugs and added some milk that Jennifer passed her from the fridge. She couldn't meet her mother's eye and didn't really know why. Kate was right when she said that it had been two years now, and that Jennifer had been lonely since their father's death. Surely she should be pleased by the idea of her mum finding companionship, or even love? She was still relatively young and very attractive. Her life shouldn't be over by the time she reached her sixties. 'I think,' she said slowly, 'you should tell me and Kate at the same time. I don't want to know something she doesn't.'

Jennifer thought about it for a moment. 'OK,' she agreed, although she knew she would find it harder talking to Kate, now that she suspected that Hugh's son and Kate's Jack might be one and the same. *Maybe I should confirm that first,* she thought, suddenly glad of the reprieve Amy had given her. It could turn out that Hugh's son was someone different altogether. That she had been worrying about nothing.

Chapter 39

Kate glimpsed Sarah standing on her own across the playground and decided to grab the opportunity to speak to her. 'Hi, Sarah,' she smiled, jogging over to join her, feeling uncharacteristically nervous. 'I feel like I haven't seen you for ages. How are you doing?'

'Good,' Sarah nodded, glancing at Kate before turning her attention back to the classroom door through which the children would come bustling out in just a few minutes. 'I've been really busy,' she added, in a clipped tone.

Kate's spirits sank. She knew from the numerous unanswered texts and phone calls that Sarah had been avoiding her for months now, and it hurt her more than she could ever have imagined. She and Sarah had been such firm friends and had always been there for each other when things got tough. When Sarah had discovered that her husband was having an affair with his secretary and threw him out, she had been almost suicidal, but Kate had spent endless nights with her, letting her talk and cry until gradually she had started to come back to life again. Similarly, Sarah had been there for Kate when her dad died, and had seemed to know exactly what to say at just the right moment. Kate couldn't imagine how she would have got through the last couple of years without her support.

'Sarah ...?' she said as she followed the other woman's gaze towards the still-closed classroom door. 'I know something's wrong but I honestly don't know what it is ... Have I done something to offend you? Because if I have, I wish you'd tell me, so that I could at least apologise!' Kate could feel her voice wobbling as her emotions threatened to overwhelm her.

Sarah shrugged and pulled her jacket more tightly around herself, but still didn't reply.

'Please, Sarah, tell me what's wrong.'

Finally, Sarah tore her gaze away from the door and looked at Kate, her expression causing Kate to recoil slightly. She looked as if she would happily stab her if she had a knife handy.

'I think you know,' Sarah began, in an alarmingly deliberate voice, '*exactly* what's wrong.'

Kate flinched under Sarah's uncompromising stare. 'I don't!' she cried. 'I just know that you're avoiding me and that you're acting as if you hate my guts!'

Sarah's bright blue eyes narrowed as her blonde hair blew around her face in the warm breeze of an early summer's day. 'I don't hate you,' she began, again in the monotonous tone that was seriously beginning to scare Kate. 'But I *do* despise you.'

Kate gasped and took a step back. 'Jesus!' she whimpered. 'Why? What have I done?'

Sarah emitted a derisory snort. 'Yes, little Miss Goody-two-shoes ... who'd have thought it, eh?'

Kate took a shuddery breath and tried to think calmly. 'Look, Sarah, I promise you that I have got absolutely no idea what the hell you're on about . . .'

Just as she finished speaking, Sarah reached into her large, cream leather tote bag and began rummaging around furiously, before pulling out her iPhone. She started punching the screen with her finger – so aggressively that Kate could hear a succession of tiny thuds – all the while her mouth set in a thin line as her eyes scanned the screen. Finally, she gave a nod of satisfaction and turned the phone to face Kate, her eyebrows raised in two perfectly shaped arches. 'Maybe this will help to jog your memory?' she said, a sinister tone having crept into her voice.

Kate's eyes dropped towards the small screen that Sarah was thrusting towards her in an almost triumphant gesture. On the screen, she could see her mum's Clio, parked in an open-air car park in town. *Is that all?* she thought, beginning to relax slightly, when she noticed the two figures in the front seat, kissing. She felt her head begin to swim as realisation dawned.

'Look familiar?' snapped Sarah.

Kate closed her eyes and put her hand up to her forehead. This couldn't be happening.

'I think that's what's known as being banged to rights,' Sarah said icily.

'No.' Kate shook her head vehemently. 'No, it's not what it looks like at all.'

'That's exactly what my fucking bastard of a husband said when I confronted him with the evidence of *his* affair!' Sarah replied, her voice cracking slightly as she spoke.

Kate opened her eyes and met Sarah's, her heart

contracting at the pain she saw there. 'I know what you must think, after what Robert did to you,' she began, 'but I am not, and never have been, having an affair with Jack. Please, Sarah, you've got to believe me.'

'Ah, but that's the problem,' Sarah shot back. 'I don't believe you.'

Kate took another deep breath, her mind casting around for a way out of this hellish situation. 'How did you get those photos?' she said at last, trying to divert Sarah's attention in a different direction.

'I saw you, in town that day. You'd made such a big thing about wanting to go shopping on your own that I had thought it was suspicious. So I followed you,' Sarah said, matter of factly.

Kate frowned and shook her head, still struggling to understand.

'Well, I knew damn well there was something going on with you two – Jack more or less told me so himself!'

'No!' Kate cried in frustration. 'That's not possible. How could he have told you something that isn't true?'

'But it *is* bloody true, isn't it?' Sarah's voice had hardened again and she was looking at Kate in disgust. 'The camera never lies, Kate! Don't forget I've got experience of finding out cheating, fucking liars!'

Despite herself, Kate stole a glance around the playground to make sure none of the other parents was listening. To her relief they all seemed to be engrossed in their own gossipy conversations.

'Worried what other people might think, are you?' Sarah said nastily. 'I'd worry more about what Miles thinks if I were you.'

Before she knew it, a giant sob had escaped from Kate's mouth. 'No!' she said with a gulp. 'Please, Sarah, don't show him those photos. It'll only hurt him.'

'Shame you didn't think about how much it would hurt him when you were fucking someone else behind his back!'

'Sarah, *you* listen to *me*,' Kate said, pointing a shaking finger at Sarah and surprising herself with her vehemence. 'I have *never* cheated on Miles and I never would! Yes, I felt attracted to Jack and he said he felt the same for me but I told him – *that* day – that it could never happen. That I loved Miles and the children too much to hurt them and that we would have to put a stop to it before it began.'

'Yeah, it really looks like you were telling him that, when you were in the middle of snogging his face off!' Sarah sneered. 'You're a liar, Kate. Jack told me that you and he were having a relationship and that's why he didn't want to see me again. He said it wasn't fair!' She almost laughed, but Kate could still see how hurt she was by the look in her eyes. 'And how could you do that to Miles? He worships the ground you walk on and he loves you to bits – Christ, have you any idea how much I'd kill to have a husband like that? How millions of women would kill to have a husband like that?' Tears filled Sarah's eyes as she spoke. 'You are so bloody lucky to have someone who loves you unconditionally and who would never cheat on you. And what do you do? You throw yourself at the first available man who looks in your direction, *that's* what. You make me sick to my stomach.'

Kate could feel tears welling up in her eyes as Sarah spoke. She wiped them away quickly, still hoping that no one else would notice that they were having such a terrible row. 'Look, Sarah,' she began, trying to contain her emotions and calm her racing heart, 'I totally understand how this looks. But I swear on my children's lives that I did not have an affair with Jack.' She saw a flicker of hesitation and confusion sweep across Sarah's eyes. 'You know me better than most people,' she continued. 'So you know that I would never, ever swear on my children's lives if something wasn't true. Don't you?' she pressed, her eyes pleading with Sarah to believe her.

Sarah looked away. 'I guess so,' she said at last, after a long pause. 'But why would Jack say that if it wasn't true?'

'I don't know,' Kate replied honestly. 'All I know is that I told him that day that we couldn't see each other again and we haven't. You could have followed me every single day for the past few months and I wouldn't care, because I've got nothing to hide.'

Sarah's shoulders seemed to sag slightly. 'I just felt so hurt,' she muttered, her voice cracking.

'Oh, honey, of course you did,' Kate said, reaching out and putting her hand on Sarah's arm. She wondered if she would shrug her off but she didn't, so Kate left it resting there. 'I totally understand how it must have looked, but I put a stop to it before any real damage could be done.'

'I meant that I felt so hurt by him,' Sarah said, looking at Kate, this time with a slightly sheepish expression. 'I really liked him, you know.'

'I know, and I would have been so happy for you and him to have made a go of it. I feel terrible that he finished it.'

'Oh, well.' Sarah shrugged and gave a watery smile. 'I always knew it was you he was after all along.'

'I'm so sorry,' Kate said, meaning it. She would have given anything to force Jack to fall for Sarah. At that moment, the classroom door opened and children began filing through it, out into the sunshine. Kate gripped Sarah's hand, aware that she only had a few moments to say what she needed to say. 'But, Sarah, please don't show Miles those photos. It would destroy him. And it would destroy me. You're right that I'm lucky to have him and I'm going to do everything in my power to show him that from now on. Please don't do it.'

Sarah looked back at Kate for a moment as if weighing up what to say. Finally, she spoke. 'I just wanted to make you realise what you could have lost.' She looked away again as if she was considering what else to say. Kate's skin prickled uncomfortably as she waited for Sarah to continue; she didn't like the feel of this. 'Do you promise you will never, ever see Jack again?' Sarah said at last.

Kate nodded vehemently. 'Of course! I would have no reason to see him. I swear.'

'OK, well, good,' Sarah said, her tone softening.

Kate bit her lip to stop the tears that had flushed into her eyes from spilling down her cheeks. 'Thank you,' she whispered as Josh sauntered towards her, smiling shyly and looking like a miniature version of his dad, as if to emphasise what Sarah had just said.

Kate hugged him tightly, loving the smell of his hair and the feel of his warm body in her arms. 'Aw, Mum,' Josh complained unconvincingly. 'Get off!' As she let go of him, she looked up and caught Sarah's eye. 'Come on, Josh,' she said, 'I want to get home and cook Dad something extra special for supper tonight.'

Chapter 40

'What would you like to drink?' Ian asked Amy as they entered the pub. They had come to a quaint, 'olde worlde' place that was a few miles off the beaten track in a village called Brickley, where Ian lived.

'Er ... a gin and tonic, please,' said Amy, racking her brains for what to order. She had a feeling that her favourite tipple of a Bellini might not be on offer out here, in the middle of nowhere.

'Great, you take a seat and I'll get the drinks.'

Amy watched him striding towards the bar and looked around her in confusion for somewhere to sit. What the hell was she doing there? She had been honest with Ben about where she was going and he hadn't seemed to mind at all but she still felt guilty: as if she was doing something she shouldn't.

Ian had been persistent in asking her to go for a drink with him and she had felt under pressure to accept, even though she didn't particularly want to. Miss Swanley was clearly suspicious about their blossoming friendship and Amy didn't want to give her any more ammunition. Plus, although she thought Ian was great fun and the fact that he was so good at his job made him very attractive, she couldn't bear the thought of anything else coming between her and Ben. They were very slowly starting to get their relationship back on track, and Ben had started to emerge from the dense fog of depression he had been hiding under. He was starting to take notice of her and the children again and, more and more, she could see glimpses of the old Ben shining through. He smiled more often, spent less time sleeping and more time helping Jennifer around the house and garden. He had recently felt able to drive again too, and so was able to go to the supermarket, or drive the children to their after-school clubs.

'Here you go,' Ian said, placing a gin and tonic on the small wooden table she had chosen to sit at. The pub was fairly empty as it was very early on in the evening but even so, she still imagined that there were dozens of prying eyes trained on them from all directions as people wondered what they were up to. However, as she glanced around her quickly, all she could see was a fat, bearded old seadog of a man perched at the bar, staring unseeingly into his beer, and two middle-aged salesmen who were obviously booked in for the night and were already surrounded by an impressive collection of empty pint glasses.

'Thanks,' Amy muttered, feeling awkward.

'So,' Ian began, settling himself in the chair opposite her. 'How's it going? You can be honest now that we're not on school grounds,' he added, picking up his bottle of beer and taking a long sip. He looked at her with a wide, open smile and, once again, she was struck by the whiteness and evenness of his teeth.

Amy laughed and felt herself relax. 'I love it. Honestly.'

'And how about Miss Swanley? Are you enjoying working with her?' Ian's grey-green eyes danced with mischief as he spoke.

'She's . . .' Amy cast around for the right words to use: she didn't want to slag off her colleagues to her boss, not that Ian felt particularly boss-like. 'She's very passionate about the job,' she said at last.

Ian grinned. 'That's one way of putting it,' he replied. 'But, you're right, she's very committed to the job and she's very good with the children. It's just that we have had quite a turnover of classroom assistants working with her – I think she can be tricky to get on with. Believe me, I was so relieved when you applied.'

Amy's eyes widened. 'Do you mean to say that there weren't any other candidates for my job?' She could feel her hackles rising as fast as her confidence plummeted. She had felt so proud when they offered her the job: little had she known that no one else had applied because Miss Swanley had a reputation of being impossible to work with!

Ian's eyes shifted to the right, which Amy had once read was a sign that he was lying. 'No, not at all!' he said quickly, picking up his bottle of beer and taking another long sip as if to buy himself some time.

Amy didn't say anything. She just sat with her arms folded and looked at him, trying to keep her expression as neutral as possible. Sure enough, after an awkwardly long pause, he spoke. 'Well, OK, there *was* only one other candidate for the role.'

'Let me guess,' Amy said despondently. 'Mrs Skelton?'

Ian nodded and looked sheepish. Mrs Skelton was the mother of the school's most badly behaved ruffians, and she was as aggressive and rude to the children as she was to the other parents. But for some inexplicable reason, she applied for every job that came up in the school. 'As I say, you can't imagine how thrilled I was when you applied.'

'Glad I could be of some use,' Amy mumbled, feeling foolish. Of course she hadn't got the job because they thought she was brilliant. It was because she was the only candidate.

'No! Amy, sorry, you've got completely the wrong end of the stick,' Ian said, looking flustered as his words tumbled over each other. 'You would have got the job however many candidates there were—'

'Yeah, right,' Amy drawled sarcastically as she picked up her gin and tonic and took a hefty slug. The alcohol hit her instantly on her empty stomach and she immediately took another long swig, enjoying the taste and sensation enormously. It had been so long since she had drunk gin and tonic that she had forgotten how good it could taste.

'Seriously!' Ian cried, rubbing his hand over his face. 'You're very, very good, Amy! Even Miss Swanley seems to be happy with your work.'

'She hides it very well,' Amy replied bitterly, still feeling as if all the confidence that had grown inside her over the past months was now ebbing relentlessly away.

Ian shook his head. 'I promise you, if she wasn't happy with you, she would have got you out by now. She's very possessive of her pupils—'

'And very possessive of you,' Amy cut in, raising her eyes to meet Ian's.

Ian looked away, as if embarrassed. 'Yes, I suppose so,' he agreed. 'Pity she's wasting her time.'

Amy frowned, thinking it was a bit of a cruel comment.

Ian might not be interested in Miss Swanley but there was no doubting her devotion to him. She felt a pang of genuine sympathy for her irascible colleague.

'Anyway,' Ian said quickly, as if keen to change the subject. 'As I was saying, I've been very impressed by you, Amy. I seriously think you should consider training to be a teacher. You have all the right qualities and I know you'd be brilliant at it. Seeing you over these past few months, I can see what a natural you are.'

'Thank you,' Amy said quietly, unable now to get her thoughts into any kind of coherent order. A minute ago, she had felt like crap because she'd thought she had only got her job by default. Now Ian was telling her again that he thought she was so good that she could become a teacher. 'I don't know what to say,' she added.

'You need to think about it,' Ian replied. 'Talk to your husband. Your children. See if it's what you really want to do.'

'But ... the biggest issue is money. My husband isn't working, so for me not to be working either, even if it is only for a year or so; well, it's not really an option, is it?'

Ian's eyes widened. 'But that's the thing! There are all sorts of incentive schemes to encourage people to go into teaching these days. You would get money, but you'd also be getting a very valuable qualification.'

'My mum did mention something about that. But why would you bother encouraging me to become a teacher? It's no skin off your nose.'

Ian shrugged. 'A big part of my job is to nurture the staff and identify talent. I think you've got talent and, at the end of it, we could get a very good teacher out of it – if you were to come back to St Marks.'

Amy felt little bubbles of excitement starting to grow inside her. The idea of her having a proper, grown-up, responsible job was both terrifying and exhilarating at the same time. 'But I don't think I'm clever enough,' she said, thinking aloud.

'You've said that before,' Ian replied. 'And I don't know why you would think that. You're just as clever as any of the other teachers at the school – in fact, you're a damn sight *more* clever than some of them!' He pursed his full lips comically as he finished speaking, making Amy laugh out loud.

'Wow! Well, thank you for even suggesting it,' she said. Her spirits, which had been sagging only moments earlier, were now soaring with pride.

'My pleasure. Just give it some thought and talk to your family about it. But don't take too long – you could apply now and start in September.'

Amy lifted her glass and clinked it against Ian's bottle, all the earlier awkwardness between them now gone.

'Now,' said Ian, leaning forward conspiratorially. 'Obviously, I'm not doing this for entirely altruistic reasons ... there is a quid pro quo.'

'Oh?' Amy replied, her face crumpling into a despondent frown again. She should have known there would be a catch. She would always just be a pretty face.

'Yes,' continued Ian. 'I want you to tell me all the details of your fabulous life in London. I want to know all the amazing places you've been, the amazing people you've met and, most of all, I want to know if you've got any single friends you think might suit me?'

Amy almost squealed with delight. 'Yes!' she cried, clapping her hands together. 'Actually, there's this amazing woman who's a publisher. She travels all over the world but she's never had a chance to meet the right man—'

'Er, let me stop you there, Amy,' Ian interrupted her. 'Only I was rather thinking about whether you had any available single *male* friends?'

Amy gave Ian a peck on the cheek and headed for her car, having spent a very enjoyable couple of hours gossiping and regaling him with stories of her London life. He was such good company and, once Amy had known he wasn't interested in her romantically, she had been able to relax and be herself. She had two really good gay friends, Chris and Paul, in London, and spending this time with Ian had reminded her just how much she missed them. She thought she might take him for a night out on the town one weekend and hook up with them. Chris was in a relationship but Paul was single and, who knew? Maybe he'd be perfect for Ian.

She climbed into her car and started the engine. As she drove towards the exit of the pub's car park, she fiddled with the radio, trying to tune it into Radio 2. Once she found it, she looked up and, just then, out of the corner of her eye, she recognised a little silver Clio that was driving past her into the car park. She frowned and watched the car in her mirror, trying to read the number plate. She was sure it was her mum's car, but what on earth was she doing here, in this out-of-the-way place? Amy waited at the exit, poised to pull out onto the main road, still watching in her mirror as, sure enough, her mum climbed out of the car and closed the door, jauntily swinging her beloved Mulberry bag over her shoulder before striding into the pub, looking like a woman half her age.

Amy suddenly felt as if she was intruding on her mum's privacy by continuing to watch her, but she couldn't tear her eyes away. Jennifer was unrecognisable. She looked different. Younger. Excited. In love.

Arriving home, Amy was surprised to hear raucous laughter coming from the direction of the kitchen. She hung up her jacket and padded quietly to the door and peeped in. To her amazement, she saw Ben, wearing Jennifer's navy-blue-and-white striped apron, standing at the island in the middle of the kitchen, upon which Flora and Sam were perched, giggling as their dad attempted to make pizza dough.

'Zis ees how to make proh-per italiano pizza perfecto!' Ben announced in a ridiculously cod Italian accent, before picking up a slab of dough and attempting to spin it into a pizza base on the tips of his fingers, just as they had watched the chefs do in their local Italian restaurant back in Notting Hill. Predictably, his fingers split the dough and it slid down his arm in a squidgy mess. 'Oooh, I zeem to av made a loverly bracelet instead!' he cried as the children squealed with laughter. 'Or how about-a a beeeaaauuutifuuul hat?' he said, planting the ring of dough on top of his head, resulting in a little puff of flour rising from the top of his head.

'You look like you've got smoke coming out of the top of your head, Daddy!' giggled Flora, pointing at the flour cloud and covering her mouth with her hand to try to stifle her laughter.

'Mamma mia!' Ben exclaimed. 'Zen perhaps Mees Flora should wear my smoking-ah hat instead?' He whipped the dough off his head and held it out mock-menacingly towards Flora's blonde head.

'No!' Flora yelped as Ben deposited the dough onto her small head, where it immediately slipped down around her neck.

'Ha, ha!' yelled Sam, clapping his chubby little hands in delight. 'Flora's got a brand-new scarf!' at which point all three of them dissolved into helpless giggles.

Amy leaned against the doorframe, watching them. Ben – his face and hair smudged with flour – had never looked more handsome as he scooped up a child in each arm and began to spin them around the kitchen, dancing with them exactly as he had done when they were smaller. Before their whole world had fallen in on them.

Taking a step forward, so that she came into view, she caught Ben's eye, causing him to stop mid-spin. 'Oh, your beautiful mummy is home!' he said in his normal voice, smiling and gazing at her in a way that he hadn't done in months.

Amy returned his gaze, loving him more than she had ever loved him before.

Chapter 41

Jack and Hugh were already waiting in the restaurant by the time Jennifer arrived. She stood outside for a while, watching the two of them as they sat at a corner table, making occasional comments to one another but generally studying the menu, seemingly both lost in their own thoughts.

She could tell that they were father and son. Hugh was darker than Jack. Darker eyes, darker skin, darker hair. But they had the same nose and the same full, sensuous mouth. Both were tall and slim but, again, Jack's edges weren't as sharp as Hugh's. He was strikingly handsome, and Jennifer found herself shaking at the prospect of coming face-to-face with him.

Taking a deep breath, she pushed open the door and walked in, smiling politely to the maitre d', before making her way over to where the two men were sitting. Hugh spotted her first and stood up. As he did so, Jack turned his head and looked at her for a couple of seconds, before doing the same.

'Hello, Jennifer,' said Hugh, looking more awkward than she had ever seen him look before. He motioned with his hand towards Jack. 'This is my son, Jack. Jack, this is Jennifer.'

Jennifer looked up at Jack who, just like his father, tow-ered over her. 'Hello, Jack,' she said, smiling, taking his cool, smooth hand in hers to shake it. 'Pleased to meet you.' His long fingers gripped hers, reminding Jennifer of Hugh's beau-tiful, artistic hands.

'Likewise.' Jack smiled back. Although his eyes were a slightly different colour to his father's, they had the same mischievous glint and depth. 'I've heard so much about you,' he added, as they all sat down.

Jennifer felt herself reddening as she wondered just how much Hugh had told his son. 'Really?' she arched her eye-brows at Hugh, who was looking sheepish.

'Oh, don't worry – it's all good,' Jack laughed, glancing from Jennifer to his father.

'Good!' Jennifer picked up the menu and began to study it, in an attempt to calm her racing heart. She felt short of breath and slightly sick: just as she had felt all week. It was such a strange and unfamiliar situation to find herself in with Hugh. Their relationship had always been conducted in the shadows, without anyone else knowing, and it felt raw and disconcerting that someone else apart from them was now being brought into it.

She stole a glance at Jack over the top of her menu and tried to work out if he could be the same Jack that Kate had fallen for. He was definitely handsome and had the same eas-iness with himself that Hugh had always had. But he was softer and gentler than Hugh, who had always exuded a cer-tain hardness and danger. She could see why Kate would have found him attractive, especially compared to Miles who, although he was still a good-looking man, had let his looks go slightly by putting on weight.

'What do you do, Jack?' she asked, after a while.

Jack lifted his long-lashed, brown eyes and looked at Jennifer. 'Advertising,' he said, slightly apologetically.

Jennifer looked from Jack to Hugh in confusion. 'The same as you?'

Hugh nodded. 'Took over my agency, when I finally decided to pack it all in.'

'Ha!' laughed Jack mock-sarcastically. 'He'll never pack it in.' He looked at Jennifer as he spoke. 'He's too much of a control freak.'

'Not true,' Hugh countered good-naturedly. Jennifer sat back and watched them in amusement as they began to banter back and forth. Hugh had always said he had a difficult relationship with his son, but they seemed to her to be at ease with one another.

'But it must all seem a bit pathetic to you, anyway.' Jack returned his eyes to Jennifer during a lull in the banter. 'Dad says you were a doctor. That's a proper job, isn't it?'

'Oh, I don't know,' Jennifer sighed. 'There are plenty of times I would have longed for a bit of mindless excitement. The medical profession can be a bit wearing sometimes.'

Jack nodded. 'I knew someone who worked as a nurse . . .' He paused and seemed to catch himself for a moment, before finishing: 'I've just got so much respect for anyone who does your job.'

Once again, Jennifer felt as if there was a metal band around her chest that was tightening by the second, and a wave of nausea washed over her. The coincidences – if that *was* what they were – were stacking up.

'Are you OK?' Hugh said quietly, as Jack excused himself and went to the bathroom. 'You seem a little tense. Well, you always seem a little tense,' he smiled at her to take the sting out of the words. 'You seem a little more tense than usual,' he finished.

Jennifer took a deep, shaky breath. 'I don't know. I feel a bit strange. I don't know if it's the stress of meeting Jack or something, but I just feel a bit—'

Her last memory before everything turned black was of Hugh's voice coming to her as if from down a long tunnel, sounding slurred and in slow motion.

'Jennifer! Jennifer, can you hear me?'

Jennifer tried to open her eyes but her lids felt too heavy. She opened her mouth to speak but her lips and throat were so dry that they wouldn't make any sound. She could hear distant voices echoing all around her and had the sense that she was being wheeled along a bright, bright corridor: even though she couldn't open her eyes, the light was still burning into her lids. Someone took hold of her hand and she managed to squeeze it, to show that she was aware, even if she didn't appear to be responding.

'She just squeezed my hand!' said the voice excitedly and she realised it was Hugh, although he sounded very different to his usual slow drawl. The thought that he was with her made her feel strangely calm and comforted, even though it was clear something bad had happened. 'She definitely squeezed my hand!' he said again, squeezing Jennifer's hand back.

'That's good,' said another, much steadier voice as they continued their clattering journey through noisy corridors, banging through endless sets of swing doors that each swished a tiny breeze over Jennifer's face as they passed. 'Is there anyone you need to ring? Anyone else she might want here?'

'Yes!' Hugh said quickly. 'Her daughters. But I don't have their numbers . . .' He tailed off helplessly.

Jennifer squeezed his hand again to try to tell him to look in her phone's address book but, instead, he just squeezed back and stroked her forehead. 'You're going to be fine, sweetheart,' he murmured.

'Have you got her phone?' said the calmer voice, and Jennifer felt relief seeping through her.

There was a pause while Hugh let go of her hand and she could hear him rummaging through her bag. 'Yes!' he said triumphantly, after a few seconds.

'Why don't you call them?' said the voice.

There was another pause.

'Really. She'll be fine.'

'OK,' Hugh agreed reluctantly, picking up her hand and kissing it. 'I'll be with you in just a few minutes, darling,' he said, before releasing her hand. She felt his presence disappear as she continued on her journey to wherever the hell it was that she was going.

Chapter 42

Kate was washing up when the phone rang. Sunday nights were the busiest of the week in their house as she and Miles tried to get everything ready for the week ahead. Between them, they had to make sure the children's uniforms were clean and ironed and that they had done all their homework. Then she had to sort out her own uniform and Miles's work shirts, as well as planning menus for the week and writing shopping lists of whatever food they needed. It used to be that Miles would leave it all to her but he really had become a changed man: cooking, ironing and helping around the house as much as he could. So she was distracted and hoping that it wasn't someone wanting a long chat as she dried her hands on a tea towel and picked up the phone. She looked at the screen. 'Hi, Mum!' she said brightly, bending down and opening the cupboard under the sink to look for the children's lunch boxes.

'Er, it's not your mum,' said a deep, male voice that sounded strangely familiar. 'It's your mum's friend, er, Hugh.'

Kate's heart skipped with alarm as she registered that he wouldn't be calling her if it wasn't something bad. 'Yes?' she snapped, panic making her sound much more brusque than she intended. 'Sorry, I mean, hello, Hugh. Is everything OK?'

'Um, not exactly, no,' he stumbled, his voice sounding hesitant.

'Shit! Is it Mum?' Kate couldn't contain her panic any longer. She felt tiny beads of sweat breaking out on her forehead. She stood up from where she had been crouching in front of the sink and tried to take a deep breath to calm herself.

'Yes, I'm at the hospital with her. She's had a bit of a funny turn.'

'What *sort* of a funny turn?' Kate immediately felt impatient at his hesitance and his lack of clarity.

'I'm not sure,' he replied, sounding sheepish.

'Well, what were the symptoms? Describe to me what happened.' Kate's words came out like the snapping of an elastic band as she fired off her questions.

Hugh sighed on the other end of the line. 'Well, she said she felt woozy and a bit sick, then she seemed to pass out, and—'

'Pass out? Shit. Right, I'll be there as quickly as I can,' Kate interrupted him. She began to hang up, already thinking about what she needed to get to the hospital quickly.

'Kate?' he said, suddenly sounding forceful and making her jump slightly.

Kate put the phone back to her ear. 'Yes?'

'She's fine. Don't panic, and drive safely.'

Kate nodded, touched by his thoughtfulness. Miles came into the kitchen as she ended the call. 'What's up?' he said, frowning with concern as he looked at her fraught face.

Kate ran her hand through her hair and tried to focus on

what she needed to do. 'It's Mum,' she said, looking up at Miles and feeling a desperate need for some reassurance and support. 'She's had some kind of turn and is in hospital.'

Miles immediately enveloped her in his arms and squeezed her tightly. 'Oh God. OK, you go on ahead to the hospital. I'll call Sarah and get her to have the kids, and I'll follow on behind you.'

Kate's hammering heart began to slow slightly as Miles calmly collected the car keys and her handbag and led her out to the car. In a daze, she got into the car and started the engine. Suddenly, a thought struck her. 'Miles!' she called, rolling down the window. Miles turned and came jogging back to the car. 'I need to tell Amy!'

Again, Miles nodded calmly. 'Don't worry. I'll call her and tell her to be ready. You can collect her on the way.'

Kate nodded, grateful for his calm practicality, and drove off in the direction of Jennifer's cottage. By the time she got there, Amy was waiting at the gate, looking pale and worried.

'Oh God, what's happened?' she said, clambering into the passenger seat and slamming the door behind her.

'I'm not sure.' Kate tried not to sound too panicky. She knew Amy would take her lead from her and she didn't want to scare her any more than was necessary. 'Hugh said she'd had a "funny turn".'

'Hugh?' Amy scowled. 'Who's he? Her secret lover?'

'Not so secret any more,' Kate replied, trying to focus on the road so that she didn't let her panic affect her driving. 'Anyway, he's with her. He just called and said she'd had a funny turn, whatever the fuck that means. Oh, Amy!'

she gulped, tears suddenly spilling from her eyes and blurring her vision. 'I think she may have had a heart attack!'

'Oh my God!' Amy said again, but then her large eyes widened and she suddenly yelled, 'Pull over, Kate! You're driving really erratically!'

Kate opened her mouth to object but her sobs were convulsing through her by now and she swerved to the side of the road, putting on her hazard lights and turning off the engine. She reached across to Amy who leaned into her and they sat holding each other, both crying helplessly with fear for a few minutes.

Eventually, Kate let go of Amy and swallowed hard. 'This is stupid!' she said, wiping her face with the back of her hand. 'It's not doing Mum much good us sitting here, bawling. And I'm sure she's fine – we'll probably get there to find her sitting up in bed eating toast!'

Amy grinned slightly and nodded, wiping her own face. 'Yes. Come on – let's just get there as quickly as we can. I'll drive.'

The hospital car park was surprisingly full for a Sunday evening as Amy drove around under the sulphur glow of the orange lighting, searching for a space. 'There's one,' said Kate, pointing. Amy swung the car into a space between a Volvo and a Mini. They tumbled out of the car and dashed towards the sign for A&E. Kate strode towards the desk, where she recognised the receptionist from when she worked in the hospital.

'Oh, hi, Kate!' said the woman, looking up at her in surprise.

'Hi, Anne. My mum's been brought in tonight. Any idea

where she might be? Her name's Jennifer Wheelan.' Kate was pleased that her voice sounded so steady whilst her insides were being torn apart in panic.

The receptionist lifted the glasses that hung on a chain around her neck to her eyes and scanned her list. 'Ahh, yes,' she said. 'She's been taken up to Connaught.'

Kate's insides clenched with fear. 'So, it's a suspected heart attack, then?'

Anne looked up at Kate with an almost pleading look in her eye. 'I don't know,' she shrugged helplessly. But Kate knew herself that Jennifer wouldn't have been taken there if it wasn't. Connaught was the coronary care unit Kate had worked on as a nursing sister before taking up her role as heart failure specialist.

She hesitated – aware that Amy was watching her – before she turned around again. Amy looked so small and scared as she gazed at Kate. 'OK, I know where she is. Let's go,' Kate said as cheerfully as she could.

'Is she going to be OK?' Amy asked, her voice wobbling badly.

Kate nodded briskly. 'I'm sure she is. Come on, let's go and find her.'

Amy followed dutifully as they made their way through the long corridors that Jennifer had travelled less than an hour previously. As they reached Connaught ward, Kate reached out and gripped Amy's hand, as much for her own benefit as for Amy's. They both came to a halt at the nurses' station, where a pretty young Asian nurse was filling out some kind of form.

'Hi!' said Kate, over brightly, fixing the nurse with a confident smile. She didn't recognise her from her time on the ward and suspected she was relatively new. 'Jennifer Wheelan's been brought up here, I believe?'

The nurse's eyes dropped for a second. 'Yes, she's in a private room. Are you her daughters? I'll get the doctor to come and have a word.'

Amy and Kate looked at each other. Both too choked to make any sound, they nodded mutely and headed off in the direction the nurse had indicated.

As they made their way down the corridor, there was an, 'Excuse me!' from behind them, and the doctor came towards them. He had a handsome, boyish face and wild, dark hair that made him look barely old enough to have completed medical school. 'We suspect your mother has had a heart attack and had a cardiac dysrhythmia, causing her to pass out,' he said in a surprisingly deep, smooth voice. 'We need to keep her monitored. The first twenty-four hours are critical.'

Kate had heard herself uttering these words many times before, but it was so different now that she was on the receiving end of the news. 'Can I see her ECGs?' she asked. The doctor nodded.

The door to Jennifer's room had a marbled glass panel in the middle, through which they could make out the shadow of a man and hear muted voices. Kate took a deep breath and opened the door. As she did so, three pairs of eyes turned towards her. She took a second to register that the third pair of eyes were a familiar brown, framed with long, sweeping lashes. A pair of eyes that she had committed to memory and had thought about so many times over the past few months.

'Jack,' she said breathlessly, concerned for the moment that she might be about to have a heart attack herself.

It seemed as if everything and everyone in the room was suspended in time: neither moving, speaking nor breathing. Jack's face had drained of colour as he looked at Kate in shock, his mouth slightly open. 'Kate,' he whispered.

Amy's face creased in confusion. 'Do you two know each other?' she asked, her eyes darting from one to the other.

Hugh frowned as he tried to compute what was going on. 'Is this . . . her?' he asked Jack. 'It was Jennifer's daughter?' he asked again, as his face filled with dawning comprehension.

Tension hung thick and heavy in the air as everyone in the room tried to make sense of what was happening. 'I didn't know she was Jennifer's daughter,' Jack said at last, as much to himself as to the others. 'How could I have known?'

No one answered and Kate's heart continued to hammer with a mixture of shock and fear. Finally, she seemed to come to as she remembered why she was there. Shaking her head as if to clear her mind, she dragged her gaze away from Jack and went over to Jennifer, who was propped up on pillows in the bed. 'Hello, Mum,' she said, kissing the top of Jennifer's head and taking her hand. 'What's all this about, then?' she continued, already feeling tears of relief starting to trickle down her face. Jennifer's skin was grey and she looked dog-tired, but at least she was awake. Kate had expected to find her unconscious. Or worse. Much worse.

Jennifer squeezed her hand weakly. 'I'm not sure,' she croaked in a slow, groggy voice. 'I just had a really strange feeling, as if I had a tight band around my chest, and I was struggling for breath a bit. Then, the next thing I remember, I was here.' Her voice tailed off to a whisper as she finished speaking, as if the exertion was too much for her, and she closed her eyes again.

Kate stood rooted to the spot, watching her closely as a fist of fear seemed to punch her in the stomach. She didn't like the look of this.

After a few moments' silence, Jennifer opened her eyes again and sought out Amy, who was still standing stock-still by the door, looking scared and confused. 'Come here, darling,' she murmured.

Obediently, Amy walked into her mum's embrace and bent down to kiss her on the cheek as Kate shuffled to one side to make room. 'We were so worried!' she said with a gulp. 'We thought—'

'Shhh,' Jennifer interrupted, again in an alarmingly slow, groggy voice, stroking Amy's silky blonde hair. 'I'm fine. No need to worry.'

Amy began to sob into Jennifer's chest as the other three gazed on in awkward silence.

Finally, Kate looked up at Hugh. She was struck by how incredibly handsome he was, despite his age. 'Hello,' she said, standing up and shaking his hand. 'I'm Kate.'

Hugh's dark eyes examined her intently. 'Hugh,' he murmured, in a voice that reminded Kate of melted chocolate. She could see why her mum had fallen for him. She felt his long fingers wrap around her own and was reminded of Jack's beautiful, elegant fingers. Looking down at her hand interlocked with Hugh's, she suddenly twigged. 'You're Jack's father?'

Hugh held her hand for a long moment. 'Yes,' he said, 'I'm Jack's father.'

Kate dropped his hand and turned awkwardly to face Jack, who was still staring at her in shock. 'Well, I didn't see this one coming!' she said with a grimace, her eyes darting from side to side until eventually, inevitably, they met his. A tingle ran down her spine as she held his gaze, unable to look away. She had thought about him so much over the past few months that she had wondered if she had imagined him into something he wasn't; whether her memory had exaggerated what he was. But, watching him now, she realised that her memory had, if anything, made him more ordinary than he really was.

Behind her, she heard Jennifer speaking gently to Amy, reassuring her, and she jolted as she remembered again why she was there; why she was in that tiny room with her mother's lover and his son, who so very nearly had been hers.

She spun round and walked over, stopping behind Amy and putting her hands on her narrow shoulders, which were still shaking with sobs.

Jennifer looked exhausted but she gazed up at Kate with an apologetic look in her eye. 'I'm sorry,' she whispered. 'I should have warned you.'

Kate shrugged. 'You couldn't have known.'

'*But I did know!*' Jennifer wanted to shout but she was too tired. She didn't have enough energy. Instead, she allowed her drooping eyelids to close.

Calmer now, Amy took a deep breath and nodded, as if she was giving herself a good talking-to. 'Maybe we should leave her to get some rest?' she said, looking at Kate.

Kate watched Jennifer, her silver hair spread out on the stark white pillow like a fan, and agreed. 'Yes, let's go and get some coffee.' She glanced at Jack and Hugh, who were looking on awkwardly, as if they didn't quite know whether to stay or go. 'Shall we all go?'

Hugh hesitated and his face flickered with concern as he

gazed at Jennifer, who was by now sleeping soundly, her lips parting gently with each rhythmic outward breath.

'She'll be fine,' Kate told him, surprised that she already felt a need to reassure and protect this total stranger. 'There's nothing any of us can do tonight.'

Hugh nodded. 'OK. I need a cigarette, anyway,' he said, as they filed out of the room.

Chapter 43

'Well, this is weird,' said Jack, sitting down opposite Kate in the empty cafeteria. He had two pale brown plastic cups full of anaemic liquid, which Kate assumed was coffee, in his hands, and he slid one across the red Formica table towards her. Amy had gone outside with Hugh, supposedly to phone Ben and let him know that Jennifer was going to be OK, but Kate also knew she was being tactful by letting Jack and Kate have some time alone.

'We must stop meeting like this.' She tried to smile but her voice sounded strained. She had been starting to feel better about Jack but now, immediately, felt as if she was right back to square one. And discovering that his father was Hugh, the man who had managed to captivate her mother all those years ago and had captivated her again now, had thrown her into a mental turmoil.

'Did you know?' she asked, after a few seconds.

'Of course not!' he protested, looking hurt. 'Jesus, Kate, this is as much of a shock for me as it is for you.'

'It's certainly that,' she agreed. Her insides were dancing with nerves and something else that she couldn't identify.

'But I can't say I'm sorry. I haven't stopped thinking about you,' he said, reaching out his hand so that it settled just a few centimetres away from hers. Kate noticed how similar their hands looked, lying next to each other on the table top. They had the same olive skin and they both had long, elegant fingers. She longed to touch him, even for a second, but she already knew that would be a mistake.

'I know,' she said, throwing him a furtive glance as if she was terrified to look at him properly in case he somehow drew her to him even more. 'I've been the same.'

'Couldn't we just ...?' He tailed off as if he couldn't think how to finish the question.

'No,' she said quickly. 'You know I can't see you.'

'How about email?' he smiled sadly. 'Is that allowed?'

Kate thought for a minute. 'It's allowed. Well, I mean, there's no one actually stopping us. But really, Jack, why? It's only putting off the inevitable. We can't just be friends. I don't *feel* like we can be just friends,' she corrected herself.

'No. I don't want to be your friend,' he said, drawing her gaze upwards until she was held in his muddy stare. 'Why did you have to crash your bloody car that day?' he said as he laughed sadly. 'I was fine until I met you.'

'No, you weren't!' she replied as she smiled back.

'Well, OK, no, I wasn't,' he agreed, grinning slightly. 'But of all the bloody women in the world ... why did I have to fall for the one I can't have?'

Kate felt a swell deep inside her. It seemed to surge upwards towards her heart and she knew that it was in danger of bursting out through her mouth in a torrent of things she shouldn't say. She closed her lips together in a firm line as if determined to prevent anything escaping but, instinctively, moved her hand a fraction closer to his, so

357

that their fingers were almost touching. Almost, but not quite.

They stared down at their hands, both slightly stunned by the effect being in such close proximity was having on them. Kate had never experienced such pure desire before and, judging by the look on Jack's face, she sensed he was feeling the same.

'I wondered where you were!' said a voice above them, suddenly.

Kate snatched her hand guiltily away from Jack's, placing it flat against her chest in a defence gesture. 'Miles!' she cried, too loudly and too shrilly.

Miles looked at Kate curiously, before peering at Jack. 'Jack? What are you doing here?'

Jack stood up and held out his hand to shake Miles's. Miles took it reluctantly, frowning under his blond fringe. 'Shall I tell him or shall you?' Jack said, turning to Kate, who had now stood up, too.

'Tell me what?' Miles's voice had taken on a steely edge and Kate gasped slightly in fright.

'Nothing!' she said quickly as both men looked at her.

'Tell me what?' Miles said again, this time sounding as if his voice was being compressed; as if he wanted to know but didn't want to hear whatever her answer was going to be.

Kate put her hand on his arm and gestured for him to sit down: her legs were shaking so it was as much for her own benefit as his. Miles, still frowning, eventually sat down beside her. Jack hesitated, unsure whether to stay or go, before he, too, sank down, into the chair opposite them.

Kate took a deep breath as her heart continued to bang in

her chest. She felt so guilty, as if she had been caught doing something she shouldn't. 'It's just that ... when I got here this evening, Jack was already here. With his father—'

'What? I don't know what you're talking about!' Miles snapped in frustration. He was obviously expecting Kate to confess to having had an affair and wanted her to get to the point.

'Shhh. I'm explaining,' Kate continued. 'Jack's father is the man Mum has been seeing.'

Miles's frown deepened and a mask of incomprehension covered his wide, open features. 'As in a doctor, you mean?'

Kate smiled and shook her head. 'No! Not a doctor, silly. I mean romantically. As in a lover ...' She could feel herself reddening as she spoke, aware of Jack's gaze.

A tiny light of comprehension ignited in Miles's eyes. 'But ... how come ...?' He tilted his head in Jack's direction without taking his eyes off Kate, as if he couldn't bear to look at him.

'Because my father and I were out for dinner with Jennifer when she became ill,' Jack said.

Finally, Miles twisted so that he was facing Jack. He looked at him for several seconds as if weighing up whether to believe him or not. 'Where's your father, then?' he said at last. 'How come it's just you two on your own in here?' Still, there was a defensive, suspicious tone to his voice: Kate knew that the one thing Miles would never stand for was being lied to or deceived. He would be angry if there was something more to tell him but he would deal with it. What he wouldn't deal with was being taken for a fool.

'Because Amy's gone outside with Hugh, Jack's father,' Kate said quickly. 'They'll both be back in a minute.' She shot a glance towards the entrance to the cafeteria as if expecting them to materialise at that moment.

Miles's forehead smoothed slightly as his frown lessened, and Kate felt relieved. Until she noticed that Jack was watching Miles with a strange look in his eye that she didn't like: it was a cross between amusement and malice.

The three of them sat in awkward silence for a few moments until finally Jack slapped his hand down on the table and stood up, making both Kate and Miles jump sharply.

'It's no good!' he cried, running his hand through his thick, dark hair as he towered over them. 'You're obviously not going to tell him, so I will!'

'Jack ...' Kate could feel the swirls of panic beginning to grip her. 'Don't. Whatever you were going to say ... *Don't*!'

Jack hesitated, before shaking his head defiantly. 'No, Kate. He has a right to know.'

There was a strange sound from Miles as he stood up and faced Jack. 'I knew it!' he cried, his voice an anguished howl.

Kate gripped Miles's arm but he shook her off angrily and raced across the cafeteria towards the door, where Amy was just coming in.

'Miles!' she smiled up at him but the smile died on her lips as she saw his face, which was contorted with pain and already wet with tears. She watched in horror as he passed her without acknowledging her and headed out into the still night air.

Amy marched over to Jack and Kate. 'What's wrong with Miles?' she demanded, still stunned, never having seen Miles show so much emotion before.

Jack said nothing, looking away sheepishly; unable to

meet Amy's eye as Kate began to cry helplessly. 'Oh God,' she repeated, over and over again.

Amy sat down beside Kate and took her hand. 'What's happened? Kate! Tell me what's happened. You're frightening me.'

Kate looked up, finally. '*You!*' she hissed at Jack, her dark eyes blackening with anger. 'You can get out of here! I need to find Miles.' She stood up and grabbed her bag.

'Kate!' Amy yelled, still gripping Kate's hand tightly, refusing to let her go. 'Tell me what's happened!'

'*He*—' Kate's face contorted in rage as she snarled in Jack's direction, '—*he* made out that we were having an affair! Miles will never, *ever* believe me now.'

Amy's own face became a mask of fury as she digested Kate's words. 'Go after Miles!' she urged Kate, letting go of her hand and motioning into the distance. 'I'll get rid of him!' she spat in Jack's direction.

Kate dashed off, almost colliding with the automatic doors in her impatience to get away.

Amy and Jack watched her go until she was out of sight before Amy turned slowly towards him and fixed him with a furious stare. 'Happy now?' she hissed.

Jack took a deep breath and slumped, putting his head in his hands. Amy watched him for a few seconds before speaking again. 'What the hell were you thinking?' There was still white-hot anger in her voice but it had dissipated slightly.

Jack groaned from under his mane of hair. He looked up and shrugged. 'I don't know. I just saw him there and couldn't help myself. He's nowhere near good enough for her.'

'He's *plenty* good enough for her!' Amy snapped furiously.

'They were very happy until you came along, unsettling her and filling her head with all kinds of crap!'

'They were happy, were they?' Jack said, and Amy felt a shiver go through her at his tone. 'I don't think they were happy at all. But I could make her happy.'

Amy shook her head incredulously. 'God, you arrogant shit,' she said, almost smiling at the outrageousness of his words. 'I think you should go home. Go home and don't ever contact her again.'

Jack smiled sadly. 'And you think that'll make everything OK, do you? You think that if I disappear from view, she'll forget all about me and live happily ever after with Mr Boring?'

'He's *not* boring!' Amy snapped. 'He's a lovely bloke who adores Kate and is a brilliant father to their children. Until you came along, they were really, really happy.'

'I don't accept that,' he replied quietly. 'There's a connection between Kate and me that I know she's never had with him. It's not a question of me stealing her away from him. It's something that neither of us can help. When you know, you know.'

Amy's eyes narrowed. 'Yes, very moving but, unfortunately, you're also talking shit. Marriage isn't about a passing lust – that will disappear. It's about friendship, shared experiences and love. I doubt you would know anything about that, but Kate does. What she has with Miles is very precious. I just hope you haven't fucked everything up for her.'

'What's going on?' said a deep voice, and Amy started as Hugh appeared beside their table. 'I just saw Kate leaving, looking very upset.'

Amy rubbed her face. She was so tired. 'Ask him,' she

sighed, getting up and making her way out of the cafeteria. She was going to go back up to Jennifer's room and check on her.

The lights in Jennifer's room had been dimmed and her eyes were still closed as Amy entered as quietly as she could. She sat down in the chair beside the bed and looked at her mum. Jennifer's skin still had a grey tinge but there were spots of colour on her cheeks now.

After a few moments of sitting in silence, listening to her mum's rhythmic breathing, Amy stood up, unable to cope with such stillness when her mind was racing with worry. She paced up and down quietly, folding her arms around herself as a chill quivered through her body.

'What's up, darling?' croaked Jennifer, making Amy yelp in shock. 'Sorry,' she added, smiling slightly. 'I didn't mean to startle you.'

Amy grinned and walked to the bed, where she perched on the pale green cover that was tucked tightly around Jennifer's slender body. 'It's OK,' she whispered. Somehow, the setting demanded that she didn't speak at normal levels.

'So?' Jennifer prompted, raising both her eyebrows in question.

'There's been a bit of ... an incident. Downstairs.' Immediately she'd said it, Amy regretted telling her mum anything, especially as she was lying in bed recovering from a suspected heart attack. 'But it's nothing,' she added quickly.

Jennifer's dark, intelligent eyes flashed. 'Too late,' she said, taking Amy's hand in hers. 'You're going to have to tell me now, or else I'll be torturing myself thinking of all sorts of terrible scenarios.'

Amy nodded. 'I know. I'm sorry. I should never have said anything.'

'Is it Jack and Kate?'

Amy nodded again. 'I wasn't there but apparently Miles turned up and Jack seemed to think it was the perfect time to let him know that he and Kate have been having an affair.'

A gasp of horror escaped from Jennifer's mouth. 'Oh my God!' she murmured, after a few moments. 'Have they? She told me nothing had happened.'

Amy shrugged helplessly. 'She told me the same. I don't know what to think. Kate isn't a liar, I know that much.'

'Anyone is capable of lying if the situation demands it,' whispered Jennifer, guilt swamping her like a heavy blanket. *She* was responsible for a chain of events that would have a devastating effect on all their lives. She closed her eyes and groaned in mental agony.

'Oh God!' Amy cried, jumping up and looking around for help. 'Mum! Mum! Are you in pain? Shit!' The panic in her voice was making it quaver.

Jennifer opened her eyes and reached out, gripping Amy's wrist as hard as she could. 'No!' she whimpered. 'Amy! I'm fine. I'm just upset, that's all – upset about Kate.'

Amy sat back down and rubbed her wrist surreptitiously.

'Where is she now?' asked Jennifer softly, taking small, panting breaths in an effort to calm her racing heart.

'She's gone after Miles. He passed me when I was coming in. He looked so distraught, Mum. I've never seen him like that.' Tears flushed into her eyes at the memory.

'I hope they can work it out,' Jennifer whispered, closing

her eyes again as her throat constricted with unshed tears. 'For the children's sake as much as anything.'

A dense silence returned to the tiny room, punctuated only by the intermittent clicking of a clock on the wall as both of them retreated into their own private thoughts.

A gentle knock at the door broke the trance and Hugh came into the room. His eyes found Jennifer immediately and Amy was struck by the deep, intense love she could see in them. 'How is she?' he said softly, his gaze still on Jennifer.

'*She* is fine, thank you for asking!' Jennifer said in a tiny yet indignant voice, half laughing as she opened her eyes and found his.

At that moment, to Amy's relief – she suddenly felt like an intruder in something very intimate – the door opened and yet another doctor appeared. She had shiny black hair that was cut into a severe bob, and was wearing equally severe black-rimmed glasses. She glanced at Amy and Hugh before making her way over to Jennifer's bed.

'Good evening,' she said, in a husky voice with a strong accent. 'We are going to be doing lots of tests and she will need plenty of rest, so it might be a good idea for you to go home and return again in the morning.' Her voice wasn't unsympathetic but her words were delivered in a way that brooked no argument.

Amy stood up and smoothed down her jeans. 'OK,' she said, bending over to kiss Jennifer's forehead, which was soothingly warm as her lips pressed against the skin. 'But I'll be back first thing.'

She looked questioningly at Hugh, who looked as if he might be going to refuse to leave. He hesitated and shrugged slightly, looking lost. 'I might just wait downstairs,' he murmured, gazing longingly at Jennifer. Amy was touched by his obvious concern for her. It was going to take a while to get used to, but she already felt pleased that her mum had someone who was apparently so devoted to her in her life.

Hugh staying made her feel guilty for going home and, as they left the room, she suddenly said, 'I'll stay, too. If you are.'

Hugh shook his head slowly and Amy noticed as he did so how tired he looked. 'No, it's fine. You have a home to go to. I don't. So I'll stay. But I promise to call if anything happens with her.'

Amy bit her lip, still hesitant. 'Well, I guess I'll see you in the morning, then?' she said uncertainly.

Hugh nodded. 'Yes, you go,' he said, his dark eyes motioning her towards the exit.

Chapter 44

Kate struggled to see the road ahead as her vision blurred with the tears that were spilling out of her eyes and pouring down her cheeks, before pattering onto her jeans. She was shaking so much that several times she jolted the steering wheel, causing the car to swerve violently. She needed to get to Miles. One tiny moment had crystallised her feelings for him and she suddenly knew that she couldn't lose him; suddenly knew that everything in her life revolved around Miles. Any attraction she had felt for Jack had just evaporated, leaving a little trail of poison in its wake.

Somehow she managed to make it home, parking the car so badly that it was almost at a right angle to the pavement. She fell out of the car, fumbling to lock it as at the same time, she scrabbled furiously in her bag for her house keys.

As she gave the sticking front door a tiny kick to open it, her heart clenched for the familiarity of it – she had moaned so much about Miles not fixing it in the past. Suddenly she was so glad he hadn't.

The downstairs lights were on but the sitting room was empty, and Kate could see through into the kitchen that there was no one there either. She was about to race upstairs when she heard a noise from the utility room at the rear of the kitchen and looked back to see Miles emerging, carrying one of their suitcases.

'What are you doing?' she gasped.

Miles stopped in his tracks when he saw her and shot her a look that went right through her. A look that told her he despised her. Gathering himself, he pushed past her, still carrying the case in his large hands as if it weighed nothing at all. Kate tried to hold on to his arm as he passed but he shook her off angrily.

'Leave me alone!' he hissed in a voice that would have sounded angry if it hadn't caught in his throat. He gulped back a sob and bounded up the stairs two at a time. Kate followed him, feeling more frightened than she had ever felt in her life. He headed for their bedroom, where he began pulling the shirts she had ironed for him earlier in the evening out of the wardrobe and stuffing them into the case. Then he opened his underwear drawer and scooped up an armful of things, which he also tossed into the case.

'Miles!' Kate cried, sinking down onto the floor in front of him. 'Please don't do this! You don't understand!'

'I understand all too bloody welll!' he shot back, making Kate reel in shock. Miles had never raised his voice to her before.

'Miles, listen to me—' she begged, clasping her hands together in a pleading gesture.

'I don't want to hear it.' He cut her off in a strangled voice. 'I can just imagine what happened. How you must all have been laughing at me behind my back: stupid, boring, fucking Miles. Blissfully unaware that his *wife* ...' – he spat

368

the word at her – '. . . is fucking some other bastard behind his back. God, I've been such a bloody idiot!'

'No!' Kate cried, fear making her shake violently. 'No, Miles! It's not like that at all. NOTHING HAPPENED! You have got to believe me.'

'I don't have to do anything. And I don't believe you,' he said in a steelier, calmer tone that chilled Kate to the bone.

'Look at me, Miles,' she pleaded. 'I swear on our children's lives that nothing happened between me and Jack.'

Miles hesitated for a second, panting slightly with the effort of ramming things into his case. '*Our* children?' he said, looking into the distance as if lost in a sudden trance. 'They're probably not even mine.'

'Oh my God!' Kate wailed, slumping further down onto the floor. She felt sick to her stomach with fear and desperation. 'Miles, I have NEVER, EVER cheated on you. I never *would*. I love OUR children – and yes, they *are* yours – too much to ever do that. I love YOU too much,' she finished, in a torrent of tears.

Miles's giant frame seemed to dissolve as he slid down onto his knees and slumped over the bed as pitiful, agonising sobs racked his whole body.

Plucking up her courage, Kate shuffled on her knees towards him and wrapped her arms around him from behind, resting her head on his back, which was rising and falling with each convulsion. 'I love you so much,' she sobbed. 'You've got to believe me.'

After a while, Miles seemed to calm and he knelt up, shaking Kate off him as he did so. He turned so that he was sitting on the floor with his back against the bed, roughly wiping away the tears that were silently but insistently cascading down his face. 'Why would he have said what he said if it wasn't true?' he demanded.

'Because he wanted you to think that I had been having an affair with him, so that we would break up!' Kate's tone was desperate and pleading. She *had* to make him believe her; had to make him see how much she loved him.

'So there *has* been something going on, then?' Miles spat out.

Kate took a deep breath. She knew that she couldn't lie to him: that she had one chance to get this right. She literally felt as if her whole life depended on getting Miles to believe her.

'No, there hasn't been anything going on,' she began, as a shuddery breath reverberated through her. 'But he wanted something to happen. And, for a while, I wondered if I did too.'

Miles's face contorted in pain.

'But, Miles . . .' she pleaded. 'Please believe me. Nothing ever happened. I had a crush, that's all it was. A crush that has passed.'

'The thing is,' he said in a flat monotone, as the tears continued to slide down his cheeks unabated, 'I sort of knew.'

Kate didn't answer. She didn't know what to say.

Eventually, Miles looked at her. 'I knew you were fucking him.'

As Kate watched in horror, Miles pulled his mobile phone from his pocket and scrolled down. Without speaking, he handed Kate the phone. She pulled her eyes away from his contempt-filled ones, to look at the screen. There, in perfect colour, was the photo that Sarah had taken: Kate kissing Jack in the front seat of her mother's Clio.

'No!' Kate gasped in shock. 'Oh my God, no! I asked her not to show you and she promised me!' But even as she spoke, she remembered being unnerved by the fact that Sarah hadn't promised. She had simply made Kate promise that there was nothing more going on between her and Jack. 'But why . . .?' she began again, frowning. 'Why didn't you say anything?'

Miles shrugged, the gesture at odds with the pain in his face. 'I was scared to. I mean, what the hell have I got to offer you over him? He's got the looks, the money . . . I couldn't compete. So, I decided to say nothing and hope you'd choose me over him. Jesus, haven't you noticed how hard I've been trying over the past few months? How much I've been trying to impress you?'

Kate's mouth dropped open. Of course there had been a reason behind Miles's change in behaviour and, of course, it stemmed from Sarah showing him the photos. She must already have shown him by the time she and Sarah had had their awful row. 'Did you talk to Sarah about it? What did she say?' Kate's mind was reeling, both from the shock of Miles seeing the photo and from her betrayal by Sarah.

Miles hesitated and wiped his face as if trying to buy some time.

'Miles?' she prompted.

'Yes – we've talked a lot over the last few months.'

Kate felt her insides freeze. 'What? When?'

'We've met up . . . a few times. She's been a good friend. But she told me that she believed you that nothing more had happened. So I believed it too, bloody idiot that I am!'

Prickles of discomfort shot up and down Kate's spine. The white wooden painted floor beneath her felt as if it was moving and the lilac walls of the small room seemed to be closing in on her. 'Have you ...?' Her throat dried and she couldn't finish the question. Maybe because she didn't want to hear the answer.

'No,' Miles said, reading her thoughts. 'I would never do that to you. *Never*. And I couldn't do it to the kids. What a shame you didn't have the same consideration for them.'

At the mention of the children, Kate crumpled. 'No!' she wept. 'I *did* think about them and that's exactly why I didn't ...' She stopped and tried to compose herself, her whole body shaking. 'He ... he wanted a relationship but I said no. I chose you.'

Miles gestured towards his phone. 'You wanted him though, clearly.' His tone was still flat and devoid of any emotion, in contrast to the tears still pouring down his face.

Kate took a deep breath to try to calm herself, and stop the tremors coursing through her body. 'Maybe, for a short while,' she agreed, not wanting to lie to him, but not wanting to give him any cause not to believe her, either. 'Maybe for a short while it seemed as if he might offer me the chance of a more exciting life.' Miles looked at her contemptuously. 'I know!' she said, feeling disgusted with herself that she could even have contemplated it. 'I know what you're thinking and you're right. I was shallow and stupid to even think like that. But, Miles, I did sometimes feel invisible to you. It was flattering that someone was showing me some attention.' She stopped, wary of saying too much and doing even more damage.

'You've never been invisible to me,' Miles said softly, shaking his head and looking at her for the first time. 'I think you're amazing. I always have. But I've always felt like I'm not good enough for you, and that sooner or later you would find someone who was. Your dad thought it too.'

Miles was right. Michael *had* always thought Miles wasn't good enough for her. And maybe that had rubbed off on her. Had she been subconsciously trying to make her father's premonition come true? No, that was absurd, but she had to make Miles feel better. 'Think about Millie in years to come, Miles. I don't think you will ever consider any man good enough for her. It's a dad's prerogative.'

Miles's lips turned up slightly in a half-smile of acknowledgement, and he roughly wiped his face as his tears began to dry. Tentatively, Kate reached out and took his huge hand in hers, shuffling round so that she was facing him, sitting cross-legged on the floor. 'Miles, I have never thought you weren't good enough for me. There are times when I have wished you would pay me a bit more attention and help more, but certainly not that I was too good for you. You say you think I'm amazing. But you don't show it. And yes, I have noticed that you've been doing more to help recently, but that's because you did so little before.'

'So why not talk to me about it?' Miles snapped, withdrawing his hand from hers and folding it into his lap, 'instead of going off with someone else!' His voice quavered again as he spoke.

'I didn't *go* off with someone else,' Kate replied patiently and quietly. 'But it's taken the threat of it to make you notice that things haven't been perfect between us. Otherwise, I would have raised the subject and you would just have complained that I was nagging. I'm not sure I would ever have been able to make you see that there was a problem.'

Miles shrugged and they lapsed into silence, only broken

373

by the occasional sniff as they both tried to recover their emotions. Kate reached out and picked up his hand again. She held it between her two palms and gently stroked the top of it with her thumb. His skin was surprisingly soft and cool to her touch, his perfectly shaped nails were clean and his smooth, pale skin contrasted with the darker colour of her own, rougher skin.

'Miles?' she said after several minutes.

Miles shrugged again, but he kept his hand in hers and didn't try to pull away.

'Miles, will you unpack that case? There's no need for you to leave. We all love you so much.' Kate tried not to sound too pleading but it was impossible as, at that moment, all she wanted was for him to tell her that he loved her, that he believed her and that he would stay. 'Miles?' she repeated, tilting her head to try to look at his face.

Miles hesitated for a minute. 'I don't know,' he said at last. 'I feel like such an idiot. That you've been plotting and planning behind my back. That you even contemplated leaving me. Leaving the *kids!*' He was working himself up again: as Kate leaned forward and put her arms around him, she could feel his whole body shaking.

'But nothing happened!' she spoke into his chest as she nuzzled her face against him.

Miles gently pushed her off. 'If I believe you that nothing sexual happened—' he said carefully.

'It didn't!' Kate interrupted hotly.

Miles motioned to her to be quiet before continuing: '*If* I believe you ... then it's almost worse. Because you had an emotional connection with him. If you had just fucked him and that was all there was to it, maybe I could understand it.

But it was more than that. You actually contemplated a life with him. You contemplated leaving me and the kids for him. How am I ever supposed to cope with that knowledge? How am I ever going to be able to trust that you're happy with me, when you were so quick to consider leaving me for the first man that shows you any attention?'

Kate's mouth dropped open in dismay. 'But it was just a crush!' she cried. 'It was a stupid crush that's completely gone. I feel nothing for him now. It's shown me how much you mean to me, Miles. How much I love and need you. Please, darling, *please* believe me.'

Miles raised his eyes and locked them onto hers. 'I believe you,' he said quietly. 'I just don't know if I can stay with you. I think that maybe, in the short term, I should move out while we both get ourselves together.'

'No!' Kate cried. 'No, Miles, please don't leave! If you really feel you can't keep sleeping in the same bed as me, then sleep on the sofa. Or better still, *I'll* sleep on the sofa. I just don't want the kids to know. It'll absolutely kill them. And I'm so scared ...' She started crying again, helplessly this time, unable to stop the torrent of emotion that was pouring out her. 'I'm so scared,' she said with a gulp, 'that if you go, you will never come back and I know that I just couldn't cope with that. I couldn't live without you!' she finished, her last words coming out as a plaintive wail as the sobs racked through her.

'OK,' Miles said after a few minutes, 'OK.' He reached out and wrapped his arms around her. 'I'll stay. But you're sleeping on the sofa.'

Kate half laughed, half cried. 'Thank you,' she sobbed. 'Thank you.'

Chapter 45

Amy let herself into the cottage and listened for sounds of life. She felt cold, tired and shivery. She couldn't hear anything except the sound of the old clock in the hallway, ticking away incessantly, just as it always did. Ben must have gone to bed, she decided, hanging up her jacket on the over-crowded hat stand and making her way into the dimly lit kitchen.

She jumped as she entered the kitchen and saw Ben perched on a stool, slumped over the breakfast bar, apparently fast asleep. She watched him for a moment and allowed a surge of love for him to wash over her.

His full mouth was slightly open and the fringe of his soft, dark hair lifted slightly with each outward breath. As she watched him, his eyes flickered open and he looked at her in confusion for a second, before his mouth softened into a wide, sexy smile that made her insides melt. 'Hi, sweetheart,' he murmured, getting up and walking towards her, the side of his cheek still showing the imprint of his hand where he had been lying on it. 'How is she?' he asked, enveloping Amy in his arms and stroking her hair in gentle, rhythmic movements.

Amy relaxed into his arms gratefully and breathed in the

scent of him that she loved so much. 'We won't know until the morning exactly what's wrong, but she's stable.'

'Oh, thank God!' Ben said fervently.

Amy pulled away and looked up at him curiously: he was crying quietly. 'Ben?' she said in alarm. 'What's wrong?'

Ben wiped his face. 'I've been so worried about her,' he said. 'I think I've just realised how selfish I've been all these months; just worrying about myself while you've been holding everything together. And Jennifer's been so good to me. To all of us. Without her . . . well, I dread to think where we would be.'

Amy nodded and swallowed hard. She didn't want to think about how they would have managed without her mum. Or contemplate anything happening to her.

Ben drew Amy back into him and held her tightly. 'You've been amazing, Amy,' he whispered into her hair. 'I love you so much, and I so nearly lost you.'

'No.' Amy shook her head. 'You didn't nearly lose me. I wouldn't have let you lose me!'

They both laughed for a moment before Ben pulled back and looked at her again, stroking her hair back off her face. 'I'm so sorry, darling. I love you so much. I'm going to make it up to you, I promise. I'm going to make you proud of me again, like you were before.'

Amy gazed into his dark eyes and felt a little nugget of hope begin to glow inside her. The old Ben was gone and she knew he would never return. But, looking at him now and seeing the fierce intensity, determination and vitality that he once had had starting to re-emerge slowly, she felt that she might love the new Ben even more than the old one.

He leaned forwards and kissed her on the lips. Gently at

first, then more passionately. He wrapped his arms around her and lifted her off her feet as if she was weightless. She curled her legs around his waist and felt him start to harden under his jeans. Longing rushed through her and she reached for his zip and pulled it down just as he did the same to hers. Desperate now, they both wriggled their jeans out of the way as Ben placed her on the breakfast bar, and entered her. She gripped him into her with her legs around his back and came almost instantly: all the months of pent-up desire bursting out in one juddering orgasm. Ben stopped and waited as the waves of feeling washed over her, watching her with a mixture of love and lust. 'Wow,' he smiled as he began to thrust again, sending fresh shots of pleasure racing through her, 'I'd forgotten how good we are at this!'

'I'm not sure I'll ever look at that breakfast bar in the same light again,' Amy said with a grin, as she lay naked on top of Ben later, in bed. Their noses were lightly touching as they stroked each other's faces and looked deep into each other's eyes.

'No,' Ben agreed, smiling at the memory. 'I love you, Amy,' he added. 'I want to make you proud of me. You deserve a husband you can be proud of; instead of the arsehole I've been all these months. I owe you so much.'

'Shhh, I *am* proud of you,' Amy said, kissing his full lips and enjoying the pulse of lust that shot through her as she did so. 'I am proud of you for pulling yourself through it, when I know all you wanted to do was end it all.' She stopped speaking abruptly as the thought of losing Ben caused her throat to constrict sharply.

'I didn't pull myself through it,' Ben said, still stroking her face with his thumb. '*You* pulled me through it. I would never have made it without you.'

Amy didn't say anything. Instead she kissed him deeply.

'But I've decided what I'm going to do,' Ben said, a few moments later. 'You're going back to college and so am I. I'm going to retrain.'

'As what?' Amy said, loving him so much she wanted to drink him in.

'As a gardener,' Ben said shyly.

Amy pulled back and looked at him in surprise. 'A gardener?'

'A good one,' Ben said hastily. 'A proper landscape gardener – designing gardens and getting proper clients. Maybe even Sam could help me.'

'What's brought this on?' Amy said, smiling. 'I didn't know you were even interested in gardening!'

'Who do you think has been working on Jennifer's garden all these months?' he shot back, mock-indignantly. 'I've been spending hours on end out there. It's been fantastic and it's given me a new lease of life, literally.'

'Well, I suppose Sam must get it from somewhere,' Amy replied, kissing his nose. 'It's certainly not from me.'

'So ... what do you think, then?' Ben asked tentatively, as if terrified that she was going to laugh at him.

Amy ran her thumb over his forehead and down the side of his cheek, taking in the contours of his chiselled face. 'I think it's a great idea,' she said, as she allowed her legs to fall either side of him so that she was straddling him. Immediately, she felt him start to harden. 'Especially as it seems to help everything else grow too.'

*

The next morning, Amy woke up early. She slipped out of bed in the gleam of the milky dawn light that was peeping in over the top of the curtains, glancing at Ben as she pulled on her robe. She felt a little leap of excitement at the sight of his toned, tanned body contrasting with the crisp white of the bed linen. It was almost as if she had a brand new lover lying in her bed, such was the excitement of rediscovering her lust for him. He looked so vulnerable, handsome and sexy that she was tempted to wake him up and mount him there and then. But they had already made love four times that night: she didn't want to push her luck and exhaust him. Instead, she threw him one last lingering glance before slipping out of the room and out onto the landing.

Flora was emerging from her room, her blonde hair messy and matted from sleep, clutching her beloved rabbit to her chest. 'How's Grandma?' she asked immediately, her pale little forehead furrowing with a concern that Amy knew was genuine. Flora and Jennifer had grown incredibly close over the months that they had lived in Jennifer's house. After all the upheaval she had already had to endure, Amy couldn't bear the thought of her having any more angst in her life.

'She's OK, darling,' Amy said, bending to wrap her arms around Flora's stiff little body. As she did so, she felt her little girl start to relax, feeling the tension seeping out of her. Amy held her tightly for several seconds, wanting her to feel safe and secure after a horrible year of change.

Eventually, Flora pulled away and looked up at Amy. 'Can I see her?' she asked, her eyes big and dark.

Amy hesitated. 'I'm sure you can,' she replied carefully, 'but she's got to have lots of tests so it might not be today.' Seeing Flora's face cloud with disappointment, she added quickly, 'Why don't you make her a lovely card? In fact, why don't you and Sam make a card together and then you can have it ready to give her when you do go to see her?'

Flora's rosebud lips parted over her slightly gappy teeth, into a wide smile that reached her eyes and sparkled out from them. 'Yes!' she breathed excitedly. 'I'll go and get him. Sam!' she called out, rushing off towards Sam's room, where he could be heard talking loudly to himself as he always did when he played with his Lego.

Amy watched her go and had turned happily to go downstairs, intending to make some tea for her and Ben, when she heard her phone ringing in the bedroom. She dashed back but after two rings it was answered and, as she walked into the room, she could hear Ben talking in hushed but urgent tones. 'OK, we'll be right there,' he finished, before ending the call. He got out of bed and looked at Amy with an expression of concern.

'Ben?' she whispered, her heart pounding with fear. 'Who was that?'

'It was Kate,' he whispered back. He began walking towards Amy with his arms outstretched and she wasn't sure if he was coming to embrace her or lean on her for support, he looked so stricken. He pulled her towards him and held her so tightly that she could hardly breathe.

'Tell me, Ben,' she said, her throat so dry she could hardly get the words out. 'Whatever it is, tell me.'

'It's your mum' he said into her hair, as if he was terrified to look at her face. 'She's taken a turn for the worse. Kate says we need to get to the hospital now.'

Chapter 46

Kate glanced at Miles as he drove towards the hospital, while Amy and Ben huddled in the back seat looking sick with fright. Miles's face was pale and covered with a light sheen of sweat, his jaw set in a grim line. As if he felt her looking at him, he reached down and put his hand on her knee, giving it a reassuring squeeze. Kate put her hand over his and squeezed it in return, before putting her head back against the headrest and taking several deep breaths to steady herself. She had a very bad feeling about this: she knew from her time on the hospital wards that when they called the families to tell them the patient had taken a turn for the worse, it very often meant that it was already too late.

The night before, she and Miles had fallen into an intermittent sleep on top of their bed, fully clothed, so they hadn't had to get dressed when she had got the call from the hospital. She had had to pretend she knew nothing about Sarah's betrayal and had called her to see if she could keep the children and take them to school. Sarah had agreed instantly and told Kate she mustn't worry about a thing: she would take care of them. Kate had felt a flood of gratitude towards her, despite her hurt.

None of them spoke during the journey, each of them wrapped in their own private thoughts and fears. Kate twisted to look at Amy and Ben in the back seat again. Amy was clinging to Ben as if she was drowning and, even in her state of worry and distress, Kate was gratified to see that Ben seemed to have risen to the occasion and was looking after her, his arms holding her in a protective embrace.

Her heart started to beat faster as the hospital loomed into view and she automatically pulled at her seatbelt, as if desperate to be free of the restraint and get out of the car. 'I'll drop you at the front and park the car,' Miles said gently, looking at her for confirmation.

Kate shook her head quickly, suddenly panicked by the idea of him being out of her sight, even for a few moments. 'No,' she said firmly. 'We'll all go together.'

Miles looked at her for a long moment before nodding briefly and swinging into the car park. Almost immediately, they found a space and the second Miles switched off the engine, all four of them sprang from the car and walked hurriedly towards the entrance. Kate, having worked at the hospital for so long, led the way through the long corridors she knew so well and bounded up the stairs several feet in front of the other three, who struggled to keep up with her.

As she reached the ward, she slammed to a sudden halt in front of the double doors leading into it.

'Kate!' puffed Miles, looking at her quizzically as he caught up with her. 'What's wrong?'

'I can't,' she whimpered, her voice suddenly hoarse as her throat dried with terror. 'I can't go in there!'

Amy and Ben reached her and put their arms around her

so that they were encircling her completely. 'Come on, Kate,' Amy said, trying to keep her own voice as strong and steady as she could manage, despite feeling just as terrified as her sister looked. 'It'll be fine. She'll be fine.'

'She won't.' Kate shook her head roughly. 'You and I both know she won't!' Kate's knees began to buckle as she spoke and she felt herself falling.

Just as she was about to sink to the floor, Miles caught her in his strong arms and lifted her up. 'It's going to be OK,' he said. Something in his voice made Kate look up. His eyes were boring into hers and she felt as if he was holding her up with just his look. 'It's going to be OK,' he repeated.

Kate grasped hold of his hand and nodded. 'OK,' she whispered, turning towards the door and, after taking a deep breath, she pushed it open. She walked purposefully towards the nurses' station, still clutching Miles's hand with Amy and Ben following just a few paces behind them. 'My mum,' Kate began, 'Jennifer . . .'

One of the nurses stood up and came round to the front of the desk. 'Hi, Kate,' she said kindly, putting her hand on Kate's arm. 'She's in a private room. I'll take you to her.'

Kate looked at the nurse in confusion. 'You mean she's OK?' she stuttered. 'She's not . . .?' She stopped, unable to find the words.

The nurse shook her head. 'No, no,' she said quickly. 'But she's quite poorly, though.'

Kate's heart plummeted again. Yet another euphemism she was used to using herself with relatives. 'Quite poorly' meant very seriously ill. It meant Jennifer might not make it.

They followed the nurse towards a private room where Jennifer was now hooked up to numerous machines and covered in wires. The cardiac monitor at the side of the bed beeped intermittently. Hugh was standing off to one side looking down at her, his hand over the bottom half of his face. As they entered the room, he looked at them with dark eyes that seemed to have retreated back into their sockets. His face was hollow and pale, exacerbated by the stubble that seemed to have grown into a beard overnight. He didn't speak, but nodded slightly towards them.

Kate walked over to him and placed her hand on his arm. 'What happened, Hugh?' she whispered, unable just yet to look at her mother lying in the bed.

Hugh shook his head and held both palms face up in a gesture of helplessness. Finally, Kate allowed herself to look at Jennifer properly. Her breathing was shallow and her skin was a mottled grey. Her eyelids fluttered slightly as she seemed to drop in and out of sleep. Or consciousness: Kate wasn't entirely sure which.

Amy and Ben had made their way around to the other side of the bed and had perched on the edge, Amy taking Jennifer's hand in hers and stroking it. Ben's face crumpled immediately but he seemed to regain control of his emotions as quickly as he lost them, and put his arm protectively around Amy's shoulders.

Kate looked back at Miles, who was waiting by the door, still apparently frozen with shock at seeing Jennifer. She caught his eye and gestured to him to come towards her, which he did immediately, pulling her into an embrace. The room fell into silence, save for the beeping of the monitor, as they all struggled with their emotions, none of them knowing how to deal with such a shocking, awful situation.

After what seemed like hours, a whistling sound cut through the heavy silence and they all looked at each other in confusion. 'It's her!' cried Amy, looking at Jennifer in surprise.

As all their heads turned towards Jennifer, her eyes flickered open. She made a moaning sound and her eyes widened when she saw Kate, as if she was in pain.

'Mum!' Amy shouted in panic, leaning forward so that her blonde hair fell across Jennifer's chest. 'Mum, what is it? Are you in pain?'

Kate gently pushed Amy back again. 'Give her space,' she said, looking in concern at the monitor.

Suddenly, Jennifer spoke. 'Kate, there's something you need to know.' Jennifer struggled, looking searchingly at Kate and Hugh as the monitor beeping became more erratic. Kate leaned over to press the emergency button beside Jennifer's head but Jennifer gave a loud, anguished cry and shook her head slightly. Kate hesitated, her hand in mid-air, and looked at her mum, quizzically.

'I'm going to get help,' she said.

'No.' They could hardly make out Jennifer's words as she spoke. 'Not yet.'

Amy burst into noisy sobs. 'No?' she cried. 'Call for help, Kate! For fuck's sake, do something!'

'No,' Jennifer said, more clearly this time, her voice still sounding tinny but stronger.

Amy's mouth dropped open mid-sob but she immediately quietened.

'Hugh,' Jennifer murmured.

'Yes, darling, I'm here,' Hugh said, stepping forwards out of the shadows and surprising them all. They had almost forgotten he was there: he had seemed to blend into the walls since they had arrived.

'Kate,' Jennifer continued, as if each word was wrenched from her.

'Yes?' Kate perched on the bed and took her mum's hand in hers, frowning in confusion. She desperately wanted to press the bell for help but she also sensed that it was the most important thing in the world right then to listen to whatever Jennifer was trying to tell her.

'I think Hugh . . .' Jennifer stopped speaking as the effort became too much.

Kate wanted to scream with frustration. 'You think Hugh what?' She tried not to let her desperation sound in her voice but it was impossible to hide.

'May be . . .'

All of them held their breath and Hugh seemed to shrink a little as they waited.

'Your fath . . .'

'Shit! She's in VF! Get the crash trolley!' shouted Kate, suddenly. Amy looked at the heart monitor, which was going haywire, then at her mum, whose eyes had rolled back into her head.

'Ben, Miles, fucking *do* something!' she screamed.

The emergency buzzers resonated loudly as the crash team rushed in. Medics and nurses vied for space in the small room. Kate automatically assumed her role as she had so many times before; only this time it was her own mother she was trying to resuscitate.

'VF confirmed, shocking 150 joules. STAND CLEAR!'

she shouted as she placed the defibrillator paddles on her mother's chest. Jennifer's body jolted in the bed and there was a pause as the team looked at the cardiac monitor.

A doctor Kate knew well grabbed her arm. 'Kate, let us take over.'

Kate glanced at him, blindly. He looked at the nurse next to him, and Kate allowed herself to be led meekly from the room, towards the relatives' room, where Amy, Miles, Ben and Hugh had been ushered to wait. They could still hear the sounds of the doctor shouting instructions to the crash team: 'No pulse, continue CPR!'

Silence swallowed up the room as each of them tried to compute what Jennifer had just said. Kate reeled back and into Miles's waiting arms. 'No,' she whispered, before shooting a glance at Hugh, who seemed to be almost cowering under her gaze. All at once the room seemed to close in on her. 'No,' she repeated, turning to face Miles and burying her face in his big, strong chest.

'Kate . . .' Hugh began, his deep, resonant voice filling the room, 'Kate, listen,' he said.

Kate turned her face and looked at him in disgust. 'No, *you* listen,' she hissed. 'She's delirious. She doesn't know what she's saying. You are *not* my father. You're not even fit to lick the boots of my father.' She whimpered slightly as she spoke the last word.

Suddenly, she realised that the distant shouting had stopped. Seconds later, the doctor came into the room and immediately she knew. 'I'm sorry, Kate, we did all we could,' he said simply.

Kate looked at Amy and their eyes locked in horror.

'I want to see her!' Kate cried, and pushed past him back

to the side room where nurses were trying to clear up the debris from the resuscitation attempt. Her gaze fell on her mother, lying in the bed, looking smaller and older than she had ever seen her look. She was still taking a gasping breath every minute but Kate knew this was just Cheyne-Stokes breathing – the death rattle – that she had witnessed so many times before. She stumbled out of the room back to the relatives' room.

Hugh looked at her in confusion. Amy was crying pitifully while Ben held her tightly and rubbed her back, his own face a picture of distress. Miles put his arms back around Kate and hugged her, while Hugh shuffled from foot to foot, looking and feeling as if he didn't know what to do with himself. He looked at Kate warily, feeling scared of what she might do next. He could sense her white-hot anger coming off her in waves. Over her head, Miles met his eye with a look that seemed to be warning him off.

Kate groaned slightly as Amy came towards her and grasped her hand, pulling her out of Miles's embrace. 'We need to go back in there,' Amy said, swallowing hard and motioning towards the room where the last few moments of Jennifer's life were ebbing away.

Kate shook her head. 'I can't!' she wailed. 'I can't!'

Amy stroked her sister's hand gently. 'You can and you must,' she told her, sounding so much stronger than she felt. 'We need to do it.'

Kate blinked twice before nodding. 'OK,' she said, pulling herself together and gripping Amy's hand tightly.

Amy opened the door and pulled Kate back into the room. One of the nurses looked at them both as they stood at the foot of Jennifer's bed.

Kate cleared her throat. 'Can you leave us?' she said, shooting a look at Amy, whose eyes were now wide and terrified.

The medics exchanged glances before nodding and backing away, melting out of the room so that Amy and Kate could move either side of Jennifer. A faint, intermittent beep emitted from the monitor and Kate knew they didn't have long left: their mum was slipping away from them. She reached up and switched the monitor off, as it was only confirming what they already knew.

She leaned down so that her face was millimetres from Jennifer's. She could smell illness emanating from every pore; she could smell death encroaching. She had seen and smelt it so many times before. Now, it was her own mother whose life was ebbing away.

She pressed her lips to Jennifer's skin, which felt dry and papery to the touch. 'I know you can hear me, Mum,' she said. 'And I need to tell you something too.' She stopped and swallowed several times, her voice suddenly unable to form the words.

She glanced up at Amy, who had lain down on the bed beside her mum and was holding her tightly, tears streaming silently down her face, forming a wet patch that was spreading into ever wider circles on the pale green sheet. Amy met Kate's eye and nodded almost imperceptibly.

Kate held her look for a moment before turning back to face Jennifer, whose eyes flickered open for a split second, almost as if to encourage her to continue.

Kate reached out and stroked her mother's forehead. Once again, she leaned in and put her lips to Jennifer's ear. 'Amy and I are here,' she said, and her voice cracked, before she took a quick deep breath and recovered in time to continue without a pause: 'And we will be OK. We will love and look after each other, just like you've loved and looked after us.' Again, she had to stop when her throat constricted with tears that would only be shed much, much later.

'Go on, Kate,' Amy whimpered. 'Please go on.'

'And whatever happens, we will be OK. It's OK, Mum. You can let go. We will never stop loving you.'

Jennifer's breathing seemed to still at Kate's words. Kate copied Amy and lay down on the bed on their mum's opposite side and wrapped her arms over her, so that she was linking arms with Amy across her. A few minutes passed before Kate lifted her head and kissed Jennifer's cool cheek. 'She's gone,' she whispered to Amy, who let out a long, slow, anguished moan.

Several more minutes passed before the door opened and a nurse came in. She walked over to Kate and put her hand on her back. Kate nodded and, without saying anything, she shuffled into a sitting position, swinging her legs off the bed. Amy was crying quietly and Kate walked around to her side of the bed to put her arm around her sister. 'Come on, Amy,' she said gently.

Amy let out another anguished cry before rolling over to face Kate and putting her arms out, like a small child. Kate reached down and hugged her tightly. 'It's going to be OK,' she said quietly.

As they shuffled out into the obscene brightness of the ward they were met by Miles, Ben and Hugh, who were leaning against the wall in various states of dishevelled distress. Kate shook her head and gently pushed Amy into Ben's arms – as if she was handing her over – while Miles rushed towards her and pulled her to him. As he rocked her backwards and forwards, stroking her hair and repeating 'I'm so sorry', Kate became aware that Hugh had slumped to the floor with his head in his hands, and was sobbing silently.

She gently disengaged herself from Miles's embrace and turned towards Hugh. After hesitating for a moment as she looked down at his crumpled form, she knelt down in front of him and put her arms around his shoulders. He resisted at first, but gradually his stiff body seemed to soften slightly and he allowed himself to be pulled forwards so that his head was resting on her shoulder. His whole body was racked by sobs as Kate held him gently: she could see and feel how much he had loved Jennifer. Whatever the story – and Kate wasn't ready to hear it right then – she already knew that he had truly loved her mother.

Chapter 47

They buried her in the same wood as Michael, as close as they could get to the same spot. The day dawned bright, clear and warm, the Suffolk skies wide and blue, flecked with wispy licks of cotton-wool clouds. The river below the wood sparkled and danced and glinted, apparently oblivious to the sadness of the occasion: much like the day they buried Michael.

Kate and Amy had specified that the day should be family only but, as they reached the burial wood, Kate sat up straight in the car as she recognised a tall, angular figure standing with his hands in his pockets, his head turned away from the bright sun.

'I thought he should be here,' Miles said quietly. Kate looked at him sharply. 'I thought he should be here,' he repeated, his eyes gentle but firm.

Kate looked away, out of the window into the distance. Miles reached out and took her hand. 'She would have wanted him here,' he added. She nodded, her emotions swirling.

'Hello, Hugh,' she said carefully as they got out of the car. Hugh smiled and Kate thought it was the saddest smile she had ever seen, his dark eyes black with sorrow and loss.

'Shall we go, then?' said Amy, coming up and putting her hand on Hugh's arm.

As they made their way through the trees, the children clutching posies of the wild flowers that Jennifer had loved so much, Kate felt glad that there were so few of them there. There was no church to fill: just a small, pretty clearing dappled with sunlight that provided shafts of warmth in the cool stillness of the early summer afternoon.

After the simple, moving ceremony, they snaked back up through the wood, all of them – even Sam – silent with the weight of their grief. Amy reached down and took his small hand in hers. He turned his chubby little face up towards her and her heart wrenched at the sight of the tears streaking over his cheeks. Ben picked up Sam's other hand and ruffled his hair at the same time. Over his head, he met Amy's eye, both of them knowing that it was Sam who would miss Jennifer most.

She looked around for Flora and reached back to take her hand too, but Flora was concentrating hard on her footsteps and didn't appear to notice. More contained than her brother, even in her walk Amy could feel her pain. Finally, Flora glanced up and caught Amy's eye. Amy smiled at her questioningly. 'Are you OK, darling?' she asked gently. Flora nodded and took Amy's outstretched hand. 'Are you OK, Mummy?' she replied.

Amy took a deep breath. 'Yes,' she said. 'I'm OK. I think we're all going to be OK.'

'You need to talk to him,' Miles said, as he and Kate made their way up the hill; Millie and Josh walking silently together up ahead of them. They had left Hugh for some time alone at the grave.

'I know,' Kate said. 'I'm just not sure I'm ready, that's all.'

'I don't think you'll ever be ready,' Miles said gently. 'But it's something you have to do.'

Kate looked up at him and linked her arm through his, feeling so glad of his strong, steady presence. She looked up at his wide blue eyes and blond hair and decided he had never looked more handsome; she felt as if she had fallen in love with him all over again during the past week and a half. Their marriage had wobbled badly but she already knew that they were going to come through it stronger than ever. She couldn't imagine being without him now, instead of feeling as though she had settled for second best.

At the top of the hill, they gathered and waited in the sunshine, all of them subdued. Finally, Hugh's dark figure appeared through the trees, his head bowed and his hands in his pockets as he emerged out of the shadows and into the sunshine. He hesitated, blinking quickly as his eyes adjusted to the brightness, before making his way over to Kate, his shoulders slightly hunched and his face a picture of pure grief.

Kate turned to face him, wanting to tell him that she didn't want to see him again and that he should cease all contact with them but, when she looked into the deep, dark eyes that had so captivated her mother, she found her resolve melting away. 'What do we do now, Hugh?' she asked, her voice cracking with distress, her face mirroring the look on his.

Hugh stared back at her, looking lost. 'I think we go home,' he said.

Epilogue

She pulled the folded white sheet of paper out of the envelope and carefully ran her fingers over it, her heart banging with fear, before quickly opening it and reading what was printed in a heavy black typeface. She folded the paper again and swallowed the lump that had formed at the back of her throat, as she waited for the threat of tears to subside. Gradually, her heart slowed and the ice that had been coursing through her veins seemed to melt away. All she felt now was a calm acceptance of what she had always known.

There was a click followed by a dull thud as the blue door at the top of the stone steps behind her opened and closed. She didn't look round. She knew it was him, and she waited as his footsteps scuffed hesitantly down towards where she was sitting on the bottom step. It had grown cold, and she could feel that her teeth were about to start chattering. In the crowded car park in front of her, the cars continued their slow waltz as they moved in and out of spaces, each one bringing with it a new story to unfold before her.

'Well?' he said, sitting down beside her. She instinctively leaned slightly away as he stretched his long legs out in front of him, his dark brown boots crossed at the ankles. He dug deep into the pocket of his charcoal cashmere coat and retrieved a packet of cigarettes. Taking one out and putting it between his lips, he hesitated, before offering the pack to her.

She looked at him and smiled slightly, before shaking her head. He had become so familiar to her over the past months. They had spent many hours together, talking about the past; about what happened back then and what might happen in the future. 'I know,' he said suddenly, startling her.

'Know what?'

'What you're thinking. You're so like her. I always knew what she was thinking, too.' He deftly lit the cigarette and took a long, deep drag on it before exhaling in tiny smoke rings that rose and faded quickly into the chill, clear morning air.

She watched him, mesmerised, as she imagined her mother watching him too, down in the depths of the past. 'I miss her.'

He nodded and, as he did so, his head seemed to drop slightly. His cheekbones became more pronounced as he sucked hard on the cigarette again and he turned his head very slightly to one side as if trying to conceal his face from her. But still, she caught a glint of sorrow in his dark eyes.

They sat in silence for several more minutes, each lost in their own thoughts. Above them, a flock of birds swooped and dived through the wide sky, en route to somewhere warmer. At last he spoke: 'Are you going to read it, then?'

She turned the folded piece of paper over in her hands. 'I've read it,' she whispered.

He shot her a look of fear. 'And?' His eyes were huge chasms of desperation, dark and deep in their sockets.

'I don't know if I can tell you. I think I might want the words to be left unsaid.'

A siren blared rudely as an ambulance screamed into the car park and disappeared out of view towards the A&E department. She would never see an ambulance now and not think of her mother.

'We've come this far,' he said at last in a gravelly voice, as he finished his cigarette and dropped it to the ground, before grinding it out under his boot. 'What have you got to lose?'

What *had* she got to lose? 'My past,' she smiled sadly.

She didn't look at him but she felt him nod. 'What do you think she would have wanted you to do?'

She thought about it for a moment as she watched a young woman get out of her car, before bending to lift out a brown-haired, blue-eyed toddler with her hair in bunches, who made her think of Millie. 'I think she would want us both to know the truth.'

He sighed. 'So do I. It was the not knowing that tortured her.'

Tears pricked her eyes and she blinked twice, before inhaling deeply. The slightly burnt smell of autumn filled her nostrils, making her instantly nostalgic for the bonfire nights of her childhood – gazing up at Michael, his face framed against the inky night sky as he lit the sparklers that he would then carefully place into the mittened hands of his daughters: her first, then Amy. Michael, with his silky blond hair and blue crinkly eyes, who loved his wife and daughters with an all-consuming passion and, in return, was truly loved by them.

Kate looked up at Hugh, who had spent decades not knowing that he had a daughter somewhere – who, in turn, hadn't been aware of his existence. He had loved and lost her mother not once, but twice. His pain was written in the lines on his skin, in the flecks of silver in his hair and in the blackness of his eyes. But it wasn't over. They still had time to build something between them. It wouldn't make up for the lost years, but it might help them both to heal.

She reached out, took his hand in hers and turned it over so that it was facing upwards. She placed the still-folded piece of white paper on the rough skin of his palm and curled his fingers over it.

He gazed at it for a few seconds before raising his eyes to meet hers with a quizzical expression.

'You read it,' she said. 'Consider it an I.O.U.'

wahanda
YOUR HOME FOR HEALTH & BEAUTY

Bit of a beauty addict, fitness fanatic or yoga guru? Then meet **Wahanda** – your new best friend. With more spas, salons, treatments and practitioners listed than any other site, **Wahanda** offers an interactive community where you can voice your recommendations, write reviews and connect with industry experts.

As well as inspiring content, **Wahanda** offers savings on thousands of health, beauty and fitness offers, daily MobDeals plus their signature **Wahanda** Spa Gift Vouchers. So next time you need spoiling, visit Wahanda - your home for health and beauty.

Come and say hello:

Become a fan at
Facebook.com/Wahanda

Follow us at
Twitter.com/Wahanda

Visit us at
Wahanda.com

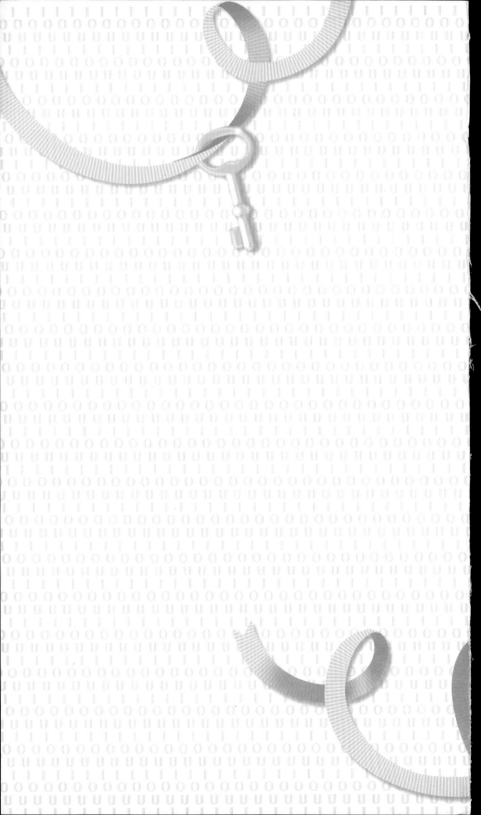